CYPRESS RUN

Cypress Run

Book One of the Cypress Run Quartet

T. N. DAIGLE

Scribomancer Guild Press

Published by Scribomancer Guild Press
Largo, Florida

Edited by Serena Daigle
Cover and interior design by Phantazmagoria Productions
Map by T. N. Daigle

ISBN: 979-8-9950379-0-3 (paperback)
ISBN: 979-8-9950379-1-0 (ebook)
ISBN: 979-8-9950379-2-7 (large print)

Library of Congress Control Number: 2026906002

First edition
10 9 8 7 6 5 4 3

Printed in the United States of America

For my dad.

And for everyone who took the time
to answer the question:

"Soooo, what did you think?"

Much love.

– TND

Prelude

THE NEW SHERIFF

November, 1883

CHAPTER ONE

The Arrival

"When's the new sheriff coming?" Jimmy blurted, abandoning all pretense of attention to his arithmetic lesson.

Young Jimmy Smith had turned around in his pew for the third time to peer toward the door, while Sarah Mills tapped her slate pencil against the wooden bench in a rhythm that matched the hammering from the courthouse construction outside.

The chalk dust danced in morning light streaming through the schoolhouse windows as Ellie Harper—a petite woman whose voice could rein in a stampede if it had to—wrote a new set of practice sums on the chalkboard and pretended not to notice her students were fidgeting like trapped rabbits. She swiped at the honey-brown strands that had escaped her braid and stepped back to inspect her work.

"Sheriff Bracken's train arrives at ten," Ellie replied, hazel eyes sharpening with irritation as she wiped chalk dust on the sturdy blue cotton of her skirt. "Now, who can tell me seven times eight?"

"My pa says he's from Chicago," this from Billy Hutchins, who'd spent the morning sketching what looked suspiciously like a pistol on his slate. "Says Chicago sheriffs shoot first and ask questions after."

Mary Kate sneered at Billy, unimpressed. "Silly, they don't have *sheriffs* in Chicago. They have *police detectives*. I've read all about them."

Ellie set down her chalk and surveyed the room. Twelve pairs of eyes stared back at her, bright with excitement and completely uninterested in multiplication tables. Every child in Cypress Run sat in that makeshift classroom, but their minds had clearly wandered to the train depot and the stranger who would arrive on the morning rails.

"That's enough for today." The words left her mouth before she'd fully decided to speak them. "Go on home. Mind yourselves around the construction."

The children didn't need to be told twice. They scattered, their voices rising in excited chatter as they spilled out into the humid morning air.

Ellie gathered her teaching materials and headed across the churchyard to the path that would take her to the clinic on Main Street.

The clinic smelled faintly of alcohol and camphor, the air still except for the scratch of a pen. Dr. Diego Delgado—a man shaped as much by the Cuban sun as by his years of frontier duty—looked up from his ledger, reading glasses balanced low on his nose, sleeves rolled precise, and eyes dark with a calm intelligence.

"Let me guess," he said, wry as a cat watching a dog chase its tail. "Arithmetic proved less fascinating than the looming specter of our shiny new sheriff."

"Couldn't get them to sit still if I'd nailed their feet to the floor." Ellie hung her satchel on its peg and twisted her braid up to pin it into the practical bun she wore when helping the doctor in the clinic. "Half the town's acting like the President's coming to visit."

"Can't say I blame them. It isn't often we get assigned an elected official without actually going through the election process. Been a whole two weeks since Judge Hartwell announced it. Long enough for all sorts of wild stories to take root."

"The children are half-convinced he's a dime novel hero finally settling down after too many adventures." Ellie moved to the medicine cabinet and began organizing bottles that didn't need organizing. "What kind of stories have you heard?"

"Oh, the usual frontier nonsense. Gunfighter from Texas. Federal marshal with a grudge. Some say he's a big city lawman who shot an innocent man." Diego's voice carried the weary skepticism of a man who'd heard too many tall tales. "Mrs. Mills swears he's seven feet tall and carries two revolvers."

"Mrs. Mills thinks the railroad's bringing Yankees to steal her chickens."

"True enough." Diego stood and walked to the window facing Main Street. The skeleton of the new courthouse rose beyond the saloon, cypress timbers climbing toward a roof that existed only in the surveyor's plans. "My question is whether this mysterious sheriff is a step up or a step down from our last one."

Ellie rolled her eyes. "Don't get me started on Sheriff Brown. Nobody could be a step down from that man. Didn't make it past one shootout."

"You say that as if you would have done any better with the Carter gang using you for target practice."

"You're right, I can't say whether I would have done much better. But at least I would have shot back instead of running off, which would have been a step in the right direction."

Diego chuckled and shook his head, eyeing the construction site across the street. "Sometimes I wonder if all this progress is worth the trouble it brings," he said.

Ellie joined him at the window, watching workers guide timber into place while the foreman shouted instructions that carried on the morning breeze. "You think the railroad's bad for us?"

"Good. Bad. Hard to say. Change is change." Diego adjusted his spectacles. "And change is coming whether we want it or not, Ellie. Only question we get to decide is whether we meet it head on or hide in the sand and hope we don't get washed away in the tide."

A train whistle echoed in the distance, long and mournful across the pine flats.

Ellie untied her apron and put it on the hook. "I'm going to meet that train."

"Professional curiosity?"

"Something like that."

Diego reached for his hat. "I'll come with you. If our new sheriff is half as dangerous as rumor suggests, someone's going to need medical attention before the day's out."

"Especially if Mrs. Mills is right about those two revolvers he's supposedly carrying."

"*Dios mío*, let's hope she's wrong about this one."

At the depot, Judge Hartwell stood rigid as a courthouse pillar, her silver hair pulled back so severely it could have been carved from marble. She clutched a leather portfolio against her chest and watched the approaching locomotive with the expression of someone expecting damnation, or at the very least a death sentence.

"Mrs. Harper, Dr. Delgado." Hartwell's greeting carried an edge sharper than usual. Her gray eyes darted toward the approaching train, then back to them. "I trust you're here to welcome our new sheriff?"

"Wouldn't miss it," Ellie said, glancing around at the gathering crowd—shopkeepers, dock workers, curious children pressed against the platform railings. "Whole town's curious to meet him."

Hartwell's mouth tightened. "Yes, well. Curiosity may be... premature." She cleared her throat, the sound lost in the growing rumble of the locomotive. "I should mention—Sheriff Bracken arrives with certain... *complications* to his record."

Diego raised an eyebrow. "What kind of complications?"

"The big city variety." Hartwell's fingers drummed against her portfolio. "There was an incident. The details remain murky, but it involved a politician's son and a poker game that went poorly."

Diego squinted against the glare. "And by 'went poorly,' I take it you mean that our new sheriff survived the poker game and the other man didn't?" he asked.

"Self-defense, supposedly," Hartwell continued over the noise. "But the timing was too coincidental to be anything other than suspicious; the young man was involved in a police investigation just before he was killed."

The locomotive trundled into the station, belching steam and cinders across the platform before hissing to a stop. Passengers began disembarking.

Ellie watched the stream of passengers, none of whom looked particularly sheriff-like. "You think he killed a man to cover up a crime?"

"I think Chicago wanted him gone, and we were the most convenient dumping ground." Hartwell's voice dropped.

"Meaning?" Diego pressed.

"Meaning we're getting a man other jurisdictions wouldn't take. The governor made it clear: Everfield County gets Thomas Bracken—or we get no sheriff at all."

The platform gradually emptied. The depot fell quiet except for the tick-tick-tick of cooling metal.

"Maybe he missed the connection?" Ellie suggested.

Then a figure emerged from the last car, moving with the careful deliberation of a man nursing a substantial headache.

"*Madre de Dios,*" Diego muttered. "Please tell me that's not him."

It was hard to say which piece of his outfit looked the most ridiculous in the sweltering humidity of Central Florida: the black wool frock coat, the blue jacquard vest, the starched white shirt collar, or the shiny laced up shoes—it was an ensemble that belonged in a fancy Chicago gambling parlor where the cooler climate would have allowed him to look distinguished, but here in the muggy heat of Cypress Run, he just appeared wilted and miserable. The odd outfit was made even more incongruous by the overly large canvas duffel that hung from one shoulder.

He paused at the bottom of the train steps, swaying slightly and squinting against the brutal sunshine like a cave creature dragged into daylight.

"Dear Lord," Ellie whispered. "Is he drunk?"

"More likely heat exhaustion," Diego observed, studying the man's posture, the careful way he held himself. "He looks like he's about to collapse, or attend a funeral. Probably his own if he doesn't do something about that coat."

The platform cleared around the figure in black, leaving him isolated in a pool of suspicious stares and uncomfortable silence. Children peeked around their parents' legs while shopkeepers exchanged meaningful glances.

The man attempted to straighten his shoulders, which only emphasized how thoroughly the heat had defeated him.

Judge Hartwell's mouth formed a thin line. "Mr. Bracken, I presume?"

The man in black turned toward them, and Ellie got her first clear look at the new sheriff. Long, angular face with a lean jawline that hadn't seen a razor in a day or two, dark auburn hair that may have been combed at some point but was now tousled and damp with perspiration, and bloodshot green eyes that couldn't help flicking from one detail to the next, even while being assaulted by the worst of the afternoon sun. If she were being honest, Ellie might have admitted that he could have looked handsome if he hadn't also looked like he'd been dragged behind the train instead of riding inside it.

"Judge Hartwell." His voice carried a Northern accent as sharp on the ear as rye bread was on the palate. He attempted what might have been a polite nod. "Grateful to finally meet you in person."

"Indeed." Hartwell's tone could have frozen the Everglades. "I trust your journey was... comfortable?"

Bracken glanced down at his wool suit, then back at the judge. "Well... I'll tell you truthfully, I almost got burned alive once, and I am looking back on the memory with an unexpected amount of nostalgia for how chilly it was in comparison."

Hartwell seemed unimpressed by the man's attempt at wit. "Well." She cleared her throat. "May I introduce Mrs. Eliza Harper and Dr. Diego Delgado? Dr. Delgado is our local physician as well as the county coroner. And Mrs. Harper is both his nurse as well as the school teacher here in Cypress Run."

"I'd say it was a pleasure," Bracken said, "but that seems like a very strong choice of words today. I do look forward to getting acquainted when it's not..." he trailed off, waving his slouched felt hat vaguely at the sun as if it had personally offended him, "...whatever *this* is."

Ellie and Diego made their pleasantries before making their excuses to retreat. This was definitely Hartwell's show now. The judge could handle whatever mess the government officials had dumped on their doorstep.

"Perhaps," Hartwell said, her voice carrying across the platform, "we should discuss your accommodations somewhere with shade."

"I'd be much obliged." Bracken hefted his duffel and gestured weakly toward the town. "Lead the way, Your Honor. Just... slowly, if you'd be so kind."

Judge Hartwell ignored the request and set a brisk pace down Main Street, her heels clicking against the wooden boardwalk. Behind her, the new sheriff followed a half-step back, hop shuffling occasionally to quickly catch up again when he fell behind, his duffel slung over one shoulder and his free hand occasionally reaching out to steady himself against a post or rail.

That black wool suit was drawing stares from every porch and doorway they passed—exactly the kind of spectacle Hartwell had hoped to avoid. The man was a walking advertisement for poor judgment, and she had the distinct pleasure of having to explain why good judgment mattered in this jurisdiction.

"Let me be clear about your situation here, Mr. Bracken," she began without preamble, her voice carrying the authority of the bench even in casual conversation. "You are here because the previous sheriff abandoned his post, not because anyone requested your particular... expertise."

"Understood." He squinted at the storefronts they passed, his steps slowing as they passes the general store where his eyes flicked from the bullet gouges in the wood, to the fresh paint on the door. He shuffle hopped to catch up again.

At least he wasn't arguing. Yet.

"You didn't come to us recommended," Hartwell continued. "You came to us because we needed a body with a badge and men in powerful positions—with agendas they have not chosen to share—decided you would be suitable."

"That does seem to be a fair assessment of the situation. Mighty grateful you took the time to summarize it for me." He tugged at his starched shirt collar, already darkened with sweat. "Though I have to ask—when you say 'abandoned,' are we talking about a strategic retreat to greener pastures or did he just decide he preferred breathing to badge-wearing?"

There it was—that flippant Chicago mouth she'd been warned about. Judge Hartwell kept walking, noting how his sharp green eyes didn't settle on one space for very long, focusing briefly on every building and every watching face along the street before moving on to the next thing.

"The Carter gang shot up the Sheriff's Office. Your predecessor was last seen heading for Tampa at a full gallop. Which brings me to my first expectation. I will not tolerate any sheriff in my jurisdiction who resembles the stereotypes associated with big city police work—corruption, excessive force, or playing favorites with local interests."

His survey of the watching faces paused. "Well, Your Honor, if I run across any corrupt, trigger-happy, bribe-taking lawmen wandering around your swamp here, I'll be sure to pass along your message."

Her mouth twitched. The man had brass, she'd give him that. Whether that was an asset or a liability remained to be seen.

"Everfield County is attempting to build something civilized here. We have railroad investors watching, state officials taking notes, and a new courthouse taking shape." She gestured toward the half-built courthouse rising from the town square like a promise. "That represents order, Mr. Bracken. Law that doesn't depend on who's fastest with a gun or smoothest with a bribe. That represents six months of civic investment and railroad confidence."

She let her voice harden deliberately. "Those investors expect their money protected by competent law enforcement, not some scandal-ridden exile looking to drink away his Chicago troubles."

"Ah." Bracken met her eyes for a moment, jade green and sharp as glass despite looking like somebody had thrown sand in them. For a moment, Hartwell thought he was going to say something about those Chicago troubles, but the man smiled and looked away. "Speaking of drinking away troubles," he said, nodding politely to a laborer who wouldn't stop staring, "I'm assuming that 'room and board' doesn't actually cover the occasional saloon beverage, so when could a sheriff new to this jurisdiction reasonably expect his first wages?"

Judge Hartwell stared at him with an eyebrow raised. Was he truly this obtuse, or was this some sort of test of her patience?

His playful grin faltered, and he stammered a little on the recovery. "Or maybe I should let you get to know me better before I start making tasteless jokes. Message received and understood; question withdrawn."

At least he could recognize when he'd overplayed his hand. She rolled her eyes and resumed walking, pointing out landmarks with the efficiency of a land surveyor. "Mrs. Wyatt's boarding house—the closest thing Cypress Run currently has to a hotel. Our more respectable city patrons and passers through pay for rooms there. Dr. Delgado's clinic—where you'll likely become a regular patient, I suspect, if you don't learn to keep track of how fast your tongue is wagging. The Cypress House Saloon—our primary source of Saturday night disturbances, and most certainly *not* an establishment covered by the 'room and board' clause in your contract."

The sheriff's office squatted at the end of Main Street like an afterthought—a simple clapboard building with a covered porch and a single barred window. A hand-painted sign reading "Sheriff" hung crooked above the door. She watched Bracken take it in with what might have been resignation. He reached out and prodded at one of the bullet holes in the timber frame, picking at a loose splinter around the edge, then took a deep breath and crossed the threshold.

The interior matched what she assumed were his lowered expectations: a desk, two chairs, a gun rack, and a potbellied stove that would be useless against the heat but might prove valuable come winter. A door at the back led to the jail.

He pushed through and stopped short. Two cells stood side by side along a narrow corridor, their iron bars painted black and solid as a bank vault. The cell closest to the door contained a cot, a washbasin, and a small table with crooked legs that might have been a nightstand.

"Cozy." He set his duffel on the bed and tested the mattress with one hand. From the look on his face and the suspicious shape of the mattress, the bedding was clearly less than ideal. "Tell me, Your Honor—do all your lawmen sleep in jail cells, or did Chief Killigan honestly give me that bad a recommendation?"

"Practical economy. The county provides a building, not luxury accommodations." She surveyed the cramped space with obvious distaste, though she had to admit the symbolism wasn't lost on her either. "But I trust a man of your... flexible moral background can adapt to frontier conditions."

"Well, at least if I arrest myself for excessive drinking, I won't have far to stumble." He sat heavily on the bed, which creaked ominously under his weight. "And it's definitely an improvement over my last apartment. It's free and not a single rat that I can see."

She studied him through the bars, noting the brittle edge to his smile.

"Your first priority is establishing order without antagonizing the railroad surveyors, cattle ranchers, or dock workers. Think you can manage that?"

"Sure thing. I'll just politely ask everyone not to commit any crimes for the foreseeable future. Then I won't have to antagonize anyone." He loosened his tie with a grimace. "Any other priorities you need me to manage?"

Judge Hartwell watched him through the bars, her expression carefully neutral. He was either the most reckless man she had ever set eyes on, or clever enough to hide sharp instincts behind careless humor.

"The town council meets Thursday evenings at the church. I expect you to attend."

"Wouldn't miss it." He folded forward, resting his elbows on his knees and pressing his palms to his eyes, evidently still fending off the headache from earlier. He groaned, then forced himself to sit up straight again, shooting her another of his little half-smiles. "Anything else?"

Her expression remained unchanged. "Don't disappoint me, Sheriff. I already don't expect much, so the bar is as low as it can be set. But please, God, don't disappoint me."

She left him sitting in his cell-bedroom, her heels clicking purposefully down the boardwalk. Whether Tom Bracken would prove to be Cypress Run's salvation—or just another disaster they couldn't afford—remained to be seen. But one thing was certain: he was her responsibility now, for better or worse.

CHAPTER TWO

Welcome to Cypress Run

Bracken sat on the bed in his cell long after his boss had left, wondering if exile to a Florida swamp was really better than whatever fate he had dodged by fleeing the political fallout of his actions in Chicago. When he finally forced himself to move again, his first order of business was shrugging out of his black coat. The garment peeled away from his shoulders like shed skin, revealing a well-worn leather shoulder harness holding a pair of holsters against his chest. Two mismatched Colt .45s sat snug against his ribs, their grips darkened by years of handling. He draped the coat over the back of the desk chair and rolled his shoulders, working out the kinks from the long train ride.

His canvas duffel bag landed on the desk with a solid thump. Bracken pulled the drawstring loose and began extracting his worldly possessions. The small bundle of clothes came out first. He looked around the spartan office for someplace to store them, then realized the futility of the search.

"Well. That's a problem."

The desk drawers yielded nothing but dust and a few scattered paperclips. A small bookshelf held only a bible and what appeared to be a guide to Florida wildlife. The filing cabinet stood against the far wall like a metal monument to bureaucracy. Bracken tugged the top drawer open and peered inside. Empty as a politician's promise.

"Perfect." He began folding his shirts into the top drawer, treating the filing cabinet like the world's most official chest of drawers. He never thought he'd be the sort to organize his clothes alphabetically, but there it was: shirts, trousers, undergarments, vests.

From the bottom of the duffel, he extracted a mahogany case roughly three feet long. The brass fittings caught what little light filtered through the dusty windows. He set it carefully against the wall behind his desk, then pulled out a leather rifle scabbard. The slide-action Colt Lightning inside stacked neatly into the office gun rack, joining the dusty weapon already hanging there. Later tonight, he'd give them both a good cleaning; his own Lightning could use the love, and the other rifle... well, it would be nice to know whether it was strictly decorative *before* someone needed it for something useful.

The canvas bag that contained his gun cleaning kit and boxes of ammunition, he stored in the desk's bottom drawer, the metallic rattle of cartridges unnaturally loud in the quiet office.

A small stack of sheet music followed along with three books that completed his literary collection: a volume of Shakespeare's comedies, an extremely well-thumbed and dog-eared copy of "Elements of Geometry and Trigonometry" by Charles Davies, and a random dime detective novel with a lurid cover that he hadn't had time to tear into yet—but judging by the Main Street in this town, it was only a matter of hours before he'd miraculously find the time to read it cover to cover.

Bracken stacked the books on the small shelf and tucked the sheet music into a desk drawer. The entire unpacking process had taken less than ten minutes, a testament to either efficient packing or a life lived light.

He studied his new domain with hands on his hips—one desk, two chairs, a filing cabinet full of clothes, and a gun rack. Not to mention his own personal jail cell in the back. That was a lovely touch. The office looked exactly the same as when he'd arrived, except for the coat draped over the chair and the billiard cue case leaning against the wall. His entire existence had been absorbed into the space without leaving a mark.

"Home sweet home," he muttered with a sigh.

And that, he decided, was enough sentimentality for one afternoon. It was time to see what passed for civilization in this godforsaken swamp.

He grabbed his coat and shrugged back into it, the familiar weight of the wool draping just right to settle the shoulder holsters into place. The jacket hid the weapons completely, returning him to the appearance of a traveling death salesman or perhaps a very serious accountant.

The lights of The Cypress House Saloon beckoned from across the dusty street where the sound of piano music promised whiskey, shade, and the kind of conversation that might teach him which locals were worth trusting and which ones would put a knife between his ribs for sport.

Bracken locked the office door behind him and headed toward the sound, figuring that if he was going to be the sheriff of this town, he might as well meet the people he'd be sheriffing.

Jennifer Starr had seen every type of man walk through her fine wooden screen door in the six years she'd owned The Cypress House. Cattlemen with dust in their beards and murder in their eyes, railroad workers flush with payday whiskey money, drifters who'd kill you for the coins in your pocket, and smooth-talking gamblers who'd take your ranch with a smile. She could read them all like yesterday's newspaper.

But the man who stepped through her doors at half past three looked like he'd wandered out of a men's fashion catalog and onto the wrong side of the Mason-Dixon line. Black wool frock over a fancy blue vest buttoned tight despite the swamp heat, white shirt that might have looked sharp before he began to sweat through it, and shoes that had never seen honest mud. The man paused just inside the doorway while the screen shut softly behind him, blinking against the saloon's perpetual haze of pipe smoke and lantern light.

Jennifer watched him from behind the bar, polishing a glass that didn't need polishing. His shoulders dropped the moment he cleared the threshold, like a man finally allowed to breathe. His eyes swept the room with the calculating precision of a cardsharp, cataloging exits and potential threats, evaluating the action at the three card tables and the subtler action up the stairway.

But when his gaze landed on the billiard table in the back corner, something shifted in his posture entirely.

Relief. Pure, desperate relief flooded his features for exactly three seconds before he caught himself and straightened. His hands flexed at his sides like he was fighting the urge to grab a cue stick and never let go.

Instead, he walked straight to her bar with measured steps, each one deliberate as a chess move.

"Whiskey," he said, settling onto a stool. "The good stuff, if you've got it. The bad stuff if you don't."

Jennifer reached for a bottle of Kentucky bourbon she kept for customers with taste and deeper pockets. She poured two fingers, then set the bottle down with a deliberate *thunk*—close enough he could read the label, far enough he'd have to ask for more.

"Fresh off the train, I'm guessing."

He nodded and reached inside his coat where, instead of a wallet, he had a small fold of bills stuck to the lining with a straight pin. As he worked it loose, his coat fell open just enough to reveal the shoulder holster strapped across his chest.

Jennifer slid the glass toward him and tapped the bar with one knuckle. "You ever consider buying yourself a billfold?"

The stranger's mouth quirked into a genuine smile. "I *do* have a billfold. Just never has any money in it."

"Lost it gambling?"

"Nah. Just makes the pickpockets back in Chicago happy if they know they can borrow it from me from time to time when they really get the itch to lift something. I usually get it back in a day or two."

He unpinned a dollar bill and held it out.

"Landlady only had to throw her shoes at me once before I learned to keep the rent money tucked away in other places."

Jennifer plucked the bill from his fingers and made change at the till. "Your landlady. In Chicago?"

"That's the one. Don't worry, I settled up with her before I left. No need to worry about her hunting me down and flinging shoes across your bar." He gestured around the saloon with his whiskey. "Speaking of satisfying financial arrangements, though, does Cypress Run have anything similar I should worry about?"

"We've got our share of light-fingered folks, but they tend toward bigger game than pocket change. Cattle, lumber, the occasional shipment of goods that falls off a wagon."

Jennifer pulled out a rag and wiped down the countertop nearby where a patron hadn't quite got all the beer to his mouth, studying the stranger out of the corner of her eye as she did. The smile was real enough, but his eyes never stopped moving, flitting from one potential trouble spot to the next almost as well as Jennifer did—and she owned the place.

"You planning on staying in Cypress long enough to worry about our local talent?"

"That depends on a number of things, I suppose, including how much I have to worry about."

"Sugar, in my experience, you should always be worried."

She leaned forward, elbows on the bar, and let the posture do its work. He glanced—quick, polite—then met her eyes again without lingering.

"I imagine worrying's half the fun with you," he said. "I'm just trying to keep an eye out for the kind that's *not* so much fun."

"Well," she said, leaning into her Savannah drawl, "we've got Two-Finger Jake who thinks he's clever lifting wallets during church service, but he's dumber than a bucket of rocks. Old Maria runs a decent shell game down by the docks, but she's honest about being crooked, if that makes sense. Then there's the railroad crew—they'll steal anything that ain't nailed down and half the things that are."

The stranger sipped his bourbon and made an appreciative sound. "Anybody I should watch out for special?"

"Depends on a number of things, I suppose," she grinned as she volleyed his earlier words back, "including who's asking."

Jennifer leaned forward, inviting confidence with proximity, her smile warm enough to hide the sharp teeth underneath. "We don't get many strangers through here who dress like riverboat gamblers and pin their money to their clothes. You selling coffins or buying trouble?"

"Neither, if I'm lucky." He took a sip of the whiskey. "Name's Tom Bracken. Everfield County's new sheriff, for better or worse."

Jennifer had figured as much the moment Judge Hartwell walked him off that train platform looking like she'd swallowed a live toad. "Jennifer Starr. I own this establishment and most of the gossip that comes with it."

"It's very nice to meet you, Miss Starr."

Jennifer grinned, appreciating how his voice had dropped to a flirtatious purr. "Normally I'd tell you to just call me Jennifer, but I do like the way you say, 'Miss Starr.'"

"How about we split the difference with 'Miss Jennifer?'"

She smiled. "I think I could be agreeable to that."

"Miss Jennifer, then. Any other local customs I should be aware of? Besides creative pilfering techniques."

"Judge Hartwell probably told you about the railroad coming through. That's stirring up all kinds of interesting negotiations." Jennifer's smile never wavered, but her eyes cooled. "Men with more money than sense, making deals that don't always account for existing arrangements."

"Existing arrangements?"

"Every town's got its ecosystem, sugar. You mess with one corner, the whole thing shifts. Sometimes violently."

Bracken nodded slowly, and Jennifer could tell that he'd taken her warning to heart.

"Well then," he said, raising his glass. "Here's to understanding the local ecosystem."

"You play?" She nodded her head toward the corner. The sheriff followed her gaze to the green felt, where one of the men was lining up what looked like an impossible bank shot. Bracken actually winced when the man missed it, even though it was obvious he was going to.

"Little bit," he grudgingly admitted.

"'Little bit,' he says." Jennifer laughed. "Honey, I've seen that look before. You're practically undressing that table with your eyes."

"Your table's very pretty."

"Mmm-hmm." She refilled his glass without being asked. "Well, Sheriff, a man's got to have his vices. Some folks drink, some gamble, some chase women. Long as you keep the peace in my establishment, I don't much care if you want to show off your stick work."

The double meaning wasn't lost on him. He grinned—actual dimples this time, not the practiced charm. "I'll try to keep my demonstrations tasteful."

"See that you do." She tilted her head, considering him. "Though I've got a feeling, Sheriff, that 'tasteful' isn't a word that follows you around much."

He raised his glass in concession. "You'd be surprised how often I prove people wrong."

"No," Jennifer said, her smile sharpening, "I really wouldn't."

The screen door swung open, swirling around a gust of humid afternoon air, and announcing the arrival of three men who looked like they'd spent the day wrestling cattle. They moved with the particular swagger of cowhands with fresh pay burning holes in their pockets, scanning the room for opportunities to lighten their financial burden.

"Speaking of trouble," Jennifer murmured. "That's Lloyd Hendricks and his cronies. They drive cattle for the local farmers when the mood strikes them, and they've got about as much sense as God gave a turnip. Fair warning—they don't much care for authority figures."

Jennifer and Bracken both watched the newcomers push toward the billiard table, where they began loudly critiquing the ongoing game. One of them, a tall man with tobacco-stained teeth, shoved a lumberyard worker and backed him against the billiard table, thick fingers jabbed into the smaller man's chest while his two cronies flanked him like hunting dogs waiting for the word. The bullied man clutched his hat in both hands, sweat beading on his forehead despite the saloon's shade.

"Two weeks' wages, Murphy," Hendricks growled, loud enough for half the bar to hear. "You said you'd have it yesterday. Yesterday came and went, and here we are."

Murphy stammered something about needing more time, about his wife being sick, about the logging crew cutting his hours. Jennifer had heard it all before. The man was a decent sort when sober, but he had the worst luck with cards this side of perdition. Hendricks, on the other hand, was exactly the kind of customer she tolerated because his money spent as well as anyone else's—but barely.

Bracken finished his whiskey in one smooth pull and set the glass down with deliberate care. "Well," he said, straightening from the bar, "This has been a real pleasure, Miss Jennifer, but I figure it's time I should go earn my pay."

Jennifer leaned forward on her elbows. "You sure about that? Hendricks brought two friends, and they're not the talking type."

"Always best to introduce yourself proper." Bracken's smile held no warmth. "Set up good relationships with the neighbors."

He strolled toward the back corner like he was heading to Sunday service, hands loose at his sides, that heavy wool frock coat swaying with each step. Jennifer noticed how the other patrons tracked his movement—some curious, some wary, all waiting to see what the new sheriff was made of.

"Afternoon, gentlemen." Bracken's voice carried just enough to cut through the tavern noise. "Couldn't help but notice you're having a spirited discussion."

Hendricks turned, sizing up the stranger in the undertaker's coat. "This ain't your business, mister. Just collecting what's owed."

"Tom Bracken. Everfield County Sheriff." He pulled back his coat just enough to reveal the badge pinned to his vest. "And everything in this town's my business now."

The two cronies exchanged glances, but Hendricks erupted in laughter. "Sheriff? You look more like a peacock at a barn dance, all dressed up and nowhere to go. Why don't you scuttle off and let the real men handle this?"

Bracken glanced at the billiard table, running his finger along the felt edge like a man appraising fine silk. "Tell you what, Mr. Hendricks. You seem like a sporting man. How about we settle this civilized-like?"

"What'd you have in mind?"

"Game of eight-ball." Bracken selected a cue from the wall rack, testing its weight and balance. "I win, you forgive Mr. Murphy's debt and buy a round for the house. You win, I'll pay what Mr. Murphy owes out of my own pocket and cover your drinking for the rest of the evening."

Jennifer saw the calculation flicker across Hendricks's face. Free drinks for his crew versus one game against a city boy who probably learned billiards in some fancy Chicago parlor. The cattleman's grin spread wide as a gator's.

"You got yourself a deal, Sheriff." Hendricks grabbed his own cue and chalked the tip with theatrical flair. "Hope you brought more than five dollars to this town."

Bracken rolled the chalk between his fingers, coating them white as bone. "Oh, I think I can cover it."

Murphy pressed himself against the wall, clutching his hat like a life preserver.

Jennifer watched Bracken chalk his cue with unhurried care. The saloon had gone graveyard quiet—even the piano player had stopped mid-song to crane his neck toward the back corner. Money was about to change hands, and in Cypress Run, that always drew a crowd.

Hendricks broke with the confidence of a man who'd hustled railroad workers out of their paychecks since the war ended. The balls scattered across green felt like buckshot, two solids dropping into corner pockets. He circled the table with a predator's swagger, chalking his cue between shots.

"Your boy Murphy here owes me fourteen dollars," Hendricks called to the room, lining up his next shot. "Figured the new law might want to know the kind of deadbeats he's protecting."

Bracken leaned against the wall, studying the table layout with undisguisable interest, the same look in his eyes that a cat got when a colorful bird caught its attention; Jennifer was certain if Bracken had a tail, it would be twitching in anticipation of easy prey.

When Hendricks missed his third shot—a tricky bank that would've impressed a circus performer—the sheriff stepped forward and surveyed his options.

"Fourteen dollars," Bracken mused, selecting his target. "That's two weeks of Mr. Murphy's logging wages?"

"Three, the way Old Pete's been cutting hours." Hendricks crossed his arms, confident the stranger was about to learn an expensive lesson about frontier justice.

Bracken's first shot dropped the nine-ball clean into the side pocket. His second sent the twelve spinning off two rails before it found home in the corner. By his fourth shot, Hendricks had stopped smirking. By his sixth, a bead of sweat traced down the logger's temple.

Jennifer found herself leaning forward despite her best efforts to maintain professional detachment. She'd seen plenty of men play billiards in her establishment, but Bracken's movements around the table held the fluid grace of a man who'd spent more hours with a cue than most men spent with their wives. No wasted motion, no showboating—just one ball after another disappearing into leather pockets while Hendricks's confident grin slowly curdled.

The eight-ball sat trapped behind two of Hendricks's solids, an impossible shot that would require either magic or angles that defied common sense. Bracken studied it for a long moment, rolling chalk between his fingers like prayer beads.

"Corner pocket," he announced, pointing his cue toward the far end of the table.

The room held its breath. Bracken's stroke sent the cue ball careening off three cushions in sequence, clipping Hendricks's ball just enough to nudge it aside. The eight-ball rolled forward with agonizing slowness, caught the corner pocket's lip, and dropped from sight.

The silence stretched until Hendricks's curse broke it like a gunshot.

"Aww, dammit." The cattleman threw his cue onto the table where it clattered against the remaining balls. "Where'd you learn to shoot like that?"

Bracken set his own cue neatly in the rack, almost with a reverence. "Picked it up from a math book, if you can believe it. Good game." He extended his hand. After a beat, Hendricks took it, grip uneasy but firm.

"Well then, gentlemen," Bracken went on easily, his voice carrying over the hush, "looks like our wager's settled. Mr. Hendricks, the house is owed a round. Mr. Murphy... seems your slate's been wiped clean."

Hendricks dug into his vest, every motion reluctant, while his cronies scuffed their boots at the floorboards. A few bills slapped onto the felt with the weight of execution.

"Round for the house," Hendricks muttered.

"Much obliged," Bracken said, touching the brim of his hat. Then, almost as an afterthought, his green eyes flicked to the bar and back. "And for being such good sports, Miss Jennifer will pour a drink for Mr. Hendricks and his men on *my* tab."

The cattle driver blinked in surprise, then gave a grudging nod. A single whiskey apiece didn't balance the scales, but it kept him from being the butt of every joke tomorrow.

The saloon erupted in noise, laughter and jeers in qual measure, and boots stomping toward the bar. Murphy, pale as chalk, clasped Bracken's hand with both of his before stumbling for the front door like a man just released from the gallows.

Jennifer poured the first glasses herself, hiding her smile behind a neutral curve of lips. Bracken had walked the knife's edge—shamed a man without making him an enemy, bought goodwill with a gesture that cost him little but earned him plenty.

And when she looked back across the room, she noticed his shoulders had loosened, his stride carrying an easy swagger as he returned to his original spot at the bar, like he'd just remembered something good he'd left behind in Chicago and finally found again on her billiard table.

"Well now," Jennifer said, refilling his glass without being asked. "That was quite a show. You hustle pool for a living before you took up law enforcement?"

"Just a hobby. Little practice, lotta patience. Or the other way around." He swirled the whiskey, watching the amber liquid catch the lamplight.

"Hendricks has been running that same con on newcomers for two years."

"Figured as much. Man like that doesn't challenge strangers to billiards unless he's used to winning." Bracken picked up his glass but didn't drink. "Question is, how much of that debt was real and how much was Murphy getting worked over for sport?"

Jennifer considered her answer while she wiped down glasses. In most towns, she'd play it close to the vest with a new lawman, see which way he leaned before revealing too much. But something about the way Bracken had handled Hendricks—firm without being cruel, clever without being vindictive—suggested he might be worth trusting.

"Murphy's good for about half of what Hendricks claimed," she said finally. "The rest was interest and fees that somehow kept growing every time they talked."

Bracken nodded like that confirmed something he'd already suspected. Bracken straightened, rolling his shoulders to work out the tension from leaning over the table. "Speaking of which, I don't suppose I could trade my share of Hendricks's largesse for something more substantial? Been living on train coffee and stale biscuits for three days, and I think my stomach's preparing to file a formal complaint."

Jennifer laughed, the sound carrying genuine warmth. "Sugar, after that display, I'd be happy to rustle you up something decent. We've got beef stew that's been simmering all day, fresh cornbread, and I think there's still some of that apple pie Mrs. Henderson dropped off this morning."

"Sounds like heaven on a plate."

"Coming right up." She turned toward the kitchen, then paused. "Fair warning though—word's going to spread about tonight faster than wildfire in August. By morning, every card sharp and pool hustler within fifty miles is going to know there's a sheriff in Cypress Run who can make balls dance to his tune."

Bracken's grin held no trace of concern. "Let them come. I could use the entertainment."

"Careful what you wish for, Sheriff. This town's got more than its share of folks looking to prove themselves against anyone fool enough to claim they're faster, smarter, or luckier."

"I guess it's a good thing I never claimed to be any of those things."

Act One

THE SURVEYOR'S END

CHAPTER THREE

The Crime Scene

Bracken stood on the boardwalk just outside of the saloon feeling something approaching optimism. A hot meal, good whiskey, and his first decent billiards game since leaving Chicago—it had unwound a knot of stress he hadn't even realized was there.

The afternoon sun had gotten lower, and he no longer felt like he was wedged between Satan's ass cheeks. He could even see the street in front of him, now that the sunlight wasn't jabbing ice picks into his eyes. It seemed as good a time as any to take a stroll and see what sort of place he'd been sentenced to.

The sound of children's voices cut through his woolgathering—not the usual playground chatter, either. These voices carried the pitch of fear wrapped in excitement that every lawman learned to recognize.

Bracken followed the sound around the corner of Cotton's General Store and found a cluster of five children, the oldest not more than seven or eight, huddled near the wooden steps, all talking at once in that breathless way kids had when they'd stumbled onto something bigger than their usual mischief.

"—tell you it was a body, Jimmy! I seen it plain as day—"

"You're full of beans, Mary Kate. Bodies don't just float around—"

"This one did! All chewed up like something got at it—"

Bracken slowed his approach. The children hadn't noticed him yet, too caught up in their heated debate over whatever they'd stumbled across. A girl with pigtails clutched a sodden hat in her hands, wringing water from its brim.

The conversation died the moment they spotted Bracken approaching. Five pairs of eyes went wide, and the group instinctively shuffled closer together like a school of minnows sensing a predator.

Bracken stopped a good ten feet away and studied their faces.

"Afternoon," Bracken said. When none of them responded, he lowered himself to sit cross-legged in the dirt, deliberately making himself smaller. Bracken watched the kids watching him.

Asking flat out where they saw the body was about the easiest way he knew to *not* get the information he needed. They'd clam up and close ranks. He'd have to get them to talk voluntarily. Like any interrogation, it was just a matter of finding the correct angle and applying just enough pressure to sink the ball without scratching.

He removed his own hat and set it beside him. "Name's Tom Bracken. I'm the new sheriff here. Which probably makes me about as fascinating as a rat on a church pew, I reckon."

A few nervous giggles broke the tension.

"That's a fine hat you got there," he continued, picking up a stick and pointing with it before drawing meaningless patterns in the dirt. "Yours?"

The girl with the pigtails shook her head.

"Looks like it's been swimming," Bracken continued. "Hat tell you how it learned to do that?"

A giggle escaped before she could stop it. "Hats can't talk, mister."

"Ah, that explains it." Bracken picked up his own hat and studied it with exaggerated seriousness. "I've been wearing this particular hat for near on two years now, and it hasn't told me a single useful thing. I just figured it wasn't much of a conversationalist. Guess that was pretty silly of me, huh?"

That earned him a few more giggles, and he saw shoulders start to relax.

"Well, if a hat can't talk... How are we going to find out how it learned to go swimming? Think we could ask its owner?" He drew what might have been a very sad horse or a very happy cow.

The girl shook her head so hard, her pigtails flailed.

"No? That's a shame. Think it's got any friends? Maybe we could ask them. Think you could show me where you found it?"

The other children began creeping forward, drawn by curiosity and the strange sight of a grown man making pictures in the dirt like he had all day to waste.

"We was just playing by the water," the girl said eventually, her voice barely above a whisper. "At Gator Creek, down past the cypress grove where Mama says not to go 'cause of the gators."

"Mamas are usually pretty smart about things like that, but sometimes they aren't all that much fun," Bracken agreed solemnly. "If I promise not to tell your mamas that you were having fun and not being so smart, think you might tell me what the hat was doing when you found it?"

"It was floating," piped up a freckled boy with dark hair. "Right near where we seen—" He clammed up as the girl shot him a warning look.

"Near where you seen what?" Bracken kept his voice casual, still focused on his stick drawing. "More hats? Whole hat parade maybe?"

"A man," the girl whispered. "Floating face down. His chest was all torn up like something with big teeth got him."

The stick went still in Bracken's hand. He looked up slowly, meeting her frightened gaze directly for the first time. "That's a mighty scary thing to see, Miss. I'm very sorry you had to see something like that. You think maybe it could have been something else? A log or... or somebody trying to get rid of their mama's prize rug before she discovered they spilled some ink on it?" That got a little bit of a giggle. "Nothing like that, huh? You definitely saw what you saw?"

She nodded vigorously. "Billy said he was just sleeping, but sleeping folks don't float. And they don't bleed like that."

"Well, do you suppose it might help if I went and had a look?" Five children all nodded in the affirmative, so Bracken stood and dusted off his pants with his hat. "Think you kids could show me this hat swimming spot?"

The children exchanged uncertain glances, and he could see the debate playing out on their faces. Adventure versus safety, curiosity versus the ingrained warning to stay away from the creek after dark. The girl looked down at the soggy hat in her hands, then back up at him.

"You won't tell our folks we was where we wasn't supposed to be?"

"Far as I'm concerned, you were being good citizens reporting suspicious hat activity." He winked. "That's sheriff business. Confidential."

The children led Bracken through a maze of cypress knees and Spanish moss. The barely-there path that wound between palmetto scrub and stands of saw grass, sweat already collecting under his hat band despite the canopy overhead. The air grew thick with the smell of rotting vegetation and stagnant water, punctuated by the occasional splash of something large disturbing the surface. The children's voices dropped to whispers as they approached the water.

"There," Jimmy said, pointing toward a bend in the creek where a fallen log created a natural dam. "Right by that big cypress."

Bracken saw it immediately—a dark shape bobbing face-down in the tea-colored water, arms spread wide like a man trying to embrace the whole swamp. Even from twenty feet away, he could make out the torn fabric of what had once been a shirt and the pale gleam of exposed skin beneath.

"Oh, that's going to be awful," he muttered, not at all relishing the thought of wading into that murky water to retrieve the body. He began shrugging out of his coat. "Alright, kids. I'm going to need you to stand way back from the water while I—"

A splash cut him off. The dark-haired boy with freckles had already waded knee-deep into the soupy water, pushing through lily pads and duck weed toward the floating corpse.

"Hey, kid! Get outta there!" Bracken called out, his voice sharp with alarm. "Come back here!"

One of the older girls yelled, "Nate, you get out of there right now!"

The boy—Nate, it would seem—ignored them both completely. With the grim determination of someone who'd made up his mind, he grabbed hold of the corpse's shirt and began to drag it toward shore. "Can't leave him floating out here," the boy called back, his voice steady despite the circumstances. "Ain't right."

"Kid, I appreciate the sentiment, but if you get hurt out there, your mother'll use my hide for a throw rug." Bracken took a step toward the water's edge.

The kid glanced back with brown eyes that held too much knowledge for a boy his age. "Already got him halfway. Might as well finish."

The boy gave one final push, and the corpse bumped against the muddy bank with a wet sound that made two of the younger children step back. Nate waded out, water streaming from his pants legs, and wiped his hands on his shirt like he'd just finished hauling in a particularly uncooperative catfish.

"Much obliged," Bracken said, studying the boy's face. No tears, no trembling—just the practical acceptance of someone who'd seen death before. Either this kid was tougher than rawhide or he was in shock. "You always this helpful with dead folks?"

"Mama says you help when you can, even when it's ugly."

"That's a very excellent philosophy. But next time, let the grown-ups handle the corpse-wrangling, understand?" Bracken studied the boy's face, noting the stubborn tilt of his chin. "You got a name?"

"Nate Harper."

Harper. Bracken nodded—same name as the schoolteacher Judge Hartwell had introduced him to at the train. The resemblance was there too, in the shape of the eyes and the faint dusting of freckles.

"Well, Nate Harper, you just saved me from having to swim in swamp soup, so I owe you one." Bracken turned his attention to the body, now visible in the shallow water.

The chest wounds were extensive—four parallel gashes that had opened him from collarbone to sternum. Could've been claws, could've been something else entirely.

"Who usually comes running when there's a medical problem around here?" he asked, not looking up from the corpse.

"Dr. Delgado," one of the girls piped up. "He looks at dead folks to figure out what killed them. Miss Harper helps him sometimes."

"Miss Harper being this one's mama?" Bracken nodded toward Nate.

"She's our teacher," Jimmy said. "And she helps the doc with sick folks, too. She knows about blood and such."

Bracken looked at the group of children, all staring at him with expectant faces. He needed to secure the scene, examine the body, and figure out whether they were dealing with an animal attack or something worse. But first, he needed the people who actually knew what they were doing.

"All right." He straightened and pointed at Jimmy and the girl with braids. "You two—Jimmy and... Mary Kate, right?—I need you to run and fetch Dr. Delgado and Miss Harper. Tell them the new sheriff needs them down at Gator Creek, and to bring whatever they use for looking at dead folks. Think you can do that?"

Both children nodded vigorously.

"Good. Rest of you, we're gonna wait right here and make sure nothing disturbs our friend in the water. And Nate?" He fixed the boy with a stern look. "No more swimming until we figure out what made those holes in his chest."

The two messengers took off at a run, leaving Bracken alone with three children and a corpse. He pulled out his pocket watch and checked the time. Half past four. The sun would be setting in only an hour or two, and he had a feeling this particular investigation was going to require more daylight than Florida was willing to provide.

"Well," he said to no one in particular, "so much for a quiet first day."

The sound of voices carried across the water before Ellie and Diego reached the creek bank. She'd been making her rounds at the clinic when word reached her that some of the younger children had stumbled across something down by Gator Creek—something that required the new sheriff's attention.

"Should've known he'd be trouble," Diego muttered beside her, adjusting his grip on his medical bag. "First day on the job and the man's already tripping over bodies."

Ellie pushed through the cypress grove and stopped dead.

"Nathaniel Harper!" Her voice cracked like a whip across the water.

Two figures crouched beside what was unmistakably a corpse: the tall man in the black coat from the train station, and her son. Her dripping wet son, water still plastering his shirt to his chest. All while four other children clustered around watching, all far too close to the water's edge.

Both figures looked up from examining the corpse. Nate scrambled to his feet, and the guilty expression that crossed his face told her everything she needed to know. He'd been here the whole time. Close enough to touch whatever was floating in that creek.

Diego caught her arm as she started forward. "Ellie—"

She shook him off and stalked toward the water, fury building with each step.

The man in black—Sheriff Bracken—straightened with what might have been a sheepish expression. "Mrs. Harper, I'm afraid we weren't properly introduced earlier." The stranger pulled off his hat in a courteous gesture and extended a hand. "Tom Bracken, the new—"

"I don't care if you're the President of these United States." Ellie's voice pitched low and dangerous as she took in the scene—her son soaked to the skin, the other children clustered too close to the water, and a dead man sprawled face-up on the muddy bank. "Do you have any idea what lives in that water? Do you know what time of day it is?"

The sheriff gave up on the offered handshake and glanced around, clearly confused. "It's... evening?"

"It's gator hunting time, you absolute imbecile!" She grabbed Nate's shoulder and pulled him further from the water's edge.

"Gator hunting?" Bracken asked.

"Prime feeding hours," Diego explained. "They hunt anything that moves near the water, especially when it's getting dark."

"Ma, we were just—" Nate started.

"Not a word. Not one word from you, Nathan Harper. You know better." She didn't take her eyes off Bracken. "What in God's name were you thinking, sending a child into that water?"

"Mrs. Harper, I can explain—"

"Can you?" Her voice came out flat and deadly calm. "Can you explain why *my son* is kneeling next to a corpse in gator-infested water? Can you explain what you were thinking when you let children—*children!*—get close to a dead body at a gator attack site?"

"I'm pretty sure this wasn't an animal attack, actually." Bracken's voice carried a note of strained defensiveness as he crouched back down beside the body. "See, if you look at the wound pattern here—" He pointed with his left hand toward a series of cuts across the dead man's chest. "These are too clean for teeth, more like a knife—"

"That's not the point!" Ellie spun to face him, and Diego watched with grim satisfaction as the cocky sheriff rocked back on his heels. "There are live gators in this water. Right now. Hunting. And you had my son standing knee-deep in their dinner table."

Diego cleared his throat. "She's right, Sheriff. Alligators are most active during twilight hours. They'll take anything—deer, wild pig..." He looked pointedly at Nate. "Curious children."

Bracken's expression shifted between several unreadable emotions, but Diego was sure that he saw confusion, embarrassment, and defensiveness all muddled in there somewhere. He used his left hand to brace himself as he shifted his feet underneath him so he wouldn't overbalance when he leaned forward again. "I wasn't... well... I mean, how dangerous can they really—"

The water erupted.

A six-foot gator lunged from the shallows with shocking speed, jaws snapping shut around Bracken's outstretched forearm with the sound of a bear trap snapping shut. The sheriff let out a yelp that was part surprise, part pain, and all terror as teeth punched through fabric and skin, grinding against the bones of his forearm. He tried desperately to yank his arm back, but one hundred pounds of predatory muscle had already decided to drag him into the black water.

His world narrowed to the prehistoric eyes staring up at him and the fire shooting through his left arm. Without thinking, his right hand swept to his holster, the Colt clearing leather in one smooth motion.

The first shot punched into the gator's back with a wet thump, the report echoing across the water like thunder, sending every bird in the cypress canopy into shrieking flight. He fired again, catching it closer to the spine. The creature didn't even flinch; if anything, its jaws ground down tighter as it tried to spin him into the water.

Bracken's boots slipped in the mud and panic clawed at the edges of his vision.

"Sonofabitch—"

The thing was going to drag him under, and he'd drown in three feet of creek water on his first day as sheriff.

Bracken flipped the gun in his grip and brought the butt down hard on the gator's snout. The first blow barely registered, the second made it hiss. The impact jarred through his arm.

"*Let go*, you son of a—"

He hammered down again, until finally those terrible jaws popped open like a spring trap releasing.

Bracken stumbled backward, falling to the ground but he managed to keep his gun hand steady. The shots came fast and angry—*bang, bang, bang, bang*—he emptied the cylinder into the creature's skull until the hammer clicked on empty chambers.

The gator lashed its tail in the shallows, its jaws opened aggressively wide. The guttural hissing snarl made the hair all over his body stand alert with terror. And then the damned thing turned and *swam off...*

The sudden silence felt louder than gunfire. Bracken stared down at the gun in his hand, then at the spot in the water where the reptile had disappeared, his chest heaving and his left arm shaking as he cradled it to his chest. Blood dripped steadily from his fingers into the mud.

Ellie and Diego were on him fast, each grabbing him under the arm pits and dragging him away from the water's edge with surprising strength, hauling him up to his feet. Diego supported him as he swayed.

"No. No, no, *no*. That's not right. That's just not right."

"Easy, Sheriff," the doctor ordered, his voice cut through the ringing in Bracken's ears. "Let's sit you down before you fall down."

Bracken couldn't look away from the water.

"No, you don't understand, I put six shots in that thing—*six*—with a .45 at point blank range—and it just swam off? Six bullets and it didn't affect it *at all*."

"You affected it plenty, *amigo*," Diego said. "You pissed it off."

Tom finally tore his gaze away from the water to search Diego's face only to discover with real horror that in spite of the doctor's teasing, he wasn't at all joking. Six bullets from a .45 really had just pissed it off.

"Oh, sweet Jesus." His legs made the sudden decision to try their impression at a frayed length of wet rope. Diego grunted as he took more of the sheriff's weight than he was ready for.

"Easy, Sheriff, I got you."

The adrenaline was wearing off, leaving behind a throbbing ache that made his vision swim.

Diego had gotten him settled on a cypress leg and Ellie worked his coat off, then used scissors to cut open what remained of his shirt sleeve, her hands careful as she peeled the torn and bloody fabric away from the wound.

Bracken looked down at the damage, his stomach lurching. Two deep puncture wounds marked where the gator's teeth had found purchase, and the skin all the way around his forearm was already turning an ugly purple.

"How bad?" he managed.

Diego studied the damage with clinical detachment. "Couple of teeth punctured the skin, but the bone doesn't seem to be broken. I'll be able to take a closer look when we clean and stitch this properly back at the clinic."

He stood and moved out of the way, gesturing for Ellie to step in and begin field dressing the wounds. "If you think you can keep from bleeding out for ten minutes, I want to take a look at our body before our friend comes back for his dessert."

Diego was already moving toward the corpse that had started this whole mess, still sprawled on the muddy bank like discarded laundry.

Bracken followed his movement with his eyes. "Thing's a goddamn dinosaur," he said, his voice still shaky from shock and blood loss, "you people have goddamn *dinosaurs* in your creek."

Ellie paused in bandaging his arm to glare at him as if he was a special brand of idiot—which he was, in all fairness. "Gators," she said finally. "We have *gators* in Gator Creek. And yes, that is exactly what I was trying to tell you."

"There are *dinosaurs* in your creek and you people live here voluntarily."

"No, Sheriff, the dinosaurs died off. *Gators* are what survived when the dinosaurs didn't make the cut. And *we people*," Ellie said while she finished wrapping his arm with efficient, unsympathetic movements, "know better than to go poking at corpses next to gator holes at feeding time. So next time maybe you should listen when someone tries to warn you about the local wildlife."

Her expression suggested she had several choice words waiting for him once he stopped bleeding. He couldn't help but feel a little grateful that she was granting him a grace period on the lecture that he no doubt deserved—because the adrenaline was hitting him hard, leaving him shaking and hollow with far too much pain pulsing through his torn arm.

"Welcome to gator country, Mr. Bracken," she said dryly. "I hope for your sake that you're a quick learner."

CHAPTER FOUR

Just a Love Bite

Ellie set out clean bandages and towels next to the examination table where the sheriff's long frame was stretched out like a scarecrow someone had dragged through a bog. He stared at the ceiling with that blank stare that men sometimes got after tangling with something bigger than their pride.

Even the children understood how close they'd come to watching their new sheriff get dragged under. Ellie had returned them home with a firm warning to stay away from the creek—one she hoped might actually stick this time. Nate had been the hardest to pry away, full of questions about whether gators could climb trees and if Sheriff Bracken's gun was really as fast as it looked.

Diego laid out the tools he would need—forceps, scissors, scalpel... "So, what did you think of the body?" he asked conversationally.

Bracken frowned, seeming to surface from wherever his mind had gone while dealing with the pain. "What? Oh. I didn't realize we were back on speaking terms."

"Oh no, that's Ellie. She's the one not on speaking terms, and that's entirely for you two to sort out." Diego glanced toward where Ellie stood with her back turned, aggressively organizing bandage rolls. "I've just been busy dealing with the excitement."

A ghost of Bracken's usual smirk appeared. "In that case—" He shifted on the table, extending his good hand. "Tom Bracken. Sheriff of this godforsaken swamp, apparently."

"Diego Delgado. Doctor, coroner, and occasional gator bite specialist. Apparently." He shook the offered hand briefly before rolling up his sleeves and washing his hands.

"Pleased to make your acquaintance, Doc." His voice carried a hint of his earlier cockiness, though pain still tightened the corners of his eyes. "As far as the body goes, I'd rather hear your take on it first, if you don't mind. Don't want anything I got going on in my head to inadvertently put a color on the facts of the matter."

"Sensible." Diego nodded approvingly as he scrubbed even his fingernails with the soap. Infection was going to be tricky to fight off even without him introducing new germs to the wound. "Most lawmen want to tell me what I'm supposed to find before I've even looked. The victim was male, mid-thirties, well-fed. Not the right kind of calluses on his hands to be a common laborer. Clothes were quality—linen suit, leather boots that cost more than most folks here make in a month. But here's what's interesting—the chest wounds weren't from any gator."

"Oh, really?" It was impossible to miss the smug look that Bracken had aimed at Ellie. "What makes you say that?"

"Wrong pattern entirely. Gator would have grabbed and rolled, left spiral tears. These were deliberate slashes, made with something sharp. A knife, maybe, or—"

"So, just to be clear, I was *right* and this was definitely not an alligator attack?"

Ellie brought the tray of bandages and cloths over and placed it on the table a little harder than necessary. "I never said you weren't *right*, I said that it didn't matter because you were being an idiot by standing next to a corpse in the water at feeding time."

Diego cleared his throat loudly and dried his hands with one of the clean towels. "Well, at least you got your wish, Ellie," Diego said. "Our new sheriff isn't a coward."

She shot him a look that could have cracked stone.

"And a man with the fortitude to fight off an alligator probably isn't the sort to run from a gunfight," Diego continued, his tone deliberately light as he arranged his instruments on the metal tray. "Very reassuring for the citizens of Cypress Run."

"Dr. Delgado." Her voice carried the same warning she used on Nate when he tracked mud through the house.

"What? I'm simply observing that our new lawman has proven himself capable of—"

"It's not his fortitude that's in question; his survival instincts are what I'm worried about," Ellie muttered, lifting the heavy pot of boiling water from the stove. Steam rose from the surface, and she carried it carefully to the exam table, filling the basin beside Bracken's injured arm. "Fighting gators isn't bravery, Diego. It's stupidity with an extra helping of arrogance."

Bracken shifted his gaze between them, blinking owlishly. He didn't seem quite sure whether or not to believe they were actually standing there talking about him as if he wasn't sitting right there listening. "I can hear you both, you know."

"Good," Ellie said, not looking up from her preparations. "Maybe you'll listen better than you did at the creek."

Diego chuckled, "Ready for the fun portion of the evening, Sheriff?"

Bracken's eyes narrowed in suspicion. "Define 'fun.'"

"Well, it's time to get a proper look at what our friend did to you, and then we get to clean it; that's the *really* fun part." Diego began unwrapping the field dressing, his movements careful and methodical as he peeled the bloodied fabric away.

The wounds looked worse under the lamplight—deep, ragged holes where the gator's teeth had punched through muscle, the surrounding area purple and swollen from crushed blood vessels and muscle tissue. "Two puncture wounds, like I thought. Deep, but clean. And the bone's not broken. This looks more like a love bite than anything."

"Sorry, did you just say a *love* bite?"

"Believe me, if that gator had gotten a proper grip on you... I've seen them crush bone, cripple men for life. Even take an arm clean off, easy as anything. This little guy was just being curious. You got *very* lucky, *amigo*."

Bracken's jaw tightened as Diego dipped a clean cloth in the hot water and began gently cleaning around the wounds, "Lucky's one word for it."

"Another word might be reckless," Ellie added. "Or pigheaded. Arrogant. Idiotic. Take your pick."

Bracken rolled his eyes and muttered, "A teacher with a thesaurus, how original."

Ellie smiled, her voice saccharin sweet as she replied, "I'm surprised you know what a thesaurus is."

Bracken flinched, his smile growing brittle in a way that had nothing to do with physical discomfort. "Well, you know, I've seen one in passing, but they don't really hire cops that can give the politicians a run for their money. Anything more... *loquacious*... than 'man do crime' starts making the brass nervous."

Diego cleared his throat, changing the subject before his nurse and his patient started circling each other like angry yard cats. "You know, Sheriff, most men who come down from up north complain about the heat, the bugs, maybe the food.

You managed to pick a fight with our local apex predator on your first day. That takes a special kind of dedication."

"Wasn't exactly intending to," Bracken said through gritted teeth as Diego worked. "Pretty sure that dinosaur's the one who picked the fight with me."

"That *alligator* was just doing what gators do," Ellie said, finally meeting his eyes. "You were the one poking around a gator hole like you owned the place."

"That gator hole was in the middle of my crime scene, which means it's in my jurisdiction. So, yeah, legally I do own the place. At least that's what my shiny new badge says."

Diego paused in his cleaning to look between them.

"*Dios mío*, you two are going to give me a headache." He resumed his work, flushing out the puncture wounds with the hot water. "If I'm going to be stuck in the middle, that makes me the referee. As the referee, I say you each get one more volley before we table whatever *this* is for another day, hopefully a day when I'm not stuck between you two trying to save a man's arm from amputation."

Both Ellie and Bracken had the decency to look chastened; Diego counted that as a small victory in itself. "Alright, Ellie, you first."

"The gator doesn't care about your badge, Sheriff. Down here, respect is earned, not appointed."

Bracken was quiet for a moment, watching Diego work. When he spoke, his tone had shifted from defensive to reconciliatory, "So what do I need to do to earn it?"

The simple question caught her off guard. She'd been expecting him to try and get the last word, or to slip one more barb in. "Start by not getting yourself killed in the first week," Ellie said. "After that, we'll see."

Diego added. "You want respect, you could try to get through the next few hours without screaming, crying, or humiliating yourself on my table, but I wouldn't hold out too much hope for that."

Bracken looked up at him, concern flickering to life behind his eyes. "What's that supposed to mean?"

"These puncture wounds need proper cleaning before I can stitch them closed. Won't be pleasant, but it's necessary if you want to keep the arm."

"Proper cleaning—isn't that what you've been doing?"

Diego shook his head, "This was just step one, *amigo*. Next is irrigation."

Bracken had the sense to look deeply concerned. "I'm sorry, irri-what-now?"

"Gators have filthy mouths," Diego explained, reaching for the irrigating syringe. "Worse than politicians. All sorts of bacteria swimming around in there." He drew hot water into the syringe, then positioned it over the first puncture wound. "This is going to hurt."

"Can't be worse than the gator," Bracken muttered.

"Don't bet on it."

Diego squeezed the plunger, flushing out the wound with hot water. Bracken couldn't help flinching, jerking back against the table, a sound catching in his throat somewhere between a whine and a gurgle.

"Easy," Diego said, refilling the syringe. "Gotta clean out all the debris—creek water, bits of cloth, and whatever else that gator had for breakfast."

Ellie watched the sheriff's face as Diego worked, noting the way his jaw clenched and the rapid rise and fall of his chest. Sweat beaded on his forehead despite the evening's relative coolness.

"You know," Diego continued conversationally as he irrigated the second wound, drawing another sharp sound of distress from his patient, "most people who tangle with gators don't live to tell about it. Between your heroics in the saloon, and your heroics in the swamp, you've impressed the hell out of half the town already. That's gotta feel pretty good, doesn't it?"

"Jury's still out," Bracken managed through gritted teeth.

"Just think, we find you a nice amenable cat to rescue from a tree and we'll get the church matrons wrapped around your finger right alongside the school kids and the drinking class. You'll be the stuff of legends in no time." Diego reached for fresh gauze. "There. That wasn't so terrible, was it?"

The sheriff's laugh sounded more like a wheeze. "You need to borrow Mrs. Harper's dictionary, Doc. Don't think your definitions of 'fun' and 'not terrible' would get Mr. Webster's seal of approval."

Ellie couldn't help a small chuckle, in spite of herself.

Diego uncorked a bottle from his instrument tray. The sharp smell of whiskey cut through the clinic's medicinal odors.

"Alright, Sheriff. Before we continue, you're going to want a few sips of this."

Bracken propped himself up on his good elbow, accepting the bottle. "Planning to get me drunk, Doc? Because I should warn you, I'm a very cuddly drunk. Ask anyone in Chicago."

"Just enough to dull the edge." Diego's expression had turned serious, the earlier lightness gone from his voice. "What comes next is going to be worse than the irrigation."

The sheriff paused with the bottle halfway to his lips. "Hate to ask, but, uh... could you define 'worse' for me?"

"Clean the wounds properly. Remove dead tissue, foreign debris, anything that doesn't belong. The gator's teeth tore through muscle and left ragged edges inside the wounds. If I don't trim them back to healthy tissue, they won't heal clean. Basically everything that was damaged by a tooth has to get cut out." Diego picked up a pair of surgical scissors, the metal gleaming under the lamplight. "No sugar-coating it—this is going to hurt like nothing you've ever felt."

"How much worse are we talking? Scale of one to ten, where irrigation was about an eight?"

"Irrigation was a five," Diego said matter-of-factly, setting the whiskey aside. "This is the ten."

"Jesus." The color drained from Bracken's face. "I guess this is the part where I'm supposed to tell you I can handle whatever you throw at me, right? Be all tough and stoic about it?"

"No." Diego's voice carried the weight of experience. "This is the part where we both acknowledge like adults that this is going to be the most awful thing you've ever experienced. But you're going to get through it without embarrassing yourself on my table, because you and I both have high expectations of you." He paused, testing the sharpness of the scissor blades. "Once the whiskey's dulled the edge a bit, we'll get started."

Bracken stared at the instruments laid out on the tray, then took a long pull from the whiskey bottle. The amber liquid burned down his throat, and he coughed once before taking another sip.

Ellie moved closer, positioning herself near the sheriff's head with a clean cloth in her hands. "The whiskey will help, but not much."

"Wonderful." Bracken took one more drink, then handed the bottle back to Diego.

"Ready?" Diego picked up the forceps and scissors, his movements precise and professional. "I need you to stay as still as possible. Ellie's going to help."

Bracken nodded, settling back against the table. Ellie dipped the cloth in clean water and positioned herself near his forehead, ready to wipe away sweat and provide as much comfort as she could.

Diego began with the first wound, using the forceps to probe carefully into the puncture. Bracken's entire body went rigid, a strangled sound escaping through his clenched teeth.

"Easy," Diego murmured, his voice steady and clinical. "I can see some fabric fibers in here. Have to get those out or they'll fester."

The sheriff's breathing turned shallow and rapid. Sweat broke out across his forehead, and Ellie dabbed it away with the cloth.

"Breathe," she ordered, her voice firm but not unkind. "In through your nose, out through your mouth."

Diego worked with methodical precision, using the forceps to extract tiny pieces of torn shirt fabric from each wound. Each movement drew another sharp breath from his patient.

"Tell me about Chicago, take your mind somewhere that isn't here," Diego said, switching to the scissors to trim away a piece of damaged tissue. "What do you miss most since you left?"

Bracken's laugh came out as more of a wheeze. "Right now? Bullet wounds. Clean. Simple. In and out."

"That's not a very good answer," Diego chided as Ellie wiped more sweat from his brow. "Try again."

"Snow," Bracken managed, his free hand gripping the edge of the table so hard his knuckles had gone white. "It was snowing when I left. Knew I wouldn't need 'em, so gave my winter c-c-coat and gloves to the rookie just before I got on the t-train... Jesus Christ, Doc, are you cutting my arm off?"

"Just cleaning house," Diego replied, switching to the forceps to remove a small piece of fabric embedded in the muscle. "Keep talking to me, Sheriff. Heard about your exploit at the saloon earlier. Where'd you learn to play billiards?"

"Bar," Bracken managed through gritted teeth. "Irish bar on—Christ Almighty!"

"Found a bit of your shirt sleeve in there. Keep talking. What was the name of the bar?"

"O'Malley's. Used to hustle—ah, hell—used to hustle the white-collar boys for beer money." His breathing came in short, sharp bursts as Diego worked. "Oh, God, I don't like this, oh sweet Jesus..."

Ellie dabbed at his forehead again. "You're doing fine. Halfway done."

"Halfway? This is only *halfway*?"

Diego moved to the second wound, and Bracken's entire body shuddered. A low groan escaped him, followed by a string of creative profanity that would have made a dock worker proud.

"Language," Ellie chided, though without real heat.

Diego continued to work, his movements economical and unhurried despite the sheriff's increasingly labored breathing. The forceps clicked against something hard buried in the second wound.

"What's that?" Bracken asked, his voice tight.

"Piece of tooth, most likely." Diego adjusted his grip on the instrument. "Gators lose teeth all the time. Consider it a souvenir."

"Wonderful—sweet merciful Jesus, Mary, and Joseph—stop, stop, please stop—"

Diego didn't stop. "Trust me, you don't want this in here longer than it has to be."

Ellie said, "Doing good, just a little more," her voice a gentle murmur. She pressed the cloth against his forehead again, noting how his skin had gone greenish-gray beneath the sweat. His breathing had turned shallow and rapid, the kind that preceded fainting in her more squeamish patients.

"Don't you dare," she warned.

"Don't I what?"

"Pass out on Diego's table. I'm not hauling you home unconscious."

Bracken managed a weak grin. "Trying, Mrs. Harper. Room's gotten all... spinny..."

The sheriff's eyes rolled back and a long groan forced its way past his teeth as Diego probed deeper, trying to get a grip on the slick sides of the tooth. Tremors ran through Bracken's frame, and Ellie had to press the cloth firmly against his forehead to keep him from shaking too much. "There! Got it!" Diego extracted the tooth with a wet sound that made all three of them wince. "There. That's the worst of it."

Sweat had soaked through his hair, plastering it to his forehead in dark strands, and his breaths were coming in short, sharp gasps, like a panting dog on a hot day. His free hand still gripped the edge of the examination table, knuckles white as bone.

It took Diego only a few minutes more to finish and Bracken nearly whimpered in relief when Diego set aside the bloodied instruments and said, "There. Debridement's done."

"Next time I see a gator," he said weakly, "I'm buying it a drink and walking the other way."

Ellie was rubbing soothing circles on his good arm with the palm of her hand, as if he was an upset horse that needed settling. "You're doing good," she said in a low, easy tone. "Almost finished."

"Almost?" The sheriff's expression shifted from relief to something approaching despair and his body started to tense up again. "What do you mean, *almost* finished? We're not finished yet?"

"Not yet." Diego reached for a small amber bottle from his supply shelf, the glass catching the lamplight as he uncorked it. The sharp, medicinal smell of carbolic acid filled the room immediately.

"What's that?" Bracken asked, though his voice carried the weariness of a man who already knew he wouldn't like the answer.

"Antiseptic," Diego said matter-of-factly, pouring the amber liquid into a clean bowl. "Solution of carbolic acid. Dr. Lister's method—kills the bacteria that cause infection. Have to make sure the wound's nice and clean."

"I thought we already cleaned it."

"That was with water. This is the real cleaning."

Ellie saw the fight go out of Bracken's shoulders, watched him sag back against the table like a man who'd just been told his horse had gone lame with fifty miles left to town.

"Sonofabitch," he whispered.

Diego paused, studying his patient's pale face with professional concern. He reached for the whiskey bottle, uncorking it again.

"One more sip of whiskey, Sheriff. You're going to need it."

The sheriff accepted the bottle with his good hand, taking a longer pull this time. His face already looked pale and drawn, sweat on his forehead despite Ellie's ministrations.

"While I work, I want you to tell me what you observed at the crime scene. Keep your mind occupied." Diego gave him a sympathetic look, then asked quietly, "You ready?"

"Hell no. Do it anyway."

"Good man."

Diego soaked a clean cloth with the carbolic solution, the liquid gleaming amber in the lamplight. The smell grew stronger, harsh and astringent. Ellie positioned herself at Bracken's head again, the clean cloth ready in her hands.

"Here we go," Diego said, and pressed the antiseptic-soaked cloth to the first puncture wound.

Bracken's back arched off the table as a strangled cry tore from his throat. The sharp, biting pain was unlike anything from the previous cleaning—it felt like liquid lightning coursing through his arm. His free hand shot out, gripping Ellie's wrist with surprising strength.

"Sweet bloody Jesus Christ on a goddamn crutch—!" The profanity dissolved into incoherent gasping.

"Easy," Ellie murmured, not pulling away from his grip. The strength in his fingers spoke to desperation more than aggression. "Breathe through it."

Bracken whined, "You trying to kill me, Doc?"

Diego worked methodically, swabbing the carbolic acid through both wounds while his patient writhed on the table.

"If I wanted you dead, Sheriff, I'd just leave the wounds dirty and let sepsis take you in a day or two. Much less work for me."

Bracken's laugh came out as more of a sob. "Your bedside manner needs work."

"So does your sense of self-preservation." Diego set aside the antiseptic, reaching for his suturing kit. "Now, about that crime scene. Tell me what you saw."

Even through his agony, Bracken managed a weak smile. "Kind of the same thing you did, Doc. Bruising 'round the neck, pink glaze to the eyes. Strangled first, knife wounds post-mortem. Too neat, evenly spaced, wasn't done while he was alive." He trembled as he watched Diego threading black silk through his curved needle. "Wanted it to look like a gator attack."

Ellie felt Bracken's grip on her wrist tighten as Diego positioned the needle. His eyes fixed on her face instead of the approaching suture, and she found herself unable to look away from the mixture of pain and determination she saw there.

"Why fake a gator attack?" she found herself asking.

"Hide the fact he was murdered," Bracken said through gritted teeth. "See a body's been mangled by accident, nobody questions it. See one's been murdered, people ask questions, maybe notice the same things our victim was killed to keep him quiet about, start wondering about those boundary stakes that got moved—sweet saints on a sidewalk, why does *this* hurt more? Christ!"

Ellie dipped a cloth in water and wiped his forehead again. "It doesn't," she said. "You've just used up all your pain tolerance getting through the other parts, now your body's telling you it's had enough and it wants a break. But we're almost finished, you're doing good."

The needle pierced living flesh, and his words dissolved into a sharp intake of breath. Diego worked quickly and efficiently, drawing the torn edges of the wound together with careful, even stitches.

"What were you saying about boundary stakes? Moved them how?" Diego asked as if he weren't sewing a man's arm back together.

"Pulled up, moved further into the swamp. Fresh dirt around the holes." Bracken's voice had turned breathless again. "Poor bastard got killed for noticing they'd been moved."

"Why?" she asked.

"That's the question, isn't it?" Bracken's smile was tight with pain. "Start by finding out who makes money, who loses it, who gets the most pissed off when I start asking questions. See which question makes someone want to shut me up, too."

Diego paused his suturing for the first time.

Ellie felt the blood drain from her face as the full weight of Bracken's words settled in the clinic's humid air. Someone had murdered a man—not in a moment of rage or desperation, but with cold calculation. They'd strangled him, carved him up to hide their work, then dumped him in the swamp like yesterday's slop bucket. The casual brutality of it made her stomach turn.

Diego resumed his suturing, but she saw her own unease reflected in his dark eyes. They'd dealt with death before—fever, snakebite, the occasional knife fight at the saloon—but never anything like this. Never murder dressed up as an accident, cold and calculated as a business ledger.

What disturbed her more was Bracken's matter-of-fact acceptance that investigating would put a target on his own back. He spoke about someone trying to kill him the way other men might discuss bad weather—an inconvenience, nothing more.

"Doesn't that bother you?" she asked. "Knowing someone's going to want you dead for asking questions?"

Bracken's eyes found hers again, and she saw something flicker there—not fear exactly, but acknowledgment. "Course it bothers me. But being bothered doesn't stop people from getting hurt. Trouble comes for you anyway; if you know which angle it's coming from, least you can position the table 'fore it gets to you."

Diego paused in his stitching, looking between them with concern creasing his forehead. "This isn't some drunk cowboy taking swings at you outside the saloon, Sheriff. We're talking about someone who plans, who thinks ahead."

"Just means I gotta think further ahead." Bracken's voice carried a grim amusement. "Not exactly advanced trigonometry, Doc..."

Diego continued his work, drawing the black silk through torn flesh with neat movements. "What else did you notice at the scene? Besides the boundary stakes."

"Blood under the victim's nails. Right hand." Bracken's words came out clipped as the needle bit again. "He got his killer good—scratches to the face, neck, maybe forearms. Someone's walking around marked up right now."

Ellie filed that detail away, already thinking of the faces she'd see around town tomorrow. Fresh scratches would be hard to hide in a settlement the size of Cypress Run.

"Iron shavings in his boot heels too," Bracken continued, sweat beading on his forehead as Diego worked. "Fresh ones. He'd been walking around the railroad camp recently."

"Railroad camp's full of men with access to those boundary stakes," Diego observed, tying off another suture.

"And plenty of reason to want them moved." Bracken winced as the needle pierced skin again. "Murder site's about thirty yards from where we found him. Drag marks in the mud led me right to it. That's where his satchel fell—papers inside all gone. Tools scattered everywhere."

Ellie watched the sheriff as Diego worked. His breathing had grown more labored with each stitch, his grip on her wrist had loosened—not from less pain, but from exhaustion. The fight was going out of him as his body reached its limits.

"What kind of papers?" she asked.

"Survey notes, probably. Maybe correspondence about boundary disputes. Whatever it was, someone thought it worth killing for." Bracken's voice had turned hoarse. "Two sets of boot prints I could see. One's about the size of my foot, not sure who it belonged to."

Diego finished the last suture and reached for clean bandages. "There. Sixteen stitches. Not my finest work, but it'll hold."

"Please... please, for the love of God... tell me we're done."

"Just need to bandage these up properly."

"Good." Bracken's laugh came out shaky. "Don't think I've got much left in me."

Diego reached for the clean gauze. Something in Bracken's expression—a flicker of calculation beneath the pain-dulled exhaustion—made him pause. "What is it?"

"Wondering why the hell anybody would want more of that god-forsaken swamp on their property than there needs to be."

"You said someone moved those boundary stakes east, further into the swamp," Ellie said, following the sheriff's train of thought. "But the swamp isn't useful for anything, not for crops or livestock. Why would anyone want more of their property taken up by the swamp?"

Bracken closed his eyes, exhaustion making his limbs tremble. "They wouldn't. Question is: what changes if the line moves six feet one direction or the other?"

Diego began wrapping the bandages around the sutured wounds, keeping the pressure firm but not tight. "Something worth killing for, evidently."

"Railroad grade," Bracken said quietly. "Has to be. Six feet might be the difference between the rail line cutting through county land versus private property. And if someone knew where that line was going to run before the official survey was complete..."

Ellie felt a chill that had nothing to do with the evening air seeping through the clinic's thin walls.

If the railroad grade survey showed the property lines in one place and the county land records showed them in another, who would win if the dispute went to court? How many homesteaders would be kicked off their property just because they didn't have the money to face down a railroad line in a legal battle?

"Hope you don't mind, we're keeping you here tonight," Diego announced as he continued wrapping gauze around the puncture wounds, his movements precise and methodical. "Gator bites go bad fast when they decide to go bad. Fever, infection, blood poisoning—whole arm could be black by morning if we're unlucky."

Bracken's eyes tracked to him, still glazed from pain and whiskey. "Staying where?"

"Back room. Got two beds for patients who need watching. Ellie and I will take turns checking on you. Make sure you don't die and spoil my good suture work."

Diego secured the bandage with a small metal clasp. "Arm needs to stay immobilized for at least a week, so I'm going to get you a sling to wear tomorrow. Any pulling on those stitches and we start over."

"Wonderful," Bracken mumbled. "How'm I supposed to shoot with one arm?"

"Try not shooting anybody for a few days. Revolutionary concept for a lawman, I know," Diego said.

"Not people, Doc, pool. Shooting pool. Can shoot people one handed easy as anything... Couldn't reload, just means you have to aim better... Pool, though... need both hands to shoot pool."

Diego smiled, shaking his head. He finished tying off the bandage. "There. Now let's get you settled."

Ellie had already disappeared into the back room, and Diego could hear her moving around—the crisp snap of fresh linens being shaken out, the squeak of bed springs being tested. She'd done this dance before, preparing the patient beds for overnight watches. They'd both spent plenty of sleepless nights monitoring fever cases or sitting vigil over children with croup.

"Can you stand?" Diego asked, studying the sheriff's pale face.

Bracken nodded, though when Diego helped him sit up on the examination table, he swayed slightly. "Just... give me a second. Everything's spinning."

"Blood loss and shock. Perfectly normal." Diego steadied him with a hand on his good shoulder. "Take your time."

They made their way slowly to the back room, Bracken leaning more heavily on Diego than either of them acknowledged. Ellie had turned down the coverlet on the bed nearest the window.

"Arms up," she said matter-of-factly, reaching for the buttons on Bracken's shirt.

The sheriff's face reddened. "Mrs. Harper, I can—"

"You can barely stand," she interrupted, already working the buttons with efficient fingers. "And I've seen worse than whatever's under that shirt, believe me."

Diego helped ease the shirt off Bracken's good arm, then carefully worked it over the bandaged one. Removing his undershirt revealed a lean frame marked with old scars—a puckered bullet wound below his left collarbone, knife marks across his ribs, the faded stories of a hard life. And one mark much newer than the others—it could only have been a few weeks old—grazing his upper bicep. They removed shoes, socks, and trousers, leaving him in only his cotton drawers.

"Thanks. Both of you. For not letting me get eaten. Means a lot to me... Can't say this is how I wanted my first impression to go—half naked and a breath away from delirious. Helluva way to earn a reputation."

They got him settled in the bed, propped up with pillows to keep his injured arm elevated.

A weak chuckle escaped the sheriff's throat. "Step up from the cot in the jail cell. Wasn't looking forward to that." His words had started to slur slightly, exhaustion finally catching up with the adrenaline crash. "Not that I'd go outta my way to get bit just to have a better bed to sleep in. That'd be pretty idiotic, even for me."

Diego reached for the small brown bottle of laudanum from the medicine cabinet. "Few drops of this to make sure you sleep through the night," he said, measuring the dark liquid onto a spoon. "Don't want you thrashing around and tearing those stitches."

Bracken accepted the medicine without protest, his eyelids already drooping. His eyes drifted closed, then opened again with obvious effort. "Doc... tomorrow, need to go—"

"Tomorrow, you rest. Investigation can wait a day."

"Can't wait. Whoever killed that surveyor... gerrymandering a damned swamp... ward boss dividing up the stockyard..." His words trailed off as the laudanum took hold, pulling him down into sleep.

After they closed the door to let him get as much rest as he could before they had to check on him, Diego and Ellie worked in quiet efficiency, cleaning the examination area and organizing the bloodied instruments for sterilization.

"What do you make of him?" Ellie asked finally, rinsing the forceps in the basin.

Diego considered the question while he wiped down the examination table. "He's tougher than he looks." He paused, watching the water swirling pink in the basin. "And he thinks like a lawman, even when he's half-dead from pain."

Ellie shook her head, stacking the clean instruments. "He's too naive for his own good, though. I understand he didn't intentionally set out to fight a gator barehanded today, but it's common sense not to—" She looked at Diego. "He could have been killed."

"Could have," Diego agreed. "And I dare to hope that after tonight, he'll know better than to do it again. Besides, I wouldn't say he's naive so much as just... *new*. All of it's gotta be catching him flatfooted. I'm sure if one of us went for a stroll in his city, he'd have colorful things to say about our behavior there, too. My first time visiting Jacksonville, I nearly got run over by a carriage, I was so busy gawking at things. I can only imagine what a big city like Chicago would do to us naive back country yokels."

Ellie sighed. "Alright. I'll try to be patient with him."

"I'm sure he'll get his feet under him sooner than you think."

"He'd better." She'd finished cleaning and putting away the instruments and was now gathering the various pieces of clothing they'd collected from him to see what could be washed—none of it suited to the swampy heat of Cypress Run. Not to mention his ridiculous shiny shoes that didn't even cover the ankle properly. They weren't shiny anymore—the swamp had seen to that. She wasn't sure any amount of polish would make them look right again.

"We need to make sure he gets a real pair of boots. He's lucky a snake didn't bite him before the gator got to him." She huffed in exasperation. "And what kind of man has a perfectly good billfold in his pocket, but keeps dollar bills pinned to the inside lining of his coat?"

Diego raised an eyebrow then shrugged. "One who's used to dealing with a different sort of predator than gators and snakes, I suppose."

Ellie shook her head. "I'm pretty sure the shirt is a lost cause. Mrs. Dixon should be able to fix the tears on his coat. I'll see what she thinks when I take these to the laundry." Ellie folded it carefully and placed it with the other clothes.

She stretched and grabbed her shawl, wrapping it around her shoulders. "I'm going to swing by the jail before it gets too late, and see if he's got a spare set of clothes we can change him into in the morning. Then I'll stop by the pharmacy and let Nate know I'm staying here tonight, see if Simon can walk him home. Need me to grab anything while I'm there?"

"Actually, if you could have Simon run by my house and tell Julietta I'm staying, too, maybe she'll throw together a basket for our dinner. I could really use an empanada or four after the day we've had."

After Ellie had left, Diego returned to the back room to check on the patient.

"*Dios mío,*" Diego muttered as he sat in a chair by the sheriff's bedside, suddenly feeling every hour of the long day. The man was sound asleep, his temperature was elevated but not feverish, his pulse was reasonable... "Why do I get the feeling that you're going to give me gray hair before I'm fifty?"

CHAPTER FIVE

Second First Impressions

Margaret Hartwell's heels struck the wooden boardwalk outside the clinic like a judge's gavel, each step announcing her impending arrival with the dreadful certainty of a court order.

The day before had thoroughly unraveled after she'd left Tom Bracken to his own devices—first there'd been reports of the new sheriff hustling locals at billiards, then word had come that he'd somehow gotten himself mauled by an alligator before sundown. She'd spent the evening fielding questions from concerned citizens and railroad representatives, her carefully laid plans for a smooth transition crumbling faster than soggy courthouse blueprints.

This morning, she would get answers.

"Where is he?" she demanded, not bothering with pleasantries as Diego looked up from his desk where he'd been reviewing notes, his pen freezing mid-sentence.

"Judge Hartwell, good morning—" Diego began, but she cut him off with a sharp gesture.

"Don't. Just tell me where Sheriff Bracken is so I can have a word with him about his first twelve hours in my county. I need to know exactly what kind of disaster I've inherited."

Ellie emerged from the back room, closing the door softly behind her. "Judge, he's still recovering from—"

"From what? Carousing at the saloon? Or from allowing children to wade into alligator-infested waters while he stood around taking notes?" Hartwell's gray eyes flashed. "Because those are the two stories making rounds, and I'm not sure which one makes me angrier."

"Judge Hartwell, please," Ellie entreated. "He's badly injured, and recovery from an alligator bite—"

"The alligator is the least of his problems right now."

Hartwell pushed past them both, throwing open the door to the recovery room.

Tom Bracken's eyes snapped open, instantly alert despite the disorientation. Even deep in sleep, years of navigating the streets of Chicago had taught him to recognize danger even in the depths of exhaustion—as well as the sound of authority approaching with malicious intent.

Pain shot through his bandaged arm as he pushed himself upright, blinking away the fog of laudanum and exhaustion.

"Sheriff Bracken." Hartwell's voice could have frosted glass in July.

Bracken took in his situation—shirtless, wounded arm strapped against his chest with loose white bandages, facing down his new boss while wearing nothing but his drawers and a sheet.

"Good morning, Your Honor." His voice came out rough and low, like his vocal cords had been dusted with sand. "This is... not how I pictured our first morning meeting."

"I can see that. Perhaps next time you'll consider the consequences before you decide to turn my county into your personal circus."

Hartwell crossed her arms, her gaze taking in his disheveled state with obvious disapproval. "Though I suppose it was just too much to ask that the county sheriff make it through one day on the job—*one day*—before I had to find him laid up in the clinic like an invalid."

Bracken ran his good hand through his hair. He looked down at himself, then back at Hartwell, resigning himself to the fact that he was about to receive what appeared to be his very first performance evaluation while lying mostly naked in a hospital bed.

"I don't suppose you would allow me the courtesy of getting dressed before we have this conversation?" he asked.

"You couldn't even go *twelve hours* without causing disturbances all over town," Hartwell continued, ignoring his request.

Bracken glanced longingly at a pile of clean clothes folded on the nearby chair—someone must have gone to the jail and raided his filing cabinet. He wondered whether he could reach them and dress mid-conversation without making the situation even more mortifying. With one arm essentially useless and strapped to his chest, he didn't like his odds.

"In my defense," he said, tugging the sheet higher with his good arm, "it was only the two disturbances. Pretty sure there'd have to be at least four or five before you could consider them to be *all* over town. And one of them wasn't even a disturbance so much as a diplomatic resolution of grievances over a friendly game of billiards."

"Diplomatic resolution?" Hartwell whirled on him. "You hustled Lloyd Hendricks out of a week's wages like a common grifter. Exactly the sort of behavior I specifically told you *not* to engage in."

Bracken's eyes flashed, his voice hardening slightly, "It was a fair game and a fair bet. A hustle implies I used trickery to stack the odds in my favor, which just wasn't the case." He hissed as he settled back against the wall, dropping the defensive tone in favor of a more gently cajoling one, "And with regards to behavior, what you *actually* asked me to do was to not *disappoint* you—a feat which I am very confident I have succeeded at."

Hartwell's eyebrows rose. "I beg your pardon?"

"Let's be honest, you knew I was going to do something catastrophically foolish sooner or later. I'd go so far as to wager you were even waiting for it to happen." Bracken's voice gained strength as he warmed to his argument, his green eyes finding a mischievous glint despite the pain. "By getting bit by an alligator on my first day in town, I not only met, but *exceeded* that expectation in a timely fashion. Rather spectacularly, even, if I do say so myself."

"I'm struggling to follow your logic, Sheriff Bracken. Let me remind you that in every other jurisdiction in the world, professional incompetence is not typically regarded as an asset. If this is truly the argument you want to make, I'm eager to hear it."

Ellie moved closer to the bed, her protective instincts clearly warring with her annoyance at his flippant tone. "Sheriff, maybe this isn't the time for—"

"No, I know it sounds crazy, but hear me out a moment." Bracken held up his good hand, his voice carrying an infuriating note of amusement despite his obvious pain, "You have to admit, you would have been a *little* disappointed if the green-as-grass, fancy-pants city boy from the North didn't do something silly enough to write home about before the week was out. This just gets it out of the way early, so you can stop holding your breath waiting for the other shoe to drop, and I can stop tiptoeing on eggshells wondering when it'll happen... Now that I've got the 'rookie did something stupid' milestone out of the way, we can both get on with our jobs."

Hartwell prided herself on reading people—it came with twenty years of presiding over frontier circuits, watching lawyers weave lies and defendants squirm. But Sheriff Tom Bracken, propped up in that clinic bed like some disheveled casualty of war, was spinning an argument that caught her completely off guard.

She stared at him, torn between fury and grudging admiration for his sheer audacity.

"Let me understand this correctly," she said, her voice carrying the precise tone she used when probing attorneys for further detail. "You're claiming that getting mauled by an alligator on your first day on the job was somehow... a strategic career move?"

"Well, no, not exactly. Strategy is what you plan for in advance, and I promise this was completely unintentional. But as a tactical advantage? It has a lot of potential."

"An advantage?" Diego muttered. "*Dios mío*, the fever's made him delirious."

Bracken shifted against the pillow, wincing slightly but keeping his voice steady. "Think about it for a moment. You asked me to establish order without antagonizing anyone. Under normal circumstances, that'd be almost impossible. An injury like this, though, might just give me enough of an edge to make it happen."

Diego stepped closer to the bed, taking the sheriff's wrist in one hand to measure his pulse while the other checked for fever.

"Doc, I'm fine. But think about it: what's the first thing that happens when a new sheriff comes to town?"

He didn't wait for an answer before continuing, "The local tough guys size him up, pick fights, throw their weight around to see who's really in charge. The respectable folks wonder if he's going to crack down on their little indiscretions. Half the town's waiting to see if he's weak, the other half's itching to prove they're stronger."

Ellie crossed her arms, her hazel eyes skeptical. "And you think that looki ng... injured... helps with that somehow?"

Bracken's green eyes sharpened, and Hartwell recognized the look of a man building his case. "I think that looking injured as a result of surviving an attack by the biggest thing with teeth around here tells a very specific story. And now that whole song and dance of testing the new sheriff, all that posturing? That goes right out the window."

Hartwell found herself leaning forward despite her irritation. "Go on."

Bracken gestured with his good arm toward the bandaged one. "It's really hard to look tough when you're beating down on a man with an obvious injury, and nobody wants to be the son of a bitch who beat up the sheriff that nearly crippled himself standing between an alligator and a group of school kids."

Ellie and Diego shared a glance; the three of them knew that wasn't *exactly* how it happened, but the children had already started spreading that rumor. And from the slight crinkling of his eyes, Bracken had guessed that's how it might look to impressionable youngsters.

"But more than that," Bracken continued, "I won't have to prove anything to anyone else, either. No chest-thumping, no demonstrations of authority, no having to throw my weight around to establish dominance. Nobody expects a man in a sling to have to prove how tough he is. The gator already did that for me."

Hartwell felt a grudging admiration creeping up her spine—the same sensation she got when a particularly clever attorney made an unexpectedly brilliant argument. "You're suggesting this injury provides you with... diplomatic immunity of sorts?"

"That's..." Diego began, then stopped, his medical training apparently failing to provide an appropriate response. "That's not entirely unreasonable, actually."

Hartwell felt her carefully constructed disapproval beginning to crack. "But you'll still have to establish authority eventually. The sling won't last forever."

"Certainly, but by the time this comes off, it will have been more than a few weeks for all of us to get used to each other and everyone will have settled into their routines. They'll know I'm dedicated enough to do the job despite being injured, that I don't take bribes or respond to threats, and they'll know what I'm not willing to tolerate regarding the fulfillment of my duties. No posturing, no power struggles, no having to choose between looking weak and starting unnecessary fights. No antagonizing necessary."

"Meanwhile," he continued, "I get to play the role of the quietly competent lawman recovering from his injuries. Folks tend to underestimate an injured man, see him as less threatening, which means they'll talk more freely around me. And if anyone does intend to cause trouble, well... hopefully I'll have an opportunity to see it coming with time enough to prepare accordingly."

Hartwell sat back, putting the pieces of his argument together. "So, what you're telling me, Sheriff Bracken, is that all things considered, nearly losing your arm to a reptile was... beneficial... to establishing law and order in my county?"

"I'm merely suggesting that while most sheriffs just get sworn in and pin on a badge, I went and got myself professionally maimed by the local wildlife to ensure a smooth transition of power. I've gone above and beyond the call of duty in service to this job." Bracken's mouth quirked into that truly infuriating half-smile. "That's dedication you can't teach."

The room fell silent except for the soft tick of Diego's wall clock and the distant sounds of Cypress Run stirring to life outside—shopkeepers opening their doors, children heading to school, the eternal hum of mosquitoes that seemed to provide the town's soundtrack. Hartwell studied Bracken's face, searching for signs of manipulation or jest, but found only earnest conviction beneath the glint of humor.

Hartwell found herself speechless for the first time in years, questioning whether she was staring down at the most deviously practical lawman she'd ever encountered or a complete lunatic. Or possibly both.

And yet the professional accounting she'd received from Chief Killigan—the unfortunate man who'd had to supervise Bracken's termination from the Chicago Police Department—had seared itself in her mind. It'd been a political death sentence if ever one had been written. Phrases like "contempt for authority" and "unreliable and insubordinate conduct" rang in her memory like a death knell.

The silence stretched like a held breath until Hartwell grudgingly let out a sigh of defeat.

"Your logic is undeniably twisted, Sheriff Bracken. And certainly unusual. But not entirely without merit."

Ellie shot Bracken a look that he couldn't quite read. "Do you have to encourage him, Judge Hartwell?"

"I'm not encouraging anything," Hartwell said crisply. "Let me be clear, I am not fond of an argument that hinges on professional incompetence as an exemption from the normal expectations of establishing authority. It sets a dangerous precedent—what happens when the next crisis demands a sheriff who can actually function? However, it would be churlish not to acknowledge certain realities. The man I hired to manage the law in this county has, in less than twenty-four hours on the job, discovered what appears to be a genuine murder—a discovery that I would be foolish to deny might have gone completely overlooked if not for his... enthusiastic insistence on retrieving and examining the body in a timely manner." She paused, her voice taking on a sharper edge. "The question now is whether he can solve this murder without getting himself killed in the process."

Bracken shifted against his pillow, the movement sending a fresh wave of pain through his arm. "Well, when you put it like that, it sounds almost respectable."

"It sounds like I'm trying not to regret your appointment," Hartwell replied. "But since you've already established yourself as the sort of sheriff who investigates crimes instead of ignoring them, I suppose I should be hopeful."

The backhanded compliment settled between them like an olive branch—stripped of all its leaves and looking suspiciously more like a twig, but an olive branch, nonetheless.

"Thank you, Your Honor."

Ellie suddenly shook herself, as if emerging from a trance. "Judge Hartwell, is there anything else you need to discuss? Because if not, I should really change his dressing."

Hartwell had come here expecting to deliver a proper dressing-down to an incompetent fool, not to find herself being swayed by what might actually be sound reasoning from a half-naked man who'd just claimed that putting himself at a physical disadvantage gave him a much stronger socio-political standing in the long run. But that wasn't the sort of thing she was willing to admit out loud. "I... honestly, I can't remember what I came here for."

"You came here to reassure yourself that your new county sheriff intends to take his job seriously," Bracken said quietly. "I hope I was able to provide that reassurance."

She studied his face one more time, then nodded curtly. "Indeed. That must be it. Good day, Sheriff. Doctor. Mrs. Harper."

Her heels clicked across the floor with less authority than when she'd entered. The door closed behind her with a soft thud.

The moment her footsteps faded, Bracken's confident expression crumpled. "Christ, this hurts like a sonofabitch," he muttered, his voice barely above a whisper. His head fell back against the pillow with a soft thud, his good hand pressing against his forehead as if trying to hold his skull together. "Feels like someone's driving railroad spikes into my bone."

Diego moved closer, his professional demeanor replacing the diplomatic restraint he'd shown during the judge's visit. "Let me see."

The performance was over, and now came the real work—checking wounds, changing dressings, making sure his patient hadn't torn anything loose during his theatrical defense.

Bracken didn't protest as Diego carefully unwrapped the bandage, revealing the puncture wounds beneath. The angry red flesh pulled tight together by the black sutures had settled into something less alarming overnight, though the bruising around them looked like a row of dark crescent moons inked into the many other shades of bruising all over his forearm.

"That was quite a show," Diego said, not looking up from his examination. "Did you practice that speech, or does it come naturally?"

Bracken's laugh came out as more of a wheeze. "Little of both. Old desk sarge took me under his wing when I was a rookie patrolman—taught me if you can't stay out of trouble, better to focus your energy on the exit strategy instead of wondering how it was you got there. Saved my skin more than once."

Ellie set the linens on the side table, her movements efficient but gentler than before. Whatever irritation she'd harbored seemed to have shifted into something closer to reluctant admiration. "Judge Hartwell looked like you'd just explained trigonometry to her."

"Don't give me that much credit. I was mostly spinning yarn out of fairy cloth and hoping it sounded convincing." Bracken grimaced as Diego prodded gently at stitches. "Did it work?"

"She left without threatening to fire you," Diego observed, checking for inflammation and early signs of putrefaction. "So, I'd say yes."

"Oh, good."

"This is looking better than I expected," Diego said. "No signs of infection yet, though we'll still need to watch for it. You heal fast for a city boy."

"Clean living and pure thoughts," Bracken deadpanned.

"Right, clean living," Diego scoffed. "Well, take a deep breath and think pure thoughts." He dipped a cloth into a fresh bowl of carbolic solution and began cleaning the sutures.

"Jesus Christ!" Bracken hissed through his teeth as the antiseptic burned into raw flesh. "Sweet bloody hell, that stings like a Goddamned sonofabitch. Dammit. Oww. Shit."

Diego finished cleaning, then patted Bracken on the shoulder. "How are those pure thoughts treating you, *amigo*?"

Bracken flinched, even the gentle touch to the shoulder nearly overwhelming after the intensity of the antiseptic. He glared, "Never said I was a saint. And I wouldn't say no to another bottle of whiskey if *that's* how you're gonna be. Do we have to do this every time?"

Diego looked up at the ceiling. "I want you to picture something for me, Sheriff. Think of the most vile thing you can imagine. Something truly stomach turning. We're talking rotting meat, body fluids, carrion eaters, all of the worst things that make your stomach feel rancid. Picture all those things all mushed up together in a soup."

Diego leaned forward. "Now imagine that gator dipped every tooth in that rotting soup, got its whole mouth packed with it... so that when it bit you, all that rotting flesh paste could get *inside* your skin *all the way* down into the muscle fiber and tissue, so that your blood vessels—everything in there that those gator teeth came in contact with—got nice and smeared with that soup paste. Understand?"

Bracken looked at him, not blinking. Finally, he spoke, his voice a little quieter than it had been. "Twice a day, you said? For the cleaning and the dressing changes?"

Diego nodded. "Twice a day."

Bracken let out a shaky breath. "I think I can handle twice a day."

Diego smiled. "Good. I think you can, too."

Ellie handed Diego fresh bandages without being asked, their practiced rhythm suggesting this wasn't their first complicated patient. "The judge was right about one thing—half the town's already talking about yesterday. Jennifer Starr stopped by this morning asking if you were going to live long enough for her to arrange another billiards match for you. She seems to think you'll be good for her business."

"I like her already." Bracken watched Diego work, almost hypnotized by the physician's steady hands and practiced efficiency. "What's the other half saying?"

Diego finished securing the new dressing. "That any man crazy enough to wade into Gator Creek at feeding time might actually be tough enough to handle Cypress Run."

"Or stupid enough," Ellie added, but without her earlier edge.

Bracken tested the range of motion in his shoulder, grimacing at the stiffness. "I'll take either one. Reputation's reputation. How long before I can use my arm again properly?"

"Few more days of rest—*at minimum*. Maybe a week before you should be doing anything strenuous. Keep it in the sling, come back for the dressing changes twice daily, and for the love of all that's holy, don't do anything stupid."

Bracken scoffed, his eyes glinting with equal parts mischief and misery. "So, what I'm hearing is that light investigative duty is fine as long as I don't get into fist fights while I'm about it."

"That's not at all what I said," Diego growled. "A few more days of *rest*. As in laying in bed and contemplating the very real consequences of your actions, *rest*."

Bracken was already shaking his head before Diego finished speaking. "Can't do it, Doc. There's work I've got to do."

"What work could possibly be more important than healing?"

"Need to get out to that railroad camp. See if they're missing any surveyors." Bracken's voice gained strength as his focus sharpened. "That dead man didn't kill himself, and whoever did it is still walking around free."

Ellie stepped forward, her teacher's voice cutting through his determination. "Sheriff, you can barely sit up without breaking into a sweat. What makes you think you can ride out to the camps?"

"I 'think I can' because it wouldn't make a lick of sense to try and do a thing if I thought I couldn't." He grunted as he managed to push himself up and swing his legs off the bed. He closed his eyes and waited for the pain to fade back to a manageable ache. "If you don't think you can do something, you start looking for excuses why you can't and then you start talking yourself out of all sorts of useful opportunities."

Ellie covered her eyes with one hand, as if trying to keep her patience physically contained. She'd known him for less than a day and already hated his verbal wriggling. She had a feeling that getting a straight answer from the man when he didn't want to give one was going to be like trying to grab a piglet in a mud pit.

"Why, then. Why do *you* have to ride out, *today*, specifically?"

Bracken's jaw set in a stubborn line. "That surveyor's been dead at least two days. Every hour we wait gives the killer more time to cover his tracks or disappear entirely."

"You'll collapse before you make it halfway to the camp."

Diego nodded, using his 'please be reasonable' voice, "She's right. You lost blood, you're fighting infection, and your body needs time to recover. Push yourself now, and you'll end up right back on this table—or worse."

The room fell silent except for the distant chatter of children playing outside. Bracken sighed heavily, looking up at the ceiling, clearly wrestling with the contradiction between his physical limitations and his professional obligations.

"You want to know why?" he asked quietly before meeting them both with a steady look. "Because that's the job. A man's dead, I gotta find out who he was before I can figure out why and by whom. And if I do it fast enough, maybe I can prevent more people from dying over the same damn reason. Because it's my job.

"Besides," he added, the self-deprecating grin sliding easily back into place, "what kind of sheriff would I be if I let my first murder case go cold because I was too delicate to get out of bed?"

Bracken used a hand on the bed post to half-pull, half-push himself up to his feet. The room tilted slightly, but he gritted his teeth and stayed upright. "Got coffee around here? Head feels like it's stuffed with sawdust."

Ellie and Diego exchanged a look that spoke volumes about their shared exasperation with stubborn patients.

"If you're determined to be an *idiota* about this," Diego said, "then I'm sending Simon with you."

"Who's Simon?"

"My assistant, Simon Finch. Runs the apothecary for me next door, mixes compounds, keeps the soda fountain running." Diego said. "Kid's got a good eye for details and he's young enough to ride hard if you need him to fetch help."

The sheriff's mouth opened to argue, then closed as another wave of pain washed over him. The prospect of riding alone through unfamiliar territory with one usable arm suddenly seemed less appealing.

"I don't suppose Simon comes with a horse, does he? I just realized I, uh..." Bracken chuckled and shook his head. "Please don't laugh at me... I just spent all that time talking dramatically about riding out there today… I don't actually have one. A horse, I mean."

Ellie stared at him, certain she'd misheard. "Why don't you have a horse?"

"Common misconception about Chicago lawmen," Bracken said, his grin firmly in place despite the obvious pain. "People hear 'beat cops hoofin' the streets' and think we actually come with hooves. Truth is, you don't really need them in the city. You can walk most anywhere you need to go, and if you can't walk, you just jump onto a cable car. Worst case, you hail a cab."

Ellie's mind reeled. Cable cars? Cabs you could just… hail? Like calling a dog? She'd heard tales of big city conveniences, but the casual way he described summoning transportation like magic left her speechless.

"What does that mean? You can just… jump on a… what's a cable car?"

"Public transportation system… Umm, like an open-air train car, except the tracks run all over the city streets. They used to be pulled by horses, but now they've got this whole new system with giant underground cables. Big steam engines keep the cables moving under the roads, and the cars grab onto them somehow and get pulled all over town. Fastest thing you ever saw."

The deeper implications crashed over her like a cold wave. "Sheriff Bracken." Her voice came out carefully controlled, the way it did when she was trying not to throttle one of her students. "Please tell me you at least know *how* to ride a horse."

His confident expression crumpled into something painfully sheepish. "I've *seen* people riding them. Looks easy enough."

Diego's pen clattered to his desk. Ellie felt her jaw drop open despite every effort to maintain her composure. They both stared at the sheriff.

"Oh, Lord," Ellie whispered, pressing her fingers to her temples. "You're planning to investigate a murder in the Florida wilderness, and you've never been on a horse."

"I'm sure I can learn," Bracken protested weakly. "It can't be that hard, can it?"

"Excuse us for just a moment," Ellie said through gritted teeth.

She grabbed Diego's arm and pulled him toward the supply closet, practically shoving him inside and pulling the door shut behind them.

The small space smelled of dried herbs, bottles of tonics and powders crowding the shelves around them.

"Diego," she whispered, her voice strained with barely controlled frustration. "Our sheriff just admitted he doesn't know how to ride a horse. A *horse*. The single most basic requirement for law enforcement out here."

Diego pinched the bridge of his nose. "I heard him, Ellie."

"First the gator, now this—he thinks he can just show up and fumble his way through this job and it's going to get people killed—including himself."

"You're being harsh," he said quietly. "Not wrong about the danger, but harsh. He's trying—that much is clear. And a lot harder than he has to. He wants to do right by this town."

Ellie clenched her hands into fists. "Wanting to do right won't matter if he gets himself killed trying to prove he belongs here when he doesn't."

"You're wrong, Ellie." Diego's voice was firm. Not angry. Just firm. "Wanting to do right matters a lot. Weren't you the one complaining when Sheriff Brown cut and run the moment it got tough?"

Ellie wrapped her arms in front of chest, heat rising up her neck at the rebuke. "That's different. Sheriff Brown was a coward," she gestured toward the door "but that man out there is just plain hopeless."

"I think you need to look again," he said, looking at the door as if he could see through it to the man beyond, then back to his nurse. "The man can barely stand, but he's still trying to button a shirt with one hand because finding a murderer matters more than his comfort. That seems more like a man determined to do his job than one who's just hopeless."

Through the crack came the *thunk* of a falling shoe, a muttered curse, determined movement.

"He didn't come here by choice, Ellie," Diego said softly. "Hartwell said as much—some office up north washed its hands of him. That's hard on a man's pride. But he's still trying. And he's quick. He turned an alligator bite into good publicity, and handled Hartwell like a chess piece. He'll get his feet under him sooner than you think."

Ellie's shoulders drooped. "Won't help if he breaks his neck before breakfast. And being quick doesn't make him any less of a fish trying to climb trees."

"No. But he can learn—if someone here bothers to teach him instead of waiting for him to fail." Diego's eyes tightened slightly. "When the war broke out, field hospitals were staffed full of clerks and farm boys. Boys who'd been throwing up mid-surgery their first week were stitching officers back together like machines by the second. If you give a man opportunity enough, he can adapt to just about anything."

Diego continued, "You don't have to like him. Just give him a chance before you write him off as hopeless."

Ellie sighed, feeling the fight drain out of her. "You're right."

"Of course I'm right. It's one of the perks that comes with a medical license." Diego's mouth quirked into a small smile.

Diego opened the door and returned to Bracken who was examining the bandages on his arm with great interest—as if the precise angle of the gauze wrap was the most interesting thing in the room—wearing the too innocent expression of a child who had heard every word of their parents' arguing but was trying to pretend they hadn't.

The guilt hit Ellie—quick, sharp, and uninvited. She hated the feeling.

"After consulting with my nurse," Diego began, "we've agreed that any kind of riding is prohibited until that sling comes off. You can argue your way around *some* of the things I suggest if you like—things like *rest* and *light activity* that are ultimately about physical comfort and subjective to your own tolerance for misery."

Diego paused a moment to pin the sheriff with a look before continuing, allowing the full weight of his medical authority to anchor his words, "*This* is not one of those things. If you disobey this order it will likely result in your death. And if you press me on it, I absolutely will go to Judge Hartwell and have her put it in writing for you. Do you understand?"

The sheriff sighed and dropped his gaze. Whatever dignity he'd managed to maintain during Judge Hartwell's visit evaporated like morning mist. "Yes, I understand," he said quietly.

Ellie caught the sag in his posture—that of a man who knew very well when he was being scolded—and felt a twist of sympathy. "Sheriff... I'm... I'm certain you *can* learn to ride. Eventually. Most folks around here have been doing it since they were old enough to walk, so it seems much easier than it actually is." She paused, choosing her words carefully. "But accidents happen. If you fall or get bucked while you're still healing, at best—Well, no, there is no 'at best' because you would either break your neck or lose your arm entirely. This just isn't the right time to try learning."

"Makes sense—practical," Bracken said, not looking up. He shook his head. "I'm not going to fight you over it if that's what you're waiting for. I can't even—" He rolled his eyes with a huff of bitter amusement. "I can't even tie my own shoes right now. It's a pretty pathetic state of affairs. But I still have a job to do, which means that I have to find a way to make it happen. Any ideas?"

Diego gestured for him to sit back and knelt to tie the laces for him, saying, "Simon has a mule and a cart that he uses for deliveries sometimes. We'll rig it up and Simon can drive you."

"That sounds... That sounds perfect, actually. Thank you."

Diego nodded and patted him softly on his good shoulder as he rose, quietly acknowledging the look that said the thanks were for more than just the mule cart solution. He grabbed a cloth sling from the supply cabinet and began the process of fitting it to the sheriff's arm, ensuring it was supported correctly.

Ellie watched Bracken's face carefully as Diego worked the sling into position, noting how his jaw tightened when the doctor lifted his injured arm. Now that Diego had admonished her—and rightfully so—about getting irritated with his odd city-born behavior without trying to understand it, she was determined to pay better attention.

The sheriff had a habit of deflecting discomfort with humor, but his body told a different story—the slight hunch of his shoulders, the way the fingers of his good hand wouldn't stop drumming and fidgeting.

"Before we head out to meet your Simon," Bracken said, his voice carrying that forced lightness she was beginning to recognize, "any chance we could stop by a grocer's? Thought I might grab an apple or something."

Ellie blinked, certain she'd misunderstood. "For what?"

"Breakfast." He shifted uncomfortably as Diego adjusted the sling's position. "Haven't quite figured out the meal situation here yet."

Diego's hands stilled on the fabric. "What do you mean, meal situation?"

The sheriff's cheeks took on a faint flush, though he maintained his casual tone. "Well, room and board is ostensibly included in my job contract," He paused, seeming to choose his words carefully. "But then 'room' turned out to be a lumpy cot in a jail cell. I was terrified the 'board' might be rats under the floor and the stove in the corner; I just didn't have the courage to properly ask at the time."

"What have you been eating?" Ellie asked. "Sheriff, you've been here since yesterday morning. Please tell me you've had *something* to eat since then."

"Well... Had a rather good lunch at the saloon, courtesy of Mr. Hendricks losing that billiards game." His good hand rubbed the back of his neck—a gesture she was learning meant he felt foolish but was trying not to show it. "Figured I'd sort out the rest once I got my bearings. But then, uh... things came up, situations transpired, got distracted. So, I haven't quite gotten around to the 'sorting things out' part yet."

Diego's expression had gone thunderous, his usual patience with bureaucratic incompetence clearly exhausted.

"Judge Hartwell didn't discuss salary or living arrangements when you got here?" Diego asked, his voice carefully controlled.

Bracken tried to laugh it off, but Ellie caught the slight tightness around his eyes. "Oh, we discussed it. Briefly. She didn't seem keen on discussing it further. And the key to a successful working relationship is knowing when it's safe to antagonize the boss and when not to push your luck. I figure I'd best have at least one good win under my belt, prove I'm worth the trouble before I try bringing it up again."

The admission revealed far more than he'd intended it to. Ellie realized with startling clarity the uncomfortable position the man was in—trying to prove himself worthy of a job he wasn't all that confident would pay him what was owed while knowing that he couldn't give up and go back home again even if it didn't.

"Speaking of practical matters," he said quickly, gesturing down at his shoes. They had clearly seen better days even before their encounter with swamp water had destroyed the shiny leather. "Not sure my shoes are gonna recover from their ordeal. Think the general store might have a suitable replacement? Preferably something that doesn't require me to tie any laces."

Ellie caught the slight grimace that crossed his features as he flexed the fingers of his injured arm—his pride was taking as much of a beating as his body, and he was working hard to pretend otherwise.

"They'll have boots," she said quietly. "And we'll make sure you get a proper meal before we do anything else."

Diego finished adjusting the sling and stepped back to examine his work. "There. That should keep everything stable." He looked Bracken in the eye. "And I'll be having a word with Judge Hartwell about living arrangements. I'll write a prescription for a proper bed and submit it as a medical work requirement if necessary."

Bracken opened his mouth as if to protest, then seemed to think better of it. "Much obliged, Doc," he said instead, the genuine gratitude clear beneath the casual words. "Both of you."

The simple thanks carried more weight than all his earlier bravado, and Ellie found herself reassessing the man sitting before her—not just the cocky sheriff with too many jokes, but someone trying to build a life from scratch in a place that seemed determined to break him.

"I, erm—" She shook her head and brushed her hands down her skirt. "It's almost time for class and I really need to freshen up before my students arrive."

Ellie moved toward the door, then paused with her hand on the frame, turning to Diego. "Will you have time to show him around this morning? If not, I could cancel...?"

"Yeah, I've got some time. Assuming no emergencies or house calls come up. I'll take him by the store, then introduce him to Simon."

Ellie nodded. "Oh, before I forget, Sheriff, I sent your clothes to the laundry. They should have them delivered to your office by this evening. And I put the money that was inside your coat into your billfold."

Bracken grimaced. "Thanks."

She hesitated in the doorway, torn between duty and the uneasy urge to make sure he'd be all right. "Diego? Try not to let our city boy do anything too foolish?"

"I'll do my best," Diego replied, though his tone suggested he had little faith in his ability to control the sheriff's impulses.

As the door closed behind her, Bracken attempted to stand, swayed slightly, then caught himself against the wall. The movement sent fresh fire through his injured arm, but he managed to stay upright.

Bracken sighed. "Please don't be offended—I appreciate the offer of an escort—but I think I'd prefer to see what I can manage on my own, just for this morning. Where can I find this Simon of yours?"

Diego lifted his hands in acquiescence. He could understand a man hating to be reliant, wanting to find some measure of self-sufficiency. "Drugstore's just next door here. Can't miss it—there's a brass soda fountain in the window and probably some kind of chemical smell leaking out the back door."

Bracken seemed to be trying to figure out how much maneuvering it would take to get into his gun harness while wrestling with the sling. "Chemical smell?"

"Kid likes to experiment. Usually harmless, though last week he managed to blow the cork out of every bottle in the storeroom trying to improve the carbonation process."

The sheriff paused in his attempt to puzzle out the gun holster problem and looked at Diego. "You're sending me out with someone who blows things up for fun?"

"Would you rather pass out *alone* in a cypress grove? Or would you rather be with someone else driving the cart who knows how to get back to town?"

Bracken considered this, then shook his head with a shrug—who was he to judge? "Food first, coffee if at all possible," he muttered. "Then we'll see about this Simon character."

CHAPTER SIX

A Few Errands to Run

The bell above the door of Cotton's General Store jangled as Bracken pushed inside, blinking hard to clear the sting of sunlight as his eyes adjusted to the dimmer interior. He rubbed his eyes, scanning the cluttered shelves.

"Help you, Sheriff?" the proprietor asked—Mr. Cotton, if the sign outside was accurate—as he looked up from his ledger.

"Need boots. Size eleven if you got 'em." Bracken glanced down at his ruined Chicago lace-ups, leather split and still damp from yesterday's creek adventure. "Something that won't fall apart the first time I step in water."

"Got just the thing." The man disappeared toward the back while Bracken wandered the aisles, his good arm trailing along shelves of canned goods and dry goods. A tin of peaches caught his eye—the label promised 'Sweet Georgia Fruit in Heavy Syrup'—and he tucked it under his injured arm. A packet of soda crackers joined it.

"You're the one got bit by that gator yesterday?" A woman with flour-dusted hands appeared at his elbow, eyes bright with curiosity.

"Yup." He popped the 'p,' already bracing for the twenty more times he'd have to answer that question today. "Not as bad as it could have been, fortunately. Gator was just being friendly, I'm told."

"Heard you shot it three or four times."

"Six, actually. Got a little over excited and kept pulling the trigger until the chamber was empty," Bracken said, shifting the crackers to keep them from sliding. "Didn't seem to bother the gator too much, so I guess we're still on friendly terms."

Two more locals drifted over, drawn like moths to flame. An older man with tobacco-stained whiskers leaned against a pickle barrel. "That true you're from Chicago?"

"Guilty as charged."

The tobacco-stained man snorted. "Bet you city boys all think gators are just big lizards."

"Thought that yesterday, sure." Bracken met his eyes. "Was none too gently shown the error of my thinking."

The man laughed. "What brings a slicker like you down to the swamp, anyhow? They got any kind of work up in Chicago that prepares a man for sheriff work down here?"

"The kind where you learn not to turn your back on anything with teeth? Absolutely. Applies just as much to politicians as it does to gators."

That earned him a few chuckles.

The proprietor returned with a pair of sturdy brown boots, leather thick enough to stop a fang. "These'll do you. Military surplus—built for marching through mud and worse."

Bracken set his goods on the counter and fumbled one-handed with his billfold. The coins scattered, and he had to chase a dime with his elbow before the woman scooped it up for him.

"Much obliged."

The proprietor tallied up his purchases—boots, crackers, and peaches—while the crowd began to gather. Bracken knew the boots would be costly, but he'd seen first-hand what happened to beat cops who didn't take care of their feet. He wasn't at all fond of the thought of being hobbled top *and* bottom.

Still, it was almost painful to slide three whole dollars and a couple of coins across the counter. That left him ten. If he kept to two meals a day, assuming no more surprises popped up, he could just about stretch it to cover three weeks. An occasional billiards game might bring in a little extra, but that'd be impossible until the sling came off. And with Hartwell being vague as fog about the timing of his first wages, that ten dollars might have to last him anywhere from two weeks to six... or even more...

Bracken shook his head before he could spiral deeper into his thoughts and get maudlin about it. He stuffed his billfold into his pocket and studied the pile of purchases, then the awkward angle of his sling. "Don't suppose I could eat breakfast at your counter, Mr..."

"Cotton. John Cotton."

"Mr. Cotton. I'd be happy to answer a few more questions about Chicago in exchange for the trouble?"

Mr. Cotton grinned. "Sounds like more than a fair trade. Mary, grab the can opener."

Soon Bracken found himself perched on a stool, watching Mary—Mr. Cotton's wife, it would seem—pry open his tin of peaches while the growing crowd pressed closer. The sweet syrup was a shock after yesterday's bitter coffee, but his empty stomach didn't care about subtlety.

"So, what's it like up north?" The tobacco-stained man leaned forward. "Heard they got buildings tall as trees."

"Taller." Bracken speared a peach slice with his pocket knife. "Some got eight, nine stories. Makes a man dizzy just looking up. Makes him dizzier if he has to climb all those flights of stairs."

"How many people?"

"More than you'd want to meet in a lifetime. Picture every soul in this town crammed into that saloon, shoulder-to-shoulder. You pick the wrong time of day to walk to work, you get real personal with the folks walking next to you. Gotta learn to be mindful of your feet and handy with your elbows." He noticed a boy of maybe ten staring at his crackers with obvious hunger. Bracken slid the packet toward him. "Help yourself."

The boy's eyes widened, and he grabbed a handful before his mother could scold him. He offered some to her next. Soon half the crowd was munching crackers while Bracken fielded questions about snow, streetcars, and whether it was true that folks up north ate with forks at every meal.

"Will you tell us about the gator attack?" someone finally asked. "You afraid of going back in the water?"

Bracken considered this, chasing the last peach around the tin. The truth was he'd been avoiding even thinking about Gator Creek, but admitting fear to a roomful of swamp dwellers seemed unwise.

"The water was actually more pleasant than it looked, so no, I can't imagine being terribly afraid of the water," he said finally after leaning back and giving it the appearance of some good solid thought. "Truth be told, I'm a lot more nervous about meeting that gator again."

He gestured at his sling. "Doc tells me this was nothing but a love bite, but then I shot it six times with a Colt .45 and I tell you truly, the thing just winked at me. Now, back home, a stranger comes up and gives you a love bite and a wink, you gotta be prepared to defend your virtue."

He tilted his head as if considering the angles. "On the other hand, you put six rounds of lead into a fella and he just winks at you, you got a whole different set of problems. But what does all that mean in gator terms? Does that mean we're in a relationship now? Should I bring it flowers next time? There's just so many questions that I'm not sure I want to know the answers to."

His verbal antics got a few more laughs than it did groans, so Bracken counted it as a win. At least the locals hopefully wouldn't suspect that their sheriff would likely have nightmares about that growling hiss and that spring trap snap for a long time coming.

Breakfast finished and the crowd dispersed, Bracken found an obliging seat and swapped out his shoes for the new boots, grateful that they seemed to fit properly. He looked sadly at his old, ruined shoes and decided that the shoestrings were at least still good, so he carefully unthreaded them and stored them in his pocket before dumping the ruined shoes in the trash.

Bracing himself for the hell outside, he exhaled through his teeth, shoved open the door, and squinted into the white Florida sunlight.

The bell over the apothecary door chimed, and heat rolled in behind the man everyone had been whispering about since dawn: the new sheriff—the one who'd wrestled a gator, lived, and somehow looked more inconvenienced than heroic. He was taller than Simon expected, lean rather than broad, like he'd traded bulk for angles. His arm hung in a sling, his face drawn against the glare outside.

At once, Simon snapped upright behind the counter, wiping his hands on his apron so fast he risked tangling himself up in it.

Three locals were perched at the soda fountain, halfway through their morning beverages, gossip silenced by the novelty that had just walked in.

"Morning." The sheriff took the end stool, setting his hat on the marble counter with deliberate care. "You'd be Mr. Finch, I'm guessing?"

Simon's pulse soared. *He already knows my name.*

"Sheriff Bracken! Yes sir, that's me—Simon Finch, apprentice to Dr. Delgado." His voice almost cracked but he pushed on. "I also run the soda fountain, though really I'm more of a chemist in training. I can make seventeen different flavors of soda phosphate, including one that glows in the dark, though Dr. Delgado says I'm not allowed to serve that one anymore after Mrs. Henderson's incident—"

"Coffee," Bracken said, gently but firmly enough to make Simon stop mid-breath. "Any chance you've got coffee? And maybe something for a headache that won't require a chemistry degree to understand?"

It wasn't unkind, just calm and intentional—the voice of a man who had a priority he needed to address.

Simon smiled anyway. "Oh. Well, no coffee exactly, but I could make you a cola phosphate? The caffeine content is actually quite substantial, and of course I use real vanilla extract, and the phosphoric acid that makes the bubbles, it helps with digestion—"

"Sure." Bracken rubbed at the narrow corner between his nose and brow and smiled with more patience than a man in pain could be expected to have. "And the headache remedy?"

"Willow bark powder mixed with bicarbonate of soda. Dr. Delgado's formula. Tastes terrible, but it works fast."

Simon busied himself behind the fountain, grateful for the chance to move. He pumped syrup, charged water, measured fizz—and tried not to think about how his hands were trembling.

"How's the arm?" he asked over the hiss of carbonation. "Dr. Delgado said the gator got you pretty good, but that you didn't pass out during the stitching—which is impressive because most folks do, even the tough ones, and—"

"Kid." The single word stopped him like a cork. Bracken reached forward and took the glass of fizzing liquid from him. "Take a breath."

Simon looked away sheepishly. "Sorry. I get excited about... well, everything really. Dr. Delgado says it's a character flaw."

But the sheriff was smiling, faint but real. "I'll let you in on a secret, kid—Doc's gonna be plenty busy coming up with opinions about my own character flaws over the next few days. You go right on ahead and be excited about everything. I'll make sure to give him bigger problems to worry about than you."

He took a sip of the phosphate, and for one agonizing second Simon waited to see if he'd grimace.

"This isn't half bad," Bracken said.

Simon nearly beamed. "Secret's in the ratio. Most folks use too much syrup, not enough acid. Chemistry's all about balance, you see, and—"

"Headache remedy?"

"Oh! Right, let me get that for you!"

Simon darted to the shelves. He found the right shelf and the jar of powdered medicine, measuring the dosage carefully into a glass.

"Right then." He could hear the sheriff, his voice weary but accommodating, "I'm guessing we're all waiting to hear about the gator? This is my third time today, so I hope you folks don't mind me keeping it short. But go on ahead and ask away."

When Simon returned with the glass of powdered medicine, the woman at the counter was already asking, "Is it true what my girls were saying? You let little Nate Harper go wading into that creek to fetch the body all by himself?"

Simon's heart stuttered. *Nate Harper. Oh no.*

He blurted before thinking, eyes wide. "You let Nate Harper go in the water? Mrs. Harper must've been furious."

"First, let me be perfectly clear—" Bracken held up his good hand, eyes steady. "I wouldn't have 'let him' go anywhere if he'd given me a choice. Kid was already knee-deep and halfway there before I'd finished telling the others to stay put."

"That boy's always been headstrong," Mrs. Patterson muttered.

"And you'd best believe that if I'd known what was lurking in there, I'd have raced in after him and hauled him out like a sack of potatoes," the sheriff added—then, with a half-grin, "But you are correct about Mrs. Harper. Furious doesn't begin to cover it. If I'm being perfectly honest, the gator was less terrifying than seeing Mrs. Harper come at me like she was going to skin me alive."

Simon had never witnessed a man invite humiliation and deflect it at the same time before. It was fascinating.

"Well?" The lumberman leaned closer. "You gonna tell us what happened with the gator, or ain't ya?"

Simon was already spellbound.

"Six-footer, I'm told," Bracken said, rubbing at the spot between his eyebrows again, trying to hide a grimace and failing. "But I wasn't about to ask him to pose for a yardstick. Decides he's got prior claim to both the body and that particular stretch of creek bank." He lifted the arm in the sling. "Turns out gators are particular about their property rights.

"Back in Chicago," the sheriff went on, voice shifting into storytelling cadence, "when you got into a property dispute between gangs, you had two choices: run like hell or start shooting. Running wasn't really an option with a gator clamped onto my arm."

Simon tried to imagine it—the splash, the scale, the sound—half horror, half admiration.

The woman gasped. "What'd you do?"

"He shot it! Six times," Simon blurted, remembering what Dr. Delgado had said. "That's what Doc told me!"

"And the darned thing just looked at me like I'd been rude at dinner," Bracken said dryly, draining his glass, "then swam off to tell its friends about the crazy Chicago lawman trespassing on his bank."

Laughter rippled around the counter. For a moment, Simon felt almost part of the legend himself—the apprentice with the front-row seat.

"Lucky it was just a six-footer," old Joseph from the lumbermill said. "Big ones'll take your whole arm clean off."

"That's what I keep hearing." Bracken said. "Makes me feel all warm and fuzzy about living here. But, now I've shared my gator gossip, seems only fair you folks return the favor." Bracken leaned forward again, sharper now. "Anyone got news about the railroad?"

The conversation shifted, and Simon listened, wiping the same glass twice over, catching every word about the surveyors, the fights, the confusion over stakes. *This* was what investigation looked like, he thought—listening hard while pretending not to.

When the opportunity presented itself, Simon blurted, "Sheriff, if you're thinking of visiting the railroad camp, I could drive you out there. I've got a cart, and I usually close the shop for lunch anyway."

"That'd be helpful, Simon. Would you be good to leave in about an hour?"

"Perfect! I'll put up a sign saying we're closed for the rest of the day."

He couldn't keep from grinning. The sheriff thought he'd be *helpful*.

Bracken reached for his wallet. "What do I owe you for the phosphate and the headache powder?"

"Fifteen cents for the cola phosphate, nickel for the willow bark. Twenty cents total."

As Simon said it, Bracken glanced down at the display case beside him—his latest object of enthusiasm, the smoked spectacles he'd ordered direct from London. They'd looked grand in the catalog, though Dr. Delgado kept muttering about charlatanism. Dr. Delgado simply hadn't had an opportunity to test them yet.

Bracken noticed. Of course he did.

"Tell me, kid," the sheriff said, squinting toward the window, "do those actually cut sunlight, or just make a fella fail to look unsuspicious?"

Simon nearly upset a glass with his excitement. "Smoked spectacles! Genuine London issue. They deflect glare, soothe the optic nerve—well, mostly. And they're medically endorsed—Dr. Delgado says so." (Or would, Simon was pretty sure, once he knew how helpful they were) Simon pulled out a pair and set them gently in front of the sheriff so he could examine them closer.

"Sounds a little on the lighter side of miraculous." Bracken lifted a pair, tilting them as though assessing evidence. "But seeing as you people don't ever seem to turn that sunshine off and it's been trying to split my skull wide open, I might be just about desperate enough to try anything."

He slid them on, stone-faced. "Well, how's the effect? More foolish than usual, or holding steady?"

"About steady." Joseph called back, and laughter rose again.

Sheriff Bracken nodded gravely. "That's about what I expected. I'm assuming that if these things don't perform as advertised—" he tapped the frame "—I reserve the right to return 'em for credit toward something stronger?"

"Of course, Sheriff!" Simon said brightly. Relief and triumph mingled in his chest—he'd *sold* one. "Though I expect you'll find immediate relief! The catalog described a number of case studies that ensured their performance."

"Here's hoping. My optic nerves could use a vacation. How much extra for these?"

"Normally, they're eighty-five cents, but I'm sure Dr. Delgado wouldn't mind if we made it an even dollar for everything together."

Bracken unclipped a dollar bill from inside his vest, handed it over like it was nothing. "Not like I had much dignity left anyway."

Simon wrote "1.00—Sheriff Bracken—Smoked Spectacles, phosphate, headache powder" carefully into the ledger. He already knew Dr. Delgado would sigh and lecture about sales ethics, but maybe he'd also say *good initiative, Simon.*

The sheriff was already wearing the spectacles as he tipped his hat to the patrons. "Much obliged for the conversation and the local news. I'll meet you at the livery, Mr. Finch."

The bell chimed again as he left, bright light flaring through the doorway.

When the shop fell quiet, Simon looked down at the empty counter, then grinned to himself.

There was willow bark to re-shelve, but also a sheriff to meet and an investigation waiting.

He reached for the 'Closed for Lunch' sign with hands that shook from excitement.

The classroom had just begun to quiet when a familiar voice came from the doorway.

"I hope you'll pardon the interruption, Mrs. Harper."

Of course it would be him, hat in hand and sling tucked neat, looking far too alive to have earned all that local gossip. And wearing something new that made her blink—wire-framed spectacles with dark lenses, smoked almost black, hiding his eyes completely. He looked absurd and somehow still disarmingly confident.

Every child in the room jolted upright. Nate was first to reach him, shouting before she could take a breath.

"Sheriff Bracken—!"

"You're alive—!"

"Hope you're not too disappointed?" he asked the clamoring children.

"We thought the gator ate you!" piped up one of the younger girls. "Jimmy said gators always come back to finish what they started."

Ellie crossed her arms, her expression stern but amusement flickering up in spite of herself. "Sheriff Bracken, you're interrupting our arithmetic lesson."

"My apologies, ma'am. Just wanted to reassure these young scholars here that the new sheriff hadn't been turned into gator bait." He held up his sling. "Got a few new scars to show for my troubles, but I'm still breathing."

Ellie didn't need the chaos, but she couldn't quite make herself stop it. The children crowded around him, eyes wide, tugging at his sleeve as though touching proof of survival. He sat in a chair to speak with them eye-to-eye, answering every question they threw at him with theatrical gravity that had them hanging on every word.

It took a few minutes of talk—and more questions than she cared to count—before he finally said, "I reckon I've interrupted your learning long enough. Mrs. Harper's got important things to teach you, and I've got some sheriff business to attend."

As the children reluctantly returned to their slates, Ellie walked him to the porch, closing the door behind her. "You scared them yesterday," she said, quietly.

He nodded. "I figured as much. I was hoping a quick look in might undo some of the damage."

"Maybe a little," she admitted. She tilted her head, studying the unfamiliar glasses. "And what in heaven's name are those supposed to be?"

He touched the frames, perfectly solemn. "Medical equipment. For the relief of optic nerves. Mr. Finch assures me they're London approved."

"I might've known," she said, shaking her head. "He's been pestering Diego for weeks about those smoked lenses."

"They seem to work," Bracken said. "Or I've gone mercifully blind. Either way, my headache's finally surrendered."

"They make you look like a villain on the cover of a dime novel."

"Small price to pay," he said, lowering them just enough for a flash of green eyes. "Spent most of yesterday feeling hungover."

"You spent a fair portion looking the part, too."

"Probably not wrong." He tipped his hat, the lenses catching twin sparks of light. "So. What's the verdict, Mrs. Harper? They told me at the shop that I didn't look any more ridiculous than normal. Do I pass inspection?"

"You're breathing," she said. "We'll call that a start."

He laughed, low and genuine, and it reached something lighter in her chest than she liked to admit.

She hid her smile behind an exaggerated sigh. "If they help, keep them. Heaven knows the sun's half the battle out here."

"I intend to. Besides, a few good stories here and there, I'll have folks convinced they make me look distinguished in no time."

"So, you met Simon then?" she asked, brisk again, folding her arms to reclaim her distance.

"I have. Little long-winded compared to some, but a fine salesman. He's driving me out to the railroad camp this afternoon. Apparently there's been trouble between the survey boys and your lumberyard, so should learn at least one interesting thing or two, I imagine."

Her stomach tightened. "Just be careful. You spun a fine story for Judge Hartwell, but if someone's already put one man in the creek, they won't hesitate to do it again."

He smiled—that half-crooked, infuriating one. "Why, Mrs. Harper, if I didn't know better, I'd say you were concerned for my well-being."

"It's a good thing you know better, then." She gestured toward the path. "Off with you. My students' arithmetic won't solve itself."

He gave a little bow, all mock gallantry behind those ridiculous glasses, and strode down the steps.

Watching him go, Ellie supposed the lenses suited him after all. They made it impossible to tell when he was bluffing.

The horses in the paddock moved with easy confidence through the Florida heat, their coats gleaming with sweat as they grazed. Bracken watched them from the rail fence, envying their simple acceptance of this place. They didn't spend their nights wondering if they'd made a terrible mistake or wake up calculating how many silver coins remained between survival and destitution. They just ate grass and endured the mosquitoes with the resigned patience of creatures born to it.

Back in Chicago, horses were for rich men and cops with better connections than he'd ever managed. Now here he was in a place where a man without a horse might as well be without legs, and he couldn't tell a saddle from a soup pot.

The irony wasn't lost on him. He'd survived Chicago's worst neighborhoods, stared down gangsters and ward bosses, talked his way out of more trouble than any reasonable man should expect to live through. He'd been a damned good cop.

But stick him on four legs and a tail, and he'd probably end up face-first in the mud before he made it to the gate. Which made him perfectly useless for frontier sheriff work.

One of the mares wandered closer to the fence, a solid bay with intelligent eyes and what looked like a permanent expression of mild disapproval. Reminded him a little of Ellie Harper, actually. The horse wore a crude brand on her flank—a simple design that looked like someone had bent a piece of iron into the shape of a...

Bracken straightened, squinting at the mark, tilting his new spectacles down so he could see the detail better. The brand was nothing fancy, just a curved piece with a notch at one end, but it looked exactly like a billiard cue rest. The kind of simple, elegant tool that kept your cue steady when you needed to make a long shot.

"See something interesting, Sheriff?"

The stable master had wandered over, a grizzled man with hay in his beard and the permanent smell of horses about him who introduced himself as Bobby Keene.

"That brand there." Bracken pointed at the mare. "Who made that?"

"That's the Circle W mark—Dunston Wooley's spread. But if you're looking to get some metalwork done, blacksmith's right next door. Jake Henley. Does good work, fair prices."

"Much obliged." Bracken glanced around the stable yard. "You mind if I borrow that brand for just a minute? Want to show Mr. Henley something."

"Sure thing." The stable master shrugged and fetched the iron from a hook near the forge. "Just bring it back before you head out—I assume you're waiting for young Simon?"

"That obvious?"

"Only two reasons a man stands around my stable staring at horses he can't ride. Either he's waiting on someone, or he's wondering what the hell he's doing in my stable."

"Could be both. Or could be he's wondering what the hell he's doing in Florida, and your stable just happens to be sitting where he's standing."

Keene laughed and Bracken tucked the brand under his good arm, headed for the blacksmith's shop, his mind already working out angles and measurements. Maybe he couldn't ride a horse, and maybe his lodgings consisted of a jail cell and whatever charity meals he could scrounge, but maybe—just maybe—if he could find a way to play pool with only one arm...

The blacksmith's forge glowed like a small sun in the shade of the covered yard outside his shop, sending up shimmering waves of heat that made even the Florida afternoon feel cool by comparison.

Henley looked up from his anvil as Bracken entered, sweat beading on his forehead despite the early hour.

"Sheriff Bracken, right? Heard about your tangle with that gator. What brings you to my shop?"

"This brand here—" Bracken held up the borrowed iron. "How much would it cost to have something similar made? Not for livestock," he added quickly, "just as a more general sort of tool."

"What kind of tool you thinking about?"

"Pool cue rest. Doc says I have to wear this sling until my arm heals, and if I can't play billiards for that long, I'm liable to go stark raving mad."

He explained his predicament, demonstrating how a pool cue rest would allow him to play the game despite his injured arm.

Bracken managed a rueful grin. "Already proved I'm not much good at staying out of trouble. I figure I better find some way to keep myself occupied before I pick a fight with something bigger than a six-foot gator."

Jake examined the brand thoughtfully, turning it over in his hands. "Interesting challenge. I could fashion something similar, maybe adjust the angle a bit for your needs. Make it out of good steel, give it some weight so it won't slide on the felt."

He quoted a price that made Bracken wince—two dollars would take a significant bite from his remaining funds. But the alternative was weeks of watching other men play, and that, he suspected, would wound his pride worse than the gator had.

And if it worked? A few careful bets might keep him from having to choose between starving and wandering around town with a collection cup and a pitiable expression on his face.

"Fair enough. How soon could you have it ready?"

"Tomorrow afternoon, if you're not particular about the finish. Day after if you want it polished pretty."

"Tomorrow's perfect. Much obliged."

Bracken returned the brand to the stable master just as Simon arrived with a mule-drawn cart, his face bright with excitement. The contraption looked sturdy enough, though the mule eyed Bracken with the same skeptical expression he'd been getting from most of the residents of Cypress Run.

"Ready for adventure, Sheriff?" Simon practically bounced on the driver's seat.

"As ready as a man can be with one good arm and no idea what he's walking into." Bracken clambered awkwardly into the cart's bed, his boots finding purchase on the rough planking. "Just promise me we're not heading anywhere that requires swimming."

"The railroad camp's on solid ground," Simon assured him, snapping the reins. "Mostly."

As the cart lurched into motion, Bracken settled back against the side rails and watched Cypress Run shrink behind them. The sun pressed down like a wool blanket, but the new spectacles were doing a decent job of keeping the worst of the glare out of his eyes, and at least he was moving toward answers instead of just collecting mosquito bites and local gossip.

The swamp had already tried to kill him once—time to see if the railroad boys could do any better.

CHAPTER SEVEN

Resolution

The cart lurched to a stop at the edge of the railroad camp, and Bracken climbed down with considerably less grace than he'd managed getting into it.

He felt strangely vulnerable in only his shirt and vest. The shoulder harness felt wrong, too—just the one gun instead of his usual pair—positioned awkwardly on his right side under his arm where he couldn't draw it with any sort of speed—or without looking like a flapping chicken. He'd had to leave the other Colt back at the office; the double holster rig just wouldn't work with the sling, but without the weight of the second Colt to balance things out, the one was dragging the harness down and making him feel lopsided.

He tugged on the left side of the leather shoulder harness to redistribute the weight and make his gun sit straighter.

It also didn't help that he usually kept his guns underneath his coat, and since his coat was indisposed until the sleeve could be repaired—

"Sheriff?" Simon's voice cut through Bracken's spiraling irritation. He hopped down from the driver's seat, his eyes bright with curiosity. "Can I ask you something?"

"Shoot."

"Why do you carry two guns? I mean, most sheriffs have just the one, don't they?"

Bracken glanced around the camp—rough men in sweat-stained clothes, the kind who sized up a lawman's hardware before they bothered looking at his badge. "Different tools for different jobs," he said, keeping his voice casual. "The one I've got on now has a four-inch barrel—clears the holster easier, so it draws fast, fires quick around corners or in tight spaces. The one back at the office has a seven-inch barrel, which gives it better accuracy at longer distances, but a little bit more cumbersome if you're trying to do things quickly."

Simon nodded eagerly. "Like having different sized hammers?"

"Something like that. Plus, two guns means twelve shots before you have to reload in a gunfight. When lead's flying, your fingers get to shaking—reloading becomes harder than you wish it was. Might not sound like much, but those extra six rounds can mean the difference between getting a pint after work or being planted in a churchyard."

"Have you ever been in a real gunfight?"

Bracken choked on a disbelieving laugh. Of all the uncomfortable questions the kid could have asked. "Never by choice," he said eventually. "I've always aspired to settle disagreements with polite conversation."

The railroad camp sprawled before them like a temporary town—canvas tents, wooden shacks, and a few more permanent structures that looked like they'd been thrown together by men who expected to move on before winter. The smell of tar and sawdust mixed with sweat and woodsmoke, and the constant ring of hammers on steel filled the air.

Workers moved with the purposeful productivity of men on a schedule, hauling rails and driving spikes under the supervision of foremen who kept one eye on the work and another on the tree line. It was organized chaos, the kind of controlled mayhem that came from building civilization one mile at a time through hostile territory.

Bracken spotted a cluster of men near what looked like the camp's main office—a wooden building with "Gulf-Atlantic Shipping & Rail Company" painted on a sign above the door. One man stood apart from the others, pointing at a map spread across a makeshift table while the others nodded and scribbled notes.

"Wait here with the cart," Bracken told Simon. "And keep your eyes open. Railroad camps aren't Sunday school picnics."

He walked toward the group, his boots crunching on the mix of sand and wood chips that covered the ground. The man with the map looked up as he approached—middle-aged, weathered, with the kind of sun-beaten face that came from spending decades outdoors.

"Excuse me," Bracken said, touching the brim of his hat. "Could you point me toward whoever's running this operation?"

"You're looking at him. Name's Garrett Samuels, camp supervisor." The man's eyes flicked to Bracken's badge, then to his sling, then to the awkwardly positioned holster. A slight smile tugged at the corner of his mouth. "Heard the

Run had a new sheriff in town. Also heard you had a disagreement with one of our local reptiles."

"News travels fast."

"Everything travels fast in a place this small." He folded the map with enviable precision—Bracken had only ever folded a map so neatly once in his life and he was certain it had been an accident. "What brings you out here, Sheriff? We running our operation a little too loud for the neighbors?"

Bracken could feel the eyes of the other workers on him, measuring, calculating. Some looked merely curious, but others carried the hard-eyed wariness of men who'd tangled with the law before and expected to do so again.

"Found a body yesterday afternoon," Bracken said, not softening the blow. "Trying to find who it belongs to."

The smile disappeared from Samuels's face. "You got a name?"

"Not yet. Was hoping you could help me get one, though. Anyone not show up for work the past couple days?"

Samuels gestured toward the office building. Bracken followed him inside and was ushered toward a chair in front of a simple desk. Samuels opened a drawer and fished out a bottle of whiskey and two glasses. After pouring out two fingers in each, he slid one to Bracken, knocked his own back, then poured himself a refill.

Bracken saluted Samuels with his glass then took a sip. It wasn't terribly good whiskey, but after being jostled about in the cart for hours, it was far more appreciated than Bracken was willing to let on.

He waited for Samuels to gather himself before asking gently, "I take it you have someone in mind?"

Samuels nodded.

Bracken waited a moment, giving Samuels an opportunity to speak—one that he seemed uneager to take. Bracken gave him a moment longer before asking, "Want me to give you a description, see if it matches the name in your head?"

Samuels shook his head, but gave him a 'go on ahead' gesture with his whiskey glass, so Bracken listed off the details, describing the man's physical traits and his clothing. Samuels shook his head again, "That's him. Dammit, Fletcher..." He shot back his second whiskey and poured himself a third.

"Fletcher...?"

"John Fletcher. He's the... Was... the Chief Surveyor in charge of establishing the railroad grade. He was a good man. A good friend."

"I'm sorry for your loss."

Samuels waved him off. "Can you tell me what happened?" he asked.

"He was murdered."

Samuels set down his glass and leaned back in his chair, studying Bracken carefully.

Bracken waited, recognizing the look of a man who had spent years managing rough crews in dangerous territory and was now trying to decide how much truth he could afford to tell a lawman. He figured rail camp supervisors and Chicago ward bosses wore different clothes but carried the same weight—men who kept order through a mix of respect, fear, and carefully distributed favors.

"Fletcher was as straight as they come," Samuels finally said. "Twenty years surveying for the railroad, never took a dime he didn't earn. Wasn't the type to cut corners or look the other way when the books didn't balance."

Bracken took another sip of the rough whiskey. "What about enemies? Man in his position, he'd have had to turn down bribes, reject shoddy work, probably step on some toes."

"Sure, but Fletcher handled it professional-like." Samuels poured himself another glass, his fourth by Bracken's count. "Wasn't the sort to make it personal."

"Except sometimes other folks make it personal for you. Anybody in particular give him trouble?"

"Well, there was that business with the lumber yard boys a few days back." Samuels' weathered face darkened. "Foreman came onto our site with about five men, all carrying axes and attitude. Fletcher, well... Fletch wasn't the type to back down from a fight, but he wasn't stupid either. Whatever the Foreman had to say, it must have been *something* for Fletch to lose his temper like that. Things got heated."

Bracken kept his voice casual, the way he would when working a table in Chicago—never press too hard, let the mark think they're in control. "How heated?"

"Heated enough that I had to send three of my boys to back him up." Samuels finally took a sip of his whiskey.

"These lumber yard boys have names that you know of?"

"Course they do. Jennings's outfit, mostly. Run by a fella named Pete Jennings. His foreman goes by Dooley—Irish fellow, big guy. About your height, maybe taller, but twice as wide. They got a camp about two miles up the Calusa."

"Who else was involved in that dustup with the lumber crew?"

"Besides Fletcher? My boys were Jack Cushing, Pete Thompson, and young Billy Crane. Good men, all of them. They'll tell you straight what happened if you want to talk to them."

Bracken filed the names away. He finished his glass of whiskey and left it on the desk as he stood. "I'd like to see where Fletcher bunked, if you don't mind."

Samuels pushed back from his desk. "Sure enough.

"His tent's just over there, past the equipment shed. Hasn't been touched since he didn't show up for breakfast on Wednesday."

They walked through the camp, past workers who nodded respectfully to Samuels but eyed Bracken with the casual wariness of men accustomed to keeping their business to themselves.

Fletcher's tent was military-neat—bedroll precisely folded, surveying equipment organized in wooden crates, personal effects arranged with the methodical care unique to decades living out of temporary quarters. A small writing desk held maps, measurement logs, and correspondence marked with the railroad company's official seal.

"Fletcher was army?" Bracken asked, noting the way the man's spare shirts had been folded into perfect squares.

"Two years with the Corps of Engineers. That's where he learned surveying. Good training for this work—army teaches you to measure twice, cut once."

Bracken examined the packed belongings. A few books on engineering and mathematics, spare clothes, shaving kit, letters from what looked like family back in Georgia. Nothing that screamed motive for murder.

He turned his attention to the writing desk and began examining the papers there.

The surveys showed disputed boundary lines, areas where Fletcher had marked discrepancies between official land grants and actual measurements. Notes in the margin indicated he'd been preparing a report for the company headquarters in Jacksonville.

"These the property lines he was checking?" Bracken asked, holding up one of the maps. "They causing problems?"

Samuels leaned heavily against the tent pole, the whiskey making his weathered face flush red in the humid air. "Fletcher was careful about his work, Sheriff. Real careful. But lately..." He trailed off, staring at the surveying equipment as if it might explain what had happened to his friend.

"Lately what?" Bracken folded the map and tucked it inside his vest. Evidence, or at least the beginning of a motive.

"He'd been staying up late, going over his measurements again and again. Said something wasn't adding up right." Samuels wiped sweat from his forehead with a grimy sleeve. "Last few nights, I'd see his lantern burning past midnight. Man was worried about something."

Bracken picked up one of Fletcher's notebooks, flipping through pages of neat measurements and sketched property lines. The handwriting grew increasingly agitated toward the end, with notes scrawled in the margins and question marks beside certain calculations.

"He ever say what was bothering him?"

"Not in so many words. But Fletcher wasn't the type to keep quiet when he found trouble." Samuels pulled out a handkerchief and mopped his neck. "Two days before he disappeared, he came to me asking about company policy on reporting land fraud. Wanted to know who he should contact if he found evidence of boundary manipulation."

The pieces were starting to form a pattern Bracken recognized from Chicago—honest man finds corruption, corruption finds honest man, honest man ends up floating face-down in whatever body of water happened to be convenient. In Chicago it was the river; here it was Gator Creek.

"I'll need to talk to those men who backed Fletcher up during the lumber yard dispute."

"They're working the grade. I can have someone fetch them if you want to wait." Samuels paused, glancing at Bracken's sling. "Though I suppose riding's not much of an option right now."

Bracken tucked Fletcher's notebook inside his vest, next to the map. Evidence was piling up, but evidence without witnesses was just paper. He needed to talk to the men who'd seen the confrontation firsthand, find out exactly what threats had been made and by whom.

"If you could fetch them, I'd consider it a courtesy. Not sure what pains me more, the gator bite itself or being 'that new guy that got himself bit.' I get the feeling that's gonna stick to me long after this thing heals up." He adjusted his hat against the afternoon sun. "One more question, though—you said Fletcher was preparing a report for Jacksonville. Any idea when he planned to send it?"

Samuels nodded grimly. "Friday—the day he disappeared, he told me he'd have everything ready to go out on the Friday morning train to Everfield Junction, then on to company headquarters from there."

The timing wasn't coincidence. Bracken had learned that much in Chicago—when honest men died, it was usually right before they could tell someone important what they'd discovered. It was starting to look an awful lot like somebody didn't want that report reaching Jacksonville.

Samuels walked off to fetch his men, leaving Bracken standing beside Fletcher's tent with nothing but the afternoon heat and his own thoughts for company. He tugged at his sling, trying to find a position that didn't make his neck ache, and wondered if he'd ever get used to the way Florida air seemed to stick to a man's skin like wet wool.

Simon appeared at his elbow, notebook in hand and eyes bright with curiosity. "Find anything useful, Sheriff?"

"Maybe. Fletcher was getting ready to send a report to Jacksonville about some boundary disputes. Timing suggests somebody didn't want that report reaching the right people."

"Like what kind of disputes?"

Bracken glanced around the camp, noting which workers were close enough to overhear. "The kind that people lose money over."

Simon's eyes widened. "That's... that's fraud, isn't it?"

"Could be." Bracken pulled out his pocket watch, noting they'd been at the camp for nearly an hour. "Question is... what did Fletcher find and who would it have implicated?"

Three men approached across the camp yard, their work clothes stained with sweat and sawdust. Samuels followed behind, making introductions as they gathered in the shade of Fletcher's tent.

"This here's Cushing, Thompson, and Crane," Samuels said. "Boys, this is Sheriff Bracken. He's investigating what happened to Fletcher."

Cushing, a lean man with graying temples, stepped forward. "Heard you found him in the creek. That right?"

"That's right. Mr. Samuels tells me you three were with Fletcher when he had trouble with some lumber yard boys. I'd like to hear your side of it."

The three men exchanged glances. Donnelly, stockier and younger than Cushing, cleared his throat. "Wasn't much of a fight, Sheriff. Mostly just shouting."

"What kind of shouting?"

"Accusations," Billy Crane said. He looked to be the youngest of the three, barely out of his teens. "Their foreman, great big fellow, came stomping into our work area claiming Fletcher had been moving boundary stakes on their timber claims."

Bracken felt his interest sharpen. "Moving them how?"

"Said we'd been shifting markers to make their cutting areas smaller," Cushing explained. "Called Fletcher a cheat and a railroad lackey. Fletcher didn't take kindly to that."

"Can't say I blame him," Bracken said. "What did Fletcher say back?"

"Told the foreman he was full of horse manure," Crane said with a slight grin. "Said every survey stake on this project had been placed according to the legal descriptions in the land grants, and if he had a problem with that, he could take it up with the land office in Tallahassee."

"That's when things got heated," Donnelly added. "Dooley started getting personal, saying Fletcher and his whole crew were in somebody's pocket. Said we were all liars and cheats."

Bracken nodded. Calling a surveyor's integrity into question was like questioning a gambler's honesty—fighting words in any professional circle. "How many lumber boys were there?"

"Five, counting Dooley," Cushing said. "All carrying axe handles, all looking ready to use them."

"But nobody actually threw a punch?"

"Fletcher shoved Dooley when the man got up in his face," Crane said. "Dooley shoved back. We stepped in to back Fletcher up, and their boys stepped in behind Dooley. Probably would've come to blows if Samuels hadn't shown up with more men."

"What ended it?"

"Dooley backed down," Cushing said. "But he made sure to get the last word. Told Fletcher this wasn't over, said the lumber company had rights that went back further than any railroad survey."

Bracken tucked that information away. Property disputes were about as common as mosquitoes. He'd seen his fair share of them in the city, where a step in the wrong direction could turn deadly and people pulled knives over which gang owned a sidewalk. It seemed they were just as much a problem out in the wilderness, where all the land in the world stretched on forever, but moving a single piece of wood could destroy a man's livelihood.

"Any of you see Fletcher after that day?"

"At supper that night," Donnelly said. "He was still steamed about it. Kept muttering about checking his measurements again, making sure everything was recorded proper."

"Said something about not letting any lumber company bullies make him doubt his work," Crane added.

The pieces were forming a clearer picture. Fletcher had been accused of fraud, had taken it personally, and had died just before sending evidence to Jacksonville that might have proven his innocence—or somebody else's guilt.

Bracken thanked the men and watched them head back to their work. Simon was scribbling furiously in his notebook, trying to capture every detail.

"Sounds like we need to pay a visit to this lumber camp," Bracken said.

Simon looked up from his writing. "You think they killed him?"

"I think somebody moved those boundary stakes, and Fletcher was getting close to proving who." Bracken adjusted his hat against the afternoon sun. "Time to find out what Dooley and his boys have to say about honest surveying."

The lumber camp was two miles up the Calusa, and Bracken had a feeling the conversation there would be considerably less cooperative than the one he'd just finished.

The lumber camp sprawled along the Calusa River like a temporary scar on the landscape, all raw stumps and canvas shelters scattered between stacks of fresh-cut timber. The air hung thick with sawdust and the sweet rot of wood shavings baking in the afternoon heat. As Simon guided the cart through the maze of lumber piles, workers paused in their loading to stare at the approaching lawman with the casual wariness of men accustomed to keeping their business to themselves.

"Things might be a little less welcoming here. Stay with the cart," Bracken told Simon, climbing down with lack of grace as before. His shoulder holster still felt wrong, the single gun dragging at his vest in a way that made him feel off-balance. "Keep your eyes open and your mouth shut."

The boy nodded, clutching his notebook like a shield.

Bracken walked toward the largest tent, where a mountain of a man was barking orders at a crew loading timber onto a flatboat. Even from thirty yards away, the foreman's Irish accent carried clear across the camp. Big as a brewery horse and twice as mean-looking, with shoulders that could have hauled logs without the benefit of oxen.

"Mr. Dooley?" Bracken called out.

The big man turned, his eyes flicking from Bracken's badge to his sling to the awkwardly positioned holster. Exactly the same as Samuels had—Bracken briefly wondered if he got himself a foot cast if he could get people to do the full cross with their eyes just by walking in a room—but Samuels hadn't looked like he could snap a man like a twig.

A slow grin spread across the foreman's weathered face.

"You'd be the new sheriff, I reckon." Not a question. "What brings the law out to an honest lumber operation?"

Bracken kept his stance casual, his weight balanced on both feet despite the sling. "Sheriff Bracken. I'd like to ask you a few questions."

"Make it quick, there's work to be done."

"John Fletcher. Railroad surveyor. Need to know when you saw him last."

"Fletcher, is it? Haven't seen him in days." He rolled his shoulders and tilted his head to the side until the bones popped. "Why? He causing trouble somewhere?"

"His boss over at the rail yard tells me he went missing a couple days ago. You and him had words a few days before that, I hear."

The grin vanished. Dooley dismissed his crew with a wave and walked over, his boots squelching in the mud churned up by countless wagon wheels. Up close, Dooley was one of the few men Bracken had encountered that he had to look up to—six-four at least, with arms like tree trunks and hands that could probably crush a man's skull without much effort.

"Had words with lots of folks. Part of the business." Dooley crossed his arms, and Bracken noticed fresh scratches along the side of his thick neck—four parallel lines that looked remarkably like fingernail marks. "Nothing more than professional disagreement. Survey stakes, property lines. Happens all the time in this business."

"Heard it got heated. Accusations of fraud, threats made."

"What are you driving at, Sheriff? Why do you care about a little professional scuffle?"

"Honestly? The fact that you threatened a man and accused him of fraud a day or two before he shows up dead, I mean... You gotta admit, the timing is..." Bracken shrugged his good shoulder, wincing sympathetically. "It just doesn't really look good, does it, Mr. Dooley?"

Something flickered behind Dooley's pale eyes—not surprise, but calculation. Like a card player deciding whether to fold or double down on a weak hand.

"Dead, you say? How's that?"

"Someone killed him. Dumped him in Gator Creek on Thursday night." Bracken kept his voice conversational. "So, you can see why I might want to get your side of the story before I make any assumptions, right? Mind telling me what you argued about?"

"Fletcher was calling us thieves. I told him we had legitimate timber rights going back three years."

"Three years is a long time. Must've been frustrating, having someone question your legal standing." Bracken looked around the camp, taking note of which faces were paying closer attention to their conversation than others. "Frustrating enough to do something about it?"

"I did do something about it. Me and some of the boys marched right over there and I told him to his face that he was the one who was a cheat and a liar."

Bracken couldn't help but notice how Dooley's massive hands kept clenching and unclenching at his sides, but he kept his tone easy and amiable, "That so? What was he lying about?"

"Boundary markers. Man kept moving stakes to favor his railroad bosses, shrinking our cutting zones." Dooley's voice carried the practiced grievance common to most of the rehearsed stories that Bracken had heard throughout his career. "We got legal claims here on this land and the cutting rights that go with it, but Fletcher's surveys don't match our deeds."

Bracken nodded thoughtfully, "Man's livelihood depends on those cutting rights."

"Damn right. We got papers. Filed proper with the County Land Office."

"Funny thing is, Fletcher was getting ready to file his own report with the railroad headquarters. Might've cleared up the whole dispute, if he'd lived to send it. Nice scratches, by the way." Bracken pointed casually at Dooley's neck. "Cat get you?"

Dooley's hand moved instinctively toward his neck, then stopped. "Brambles. This country's full of thorns."

"Sure is." Bracken smiled, as unthreatening as he could be. "Tell you what, Mr. Dooley. Why don't you ride into town with me where we can sit comfortable and talk proper? Answer a few more questions, help me get this whole thing straightened out."

The big man's face darkened. "I got work to do here."

"Won't take long. Just want to get your side of things written down, witnessed and proper."

"My side's what I told you. Fletcher and me had words, nothing more."

"Mr. Dooley, I am gonna have to insist that you come with me into town."

"I told you; I got work and I ain't going anywhere." Dooley uncrossed his arms, and Bracken caught the subtle shift in his posture—weight moving to the balls of his feet, hands loose at his sides.

"I'm afraid I'm not really asking anymore."

Tension pulsed in his fingertips—the same warning buzz he'd felt at a dozen or more rail strikes and picket lines when crowds were seconds from turning into mobs.

Dooley laughed viciously, the mirth that comes with knowing he had the upper hand. "Not sure what you think you're gonna do about it, Sheriff. A one-armed lawman against a full crew of lumberjacks? Odds don't favor the badge."

"Come on, Mr. Dooley. Let's keep this friendly."

"Friendly?" The Irishman took a step closer. "You come into my camp, accuse me of murder, and call it friendly?"

Bracken sighed. "Mr. Dooley, I can see those scratches on your neck from here. Fresh ones. The kind a man gets when somebody's fighting for their life. I'm being about as friendly as I can, given the circumstances." He kept his voice level, almost bored. "Now, you can walk to that cart with me like a gentleman, or I can drag you there like a sack of grain. Your choice."

"A one-armed man ain't taking me nowhere," Dooley growled, his massive frame casting a shadow that swallowed Bracken whole. "And if you don't climb back on that cart and ride out of here right now, I'm gonna take great pleasure in beating you to a pulp. That sling ain't gonna protect you any."

Around them, the lumber camp had gone dead quiet. Workers set down their tools and formed a loose circle, sensing blood in the water. Bracken could feel their eyes weighing him—the injured sheriff with his awkward holster and city swagger, facing down a man who could probably heave a pine log over a fence.

"Well, Mr. Dooley, I appreciate the warning," Bracken said, feeling the familiar calm settle over him, the same cold clarity that had kept him alive on Chicago's meaner streets. "But I'm taking you in whether you want to go or not."

The big Irishman's face darkened to the color of a fresh bruise. "You got stones—I'll give you that. Too bad they ain't gonna help when I—"

Dooley charged like a freight train.

Bracken sidestepped at the last instant and swung a vicious open-palm arc—delivered with the precision of a man who loved his angles and aimed for perfection.

The slap caught Dooley flush across the jaw and ear. The crack of skin on skin echoed like a rifle shot. All two hundred and eighty pounds of Patrick Dooley crashed like a felled oak into the mud and stayed there.

Silence.

Mouths hung open, feet edged back. Then murmurs spread—*Did he just? How in the world—? Sweet Jesus...*

"South Side Street Nap," Bracken said conversationally, shaking the sting out of his right hand. "Handy in a riot. Just as handy on giant lumberjacks, it seems."

"He dropped Dooley with a slap."

"Jesus Christ," someone whispered. "Is he dead?"

Bracken shook his head. "He'll wake up with a headache and ringing ears, but he'll live. Though he might think twice before bum rushing a lawman again. Now. Anyone else want to discuss this further?" Bracken surveyed the circle, meeting gazes that quickly looked away. "No? Good."

He cleared his throat, not taking his eyes off the crowd, and called out, "Simon! Need your help over here."

The boy scrambled down from the cart, his eyes wide as saucers as he approached the unconscious giant. "Sheriff, how did you...? I mean, he's twice your size, and you just...!"

"Leverage and angles, kid. David had the right idea with Goliath—can't always stop the big ones in their tracks, but a little tap at the right angle can change their trajectory. Course, David wasn't *wearing* his sling, but you gotta admit, the parallels are striking. Think you can help me get him tied?"

Simon nodded eagerly. "What do you need me to do?"

"Haven't had a chance to stock up on supplies, like proper handcuffs, so... in the meantime," Bracken pulled his shoelaces from his pocket, holding them up like a magician's prop. "We improvise."

Simon knelt, eyes bright. "That's going to work? With shoelaces?"

"Well, I wouldn't do it *every* day, but it works in a pinch. Tie them together, end to end."

The boy's hands shook slightly as he knotted the laces. "Like this?"

"Good. Now help me roll him a bit—watch out for his head, don't want him choking on mud when he comes around."

Together they bound Dooley's wrists with the makeshift tool repurposed for the occasion.

"Like tying up a feed sack?" Simon asked.

"Sort of. Feed sacks don't wake up and try to get themselves loose. This is called a constrictor knot—tightens under pressure, won't slip loose no matter how much he struggles."

When they finished, Dooley's massive hands were bound securely behind his back. Bracken tested the knots, satisfied they'd hold even against the foreman's considerable strength. "Solid enough, should keep him secure until we get him back to town. Next time we'll use real irons, spare the next guy the indignity of being handcuffed with my shoelaces, but this works for now."

He straightened and addressed the gathered workers, his voice carrying the easy authority granted by much practice and the incidental advantage of having just proved a point. "In case I forgot to mention, I'm placing Mr. Dooley under arrest on suspicion of murder, attempted assault of a law officer, and aggravated inducement of irritation. All charges currently excluded shall be deemed included as necessary. Anyone here got something to say before we take him back to town?"

The lumber crews shuffled their feet and exchanged nervous glances, but nobody spoke up. A few men removed their hats, as if attending a funeral.

One of the older workers stepped forward cautiously, hat in hand. "Sheriff, we... we didn't have nothing to do with any murder. Dooley, he runs things here, but most of us just cut timber and mind our business."

"I believe you. But your foreman's got some questions to answer, and those scratches on his neck aren't from any brambles." Bracken glanced around the circle of worried faces. "I'll need someone to help load him into the cart. And if any of you boys know anything about what really happened between Dooley and Fletcher, now's the time to speak up."

Two men reluctantly came forward to help hoist their unconscious foreman. As they struggled with his dead weight, an older logger with graying whiskers cleared his throat.

"Sheriff? There might be something you ought to know."

"I'm listening."

"Couple nights back, Dooley came back to camp late. Real late. Clothes all muddy, scratched up like he'd been fighting through palmetto scrub. Told us he'd been checking boundary markers, but..." The man glanced nervously at his fellow workers. "Well, we all knew he'd taken some boys out to start trouble earlier that day."

Bracken felt the pieces clicking into place like billiard balls finding their pockets. "Anyone else see him come back that night?"

Three more hands went up slowly.

"All right then. If you gentlemen would come by the Sheriff's Office in town sometime in the next day or two, I'd be obliged."

Bracken watched as some of the lumber workers around the periphery started breaking away to chatter to themselves, and others edged toward the tree line. Word would spread fast—the new sheriff was one-armed and city-soft, but he'd dropped a man twice his size with a single slap.

That reputation might come in handy. In the city, respect was currency, and if frontier Florida ran by the same rules, Bracken had just made a substantial deposit.

The unconscious foreman groaned softly as the two workers finally dragged him into the cart, but his eyes stayed closed. Bracken climbed up beside Simon.

"That was..." Simon's voice was awed. "That was incredible, Sheriff. How did you learn to do that?"

"Being a cop's a tough gig, kid. You learn things or you die trying." Bracken settled back against the cart seat, suddenly feeling every ache in his gator-mauled arm. "Now let's get our friend here back to town before he wakes up and decides he wants a rematch."

As they rolled away from the lumber camp, Bracken could hear the workers already spinning the tale that would be told in every saloon from here to Tampa—how the new sheriff had knocked out Big Dooley with nothing but his bare hand and a sling on his arm.

CHAPTER EIGHT

A Quiet Interlude

The late evening air hung thick and oppressive around the clinic, heavy with the day's accumulated heat and the promise of another restless night. Ellie paced between the windows, her boots clicking against the wooden floor in an uneven rhythm that betrayed her mounting anxiety. Ellie paused mid-stride, peering down the darkened street. The heat clung to the windows and to her nerves.

"They're fine," Diego said from behind his desk, not looking up from the medical journal he'd been pretending to read for the past hour. "Simon knows that route like the back of his hand."

Ellie had already stocked the linen cabinet, organized the medicine bottles, and rechecked the supply cabinet. There was nothing she could do to pretend to stay busy, so she peered out the window again. "I know they're fine. I'm just..." She trailed off. The knot in her stomach had been tightening since the sun had started to set, but she'd been trying to keep it hidden. Apparently not very well.

"You're worried about the sheriff."

"I am not!" Ellie swept a strand of honey-brown hair from her face, the gesture sharp with frustration. "Maybe... I'm worried about *both* of them." She turned back to the window with more force than necessary. "Simon's just a boy, and the sheriff's still healing—no, he hasn't even *started* healing from that gator bite, and—"

"Mmhmm." Diego closed his journal and leaned back in his chair, studying her with the careful attention of a physician reading symptoms. "I'm not sure who you think you're convincing."

"You say that as if I don't have very good reasons to be concerned." She turned from the window, hazel eyes flashing. "What if they ran into trouble? What if those people he's going to talk to decided they didn't want to answer questions?"

Diego finally looked up, his dark eyes patient but weary. "Then Bracken would talk his way out of it. Man's got a mouth on him, I'm sure you've noticed."

"Talk won't stop a labor crew with their blood up." Ellie resumed her pacing, the floorboards creaking under her agitated steps. "And he's injured, Diego. One arm in a sling, exhausted from blood loss, probably hasn't eaten a proper meal since he got here."

"Now you sound like a mother hen."

The words stopped her cold. She wheeled around, ready to deliver a sharp retort, but the gentle knowing in Diego's expression deflated her anger before it could fully form.

"I'm not—" She caught herself, jaw tightening. "Someone has to worry about practical things."

Before she could answer, movement in the street caught her eye. A cart rolling slowly through the evening shadows, a lantern swinging from its side. Even in the dim light, she could make out the hulking figure of a man slumped in the cart bed, and Bracken sitting rigid as a fence post beside Simon.

"Good Lord." The words left her in a rush as she pressed against the window glass. "Something's wrong."

Diego was already moving, grabbing his medical bag from the shelf behind his desk. Together they rushed outside, Ellie's heart hammering against her ribs as the cart lurched to a stop in front of the sheriff's office.

"*Madre de Dios,*" Diego muttered beside her. "What happened?"

Simon was practically bouncing in the driver's seat, words tumbling out before she'd even reached them.

"Mrs. Harper! You should've seen it! The sheriff arrested Dooley—that's the lumber foreman—and when Dooley tried to tackle him, Sheriff Bracken knocked him out cold with just a slap! One slap, Mrs. Harper! And the man's twice his size, but the sheriff just walloped him like it was nothing!"

"Simon." Ellie's voice cut through his excitement as she got her first clear look at Bracken. The sheriff's face was white as fish bones, his jaw clenched so tight she could see the muscles jumping in his cheek. His eyes were fixed straight ahead, glassy with pain he was clearly fighting not to show.

"Sheriff?" she said softly.

Bracken didn't respond. Couldn't respond, from the look of him.

Diego appeared at her shoulder, taking in the scene with a physician's practiced eye. "How long has he been like this?"

"Sheriff was fine after the fight, talking and joking," Simon said, his enthusiasm dimming as he noticed the adults' concern. "But he's been getting worse the whole ride back. Started shaking about a mile out, and now he won't hardly speak. And... well..."

Ellie stepped closer to the cart, noting the tremor in Bracken's good hand and the way he seemed to be holding himself together through sheer willpower. "Sheriff Bracken? Can you hear me?"

Bracken's glassy green eyes focused on her with obvious effort. He opened his mouth as if to speak, then closed it again, his jaw working soundlessly. Whatever quip or deflection he usually deployed seemed beyond his reach.

Diego frowned. "Adrenaline crash. Pushed himself too hard, too soon after losing that much blood yesterday," he said. "We need to get him inside before he collapses. Help me get the office unlocked," Diego told Simon, who scrambled down from the cart and raced toward the sheriff's building to unlock the door and prop it open.

In the cart, Dooley stirred with a low groan, his massive arms shifting against the shoelaces that bound his hands. Bracken seemed to register the movement through his haze of exhaustion and pain. With tremendous effort, he straightened enough to climb down from the cart.

Without a word, he grabbed Dooley by the belt with his good hand and dragged the semiconscious foreman just far enough off the cart that the big man's feet could find purchase on the ground. Dooley sat up, hissing in pain as consciousness slowly returned.

Bracken drew his revolver with deliberate and carefully controlled motions, the movement clearly costing him. He gestured toward the sheriff's office where Simon was holding the door wide open. "Walk."

Dooley's eyes widened as he took in his situation—the restraints, the gun, the stern-faced lawman who looked half-dead but somehow even more dangerous because of it. He shuffled forward without protest, his massive body filling the doorway as he entered the office.

Bracken followed, never lowering his weapon, and gestured Dooley into the cell. The big man stumbled inside, and Bracken locked the door with a solid click that echoed through the small office. Only then did he holster his weapon and pull out his pocketknife.

"Turn around," he said quietly, his voice hoarse. "Hands against the bars."

Dooley complied, and Bracken carefully cut the improvised shoelace restraints with his pocketknife. The moment the prisoner was secure and no longer a danger, Bracken's remaining strength seemed to desert him entirely. He walked the few steps to his own cell as carefully as a drunk trying to appear sober, then sank onto the narrow cot, curling protectively around his injured arm like a wounded animal seeking shelter.

"Sheriff Bracken?" Ellie called softly from the door into his bedroom cell. She knelt by his cot and put a hand on his shoulder. "Tom?"

He didn't answer, didn't even acknowledge her presence. He lay on his side facing the wall, his breathing shallow and controlled, every line of his body tense as piano wire—a man who had reached the absolute end of his reserves.

"What's wrong with him?" Simon whispered, his earlier excitement completely deflated.

Diego scoffed. "Stubborn fool pushed himself past his limits. Should have kept him sedated another day. You'd best believe I won't make that same mistake tomorrow."

"Will he be all right?"

"He will be. His body's demanding rest, and it's going to get it whether he cooperates or not." Diego studied the sheriff's still form through the bars. He raised his voice so the man would hear him, emphasizing the words pointedly so they would be understood even through whatever haze of pain he was in, "The only question is whether he'll listen to reason when he wakes up, or if I'm going to have to mix laudanum in with his coffee. Because I *will* drug him if I have to, *te lo juro.*"

Bracken stirred on the cot, his left arm extending slowly toward Diego. The gesture was wordless but clear—a request for medical attention delivered with the resigned cooperation of a man too exhausted to argue.

From the adjacent cell, Dooley's voice rumbled like distant thunder. "Sheriff's got sand, I'll give him that. Never had a man drop me with a single blow before. Can't believe I let a one-armed man beat me."

Neither Diego nor Ellie acknowledged the prisoner. Their attention remained fixed on the lawman who'd pushed himself to the breaking point.

Diego turned to Simon. "I'm going to need you to get a few things from the apothecary for me. And tell Julietta to send another dinner basket. We've got another long night ahead."

For the second time in two days, Diego and Ellie's morning vigil over their injury prone sheriff was interrupted by Maggie Hartwell arriving like a thunder cloud. She burst through the office door without knocking, her gray eyes blazing with the kind of fury that preceded either executions or resignations. Diego and

Ellie looked up from their coffee cups—both poured from their second pot of the morning after another sleepless night monitoring Bracken's fever and checking his bandages for signs of infection.

"He'd better have a damned good explanation this time." Hartwell demanded, not bothering with pleasantries as she swept through the door.

Diego took a sip of coffee. "Judge Hartwell, good morning—"

"Don't." She held up a hand. "His first day he hustles billiards at the saloon and wrestles an alligator. Today I woke up to reports he's been brawling in the lumber camps like a common street tough. What the hell is he even thinking?"

Ellie's coffee cup hit the desk harder than necessary, the sharp crack echoing through the office like a small explosion. Her hazel eyes flashed with a protective fire that Diego had learned to recognize as dangerous territory.

"Judge Hartwell," Ellie said, her voice carrying the same tone she used when her students pushed too far, "maybe a better question to ask is what exactly were *you* thinking when you lodged our sheriff in a *jail cell* instead of actual living quarters?"

Hartwell's eyebrows shot up. She clearly hadn't expected to be on the receiving end of an interrogation. "I beg your pardon?"

"Room and board." Ellie's voice carried the crisp authority she used when correcting particularly obtuse students. "Those words have actual meanings, Your Honor. And they typically mean slightly more than a dirty mattress in a jail cell with no extra bedding and having to scrounge crackers and tinned fruit from the general store like some kind of vagrant." Ellie continued, her hazel eyes flashing, "If I promised room and board to a ranch hand as part of their wages and they showed up from out of town to find *that* was their expected accommodation, not only would they refuse the job, but word that I was a skinflint would spread so fast that I'd never hire decent help again."

Hartwell's mouth opened, then closed, clearly unprepared for this particular line of attack.

"Furthermore," Ellie pressed on, "gossip travels in this town like water through sand. Once everyone knows the new sheriff's been living on whatever scraps he can afford and sleeping on a cot that wouldn't be fit for a dog, what kind of message is that going to send about how this county treats its law enforcement?"

Hartwell's face flushed, but before she could formulate a response, the door to the jail cells opened with a soft creak. Tom Bracken emerged, fully dressed but carrying himself like a man whose body was staging a revolt against consciousness. His good hand gripped the doorframe for support as he took in the room—two exhausted caregivers, one furious judge, the same amount of tension as a labor riot about to kick off.

"Morning," he said, his voice still rough with sleep and the aftereffects of laudanum. Bracken leaned against the doorframe, the casual gesture not quite hiding the way he favored his injured arm while he sized up the situation: the judge standing stiff as a board, Ellie with her hands on her hips, Diego trying to hide a smirk behind his coffee cup. "Judge Hartwell. To what do I owe the pleasure?"

Hartwell straightened her shoulders, squaring her stance to face her intended target. "The pleasure, Sheriff, is due entirely to me hearing all sorts of colorful stories about your adventures yesterday. The town's buzzing with gossip about you getting into a brawl with some lumberyard foreman. I came to get your side before I decide how I want to proceed. Care to enlighten me?"

Bracken's green eyes sharpened despite the lingering haze of exhaustion. He studied her face with the same calculating attention he'd use on a poker opponent trying to bluff with a weak hand. "I arrested Patrick Dooley on suspicion of murder. Standard police procedure."

Hartwell recognized the statement for what it was, bureaucratic chaff that didn't actually lie while offering nothing of the whole truth. Hartwell waited, clearly expecting elaboration, but Bracken just stood there with a maddeningly patient expression that had disappointed far more imposing authority figures than she.

"That's it? That's all you're going to tell me?" she finally demanded, her voice carrying the sharp edge of annoyed disappointment. "The whole town's talking about our sheriff beating a man in a bare-knuckle brawl, and all you have to say is 'standard police procedure?'"

Bracken's mouth quirked into a half-smile that somehow managed to be both polite and infuriating. "If you want to hear more than that, Your Honor, you're welcome to buy me breakfast and I would be happy to discuss the matter in further detail like civilized people with a healthy working relationship. Otherwise, you'll have to wait for my written report preceding the trial like any other county Judge subject to standard police procedure."

The standoff stretched between them like a taut wire, neither willing to give ground. Diego watched with the fascination of a man observing two cats circling each other on a fence rail, while Ellie fought to keep her expression neutral despite the second-hand satisfaction she was taking in watching a man who'd been kicked down stand on his feet and hold his ground.

After what felt like an eternity, Hartwell turned on her heel and stalked out the door without another word. The silence in her wake was deafening.

Diego let out a low whistle once her footsteps faded. "Well, that went differently than yesterday."

"I was actually dressed today." Bracken eased himself into the chair behind his desk, his body moving like every joint had been replaced with rusty hinges. "Not gonna lie, there's something about wearing pants that makes a man more confident during conversations like these. That and I had a much stronger poker hand to play—yesterday I was maybe holding jack high, but this time I've got at least a pair of aces with the chance for a third coming on the turn."

Ellie moved to pour him a cup of coffee, her movements efficient but gentler than usual. "I wouldn't mind hearing what happened at that lumber camp."

Bracken accepted the coffee with the same reverence of a man receiving communion, wrapping his good hand around the warm cup. "Well, since you were nice enough to bring me coffee, I suppose I don't mind sharing. But I was just there asking questions mostly—that's a lot of what being a police detective is, just asking questions till someone tells you the truth. Standard procedure is you ask nicely first, then you ask less nicely if the situation requires it."

He took a careful sip, closing his eyes briefly as the warmth hit his system. "I'd gathered enough circumstantial evidence to justify being curious about Mr. Dooley's connection with our victim. When I asked him to come to town for questioning, he expressed his disagreement with my request in a more physical manner than I would have hoped for."

"And?" Diego prompted.

"And I arrested him." Bracken's tone suggested that was all the detail the situation warranted.

Ellie studied his face, noting the way his jaw tightened slightly when he moved his injured arm. "You're being awfully sparse with the details for a man who usually can't stop talking."

"Nothing much to say. Dooley took a swing, I put him down, tied him up with my shoelaces, and brought him back to town." Bracken hummed gratefully as he sipped his coffee.

"Simon's version is a lot more colorful."

Bracken shrugged. "Simon's version would look a lot less colorful if he knew it was just geometry and physics."

Diego snorted. "Physics. Right. That's what we're calling it when you drop a man twice your size with one hand."

"Same as dropping the eight ball—line it up, tap it clean, let gravity take the cue from there. Nothing to it but angles and pressure." Bracken looked back at the door leading to the jail cells. "And speaking of angles and pressure, it's a pretty straightforward case against him for Fletcher's murder, but I won't know for sure until I question him more. I feel like I'm missing something, I just don't know what."

The office door swung open again. This time, Judge Hartwell entered carrying a wicker basket that smelled like heaven—bacon, biscuits, and butter—the kind of aroma that could raise the dead... or at least tempt them to get out of bed long enough to eat. She set the basket on Bracken's desk with the measured precision of a chess player making an opening move.

"There," she announced, as if she were fulfilling a contract. "Breakfast from The Cypress House. Now talk."

Bracken's entire demeanor transformed like a man witnessing a miracle. His eyes lit up with the kind of pure joy Diego had previously only seen in his youngest daughter when presented with penny candy. He leaned forward enthusiastically, his previous pain a distant memory. He lifted the checkered cloth covering the basket and let out a sound that was half sigh, half prayer.

"Judge Hartwell, you are a woman of impeccable taste and refined negotiation tactics." He unwrapped cloth bundles to reveal warm biscuits, thick slices of bacon, hard boiled eggs, and what appeared to be orange-colored fruits of some kind. He pulled out a biscuit and took a bite that bordered on reverential. Eyes closed, he chewed and swallowed, then murmured, "Actual food... Real, honest-to-God food with butter and grease and everything and I love it."

Ellie watched him savor the biscuit with focused intensity, as though he'd been living on crackers and coffee and something as simple as a biscuit was now a culinary treasure. She felt something uncomfortable twist in her chest. Sympathy? Guilt? The maternal instinct to protect a man clearly unable to fend for himself in any meaningful way?

"Now," Hartwell settled into a chair, "the full story, as you promised."

Bracken explained everything in painstaking detail, starting with what they discovered at the crime scene and the body, the dispute between the lumberyard and the railroad line, and then finishing with the eyewitness accounts and physical evidence regarding Dooley's late night return the night Fletcher was killed.

When Bracken had finished recounting the facts of the case so far and was happily munching on a piece of bacon, eyes closed and swaying blissfully like a hypnotized snake, Hartwell leaned back, processing. "Strong circumstantial case," she said. "What's your concern?"

Bracken's expression sharpened, details taking precedence over his obvious pleasure in the meal. "Someone moved those survey stakes to alter property lines, probably to skim land for resale or redirect timber rights. Dooley claimed Fletcher was moving stakes to favor the railroad. Fletcher insisted that neither he nor any of his other surveyors had done so. But Fletcher had already been documenting boundary discrepancies between the railroad and the local lumber interests. What if Dooley's accusation was enough to make Fletcher suspicious that someone wasn't just making mistakes with the numbers?"

"So Fletcher went back to check his own work?" Hartwell asked.

"Exactly. And what if he found out it wasn't above board after all? Those stakes were moved with deliberation, not random vandalism. Someone was actively committing fraud." Bracken searched the basket for any other remnants of food. "The rail supervisor, Garrett Samuels, said he was putting together a report about the discrepancies..."

"Where's this report now?"

"That's the thing—it's gone missing. The murder site was tossed and all the papers from his satchel taken."

"You think Dooley killed him to cover the fraud?" Hartwell asked.

"Doesn't figure out that way does it? Dooley's muscle, not brains—he might've killed Fletcher out of anger, but he didn't mastermind the land scheme." Bracken pulled an orange from the basket, staring at it with a puzzled expression like it held the secrets of the universe. "Thing is, moving survey stakes for individual properties is small-time grift. I've seen people killed for less, granted, because human beings get downright awful when money gets involved... But that's a whole lot of trouble for only a few hundred dollars—unless they were covering up something much bigger."

Diego leaned forward. "What kind of bigger?"

Bracken's green eyes sharpened, the food-induced euphoria fading as his mind engaged with the puzzle. "Railroad fraud. If you can move enough boundary markers, you can make it look like the railroad owns land it never legally purchased. Or you can make it look like local landowners are trespassing on railroad property.

"Either way," he continued, "that's not hundreds of dollars. That's thousands. Maybe tens of thousands, depending on how much acreage we're talking about." Bracken twisted the orange in his fingers as he contemplated. "Question is whether killing Fletcher was just a badly timed fit of anger... or if somebody planted the idea of fraud in Dooley's head, got him riled up enough about it, and then pointed him at Fletcher like an attack dog, using Dooley as their own murder weapon of sorts."

Bracken grew quiet for a moment as he sorted information in his head, calculating angles. Finally, he blinked and almost seemed to shake himself from a trance. "Course, I could be wrong," he added, shrugging one shoulder. "Maybe Dooley just snapped and killed Fletcher over a fence line. Won't know until I question him properly."

Before anyone thought to stop him, Bracken bit into the orange the same as he would have an apple or a pear.

Ellie watched the whole disaster unfold in slow motion, like watching a child reach for a hot stove and being too late to stop it. She could see the moment the peel burst under his teeth, when the bitterness of the rind hit his taste buds like kerosene and acid.

He jerked backward in his chair, his eyes watering from the unexpected assault of flavors. A strangled sound escaped his throat—half cough, half exclamation—before he began spitting orange peel and pulp onto his desk with the urgency of a man who'd just discovered he'd chewed on a wasp nest.

Diego burst into laughter so sudden and sharp it made Ellie jump. The usually composed doctor doubled over, clutching his sides as tears streamed down his face. Even Judge Hartwell's stern expression cracked, her mouth twitching upward despite her obvious efforts to maintain judicial dignity.

"Sweet Jesus," Bracken gasped between spits, grabbing for his coffee cup and draining half of it in one desperate gulp.

"Sheriff," Ellie said, fighting to keep her voice steady as her own amusement threatened to spill over, "you're supposed to peel it first."

Bracken stared at the mangled orange in his hand like it had personally betrayed him. "Peel it? What do you mean, *peel it?* Who the hell designed a fruit you have to disassemble before eating? And why doesn't anything down here come with instructions?"

"Most people figure it out before they're thirty," Hartwell observed dryly, though her eyes sparkled with barely contained mirth.

Diego wiped his eyes with his sleeve, still chuckling. "An orange, Tom. It's called an orange. And yes, you remove the skin first—same as you would with, say, a potato."

"First of all, potatoes are not fruit; second, it doesn't kill you to eat the skin on a potato," Bracken protested, still looking wounded by the fruit's betrayal. He used the cloth that came with the basket to try and wipe the juice from his face, hands, and desk, muttering darkly, "And third, what the hell kind of fruit tries to kill you when you eat it?"

Ellie finally allowed herself a small smile. Despite everything—the murder case, the political tensions, his stubborn refusal to take proper care of himself—watching the new sheriff get defeated by breakfast fruit was oddly endearing. This was a man who was slowly crafting a legend for himself by wrestling alligators to preserve crime scenes and felling giant lumberjacks with one arm tied behind his back—and here he was, brought low by a piece of citrus.

"Haven't you caught on yet?" Ellie asked with a smile. "You're in Florida. Everything tries to kill you in Florida."

Dooley sat slumped on the narrow cot, making the jail cell look like a child's playhouse. The big Irishman's eyes tracked Bracken's approach with the wariness of a cornered animal.

"Feeling better?" Bracken asked, leaning against the wall opposite the bars, close enough to see and make eye contact, not close enough to be grabbed and throttled. "Head still ringing?"

Dooley worked his jaw experimentally, wincing. "You got a hell of a bite to you, Sheriff."

"Lucky for you, I only save it for special occasions. You ready to have that conversation now?"

The Irishman sat back against the wall. "What conversation?"

"The one where you tell me what really happened between you and John Fletcher the night he died."

For a long moment Dooley said nothing. He sat there, jaw and fists clenching.

Bracken sighed, "Look... I got enough evidence to present your case in court and get a conviction. Right now, that case is looking like premeditated murder, like you went out there specifically intending to end a man's life. That kind of murder gets you an appointment with the gallows. Can't remember if I saw one when I was getting the penny tour of the town, but they're pretty quick to build if you're not too fancy."

Bracken shifted closer to the bars, trying to break through the stubborn silence. "But what most people don't realize is: that's not the only kind of murder there is, Mr. Dooley. If you tell me your side, tell me what *really* happened—without jerking my chain around—maybe I can make a case for one of those other kinds of murder, something that gets you time in prison instead of time in a coffin."

The big man's shoulders sagged slightly. "Christ."

"Take your time. We got all day."

Dooley stared at his hands. When he finally spoke, his voice carried the hollow tone of a man watching his life fall apart. "Word around camp was they'd found more survey lines moved. Figured if I rode out there quick enough, I could catch the bastard red-handed."

"And did you?"

"Found him by the boundary markers, all right. Had his equipment out, measuring something by lantern light." Dooley's voice carried the bitter edge of a man who'd discovered his worst suspicions confirmed. "When I confronted him about it, the bastard still wouldn't admit what he was doing. Red-handed and all, and he was still lying through his teeth."

"What did he say?"

"Claimed he wasn't moving anything. Said that someone else had been tampering with the stakes. Cool as you please, like I was the fool for believing my own eyes."

Bracken nodded slowly. "So, you lost your temper."

"Damn right I did. Man's been stealing land from under our noses for weeks, and when I catch him at it, he tries to make me out as the liar?" Dooley's hands clenched into fists. "I grabbed him by the shirt, shook him good. Told him to stop treating me like some backwoods fool."

"And then?"

"He fought back. Stronger than he looked, and slippery as a fish. We went down wrestling in the dirt, and he got his fingers up around my throat." Dooley touched the scratches on his neck. "That's when I—"

"When you what?" Bracken pressed.

"I squeezed back." The words were thick with emotion. "Harder than I meant to. By the time I realized he'd stopped struggling... He wasn't breathing anymore and it was too late to take it back."

The confession was heavier than a funeral shroud. Bracken felt the familiar hollow satisfaction that came with solving a case—mixed with the bitter irony of human stupidity.

"You take anything from his satchel?"

"No. Soon as I realized what I'd done, I just... I left him there in the bushes and rode back to camp. Told the boys I'd been checking markers but didn't find anybody."

Bracken sighed heavily and leaned back against the wall. The pieces fit, but something still nagged at him like a splinter under the skin.

"Sad fact is, Dooley, Fletcher wasn't out there committing fraud. He was investigating it." He turned back to face the prisoner. "Those reports about moved stakes? The things you told him? He took them seriously enough to ride out there and document what was really happening. He was preparing evidence for the railroad company about whoever was actually shifting the boundaries."

Dooley's face went white. "You're saying he was..."

"Trying to prove your claims were legitimate. His report would've identified the real culprit and cleared your timber rights." Bracken shook his head. "Poor bastard died trying to help you."

The big Irishman buried his face in his hands. "Jesus. *Oh, Jesus,* what have I done?"

"You killed an honest man because someone pointed you at him like a loaded gun." Bracken said. "What I need to know is, who loaded you? Who told you Fletcher was out there that night?"

"I... I don't remember exactly. Word just spread through camp that someone had spotted more moved stakes."

"Think harder. Someone had to start that rumor."

Dooley looked up, his eyes haunted. "There was talk at supper. One of the boys said he'd heard it from someone in town. But I can't recall who."

Bracken filed that information away. Murder was one thing, but murder with manipulation behind it was something else entirely. Someone had wound Dooley up and pointed him at Fletcher, then let nature take its course.

"Someone else was out there that night," Bracken said. "After you left. Someone found Fletcher's body, took his surveying reports, and mutilated his body to make it look like a gator attack."

Dooley's head snapped up. "Mutilated?"

"Multiple knife wounds, carved him up like a Sunday roast. Whoever did it wanted to make sure people took his death for a gator attack. People don't question why gator attacks happen, but they do question why murders happen. Somebody didn't want people asking why Fletcher died and took steps to make sure nobody would investigate too closely." Bracken studied the prisoner's shocked expression. "You wouldn't know anything about that part, would you?"

"I never touched a knife. Never even thought... God almighty, somebody *mutilated* him?"

The horror in Dooley's voice rang genuine. Bracken had heard enough confessions to recognize the difference between calculated lies and raw human revulsion.

The big Irishman slumped against the cell wall, the full weight of his situation finally settling on him. "Christ almighty. I killed an innocent man."

"You killed a man who was trying to help you, yes." Bracken's voice carried no judgment, just the flat finality of facts. "Fletcher wasn't moving those stakes to cheat your company—he was trying to put a stop to who was."

Dooley closed his eyes. "What happens now?"

"Now, you sit tight until we arrange a court date and I'll make sure Judge Hartwell knows that you chose to cooperate in the investigation. In the meantime, I'll see if I can't find out who might have been tugging on strings behind the curtain."

Bracken tapped his fist lightly against the wall before returning to his desk in the front of the office. Diego had returned to the clinic, Ellie had gone to teach her school children their times tables, Judge Hartwell had gone to harass some other poor civil servant, and Bracken had his office all to himself.

He sat in his office chair, contemplating the two crimes at play. Dooley had killed Fletcher in a rage. But somebody else found him, stole his evidence, and tried to cover up the murder. One large question remained: who stood to gain the most if his report never reached Jacksonville, and who stood to lose the most if it did?

Bracken leaned back, the office quiet around him, his mind ticking away like a pocket watch.

Someone had moved the stakes. Now he just had to find who'd moved the money.

Act Two

THE SHADOWS IN TOWN

CHAPTER NINE

A Shot in the Saloon

The evening crowd at The Cypress House had settled into its usual rhythm of whiskey, cards, and loud opinions when the screen door swung open with its familiar creak. Jennifer Starr looked up from polishing glasses behind the bar, her blue eyes automatically cataloging the new arrival.

Sheriff Tom Bracken stood silhouetted in the doorway, no longer wearing that ridiculous wool frock coat, but the black trousers, the fancy blue vest, and the jauntily cocked city hat still marked him as foreign as if he'd painted "Yankee" across his forehead in red letters. At least he had the sense to pull off the dark spectacles and tuck them safely into a vest pocket.

But there was something different about his posture tonight—a quiet confidence that hadn't been there during his first visit.

The saloon went dead quiet. Every conversation stopped mid-sentence, every card game froze, every glass paused midair. Jennifer had seen this kind of silence before—the hush that fell when something significant walked through the door, demanding acknowledgment.

Bracken tipped his hat with his good hand, that familiar half-smirk playing at the corners of his mouth. "Evening, folks."

The greeting rang through the silence for a heartbeat before the low murmur of conversation resumed, but Jennifer noticed how every eye in the place tracked the sheriff as he made his way to the far end of the bar—the same spot he'd claimed during his billiards exhibition two nights earlier. Smart man. Staking out territory, making it clear he belonged here whether they liked it or not.

Jennifer set down the glass and moved to meet him. The nearby patrons pretended not to listen in, but none of them were fooling anyone.

"Sheriff," she said, setting a clean glass in front of him. "You're looking better than I expected, considering the stories floating around."

"You know what they say about stories, Miss Jennifer—they're worth about as much as you pay for them." Bracken settled onto the barstool with obvious relief, favoring his injured arm. "Out of an abundance of curiosity, what kind of stories are we talking about?"

Jennifer poured him a whiskey without being asked, studying his face in the lamplight. The humor was still there, but underneath it she caught glimpses of something deeper—the relieved satisfaction of a man who'd been tried and tested and was both surprised and pleased to find himself still standing. "Oh, the usual tall tales. Something about our new sheriff taking down Big Dooley at the lumber camp with one hand tied behind his back."

Bracken's laugh was genuine, if slightly hoarse. "Well, I reckon that part's not entirely inaccurate. One hand was definitely out of commission at the time."

The comment drew chuckles from the nearest tables, and Jennifer noticed the tension in the room ease slightly. Whatever had happened at that lumber camp, it seemed to have earned their sheriff a measure of respect.

A gruff voice piped up from two stools down—Murphy, the same lumberyard worker that Bracken had helped during his first night. "Sheriff, settle an argument for us. My friend here says it's impossible you dropped Dooley with one punch. Says a man that size can't go down that easy, not from somebody half his weight."

The man next to Murphy—a ranch hand—shook his head stubbornly. "No offense to the sheriff, but Big Dooley's fought half the lumber camps from here to Jacksonville. Hell, I've seen Dooley take a fence post to the head and keep swinging. No way some city boy drops him with one punch, not no how."

Bracken took a slow sip of his whiskey, clearly savoring both the liquor and the moment. "Well, I hate to disappoint you, Mr. Murphy, but your friend's got the right of it. I certainly did not drop him with one punch."

Murphy's face fell. "You mean you didn't—"

"Didn't punch him, no." Bracken's eyes glinted with amusement. "See, the thing about trying to punch a head that can stand up to a fence post, you're just as likely to go breaking your knuckles as you are a man's face. Now, can you imagine how pitiful a sight that would have been? Me with one arm already in a sling, showing up at the bar with the other hand in a splint? Whole town would be laughing at me till Christmas and then some. So, I did what any self-respecting city boy who didn't want to break his knuckles would have done—"

Bracken brought his whiskey glass to his lips, smiling broadly.

"—I slapped the shit out of him instead."

He downed the liquid and set the glass back on the table.

The silence that followed was so complete Jennifer could hear the piano player's fingers stumbling over the keys two rooms away. Every conversation in the saloon had ground to a halt, all attention focused on the sheriff who'd just casually admitted to felling a giant with what amounted to a firm reprimand.

Murphy's friend stared at him, his mouth working soundlessly for a moment. "You... slapped him?"

A beat—then roars of laughter broke the dam. Tankards thudded in applause, men clutched their ribs, one cowboy crowed, "Christ Almighty, sheriff laid him out with a bird-hand!" The tension melted into merriment, the story already rewriting itself louder and grander around the room.

"Back home, we call it a South Side Street Nap. Most beat cops do it with a billyclub, but I learned that open palm trick from a bare-knuckle boxer in the Irish mob. He used to play the underdog long enough to rake in the bets, then 'pow' walked away with the pot before the other guy knew what hit him."

Bracken demonstrated the motion with his good hand, a quick, sharp movement that somehow looked too casual to be so deadly. "Course, it stings like a sonofabitch, and you've really got to commit to it. Half-hearted slap just makes folks angry. But a proper one..." He shrugged. "Well, Dooley spent last night sleeping it off in my jail, so I'd say it worked well enough."

Murphy shook his head, "Damn, I'd have given my left big toe to see something like that, sure enough."

Bracken tilted his head, gaze turning thoughtful. "Come to think of it, between the two of us, Mr. Dooley probably came out on top in that confrontation, all things considered. One good smack and he got to sleep it off. Me: I had to suffer through Doc and Mrs. Harper giving me the business about pulling my stitches out. I had to listen to the both of them scold me while Doc sewed me back up again. I swear to God, my ears were bleeding worse than the gator bite by the time they were done with me."

That set the house off again—the kind of deep belly laughter that banged off rafters and spilled whiskey.

Jennifer's smile lingered, sharp as a corkscrew. She leaned close enough for only Bracken to hear, "Careful, Sheriff. You make them laugh too long and they'll start to love you. Then you'll owe them stories every time you walk in this door."

Bracken cracked a grin and twisted his empty glass. "That's all right, Miss Jennifer. You know what they say about stories, don't you?"

She refilled his whiskey. "Worth what you pay for them?"

Bracken smiled. "Ain't that the truth?" He toasted her with the glass, then downed the shot.

Bracken stepped into the humid night air, his stomach pleasantly full and his mood lighter than it had been since stepping off that godforsaken train. The whiskey sat warm in his chest, and for the first time since arriving in this mosquito-infested corner of hell, he felt that maybe—just maybe—he could make this work.

He'd promised Diego he'd stop by the clinic before turning in—let the doc change his dressing and poke at his stitches with that particular brand of medical disapproval Bracken had grown oddly fond of—so that was the direction he turned. The walk down Main Street was pleasant enough—lanterns flickering in windows, the distant sound of piano music drifting from the saloon behind him, mingling with the chorus of frogs and insects that never seemed to sleep in this place.

He could almost pretend life in Cypress Run might steady out eventually, given enough time—until gunfire tore the night apart—a single crack like a whip in the dark.

Bracken's hand moved before his brain caught up, Colt sliding free from where he'd tucked it inside his sling. The second shot followed a few heartbeats later with a third so close behind, it might have been an echo. But the screaming that erupted from the Cypress House was real enough.

People poured from the saloon like cattle through a stock chute—men stumbling, women shrieking, someone shouting about blood.

A woman in a torn dress stumbled past him, blood streaming from her temple. Behind her came Murphy, his face white as milk.

"Sheriff!" Murphy grabbed his good arm. "Someone's shooting up the card tables!"

Bracken fought upstream through the chaos, his injured arm getting knocked and jostled as panicked patrons shoved past him. Pain shot up to his shoulder, but he gritted his teeth and pushed forward.

The screen door hung crooked, torn half of its hinges. Inside, the familiar haze of pipe smoke had turned acrid with gunpowder. Overturned chairs and scattered cards littered the floor. A barmaid sat against the far wall, clutching her shoulder and sobbing while Jennifer knelt beside her with a bar towel pressed to the wound.

Near the back poker table, a man in a checkered vest lay sprawled across his chair, arms dangling. Blood pooled on the green felt, mixing with scattered coins and playing cards.

Another patron—a railroad worker that Bracken recognized from the camp—sat on the floor holding his leg, cursing creatively between gasps of pain.

"Shooter went out the back!" Jennifer called without looking up from the barmaid.

"Sonofabitch," Bracken muttered, and gave chase.

He burst through the back door just as a muzzle flash lit the alley. The wooden doorframe exploded beside his head, close enough to feel the splinters slice into his cheek. Bracken ducked left, taking cover behind a stack of empty beer barrels as a second shot rang out.

"Three and two makes five," he counted aloud. Most men carried six-shooters, which meant one left—unless the bastard was smart enough to reload. He pulled off his hat and tossed it into the alley. The hat sailed through a shaft of moonlight like a lazy bird.

The shooter took the bait—his last shot cracked out, wasted on felt and shadow.

Bracken broke cover, sprinting across the alley. The man was already running again, stumbling toward the skeletal frame of the new courthouse where Judge Hartwell's grand vision rose in half-built timber and abandoned scaffolding.

Bracken followed, his boots hitting packed earth as he closed the distance. The shooter disappeared into the maze of construction materials—lumber stacks, tool sheds, and the deep foundation trenches that would someday hold the building's weight.

Moonlight filtered through the wooden skeleton above, casting a lattice of shadows that could hide a dozen men. Bracken slowed, his Colt raised as he picked his way through the construction site. Somewhere ahead, bootsteps hit gravel, fading, mingling with the hammering of his own pulse.

His breathing sounded too loud in the sudden quiet, and sweat stung his eyes despite the night's relative cool.

A board creaked somewhere to his left. Bracken pivoted toward the sound, just as his boot caught on a coil of rope he hadn't seen in the darkness.

He hit the ground hard, pain flaring through the bad arm like fire. Tools scattered around him—hammers and saws clattering like dice across a poker table. By the time he rolled to his feet, cursing Chicago and Florida and his own damn clumsiness, the night had gone silent again.

The shooter was gone.

"Dammit."

Bracken stood in the skeletal courthouse, surrounded by the bones of Judge Hartwell's justice, holding his Colt and nursing his throbbing arm. Somewhere in the distance, he could hear voices calling his name—probably Diego and half the town, drawn by the gunfire.

He holstered his weapon and looked around at the construction site that had cost him his quarry. In the morning, he'd come back and search for tracks, for dropped shells, for anything the shooter might have left behind. But right now, all he had were questions and the bitter taste of failure.

Diego had barely closed his clinic door when the first gunshots had been fired. Even muffled by wooden walls and distance, the sound was unmistakable to a war veteran.

Diego ran.

By the time he reached The Cypress House, people were spilling out like blood from an artery. He pushed through the chaos into the smoky interior.

The scene crystallized in an instant: a dead man slumped over the poker table, cards scattered in a pool of blood. A railroad worker sat propped against the wall, both hands pressed to his thigh where crimson seeped between his fingers. And near the bar, a young woman in a torn dress sat sobbing while Jennifer Starr tried to staunch blood flowing from her upper arm.

"Let me." Diego knelt beside the girl, whose face had gone gray with shock.

"Thank God," Jennifer muttered, moving aside. "She's bleeding something fierce."

Diego opened his bag, pulling out exactly what he needed by feel alone. The wound was messy but not fatal—muscle damage, some torn vessels, but no major arteries hit. He pressed clean gauze against the entry and exit wounds while the girl whimpered.

"You're going to be fine," he said gently. "Just a flesh wound. Painful, but it'll heal."

Behind him, he heard familiar footsteps and turned to see Ellie entering the saloon, her own medical kit in hand. She surveyed the carnage with the same grim determination he recognized from their work together, then moved straight to the railroad worker.

"How bad?" she asked, kneeling beside the man.

"Leg wound," the worker gasped. "Burns like hellfire."

Diego worked quickly, murmuring soothing words of encouragement, while he cleaned the girl's arm and Ellie examined the bullet wound in the worker's thigh.

The air stank of cordite, blood, and spilled whiskey. The saloon's normal din had been replaced by nervous murmurs and the scrape of overturned chairs being righted. Even the piano sat silent, its bench knocked askew. Jennifer moved between the remaining patrons with forced calm, but Diego caught the way her eyes kept darting toward the back door.

When it finally creaked open, it was the sheriff himself who stepped through. His shoulders sagged, defeat written in the slump of his frame and the way his good hand hung loose at his side. He straightened, rolled his shoulders back, and tucked whatever disappointment he carried behind that familiar mask of wry confidence.

Bracken's gaze swept the saloon, taking inventory of the wounded, the overturned furniture, the blood on the poker table. When his eyes found Ellie, who was helping the injured railroad worker bind his leg, he crossed to her without hesitation.

"How can I help?"

Ellie didn't look up from her patient. "You could start by actually *catching* the man who shot up the saloon."

Bracken flinched as if her words had been a bucket of cold water she'd smashed in his face. Diego saw it in the way the sheriff's jaw tightened, the sudden stillness that gripped his frame. For a heartbeat, something raw and wounded flickered across his features before he schooled his expression into stone.

Diego threaded his needle with more force than necessary. The girl had meant it as a quip—her way of dealing with stress—but it had found its mark with surgical precision.

Bracken turned away from Ellie and approached Diego's makeshift medical station. "Doc, anything I can do here?"

Diego considered the request. The sheriff looked like he needed something to occupy his hands, some way to channel whatever frustration was eating at him. "Hold this compress while I stitch. Keep steady pressure, don't let her move."

Bracken moved into position beside the barmaid, his touch surprisingly gentle despite the obvious tension coiled in his shoulders.

Diego had just begun the first stitch when Judge Hartwell strode into the saloon like an avenging prosecutor, her steel-gray eyes taking in the scene with the cold calculation of a hanging judge. Her gaze swept over the wounded, the blood, the scattered tables and chairs, before settling on Bracken.

"Sheriff Bracken." Her voice carried the crisp authority of a woman accustomed to having her words carved in legal stone. "Would you care to explain how a gunman managed to shoot up the busiest establishment in town while you were apparently nowhere to be found?"

Diego felt Bracken's hands go rigid on the compress. The saloon fell silent except for the soft whimper of his patient and the distant buzz of insects beyond the doors.

"Your Honor, I was—"

"Don't bother," she snapped. "I can smell the whiskey from here. A saloon, a card table, men drinking, somebody dead before the night was over—does any part of this sound familiar? Tell me, Sheriff, how much more of Chicago do you plan to bring to my county?"

The room seemed to inhale as one.

Ellie's bandages were suspended mid-tie, and Diego's stitching hand froze above the thread. Bracken's jaw flexed, his teeth grinding so tightly together, it was a miracle he didn't chipped any of them from the force of it.

Hartwell stepped closer, boots clicking through the spilled whiskey. "Three people wounded," she continued, voice rising with each word. "One man dead. And the shooter—your shooter—walked out the back door and into the street as casual as a Sunday stroll."

"I gave chase," Bracken said through clenched teeth, voice carefully controlled. "Lost him in the courthouse construction."

"Lost him?" Hartwell's tone could have frozen whiskey in July. "I can't wait to hear what your excuse is this time. All I can say is that it'd better be damned good. I promised this town a lawman—not a repeat performance of the scandal that got you sent here in the first place."

That did it.

The last line landed like a backhand across the room.

Diego watched Bracken's composure finally crack. Not violently. He just went still—completely still—his jaw locked, eyes gone cold as broken jade. The blood drained from his face until he was as white as a shark's underbelly. When he spoke, his voice carried a dangerous quiet that Diego recognized from his time in the war, from men pushed past what they could tolerate.

"Judge Hartwell." Each word was enunciated with the diction reserved for delivering threats to people who couldn't be threatened. "Perhaps you'd join me in the kitchen for a private word."

The challenge reverberated in the air like the warning growl of a nearby gator. Diego resumed his stitching, but every nerve was focused on the tableau playing out beside him. Hartwell's eyebrows rose, perhaps surprised to find steel beneath the sheriff's usual sardonic deflection.

"By all means, Sheriff. Lead the way."

Bracken handed the compress back to Diego without a word, his movements controlled but radiating barely leashed tension. As the two authority figures disappeared toward the kitchen, Diego caught Ellie's eye across the room. She looked troubled, her earlier sharpness replaced by something that might have been regret.

Diego tied off his suture and reached for the bandages. Whatever words were about to be exchanged in that kitchen, he suspected the real bloodshed in the Cypress House was just beginning.

The saloon had fallen into an eerie stillness—everyone pretended to clean up the scattered debris from the shooting, but their movements were careful, deliberate, designed to make no noise.

Inside the kitchen, voices sharpened but stayed low—the brittle calm of two people who both knew the next sentences could not be unsaid.

"Judge Hartwell," Bracken's voice carried first, deliberately quiet but sharp with controlled anger, "next time you've got a grievance with me, I'd appreciate you taking it aside, not airing it to half the town. What you just did undermines the badge you appointed me to wear—and it will not happen again. Are we clear?"

Diego caught Jennifer pausing in her sweep of broken glass, the broom suspended inches from the floor. Even the injured railroad worker had stopped adjusting his bandages.

"Your job, Sheriff Bracken, is to make sure things like this don't happen," Hartwell's crisp tone cut back. "If you'd been more diligent—"

"How much more diligent am I expected to be?" Bracken's voice rose slightly, exasperation bleeding through his careful control. "I've been here all night. The shooter waited for me to step outside—two minutes, that's all. You tell me which man could have stopped that."

Diego tied off the bandage with steady fingers, though his pulse quickened. He'd seen men pushed to their limits before—in the war, in surgery, in the dark hours when families lost loved ones. Bracken had that particular edge now, the brittle iron of patience that had worn thread-thin.

"Perhaps one who wasn't drinking on duty."

Bracken's laugh filtered through the walls—not a pleasant sound. "I'm neither intoxicated or inebriated," Bracken replied, his voice tight. "And all due respect, Your Honor, that's just about the dumbest charge I've ever heard."

"I beg your pardon, but just who do you think you are? I will not be spoken to that way by an officer under my jurisdiction."

"I'm almost surprised you have any officers at all under your jurisdiction, the way you're talking. Drinking on the job? Would you be chewing my hide if I'd been sleeping on the job instead? I took this badge on your contract, and that contract says I'm on call every damned hour of the day. You know what it doesn't say? That I don't get to be human once in a while. You want a man who never eats, never sleeps, never sets foot in a saloon? Hire a ghost—or adjust your damned expectations."

"My expectations are just fine, Mr. Bracken. From what your chief wrote, I expected the bottom of the barrel—and you're meeting those expectations perfectly."

The words seemed to suck the oxygen from the room in one collective gasp, loud enough to muffle whatever it was that Bracken had said in reply.

Diego saw several patrons exchange glances, eyebrows raised. Even Jennifer froze mid-motion, her blue eyes fixed on the kitchen doorway with predatory interest.

"The higher-ups back in Chicago might've tried to bury the truth about why you were sent here, but I read every word of Chief Killigan's fitness report. He warned me I was getting a man who needed a leash—and I see he was right. He called you a disaster the city was glad to be rid of."

Diego winced. The sheriff's reputation in Chicago was already whispered speculation—now with Judge Hartwell broadcasting his disgrace to half the town, it would be confirmed gossip by sunrise.

Bracken's reply came low, fierce, controlled. "Careful where you swing that gavel, Your Honor."

"Why? Have I struck too close to the truth?" Her tone rose, brittle and furious. "It astounds me that a man exiled from an entire city for one drunken gunfight in a saloon is present in my town for less than a week before another man lies dead from yet another shootout in another saloon—tell me, Sheriff, what pattern am I supposed to see?"

The silence that followed carried weight—the kind of silence that makes people stop pretending not to listen. Jennifer's broom froze mid-sweep. Ellie's head lifted.

His voice wasn't raised, but the fury in it came through like the charge before lightning. "Your Honor, I am contractually obligated to never speak of the circumstances preceding my transfer here. You want to crucify me for what happened in Chicago—a city so far out of your jurisdiction it's across the damned country—that's your prerogative. But don't stand out there telling a room full of people that I failed them just because I wasn't in two places at once."

He let the next words cut like steel. "And while we're at it, here's a word of advice: if you actually care about those ideals you claim to support—law, order, and justice—stop taking your cues from the brass in Chicago. Because the brass in Chicago are exactly the kind of bastards who force cops to sign nondisclosure contracts before sending them into exile. You can make any assumption you want from that."

The silence that followed stretched tight as a hangman's rope. Diego finished with Maria's bandage and helped her to a chair, his movements automatic while his mind processed what had just occurred.

Footsteps approached the kitchen door. Diego quickly bent over his medical bag, pretending intense focus on organizing his instruments. Around the saloon, everyone suddenly found urgent tasks—Jennifer polished glasses, the cattlemen righted tables with exaggerated care, and even the injured railroad worker developed a fascination with his bootlaces.

The kitchen door swung open and Bracken emerged, his face a carefully composed mask. He paused for just a moment, taking a long, measured breath that seemed to pull some internal armor back into place.

Diego watched the sheriff's shoulders straighten, watched him transform himself from wounded man to investigating lawman through sheer force of will. But he'd seen the cracks in that armor now, and he suspected they ran deeper than any alligator bite.

Without acknowledging the room full of eyes pretending not to watch him, Bracken walked to the poker table where the dead man still slumped in his chair. Cards scattered around the felt surface like fallen leaves, some stained with blood that had already begun to darken.

Diego watched the sheriff's hands as he began examining the corpse—steady, methodical, professional. But something in the rigid line of Bracken's spine suggested the man was running on pure stubborn pride now, as he tried to recover from Hartwell's public dressing down.

Diego caught Ellie's eye across the room. She had gone very still, her usual bustling efficiency replaced by something that looked uncomfortably like regret—she'd thrown the first jab about catching the shooter, never guessing Hartwell would follow it with a public flogging.

We broke him, Ellie's expression seemed to say. *Both of us.*

Jennifer moved between the scattered chairs with feline grace, but Diego noticed how her blue eyes tracked every movement at the poker table. The saloon proprietor had built her business on reading men's tells, and she was studying Bracken like a particularly dangerous hand of cards. She'd seen lawmen break before—usually right before they started taking bribes or drinking themselves into early graves.

The judge emerged from the kitchen a moment later, her steel-gray eyes sweeping the room with the authority of someone accustomed to having the last word. She paused beside Bracken at the poker table, but he didn't acknowledge her presence.

Diego closed his medical bag with a soft click. Whatever was brewing between the sheriff and the judge, it had just gotten considerably more dangerous than any gunfight.

Finally, Judge Hartwell spoke, her words tight and clipped. "I would like to meet with you in the morning to go over the details of your investigation. I expect you—" She cut herself off, her face working through a complicated series of emotions. "No, I *trust* you will have found some useful information to share by then. 8 a.m., your office?"

Bracken was silent for several seconds, not turning to face her. His voice was breathy when he finally spoke, with none of the earlier steel bolstering it up, "Sounds agreeable, Your Honor."

"Good." She nodded decisively. "I'll provide breakfast. As per our previous agreement."

She left, taking the thunderous energy with her and leaving a broken and subdued room in her wake.

At the poker table, Bracken continued his examination with methodical calm, but something fundamental had shifted. The bravado that had carried him through challenge after challenge since he'd stepped off the train had been completely stripped away, leaving behind the rigid professionalism of a man who was no longer proving only to himself that he was capable of doing this job—but to everyone watching as well.

"Hey, Doc," Bracken called softly. "No rush, but when you get a minute, would you mind giving me a consult here? Pretty sure this poor bastard wasn't an accident."

CHAPTER TEN

Smoke and Mirrors

Diego approached the poker table, his medical bag in hand and his expression grim. The crowd had given them space, but he could feel their eyes tracking every movement, every word. In a town this small, tonight's events would be dissected and reassembled into a dozen different stories by morning.

The dead man slumped forward in his chair, cards scattered beneath him like fallen leaves. Blood had pooled on the green felt, already beginning to congeal in the humid air.

"What do you see, Sheriff?" Diego asked, setting his bag down beside the table.

Bracken shook his head, stepping back from the corpse to give Diego room. "Coroner gets to go first, same dance as before. Just 'cause I'm not sobbing like a schoolgirl this time doesn't change the steps."

"Don't sell yourself short, Sheriff," Diego said, voice raised enough to be heard by the room, but not enough to be obvious about it. "You were only sobbing like a schoolgirl because I was digging a gator tooth out of your arm at the time. And you still kept your wits in order—impressed the hell out of me, if I'm being honest."

Bracken glanced down at him, the tight lines around his eyes and mouth easing a fraction as he recognized the theatricality of the gesture, as well as the vote of confidence that it conveyed.

Diego leaned over the corpse to get a closer look.

"Gunshot wound to the base of the skull, just above the spine. Clean entry, exit wound through the jaw," Diego murmured, gently lifting the man's head to examine the angle. He leaned closer, studying the charred edges around the hole. "Powder burns. Close range—maybe two inches. Point blank shot from above and behind." Diego looked up and met Bracken's eyes. "You're right. This was an execution."

"That's what I figured." Bracken moved to stand behind the dead man's chair, pantomiming a pistol. "First shot, right here. Clean, professional—one and done." He mimed the gunshot, then swung the invisible weapon across the room. "Second and third shots were for cover—close together, shooter didn't care where they went. Just wanted every man diving to the floor so they'd miss his exit."

Diego nodded. "Makes sense. But this fellow—something's off."

"How so?"

"Clothes don't fit the hands." Diego lifted one into the lamplight. "Rough shirt, canvas trousers, mill boots, yet no calluses from lumber, no splinters, no sawdust under the nails. These are clerical hands." He turned the fingers. "Ink stains at the tips—pen work. Bookkeeper, not laborer."

Bracken leaned closer, his green eyes sharp as they looked over the puzzle pieces. "Check again, Doc."

Diego frowned and examined the hands more carefully. On the middle finger: a long, well-developed callus right where a trigger guard would catch. Another thickening of skin between thumb and index finger, with gun powder stained into the creases.

"*Carajo*," Diego muttered. "Not a clerk then. Gun handler—maybe an outlaw."

"Or a lawman," Bracken said quietly. "Outlaws don't keep ledgers. Lawmen do."

Diego looked at him sharply.

"Think disguise," Bracken added. "A gun hand wouldn't dress down unless he had reason to blend. Most shootists I've met crave the spotlight. Pretending to be millfolk? That's deliberate."

Diego studied the dead man's shirt and trousers with fresh eyes. Bracken was right—the garments looked appropriately rough but lacked the specific wear patterns of actual labor. No pitch stains, no fray at the cuffs. Costume, not uniform. "What kind of lawman hides as a mill worker?"

"The kind hired to sniff around railroads," Bracken answered. "Pinkerton detective."

Diego had heard stories about the Pinkerton Detective Agency—private investigators who worked for railroad companies, mining interests, anyone with enough money to buy their particular brand of justice. If one was dead here, it meant the railroad had called in private muscle. "A Pinkerton agent executed in our saloon." Diego stood up, his expression troubled. "Sheriff, what exactly have we stumbled into?"

Bracken stared down at the dead man. When he finally spoke, his voice carried none of its usual sardonic edge. "Something a hell of a lot bigger than boundary stakes and timber rights."

"*Dios mío*," Diego said softly. "This just got a lot more complicated."

Bracken crouched next to the body, examining the man's jacket, his earlier deflation replaced by focused curiosity and a new angle to work. "Gets better. Whoever killed him was looking for something he had, but didn't find what they were looking for."

"How can you tell?"

"They went through his pockets, ripped the stitching here on this one." Bracken pushed the coat open, fingers tracing the seam of the inside lining. "And I know they didn't find it 'cause it's still in his coat. Ah! Here: hidden pocket."

He slipped a small notebook free of the inside lining and waggled it triumphantly. "Well, let's take a look, see what our friend was hiding that got him killed."

Bracken opened the notebook carefully. Diego leaned in beside him, their heads nearly touching as they examined the cramped, methodical handwriting by lamplight.

"This isn't mill accounting," Diego said. "Precision hand, consistent ink—a clerk's script."

Bracken flipped through. Each line listed initials and two sets of numbers: one in scrip, one in cash. "'P.D.—3 scrip + 5 cash.' 'H.L.—2.5 scrip only.' 'O'M.—2 .75 scrip + 4 cash.' Notice anything?"

"The cash doesn't match wages," Diego said. "And some names repeat."

"In Chicago we called this a pad," Bracken said. "Boss pays select men hush money to keep quiet about what they shouldn't be seeing. Classic protection racket."

Diego turned a page. A rough sketch of the mill yard sprawled across it, arrows marking routes and scrawled notes: *night-shift meetings, unmarked deliveries.*

"He wasn't just recording bribes," Diego murmured. "He was documenting an entire operation. Look at these margin notes—'Pay chest opened early, discrepancy $28.' 'Unmarked cigar boxes arriving at dock.'"

Bracken studied the diagram more closely. "This puts the lumber mill right in the middle of whatever got Fletcher killed. Our Pinkerton friend here was tracking money moving through the lumber operation—money that didn't belong on any legitimate payroll."

"You think Fletcher stumbled onto this?"

"I don't think so." Bracken closed the notebook, his expression grim. "Fletcher's concern was primarily the survey stakes for the railroad grade. This ledger looks like bribes and a smuggling racket. Only thing they have in common is proximity; someone was moving the survey stakes onto the lumber camps, setting up a long game to steal the timber rights out from under the lumber mill's nose."

Diego frowned. "Except if the lumber mill is fronting a smuggling operation, whoever's bankrolling that side of the business has to have opinions on the railroad sniffing around where it isn't wanted, trying to steal their land."

"Which leads us to our dead friend here. So, we have a dead Pinkerton detective investigating systemic bribery and possible smuggling at the lumber mill, and a murdered railroad surveyor investigating land fraud at the railroad camp," Bracken said, tucking the notebook inside his trouser pocket. "I'm getting that itchy feeling that says this is shaping up a lot like a turf war, but I haven't the first clue who the ward bosses are down this way."

"Ward boss? You've used that term before, I think, but I'm not familiar. Is that like our foreman in the jail cell over there?"

"Oh, God no. Umm." Bracken frowned, wracking his brain. "Ward boss is the guy in charge of a chunk of the city... Say... All right, picture Chicago as a human body—each limb a ward, each limb run by its own boss. Except there's not really a brain boss, so if each limb had it's own brain... Shit. That made more sense before I said it out loud..."

Diego smirked. "It's close enough I can follow. So, the left arm ward boss, what does he do?"

"He controls everything. And I mean *everything*. He controls the people, which means he controls the votes, which means he controls the politicians that represent his ward. Because he controls the politicians, he's got impunity from the law, for the most part. All the businesses in his ward, they gotta jump where he tells them, pay their protection fees. Otherwise his thugs come around, break up the shop, break up some kneecaps, maybe both if he's really feeling cross. Which means if you cross a ward boss, then suddenly none of those businesses have permission to do business with you, and you don't eat until you're back in his graces."

"And I take it the left arm ward boss and the right arm ward boss have to maintain their boundaries to keep control of all these things? And when one starts chipping at those boundaries, that's what starts a turf war?"

"That's about the size of it."

"So, knowing who the ward bosses are..."

"Essential as knowing how to tie your shoes. You don't show the right amount of respect to the wrong guy, you find yourself floating belly down in the river sooner rather than later."

Diego looked at the body in front of them, arranging the new information in his head. "So, the ward bosses are the players. Everyone else is just a piece on the board, and we're still staring at the opening pawns—no idea yet who's moving which side."

Bracken stared at him, then sighed. "Should've known you were a chess man. Your metaphor's accurate, if mildly disappointing."

"Oh? You think you can do better with billiards, *amigo?*"

"Easily," Bracken said. "Solids are the railroad; stripes are the lumbermill. Ward bosses are the ones holding the cue sticks, and we need to figure out who they are—and what the cue ball is—before they use it to sink our eight into the pocket."

Diego arched a brow. "Too much to hope that the cue ball isn't us?"

Bracken smirked. "Wouldn't bet on those odds, Doc." His mouth curved into a cold smile. "But we've got one advantage: the lumbermill bishop left the ledger behind when he took out the railroad rook. Means we know something they don't know we know... even if we don't know what it is yet."

Diego narrowed his eyes. "Sounded smarter in your head, didn't it?"

"...Yeah."

"Thought so." Diego glanced around the saloon. "I'm going to check on my other patients here, then I still need to change *your* dressing. And have someone bring the body to the clinic so I can take a closer look at it."

Diego paused, catching sight of Ellie standing at a respectful distance, medical bag in hand. "Actually..."

Bracken followed his gaze and wilted. "No."

"There's only one of me, and Ellie is my assistant."

"Please, no?"

"Changing dressings is precisely the sort of task she's both talented at and useful for."

"But you know she—" Bracken stopped himself. "She doesn't—" He dropped his head. "You wouldn't really do that to me, would you?"

"Sheriff, I haven't had dinner with my wife and daughters or slept in my own bed since the day you stepped off that train. You'd best believe I would."

Bracken had the decency to look slightly ashamed. "Sorry," he muttered. "Hadn't realized."

"You had enough on your mind at the time," Diego said. "Now you're going to let Ellie change your dressing, and you're not going to make a fuss about it. Are you?"

Bracken sighed in defeat. "No, sir."

"*Bueno,*" Diego said, turning away to go give Ellie her instructions.

Bracken stood and stared at a spot on the floor. Huffing out a breath, he righted a nearby chair and pulled it closer to the billiards table, laid his gun on the felt, and rested his chin on his good forearm. He didn't look up when Ellie approached the makeshift examination area with her medical bag—just extended his injured arm toward her without a word, quietly inviting her to do her worst.

"Alright," she said, setting her bag down beside his chair. "Let me see that arm."

The silence felt strange coming from him—no quips about her bedside manner, no jokes about gators, no deflection at all. Just quiet resignation.

She began unwrapping the bandage, noting how he held himself perfectly still. Usually he fidgeted or made conversation to distract himself from the discomfort, but tonight he stared at a fixed point on the wall like a man enduring penance.

"You're awfully quiet," she said, peeling away the outer layer of gauze. "That's not like you."

He said nothing.

"Cat got your tongue, Sheriff?"

"Can't imagine what you want me to say, Mrs. Harper." Bracken's voice straddled the line between resigned and too exhausted to care. "Doc said he'd sic you on me whether I cooperated or not, so I figured I'd save us both the trouble and just keep my mouth shut."

Ellie frowned and continued her work, removing the blood-spotted inner dressing. The wounds came into view, and her breath hissed between her teeth. The puncture sites looked angrier than they should, red and slightly swollen around the edges. Worse, she could see where stitches had torn—one from each of the deeper wounds, leaving small gaps that had bled freely.

"How in heaven's name did you manage to pull stitches again?" She tried to keep the exasperation out of her voice and failed. "Diego just put these in this morning."

Bracken finally looked up, his green eyes flat and tired. "Honest answer? It was either when I had to dive behind a barrel to avoid getting shot, or when I tripped over construction debris in the dark while I was letting the shooter get away clean." He shrugged his good shoulder. "Dealer's choice."

The bitterness in his voice caught her off guard. She'd expected one of his deflecting jokes, some quip about gator wrestling or Florida's hostile wildlife. Instead, he sounded like a man cataloging his failures.

"Sheriff—"

"Mrs. Harper," he cut her off sharply, "I was under the impression that not being a complete failure was a prerequisite to civil conversation in this county, and that we weren't on speaking terms again until I caught the man who shot up the saloon. If you could just finish doing what you have to do, then I can go back to not bothering you. Or trying not to bother you, anyway. Success at much of anything hasn't been my forte lately."

Ellie sucked in a breath. She'd meant her earlier comment as a sharp quip, the kind of verbal sparring they seemed to fall into naturally. But hearing it thrown back at her with such self-recrimination made her stomach twist with guilt.

"That's not what I—" she stopped herself. Because she had said it, hadn't she? Right before Judge Hartwell's public humiliation had caused him to bleed his pride all over the saloon floor.

She resumed her work with careful, gentle movements, cleaning the torn stitches where his reckless chase had reopened the wounds. The silence stretched between them, thick with hurt feelings and stubbornness.

"That's not what I meant," she said quietly, her voice losing its usual crisp authority. "Earlier, when I said that about catching the shooter. I was just—"

"Worried about your patients. I know. I get it." Bracken's tone carried no accusation, just bone-deep weariness. "Can't say I blame you for it. But that doesn't make what you said any less true."

She'd spent years nursing wounded men, reading the spaces between their words. Bracken wasn't just tired from the day's chaos. This was the weariness of a man who'd been fighting to prove himself worthy of basic human decency and kept losing ground.

"Sheriff... Tom." Her voice came out gentler than she'd intended. "I was scared. When I heard those gunshots, and then you came back bleeding again..." She resumed cleaning his wounds, her touch careful. "I don't handle fear well. I get sharp with people."

Bracken finally looked up, eyes searching her face for something—maybe sincerity, maybe pity he could armor himself against.

"Afraid I'd get myself killed before catching your shooter?"

"Afraid you'd get yourself killed, period." The admission slipped out before she could catch it, honest and unguarded.

They stared at each other for a heartbeat, the saloon's din fading around them. Then Bracken's mouth quirked into something almost like a smile.

"Well. I'm sure there's some context where that might be considered flattering, Mrs. Harper."

She began rewrapping the wound with a clean bandage. "You shouldn't have been chasing anyone with your arm like this."

"Probably not. But I also shouldn't let shooters waltz out of saloons without at least making them work for it." He shifted in his chair, wincing as she tightened the bandage, shaking his head with dark amusement. "Pathetic state of affairs, but it's what I've got to work with."

Ellie's throat tightened at the defeat in his voice. She'd heard that same hollowness from her students when they'd failed too many times in a row, when the effort itself started to feel pointless.

"You know," she said, securing the bandage with neat, precise movements, "when Nate falls off his horse, I don't tell him he's a failure. I tell him to get back up and try again."

Bracken flashed what might have been a smile if it had carried any warmth. "You'll have to wait at least a few weeks before you can give me the same advice. No falling off horses until the sling comes off. Doctor's orders, remember?"

"I think you're avoiding the point I'm trying to make."

"Oh? What's that?"

She met his eyes, holding his gaze steady. "Judge Hartwell was wrong to tear you down in front of everyone. And I was wrong to take a shot at you when you were already bleeding. And my point about Nate and the horse is that he keeps trying because he has someone in his corner believing that he can succeed if he keeps at it. Maybe I'm offering to be in your corner."

For a moment, something flickered in his green eyes—surprise, maybe gratitude. Then the familiar mask slipped back into place, though it sat less securely than before.

"Appreciate the sentiment, Mrs. Harper, but believing in me might not be the smartest investment you could make right now."

"You just let me worry about that, Sheriff." Ellie counted it as progress when Bracken's mouth twitched—not quite a smile, but close enough. "Try not to pull these out again before morning. Or I'll have to give you a talking to about protecting my investment."

They sat in awkward silence for a moment, the weight of unspoken apologies hanging between them like Spanish moss in still air.

Bracken flexed his arm experimentally before settling it back into the sling and tucking his Colt back into its hiding place in the crook of his elbow. "I do appreciate it. Both the patch job and... well, the gentler bedside manner this time around. Seems like an awful lot of fuss for a strung-out Chicago copper, but it is appreciated."

Ellie began packing her medical supplies back into her bag. The saloon had begun to empty, patrons drifting away now that the excitement had died down to blood stains and whispered speculation. Jennifer moved between tables, collecting abandoned drinks and surveying the damage with the resigned expression of someone who'd cleaned up after worse nights.

Diego had finished his checkup of the railroad worker and the barmaid, as well as making arrangements for the removal of the body. He set his own medical bag on a nearby table and asked, "How's our favorite patient doing?"

"Reset a couple of stitches; they should hold until morning," Ellie said, snapping her medical bag shut. "Assuming he doesn't go chasing any more armed criminals through construction sites in the middle of the night."

Bracken chuckled. "Night's still young. I make no promises."

"Sheriff," she said, her voice dropping to a tone reserved for stubborn patients and wayward students, "you need to eat something substantial and get some real sleep. Not the kind of sleep you get in a jail cell with drunks hollering next door."

"Well, when I get my first pay packet—if I don't get fired or expired before then—upgrading my lodging is top of the wish list. But until then, I don't have much choice about the accommodations, I'm afraid."

"Actually, you do." Ellie straightened, decision crystallizing in her mind. "I've got a spare room at my place. Nothing fancy, but it's got a real bed and actual walls instead of iron bars."

Bracken's eyebrows shot up. "Mrs. Harper, I couldn't impose—"

"It's not an imposition. I'm offering." She cut him off with the same authority she used to silence chattering schoolchildren. "Besides, someone needs to keep an eye on you after today's excitement, and Diego's got his own family waiting at home."

"What about Nate? Won't he—"

"Nate will be thrilled to have a real sheriff staying under our roof. He's been pestering me with questions about Chicago since the day you arrived." She softened slightly. "And honestly, Sheriff, I'd sleep better knowing you're somewhere safe instead of alone in that cell where anyone could walk in and finish what the shooter started."

Bracken studied her face, searching for pity or charity he could deflect with humor. Instead, he found something that looked like genuine concern wrapped in practical common sense—the same combination that had made her such an effective nurse.

"You sure about this, Mrs. Harper? Town's gonna talk."

"Let them talk. Half of them are drunk, and the other half will be too busy gossiping about tonight's shooting to worry about my housekeeping arrangements." She stood, smoothing down her skirts. "Besides, anyone with sense knows you can barely stand upright just now, much less pose a threat to anyone's reputation."

Bracken's mouth stretched into an uneasy smile that did little to mask his bewilderment. "Well, when you put it that way, how can I refuse such a flattering invitation?"

"Good. I'll gather my things and meet you outside in five minutes."

She walked away before he could argue, leaving Bracken staring after her retreating figure. There was something about their exchange just now that left him feeling oddly off-balance. Like he'd been outmaneuvered in a game he hadn't realized they were playing.

Diego chuckled from beside him. "Careful, *amigo*—you'll catch flies with your mouth hanging open like that."

Bracken clicked his teeth shut with an audible snap, his green eyes narrowing in genuine confusion as he watched Ellie disappear through the saloon's crooked screen door. "I'm really not sure I understand that woman entirely."

"Take my advice, *compadre*," Diego said, hefting his medical bag with one hand while clapping Bracken on his good shoulder with the other. His dark eyes glinted with amusement, the expression of a man who'd witnessed this particular brand of masculine confusion more times than he cared to count. "Stop trying before it gives you apoplexy. Some mysteries aren't meant to be solved—just survived."

Chapter Eleven

Something Real

The walk from town was mostly quiet, the kind of silence two tired people share when there's nothing left to say. They'd stopped at the sheriff's office for his shaving kit, a change of clothes, and to drop off a plate of food for Dooley, still hollow-eyed in his cell.

Now they were walking the mile or so stretch of road that Ellie walked every morning from her house to the edge of town. It wasn't a hard walk by any stretch and Bracken had been keeping pace beside her easily enough at first, but as they moved farther from the orange glow of Cypress Run's scattered lamps, he kept slowing down. Not stumbling or favoring his injured arm, just... stopping.

Every fifty yards or so, his boots would scuff to a halt on the packed dirt road, and she'd glance back to find him scurrying to catch up again. At first, she assumed fatigue—anyone would be dragging after today.

"Sheriff?" She paused again as he fell behind for the fourth time. She turned to find him standing in the middle of the road, head tilted back, staring up at the night sky like he'd never seen it before. "What exactly are you looking at up there?"

"Sorry, Mrs. Harper, just..." He gestured vaguely upward with his good arm. "I don't know... What *am* I looking at here?"

Ellie followed his gaze. Above them, the Milky Way stretched across the darkness in a broad river of light, stars thick as scattered salt. The sun had set hours ago, leaving nothing to compete with the stellar display. The sky itself seemed to glitter, the night so clear it felt thin enough to fall through. It was a sight she'd grown up with, taken for granted every night of her life.

"The stars, Sheriff. Same ones they have in Chicago, I imagine."

"No." Bracken shook his head slowly, still craning his neck. "No, they definitely don't have stars like these in Chicago."

He laughed softly. "Back home, you're lucky if you can spot the Big Dipper through all the smoke and gaslight. Maybe seven or eight other stars on a *good* night. This is..." He trailed off, searching for words and gestured broadly at the canopy above them. "How do you people get anything done at night? I'd spend all my time gawking."

Ellie noticed how small he suddenly seemed beneath all that vast darkness. Not physically—he still towered over her by more than a foot—but the confidence that usually carried him through every interaction had melted away, leaving behind someone younger than his years.

Despite herself, Ellie smiled. For the first time since she'd met him, Tom Bracken sounded genuinely awed instead of sarcastic. No jokes, no city-smart commentary. Just honest wonder.

"You get used to it," she said. "Though I suppose if you've never seen a proper dark sky before, it must be overwhelming."

"Overwhelming." He repeated the word like he was testing its weight. "Yeah, that covers it. Back home, night means gas lamps and electric lights beginning to flicker on. Makes everything sort of orange and close together. This is..." He trailed off again, blinking at the sky.

"A whole different world out here," she said quietly.

"Different everything." His voice held the same awe she'd heard in Nate's voice the first time he'd seen the ocean. "Makes a person feel pretty small, doesn't it?"

Ellie watched his profile in the starlight—angular features softened by shadows, the usual smirk absent from his mouth. Standing there beneath that vast canopy, Tom Bracken looked less like the cocky sheriff who'd knocked out Big Dooley with one arm tied up in a sling, and more like a man trying to find his place in a world that kept startling him.

"Come on," she said gently. "You can stargaze from the porch once we get home. Nate will be thrilled to show you the constellations he knows."

They resumed walking, and Ellie found herself stealing glances at the man beside her. She'd been so focused on his injuries, his reckless behavior, his irritating habit of making jokes at inappropriate moments, that she'd missed this—the part of him that could be struck speechless by something as simple as an unobstructed view of the night sky.

Maybe there was more to their sheriff than swagger and sarcasm after all.

They walked the final quarter mile in companionable silence, Bracken's pace steadier now but his eyes still drawn upward every few steps. When her small house finally appeared ahead—lamplight glowing warm and yellow through the front windows—Ellie felt something she hadn't expected.

Pride.

It wasn't much—three rooms, a loft, and weathered pine that had seen better decades—but seeing it through someone else's eyes, a man who'd spent weeks sleeping in train cars and jail cots, it looked more like home than she remembered.

"That's us," she said, nodding toward the fence line where her garden patch caught the starlight.

Bracken slowed again, but this time his attention had shifted from the sky to the modest homestead before them. In the distance, an owl called from the cypress trees, answered by another from across the clearing.

"Mrs. Harper," he said, voice careful and formal again, "I want you to know I appreciate this. More than I can properly express."

Something in his tone made her glance at him sharply. There was gratitude there, yes, but underneath it lay something that looked dangerously close to vulnerability.

"Just don't track mud on my floors, Sheriff," she said briskly, pushing open the gate. "And try not to bleed on anything that can't be washed."

Behind them, the stars continued their silent watch over the sleeping swamp.

As they turned up the path toward Ellie's house, Bracken stopped again—this time mid-stride, his head turning to track something moving through the darkness around them.

"What in God's name are those?" For a heartbeat she followed his pointing finger, not sure what he meant—then saw them, dozens of tiny lights blinking on and off like scattered sparks from a dying fire.

"Lightning bugs," Ellie said, adjusting her grip on the medical bag. "Fireflies. They come out when the air gets heavy like this."

Bracken stood transfixed, watching the insects dance through the humid night. One drifted close enough to his face that she could see the wonder in his expression when its abdomen pulsed with soft yellow light.

"I don't even have a single thing to compare these to back home," he said slowly. "Never even heard of such a thing."

"They don't bite. Just flash their lights to find mates." Ellie found herself smiling despite her exhaustion. "Nate used to try catching them in mason jars when he was smaller."

A firefly landed on Bracken's sling, pulsing once before taking flight again. He watched it disappear into the darkness between the trees, then looked at her with the same expression he'd worn beneath the stars—like a man discovering the world was far stranger and more beautiful than he'd ever imagined.

"Different world," he repeated quietly.

"Different everything," Ellie agreed, stepping onto her porch. She opened the door and turned to invite him in, but he was staring at the stars again. She shook her head with fond amusement and left the door cracked behind her, not wanting to interrupt.

Nate stirred at the kitchen table, blinking sleepy eyes as Ellie set down her medical bag. His hair stuck up in several directions, and a piece of paper with half-finished arithmetic problems clung to his cheek.

"Mama?" He rubbed his eyes with the back of his hand. "You're back late."

"Go fetch the spare quilt from the loft," Ellie said, smoothing his unruly hair. "We've got a guest tonight."

Nate blinked hard, then straightened, sleep gone in an instant. "A guest? Who?"

"Sheriff Bracken needs a place to stay that isn't a jail cell."

That woke Nate up completely. He straightened in his chair, eyes wide with excitement. "The sheriff? The one who fought the gator? He's staying here?"

"Yes." Ellie moved to the stove, checking the embers and adding kindling. "Now go get that quilt before he comes in and finds us unprepared."

Nate scrambled toward the ladder leading to the loft, chattering over his shoulder. "Wait until I tell the other kids! Sheriff Bracken's staying at our house! Does he still have the gator bite? Can I see it? Can I ask him about Chicago? And the gator? And—"

"You can ask him whatever you want once you get that quilt," Ellie interrupted, ladling beans onto three plates. "But don't pester the man to death. He's had a long day."

Nate disappeared up the ladder to the loft, his footsteps thumping overhead as he rummaged around. Ellie added cornbread to each plate and set them on the table just as the front door opened.

"Sorry about that, Mrs. Harper," Bracken said, ducking slightly under the doorframe. "Got a little distracted out there."

"By the stars," Ellie smiled, not looking up from arranging the plates. "I noticed."

She heard him shift uncomfortably behind her. "Probably looked like a fool, standing in the road gawking at the sky."

Ellie shook her head. "Probably looked like a man who'd never seen them before." She turned to face him, wiping her hands on her apron. "It's not foolish to appreciate something beautiful, Sheriff. Seeing you taken aback by a starry sky might be one of the more endearing moments of our acquaintance-ship, actually."

"Well, that's—" Bracken let out a surprised laugh, color rising in his cheeks. "I'm not actually sure how to take that."

"As a compliment." She took her usual seat at the table, noting how he stood just inside the doorway, taking in her modest home without touching anything. His gaze swept over the rough-hewn furniture, the mended quilt draped over her reading chair, the shelf of medical texts beside Nate's schoolbooks.

When his eyes landed on the photograph of her ex-husband sitting on the mantel among Nate's carved wooden figures, he lingered there a moment longer. Ellie felt her jaw tighten reflexively, but he didn't ask and she didn't explain. Some conversations could wait.

"Sit," she said, gesturing to the table. "Food's getting cold."

"I found it!" Nate's voice echoed from above, followed by the ominous thump of footsteps directly overhead. "Look out below!"

The thick blanket plummeted toward the exact spot where Bracken stood. He sidestepped smoothly, the quilt hitting the floor with a muffled whump that would have knocked him flat if he'd stayed put.

"Nathaniel!" Ellie's voice carried the sharp edge of maternal exasperation. "You don't drop things on guests!"

"Sorry, Sheriff Bracken!" Nate's head appeared at the loft opening, his face flushed with embarrassment. "I didn't know you were right there!"

"Situational awareness, kid. No harm done," Bracken chuckled, straightening his vest. "Though, you've got better aim with that quilt than some criminals I've dealt with."

Nate climbed down the ladder with the speed of a squirrel, practically bouncing as he joined them at the table. "Really? Did you have to dodge things in Chicago too? Like what? Bullets? Knives?"

"When I was growing up in the city, before they started putting in sewers and sanitation laws, you had to keep an eye to the sky to avoid getting wastewater and worse dumped on your head. Believe me, happens to you once and you never let things surprise you from above ever again," Bracken said, settling into his chair and accepting the fork Ellie passed him.

Nate bounced slightly in his chair with barely contained excitement. Before Ellie could warn him to mind his manners, the questions started pouring out. "Did you really carry two guns? How many bad men did you catch? Were there gangs like in the dime novels? Did you ever have to chase someone through the streets? What's Chicago like?"

"Nate." Ellie's warning tone carried clear instruction to mind his manners.

But Bracken seemed genuinely amused by the boy's enthusiasm, his usual guarded expression relaxing into something warmer. "What do you want to know, kid?"

"Everything!" Nate dug into his beans with renewed energy.

Bracken's voice filled the little kitchen, warm and vivid as lamplight as he answered each question with surprising patience, spinning tales that walked the careful line between exciting and appropriate for an eight-year-old's ears. He described Chicago's towering buildings and electric streetlights, the elevated trains that ran on tracks above the streets, the crowds of people thicker than any gathering Cypress Run had ever seen.

Ellie found herself watching Bracken more than eating, noting how he leaned forward when Nate asked about police work, how his hand moved expressively when he described chasing pickpockets through alleyways. There was genuine warmth in his voice, none of the performative charm he used on adults.

The man had a soft spot for children. She filed that observation away, wondering what else about Tom Bracken might surprise her.

"Nate, help me get this quilt on the guest bed," Ellie said, gathering up the heavy blanket from where it had crashed to the floor. "Then it's time for you to turn in."

Nate's face fell. "But Mama, Sheriff Bracken was about to tell me about the time he chased that pickpocket through—"

"The pickpocket will still be caught tomorrow morning," Ellie said firmly. "Bed."

Bracken looked up from where he'd been pulling a small notebook from his vest pocket. "Story's not going anywhere, kiddo. Besides, your mother's right—it's past time for young lawmen in training to be asleep."

Nate beamed at being called a young lawman, and he grabbed one end of the heavy quilt with both hands. Ellie took the other end, and together they wrestled it into the small back room that served as storage and occasional guest quarters. The narrow bed creaked as they spread the quilt over the straw mattress, Nate smoothing wrinkles with the focused attention he usually reserved for whittling.

"There," Ellie said, fluffing the single pillow. "That should do."

"Ma," Nate said quietly as they stepped back into the main room, "is Sheriff Bracken gonna stay long?"

Ellie glanced toward the kitchen table where the sheriff sat hunched over the notebook, his injured arm resting carefully on the wooden surface. In the lamplight, the angular planes of his face looked sharper, more serious than she'd yet seen them.

"I don't know, sweetheart. Depends on how long the town needs him, I suppose. Maybe how long he wants to stay after that."

Nate nodded solemnly, like that answer carried weight beyond his eight years. "I hope it's a long time."

"I hope so, too," Ellie said. "Now say goodnight and get yourself upstairs."

Nate bounded back to the kitchen, threw his arms around Sheriff Bracken's good shoulder in an enthusiastic hug that made the sheriff wince, then scrambled up the ladder to his loft.

After tucking Nate into his bed in the loft and listening to his prayers—which now included a petition for Sheriff Bracken's continued health and the safety of his gator bite—Ellie returned to the kitchen. Bracken remained at the table, turning pages slowly with his good hand.

She gathered the empty plates, moving quietly so as not to disturb his concentration. The water in the washbasin was still warm from supper preparation, and she worked methodically through the dishes, stealing glances at the sheriff's profile.

His usual smirk had vanished entirely, replaced by the focused intensity she'd glimpsed when he examined the dead body at the saloon. Every few minutes he'd pause to rub his eyes or flex his injured arm, but his attention never wavered from the notebook's contents.

The steady rhythm of washing and drying felt soothing after the evening's chaos. Outside, night sounds drifted through the windows—tree frogs calling from the cypress, the distant splash of something large moving through water, the rustle of Spanish moss in the humid breeze.

When she finished with the last spoon, Bracken was still reading, his brow furrowed in concentration.

"Finding anything useful?" she asked softly.

He looked up, startled out of his thoughts. "More than I expected. Less than I hoped," he said, fingers drumming on the table. "This detective—Morrison's his name—was tracking money. Lots of it moving in directions that don't make sense to me just yet. But I'm working on it."

He flipped to a page towards the front of the book and ran his finger down one of the columns. "There are an awful lot of initials here, too. I think the ones with three letters might be locations or drop off points and the two letters are people. There's SSS, RTE... One of them—CCT—seems to stand for something called the Calusa Cypress Trail. That one's actually mentioned a number of times, always in connection with H.C. Whoever H.C. is, he wasn't getting paid in mill scrip like the other workers."

Ellie's hands stilled on the dishes. Her heart lurched hard enough to make her breath catch for a moment, but she kept her voice steady. "Could be someone who didn't work at the mill directly. A contractor, maybe."

"That's what I'm thinking." Bracken's chair creaked as he leaned back. "You know anything about that Calusa Cypress Trail? If I find one location on a map, maybe I can trace it back to the others."

Ellie focused on scrubbing a particularly stubborn spot on one of the plates, grateful her back was turned to him. "Old hunting path along the river. Connects a few little settlements inland."

"Hunting path," Bracken repeated slowly. "Would it be useful for moving things without being seen? Cargo that maybe shouldn't attract attention?"

Her throat felt tight. "I suppose. It winds through some pretty isolated country. Not the kind of place you'd travel unless you knew where you were going."

"Or unless you were trying to avoid the main roads," Bracken said. His pencil tapped against the table—a rhythm that matched her accelerated heartbeat. "Morrison's notes suggest H.C. was using that trail for regular runs. Moving something valuable enough to pay well for."

Ellie dried her hands on her apron and turned to face him, careful to keep her expression neutral. "Smuggling's not uncommon along the waterways, Sheriff. Cuban rum, firearms, other goods that avoid the customs houses. Always has been."

Bracken looked up from the notebook, his green eyes sharp with interest. "You seem to know a fair bit about it."

"I grew up here." The words came out flatter than she intended. "You hear things in a place this small. Especially when you're treating men who get shot for being in the wrong place at the wrong time."

Bracken studied her face for a long moment, and Ellie forced herself to meet his gaze without flinching. She could see him weighing her words, deciding whether to push for more details.

Finally, he nodded and looked back down at the notebook. "Well, whoever H.C. is, Morrison thought he was important enough to keep track of. And now Morrison's dead."

Ellie turned back to the dishes, her hands trembling slightly as she stacked the clean plates. In her mind, she could see her husband's face—the easy smile he'd worn when he returned from those mysterious trips along the river trail, pockets heavy with money he claimed came from cattle sales.

H.C.—Harlan Carter.

The notebook contained evidence of her husband's crimes, documented by a detective who'd died for getting too close to the truth. And now Sheriff Bracken was following the same trail, with the same dangerous curiosity that had gotten Morrison killed.

The chair scraped softly. "Mrs. Harper?" Bracken's voice carried a note of concern. "You all right? You look like you've seen a ghost."

Ellie blinked; she'd been standing frozen at the washbasin far too long to blame on tidying. Ellie forced her shoulders to relax, hung the dishrag on its hook, then turned to face him with what she hoped was a convincing smile.

"Just tired," she said, which wasn't entirely a lie. "It's been a long day."

"Right. That it has. I should probably let you get some rest." Bracken closed the notebook, slipping it back into his vest pocket. "Thank you again for..." He gestured around the modest kitchen, encompassing the meal, the guest room, the simple kindness of offering shelter to a man who'd been essentially homeless since whatever had happened to upend his entire life. "All of this."

"You're welcome." Ellie moved toward the guest room, pausing in the doorway. "There's a washbasin and pitcher on the stand, clean towels in the drawer. If you need anything else—"

"I'll be fine, Mrs. Harper. More than fine." Bracken stood, collecting his satchel from where he'd left it by the door. He paused at the threshold of the guest room, turning back with an expression she couldn't quite read.

"Mrs. Harper, I want you to know—whatever's in Morrison's notes, whatever trail I'm following, I'm not looking to hurt innocent people. I'm after whoever killed that detective, nothing more."

Ellie's throat tightened. "I understand, Sheriff."

"Good. I just... wanted you to know." He rubbed the back of his neck, then shook his head. "Well... Good night, then."

"Good night."

The door closed softly behind him, and Ellie retreated into the main bedroom. But sleep wouldn't come. She lay staring at the ceiling, listening to Bracken moving quietly next door, and wondering how long before his search found its way to her own doorstep.

An hour later, sleep had proved just as elusive as Ellie had been afraid it was going to be, so she put on her robe and grabbed a basket of mending, then set herself up at the kitchen table. Her needle moved in steady, practiced strokes, the motion soothing her thoughts for a few stolen minutes.

The door to the guest room opened quietly, and Bracken emerged in his shirtsleeves and his bare feet, hair mussed from tossing around on the pillow but clearly not sleeping, bandaged arm held protectively against his chest even without the sling. He paused when he saw Ellie at the kitchen table, bent over Nate's torn shirt by the warm glow of the lantern.

"Sorry," he said softly. "Didn't mean to disturb you."

"You're not." Ellie didn't look up from her needle. "Can't sleep either?"

"Too much rolling around in my head." Bracken approached the table. "Mind if I sit?"

She gestured to the chair across from her. "Coffee's cold, but there's water if you need it."

Bracken settled into the chair, watching her steady stitches mend a tear in the shirt's sleeve. "How'd he manage that one?"

"Climbing the old cypress behind the schoolhouse. Again." A faint smile tugged at her lips. "I've told him a dozen times that tree's half-dead, but eight-year-old boys don't listen to sensible warnings."

"Smart kid, though. Asked good questions at dinner."

"Too good, sometimes." Ellie's needle paused. "He gets curious about things that aren't his business. Like his mother, I suppose."

Bracken leaned back in his chair. "Curiosity's not always a fault, Mrs. Harper."

"It is when it gets people hurt." Her voice carried an edge that made him study her face in the lantern light. "When it makes you chase things better left alone."

"Speaking from experience?"

Ellie resumed her stitching, but her movements had grown more deliberate. "This is a small town, Sheriff. People know things about each other. Sometimes those things are better kept quiet."

Bracken felt something shift in the air between them. His voice was quiet as he asked, "Mrs. Harper, are you trying to warn me about something?"

"I'm trying to tell you that some trails lead nowhere good." She tied off her thread and bit it clean. "Morrison found that out."

"Morrison was a detective—so am I, for that matter. It was his job—*our* job—to follow trails regardless where they lead."

"And look where it got *him*." Ellie folded the mended shirt, her hands precise and careful. "Shot dead in a saloon for asking the wrong questions."

Bracken leaned forward, elbows on the table. "Mrs. Harper, if you know something about what happened to Morrison—"

"I know that good men die when they get tangled up in other people's business." She met his eyes directly. "I know that some secrets are kept secret for a reason."

"Even if keeping them means letting killers walk free? Even if it means more people—*good* people—getting killed?"

Ellie was quiet for a long moment, her fingers smoothing the fabric of Nate's shirt. "Sometimes the cost of justice is higher than anyone should have to pay."

"Well aware of that notion, Mrs. Harper, thank you." Bracken studied her face, seeing something haunted behind her steady composure. "You're not just talking about Morrison, are you?"

The lantern flame guttered, casting dancing shadows across the kitchen walls. Somewhere in the distance, a night bird called once before the swamp settled back into silence.

Ellie's hands stilled on the folded shirt. The silence stretched between them like a taut wire, broken only by the distant croak of frogs and the soft hiss of the lantern flame.

"No," she said finally. "I'm not just talking about Morrison."

Bracken waited, sensing the weight behind her words.

Ellie continued, her voice barely above a whisper, "I'm talking about my husband."

Bracken felt something cold settle in his chest. "Your husband?"

"Harlan Carter."

The name fell between them like spilled gunpowder—bitter, acrid, waiting for the right spark to ruin someone's day.

Ellie continued, "Harper is my maiden name; I went back to using it after my husband went away. But H.C.—those initials you found in Morrison's notebook—those belong to Harlan Carter."

The pieces he'd been trying to sort into place all scattered like billiard balls after a break. Bracken sat back in his chair, studying Ellie's face in the lantern light. Her expression had gone carefully neutral, the same mask he'd seen her wear when tending wounded patients.

"Where is he now?"

"State prison in Tallahassee." Ellie's voice remained steady, but her knuckles had gone white where she gripped the shirt. "Been there three years now. Armed robbery, they said, but there were... other things. Things that never made it to trial."

"What kind of things?"

"The kind that get detectives shot in saloons." She met his eyes directly. "The kind that powerful men pay good money to keep buried."

Bracken leaned forward, his voice gentle. "Ellie, if your husband was involved in whatever Morrison was investigating—"

"Involved?" A bitter laugh escaped her. "Sheriff, my husband *ran* whatever Morrison was investigating. The Calusa Cypress Trail isn't just a smuggling route. It's *Harlan's* smuggling route. Had been for years."

The revelation hit Bracken's stomach like the first unpleasant stirring of a bout of cholera. "And you knew."

"I suspected. Harlan always had money, but never seemed to work for it. Always had friends visiting at strange hours, men who spoke in whispers and left before dawn." Ellie's fingers traced the edge of Nate's shirt. "A wife notices things, even when she doesn't want to."

"Why didn't you—"

"Report my own husband?" Ellie's voice sharpened. "To who? Half the county officials were taking his money. The other half were too scared to cross him. And I had Nate to think about."

Bracken absorbed this, watching her face. "But you're telling me now."

"Yes."

"Why?"

Ellie stared into the lantern light. "Because that detective is dead and whoever killed him is still out there. And because—" She hesitated, then continued. "You're different from the others, aren't you? You actually want to do the job right."

"I try to."

"Then you need to know what you're walking into." Ellie folded the shirt again, her movements precise and controlled. "Harlan may be in prison, but his organization isn't. Someone's still running things, still moving cargo through the Everglades. Still killing people who ask too many questions."

Bracken felt a familiar itch between his shoulder blades, the same one he'd gotten in Chicago when walking down dark alleys. "Any idea who?"

"Could be anyone. Harlan was careful about compartments—nobody knew the whole operation except him." She paused. "But whoever it is, they've got reach. Whatever Harlan was moving through that trail, it was big enough to interest the men bankrolling the railroad. Big enough to get a Pinkerton detective killed."

The lantern flickered again, and somewhere in the darkness beyond the windows, something splashed in the distant creek. Bracken found himself thinking about Dooley's confused confession, Fletcher's missing survey reports, and the neat hole punched through the back of Morrison's head.

"Mrs. Harper—" He searched her face, looking for the truth she was keeping hidden. "Ellie, why are you telling me this? Really?"

She was quiet for a long moment, her eyes fixed on the folded shirt. When she finally looked up, her expression held something he hadn't seen before—not just worry, but genuine fear.

"I don't know," she said simply. "Because I don't want another good person to die, I suppose."

The shirt stayed folded beneath her hands. The lamplight trembled between them, soft gold against shadow, and for a heartbeat she wished the world would just stay that quiet.

I don't want another good person to die.

The moment stretched longer, too long. Both of them held their breath while they waited for the chips to fall where they would.

Then Bracken's mouth twisted—that familiar shield of humor sliding back into place. "Careful, Mrs. Harper. You start talking like that and a man might think you cared about him just a little. He might even pass out from the shock of it—undo all your hard work on these new stitches."

Ellie's mouth twitched, part smile, part sigh. She knew a retreat when she saw one. "Then I suggest we don't try to test the theory, Sheriff."

The quip drained the charge between them as neatly as pulling a cork. He stood, tugging his sleeve down over the edge of his bandage. He seemed hesitant, almost reluctant to go.

"You should get some rest," she said at last, her voice steadier than she felt.

"I will," he murmured, though he didn't look convinced. "Goodnight, Mrs. Harper."

He managed a crooked half-smile, that same mix of pride and apology that undid more steel in her than she cared to admit, then turned back toward the narrow hall. The floorboards creaked once under his weight and went still as he disappeared back into the guest room.

Ellie sat unmoving, fingers tracing the neat line of her stitches. The room felt larger without him—not empty, just keenly aware of its own silence. She drew a slow breath, blew out the lamp, and let the darkness close in.

CHAPTER TWELVE

Paper Trails

Tom Bracken pushed through the jailhouse door with his good arm, a cloth-wrapped bundle tucked against his ribs. The morning light slanted through the single barred window, catching dust motes that danced like gnats above Dooley's cell.

"Breakfast," Bracken announced, unwrapping two biscuits and a thin slice of ham on a tin plate. He slid it through the gap at the bottom of the cell door to Dooley, who sat hunched on his cot like a bear nursing a hangover.

Dooley examined the meager offering like it was something he'd stepped in. "That's it? Christ, Sheriff, I've seen more meat on a picked chicken bone." Dooley picked at the ham with thick fingers. "Back at camp, breakfast was flapjacks, eggs, bacon, grits—food that'd stick to a man's ribs for twelve hours of swinging an axe."

"Complaining about the service?" Bracken leaned against the wall across from the bars, favoring his bandaged arm. "Believe me, I'd rather you were eating somewhere else on somebody else's dime, too. But you just had to go and murder a fella and now you're at the mercy of my financial limitations and whatever I can afford to feed you. So, before you go complaining *too* much about the meager state of affairs, kindly save my last nerve the aggravation by remembering that what you have in front of you is one less meal that I get to eat myself. We clear?"

He tilted his head, studying the big man through the bars. "Unless, of course, you want to use your own money to pay for your room and board. Which I'm certain you've got plenty of, seeing as you're the sort of fellow who doesn't seem to mind being paid to look the other way."

"I don't know what you're talking about."

"Really?" Bracken drew the Pinkerton's ledger from his vest pocket, flipping it one-handed to a dog-eared page. "Because this little book here tells a different story." He held it up to the bars for Dooley to see. "See these payments to 'P.D.?' Took me longer than I care to admit to realize that wasn't referring to the police department. There's only one cop in this town, and he certainly isn't getting paid *that* kind of money. But that P stands for Patrick, doesn't it?"

Dooley's jaw worked around a bite of biscuit, but his eyes had gone wary.

"'P.D.—$10, weekly arrangement,'" Bracken read aloud. "'P.D.—$25, extra considerations.' So, tell me about your involvement, Mr. Dooley. And while you're at it, maybe you could also explain some of these other names in here?" Bracken flipped a page with his thumb. "Mercer, for instance. Ring any bells?"

The lumber foreman set down his breakfast and crossed his arms. "I got nothing to say about that."

"Nothing to say." Bracken closed the ledger with a soft thud and slipped it back into his pocket. "You know what's been bothering me, Mr. Dooley? About this whole mess?"

Bracken tilted his head, sharp as a hawk sizing its prey.

"Fletcher wasn't killed on lumber yard property. Hell, he wasn't even close to it. Found him clear down by Gator Creek, remember? Now, I remember what you said: you were angry he was moving stakes so the railroad could steal the lumber mill's timber rights—put your crew out of work. You said you went to catch him red-handed. But he wasn't anywhere near where you would have caught him if it was the *lumber mill* you thought he was cheating."

Bracken pushed himself off the wall and moved closer to the cell, his voice dropping to conspiratorial. "No—something about that story doesn't line up. And you don't strike me as the sort of man who murders somebody just because his boss told him to. You're more the 'crime of passion in a fit of rage' type. Or maybe because people you cared about were going to get hurt otherwise?"

Dooley's jaw flexed; the cords in his neck showed pale against the grime. He looked away toward the wall, eyes fixed on nothing.

"So who was going to be hurt, Patrick? Did the people who pay for your cooperation tell you that you had to kill Fletcher or they'd make you pay? Make your boys pay?" Bracken leaned against the bars, close enough now that his voice barely carried beyond the cell. "Was it just your lumber crew? Or was it something more personal?"

The big man's breathing had grown shallow, but his mouth remained a hard line.

"See, I think Fletcher was documenting fraud worth more than you or I will see in a lifetime. And I think whoever's been greasing your palm decided

Fletcher was too dangerous to let live." Bracken paused, letting the silence stretch. "Question is, did they tell you to kill him? Or did you just panic when he caught *you* moving those stakes?"

Dooley's eyes flicked toward Bracken's pocket where the ledger sat safely tucked away, then back toward the wall.

"Because if they told you to kill him, Patrick, then you're not just a murderer. You're a pawn who got played by men in fine suits who'll never see the inside of a cell like this one." Bracken straightened, his tone hardening. "But if you panicked and killed him on your own, and then covered it up to protect those same men who've been paying you..."

He let the words grow and expand on their own to fill the space in the tiny jail cell.

"Either way, they're going to let you swing for it."

Bracken watched for a fracture in the stone mask of that face. The big man chewed his biscuit like it was sawdust, eyes fixed on the floor.

"Or..." Bracken said slowly, leaning back against the wall again, settling there with the air of a man ready to talk all morning. "Maybe I've got the angle wrong. Maybe you've been looking the other way for minor crimes. Little things. A bottle goes missing from a shipment here, some lumber gets misplaced there. Nobody gets hurt, you pocket a few extra dollars to keep your family fed."

He tried to cross his arms, but was hampered by the sling. "Hell, I can understand that. Times are lean, and a man's got to eat. But moving railroad stakes? That's not a little thing, is it, Patrick?"

Dooley's jaw stopped working. His eyes flicked to Bracken's face, then away.

"Because when those stakes get moved, somebody's going to lose their land. Maybe their home. Maybe their livelihood." Bracken's voice stayed conversational, but something harder crept underneath. "That's not pocket change anymore. That's people getting hurt."

The lumber foreman's massive hands curled into fists on his thighs.

"I'm thinking maybe that was a line too far for you to keep looking the other way."

Bracken stood and walked to the lone window at the end of the small aisleway in front of the cells. He stared out at the muddy street. "In Chicago, money controls everything. What gets investigated, which criminals walk, which ones hang. You learn to work the system, or the system works you over."

He turned from the window, eyes on Dooley again. "Money never made its way to my pocket, but I had to dance around it all the same. Started small for me, too. Little things that became bigger things. Crack a few extra skulls breaking a labor strike, the brass start calling you *their* kind of man."

Bracken let out a breath that sounded like a laugh. "And because you're *their kind of man*, they maybe give you some extra leeway—cases they'd usually bury 'cause they aren't 'worth the time' stay open because you play ball when it suits them. As if helping the people we're supposed to protect is some personality quirk they choose to indulge."

His voice roughened to a near whisper. "There's always a scale in your head—what your conscience can stand on one side—what good you manage to do on the other. And God knows how, but somehow you have to keep your balance in between."

He rubbed a hand over his jaw, as if trying to scrape off the memory.

"But there comes a point where you can't look the other way anymore, doesn't there?"

Bracken eased up to the bars until his shadow crossed Dooley's boots. "Brass told me to drop a case once. Said it wasn't worth the trouble. Somebody was hunting immigrant kids. The ones that nobody else seems to give a damn about. Little ones. Six, seven years old."

His good hand curled around the iron, knuckles whitening. "If I'd dropped it, he'd have kept on killing. But the bosses didn't care—to them it was just another mess in a poor ward. But I couldn't pretend those children didn't matter just because their parents couldn't afford to make a proper donation to some politician's campaign fund."

Dooley's eyes were fixed on Bracken's face now.

"So, I didn't drop it, kept digging. And when I found the bastard..." He huffed out a breath through his nose—half laugh, half disgust. "They told me to drop it *again* because the son of a United States senator isn't in the same tax bracket as the son of an immigrant. There's different rules when your old man hosts the fundraisers."

He pressed his forehead against the prison bars. "Still couldn't drop it. So I did what I did."

For a second his eyes looked past Dooley, like he was seeing a different cell somewhere further north and much colder. But then he stepped back from the bars, hand falling to his side. "Point is, Patrick, I know what it's like when you hit your deadline—that line you can't cross without losing yourself. When too many folks are bound to get hurt, and you've got to act, no matter what the day after looks like."

Dooley sat back on his bunk, shoulders sagging like a man finally dropping a load too heavy to carry. He stared at his half-eaten breakfast for a long moment before looking up at Bracken.

"You want names? All right, Sheriff. I'll give you names." His voice carried the hollow ring of surrender. "But this thing's bigger than you think. Bigger than me turning a blind eye for pocket money."

Bracken settled back against the wall, keeping his expression neutral despite the quickening of his pulse. "I'm listening."

"The bribes started small. Couple dollars to look the other way when timber shipments didn't match the manifests. Sometimes they'd ask me to put my initials next to numbers that were wrong—say we shipped forty board feet when it was really sixty. The extra twenty would disappear somewhere between here and Tampa."

Dooley ran a hand through his hair, looking older than his years. "Then they started scheduling me for night shifts when the boats came in. I'd sign off that all the lumber made it onto the river barges, but half the time they'd split the shipment. Send some downriver like it said on the papers, but truck the rest overland to some warehouse I never saw."

"Who's 'they,' Patrick?"

"That man you mentioned—Mercer runs the operation out of Rawling-Thom Export. Never gave me a real first name, just Mercer. Smooth talker, always dressed like he belonged in Tallahassee instead of Cypress Run." Dooley's hands clenched into fists. "But the money wasn't coming from him. He was just the middleman."

Bracken leaned forward. "Middleman for who?"

"Big fish down in Tampa. Shipping company called Samson & Sons. Old Man Samson's got half the legitimate export business on the Gulf Coast, but that's just the front. The real money comes from Cuban rum and cigars hidden inside lumber crates."

Rawling-Thom Export. RTE. Samson & Sons Shipping. SSS. The pieces were starting to form a picture in Bracken's mind, but it was uglier than he'd expected. Dooley stood and began pacing the small cell like a caged animal. "But then this other fellow showed up. Said he knew Fletcher was the one moving stakes to help the railroad grab land from honest working folks."

"What other fellow?"

"Harlan Carter."

Bracken's spine stiffened before he could mask it. For a heartbeat the name landed like a slug to the ribs—but Dooley kept talking, mercifully unaware. "Used to be a big name in the smuggling business before he got sent to the pen. Word was he'd broken out and was laying low in the swamps." Dooley stopped pacing and gripped the cell bars. "Man like Carter would know better than anyone if the railroad was trying to muscle in on things."

Bracken did his best to pretend that Harlan Carter was just another name and not something complicated and potentially painful. "Carter told you Fletcher was committing fraud for the railroad?"

"Said Fletcher was documenting false boundary lines to help the railroad steal property from everyone in town. Not just the lumber mill, but the whole damn county. Every family with property rights, every business owner, everyone was going to lose their land to some Tallahassee investment group funding the courthouse construction."

Dooley's knuckles were white where they gripped the bars. "Said the railroad and their political backers in Tallahassee were planning land grabs all up and down the railroad grade. The whole town was in danger of being bought out from under us for pennies on the dollar."

Bracken felt the puzzle pieces clicking together and finding their pockets. "It's not just the smuggling ring that stands to lose if the railroad gets their way."

"That's right. But the smuggling ring's the only one with the muscle to push back against railroad money and political connections." Dooley's voice dropped to barely above a whisper. "Carter said if I didn't stop Fletcher from helping the railroad steal our land, my lumber crew would be out of work and homeless inside a month."

"So you confronted Fletcher."

"I was protecting my boys. I thought Fletcher was the enemy." Dooley's voice cracked. "Carter made it sound like Fletcher was some kind of carpetbagger come to steal everything we'd worked for. And Carter's a local. He's a homesteader. He stands to lose just as much from the railroad as anyone else. So, why wouldn't I believe he was telling the truth? I never knew Fletcher was trying to help us."

Bracken paced slowly across the floorboards, his mind racing through implications. A prison breakout nobody had reported. A man with connections to both the smuggling operation and enough local knowledge to manipulate honest workers like Dooley. Bracken felt the familiar chill of a case turning darker than expected.

"Mr. Dooley, if you can put names to some of the entries in that Pinkerton's ledger and help me find the people I need to talk to in this smuggling ring, I can present you as a cooperating witness. Get your charge knocked down from first-degree murder to manslaughter."

Dooley looked up with something that might have been hope. "You'd do that? You'd speak in front of the judge for me?"

"You killed a man, but you were played by people who knew exactly which strings to pull." Bracken picked up the ledger and moved closer to the cell. "Help me catch the puppet masters, and I'll make sure Judge Hartwell knows you were as much a victim as Fletcher was."

"Sheriff... you gotta know. These aren't the sorta men you drag into a jail cell. You chase after them like you done me, you're gonna get yourself killed faster than if that gator was being serious with you."

Bracken leaned back against the wall, looking up at the ceiling. "I'll let you in on a secret, Mr. Dooley, I already chose to get myself killed once—when I decided to put myself gun to gun with the son of a senator."

He shook his head with a rueful chuckle. "All things considered, I should have been sent swimming in the river wearing a pair of cement shoes—that's just how things work in the city—and the fact that I wasn't... well, it truly surprises the hell out of me. Tell you the truth, I figure everything that comes along after that point is just borrowed time to enjoy."

Bracken shrugged his good shoulder with a smile. "Or who knows, maybe I did die that day and got sent to Hell; it's certainly hot enough here for it." The carefree mask of good humor slipped back into place. "But if I'm going to get caught between the big money behind the railroad and the big money behind the smuggling—regardless of anything I choose to do—I figure I'd rather go out banking the shot than lagging the cue. May as well see just how many crooked bastards I can piss off between now and Judgment, huh?"

Dooley stared through the bars for a long moment, like a man trying to decide whether the other side of the law was really any drier ground at all. Dooley nodded slowly. "What do you need to know?"

"Start with Mercer," Bracken said. "Rawling-Thom, Samson's men—and then you tell me how to find Harlan Carter."

Diego pushed through the screen door of The Cypress House—freshly reattached with new screws, courtesy of Jake Henley—the crumpled note clutched in his fist like evidence of a crime. The saloon smelled of stale beer and fresh sawdust. The rhythmic crack of billiard balls and the murmur of early morning drinkers gathered around the pool table drew him to his quarry.

Sheriff Bracken stood at the far end, sling cinched tight around his left arm, a pool cue balanced in his right and supported on the table by a contraption that looked like a metal bridge with smooth grooves along the top—the unmistakable handiwork of Jake Henley. A modest crowd of railroad workers and cattlemen nursed their morning whiskey or coffee while watching Bracken line up what appeared to be an impossible bank shot. A few tossed coins into the mason jar perched on the rail.

"Five-ball, corner pocket, bank shot off the eight," Bracken called, chalking his cue with his good hand. The ball ricocheted perfectly off the cushion, kissed the eight, and dropped into the corner with a soft *thunk*. A few appreciative murmurs rippled through the watchers as more coins clinked into the jar.

"Sheriff Bracken." Diego's voice cut through the congratulations like a scalpel through skin.

Bracken looked up, his grin faltering slightly when he spotted the paper in Diego's hand. "Morning, Doc. Come to witness the miracle of mechanical engineering? Jake's cue rest here is revolutionizing one-armed billiards throughout Everfield County."

Diego held up the paper. "Really?"

Bracken shrugged, repositioning the cue rest so he could line up the six-ball. "Figured the judge would want to know where to find me." He paused, glancing at Diego's face. "Though judging by your expression, I'm guessing she didn't appreciate the humor."

"You're fortunate I reached your door first and removed this—your masterpiece of professional suicide—before she could read it."

Diego held up the crumpled note and read aloud: "Gone drinking. Back before the gators get snappy. Sheriff T. Bracken." Diego glared at him. "Do you really have this much of a death wish? Because this is certainly an efficient way to go about it."

The six-ball dropped clean into the side pocket. Bracken straightened, rolling the chalk between his fingers. "Death wish? Come on, Doc. I'll admit it seemed funnier at the time, but levity aside, I'm stone sober and conducting official business. This is practically a church social compared to my usual morning routine."

Diego's gaze shifted to the tip jar, now heavy with coins and a few crumpled dollar bills. "And what exactly is this official business?"

"Economics." Bracken gestured at the jar with his cue. "Got a lumberjack in my jail who needs feeding between now and his court date. County budget doesn't stretch to three meals a day for prisoners, and this is the only trade I know that pays in cash."

"You're hustling pool to buy food for your prisoner?"

"I am not *hustling*," Bracken said—the words a shade too sharp. Then he caught himself and reined it back with a crooked smile. "I'm demonstrating feats of skill and practicing trick shots for the entertainment of the fine citizens of Cypress Run. The tips are simply their way of showing appreciation for quality marksmanship. Nobody's being *cheated* of anything."

He shot Diego a sidelong glance, then chalked his cue again, eyeing the seven-ball. "Besides, Dooley's given me information I needed, and an empty belly is poor thanks for useful information. I can't always manage it, but I do try to keep my side of the scale balanced."

Diego watched Bracken line up his next shot, the cue rest keeping his aim steady despite the sling. "You realize Judge Hartwell is going to take one look at this and assume you've started drinking before breakfast."

"Judge Hartwell's going to assume I've done something wrong regardless," Bracken said, sending the seven-ball spinning into the corner pocket. "Might as well give her something interesting to complain about."

The saloon doors swung open with their familiar squeak. Jennifer emerged from behind the bar, wiping her hands on her apron and nodding toward the entrance. "Your judge is coming up the walk, Sheriff. Looks about as pleased as a wet cat."

Bracken pocketed the eight-ball with a flourish, earning a small cheer from his audience. "Well, gentlemen, show's over. Doc, you might want to stand back. When Hartwell gets wound up, she tends to spray shrapnel." He began breaking down his cue one handed, sliding the pieces into their case with as much care and precision as his current handicap allowed him.

"This is not going to end well," Diego muttered.

Bracken placed his new cue rest on the wall rack, making a home for it with the house cues and the extra chalk. "Doc, in my experience, nothing in this swamp ends well. But at least Mr. Dooley gets more than a biscuit and a slice of bacon for dinner tonight."

Judge Hartwell's silhouette filled the saloon doorway like a storm cloud blocking the sun.

She stepped inside with measured dignity, her steel-gray eyes taking in evidence—the jar of coins on the billiards table, the wooden case that Bracken hurried to shut, and his carefully innocent expression—with the thoroughness of a prosecutor cataloging evidence.

"I rather expected I'd find you here, Sheriff."

Her tone carried no surprise, only the weary resignation of someone who'd long since stopped expecting pleasant surprises from life. She moved to an empty table near the bar, settling into a chair with the authority of someone claiming a courtroom bench.

"Ms. Starr, would you prepare three breakfast plates? We have business to discuss, and I rather suspect I'll need something to bolster my fortitude."

Jennifer nodded, already moving toward the kitchen. "Coming right up, Judge."

Bracken grabbed the tip jar and came to join Judge Hartwell at the table. She watched him carefully tip out the contents in front of him, her expression suggesting she'd discovered something particularly distasteful on the bottom of her shoe, but Bracken made no move to explain himself. Instead, he methodically counted out the money, arranging it into neat stacks—silver coins here, copper there, the few dollar bills smoothed flat, completely ignoring her obvious disdain for his morning's work.

Diego shifted uncomfortably between them, sensing the pressure shift, like the charged air before a thunderstorm.

"The dead man from last night was the target," Bracken said without preamble, his attention still focused on organizing the currency. "Pinkerton agent named Morrison investigating a smuggling operation that runs through Rawling-Thom Exports. Man named Mercer's been using the Calusa Cypress Trail to move contraband—Cuban cigars, rum, possibly worse."

Both Hartwell and Diego stared at him, the judge's coffee cup paused halfway to her lips. The casual way Bracken delivered this information, while counting pocket change in a saloon at nine in the morning, seemed to violate several laws of professional conduct.

"Morrison was gathering evidence when somebody put a bullet in his head. Professional job, execution style," Bracken continued.

"Discretion really isn't your strong suit, is it?" Diego observed, glancing around the saloon where Jennifer was pointedly not listening while she prepared their breakfast.

Bracken looked up from his coin stacks, genuinely surprised. "Discretion? I can do discretion, Doc, when the situation calls for it. But this week isn't a discretion sort of week. Fletcher and Morrison were both trying for discreet, and look how that worked out for them." Bracken settled into his chair, adjusting the way his sling pulled at his neck. "If the whole town knows I'm barking at the door of a smuggling ring and I end up dead, everyone's going to know who to blame. Which makes killing me a bad business decision. County sheriff murdered by smugglers is a bad headline if you want people to stay out of your business interests."

He scooped the coins into his pocket, leaving the dollar bills on the table. "Avoiding bad publicity—any publicity—might entice them to behave accordingly."

Hartwell's eyebrows rose incrementally and she set down her coffee cup. "You're... announcing your investigation to prevent violence?"

"Hard to call it a tragic accident when half of Cypress Run knows what I was getting myself into and who I was planning to see." Bracken's mouth curved into what might charitably be called a smile. "Assuming a freight boss runs his outfit like a ward boss back home, a little advance notice says I know I'm walking onto another man's turf—and that I mean to tip my hat politely before I kick the door in."

"And who exactly are you planning to visit?" Hartwell's voice carried the sharp edge of judicial authority.

"Mercer, for starters. I'm given to understand he's running the Rawling-Thom operation." Bracken leaned back in his chair. "Figured I'd introduce myself properly. Let him know the new sheriff is keen on maintaining good community relations."

Diego shook his head slowly, sighing into his coffee. "Your idea of diplomacy worries me."

Bracken smiled. "In my experience, that's how you know it's working."

Diego gave him a long look—the kind reserved for a man already responsible for several of his gray hairs and intent on cornering the market. "There's a fine line between clever strategy and elaborate suicide, Tom."

Jennifer appeared with three steaming plates of eggs, bacon, and grits, setting them down with practiced efficiency. Bracken nodded his thanks before picking up the thread again. "The way I see it, they know I'm coming anyway. Whoever killed Morrison was searching for his notebook before they vanished—they have to realize somebody else took it, probably read it, and that their operation's blown. My arrest of Mr. Dooley wasn't exactly quiet, either."

Hartwell arched a brow. "So instead of investigating quietly—"

"Back in Chicago," Bracken cut in, "we had a saying: sometimes the best way to avoid getting shot in a dark alley is to make sure everyone knows you're walking down it. They understand that killing the sheriff might solve one problem but create ten worse." Bracken picked up his fork with his good hand. "This way, when I knock on their front door later today, they'll be expecting a conversation, not a fight."

Judge Hartwell studied him with the intensity of someone trying to solve a particularly complex legal brief. "And if they decide a conversation isn't in their best interests?"

"Then they can inform me of that preference before I arrive," Bracken said pleasantly, "and I'll respond with my disinclination to honor it." He poked at the pale mound of grits on his plate. "What the hell am I eating, anyway? This looks like wall plaster."

Jennifer, already halfway back to the counter, called over her shoulder, "Eat it while it's hot, Sheriff—don't want 'em to congeal on you."

"That doesn't make me feel better!" he called back.

Judge Hartwell nearly choked on her coffee at the sudden change of subject. "Grits, Sheriff Bracken. They're called grits."

"I'm sorry, did you say *grits?*" He shook his head in bewilderment. "Well, now it *sounds* like wall plaster."

Diego shook his head. "Better get used to it, *amigo*. It's a common breakfast food up this way. You'll be having grits for breakfast nine days out of ten."

Bracken shrugged and put a forkful in his mouth, eyebrows scrunched together as he pondered the texture before swallowing. "Tastes slightly better than wall plaster. Slightly."

Hartwell struggled to contain a smile. "It's a type of porridge, Sheriff. It tastes like whatever you mix into it. Butter and salt, usually, or gravy. But some folks add a bit of milk and molasses to theirs if they want something sweeter—"

"Or if they want to get shot," Diego added. "Are you trying to get him shot?"

"He's a Northerner. People expect Northerners to be strange."

"There's strange and there's sacrilegious. As one transplant to another, never sweeten your grits. Here." Diego slid the crock of butter over to him.

Bracken used a knife to cut out a dollop of butter and mix in with the grey, goopy substance. He tried again, eyebrows raising in surprise. "Alright, you got me. That's a good bit better, now."

Judge Hartwell leaned back in her chair, appraising her sheriff. "You know, Sheriff Bracken, I'm beginning to think that lawmen from Chicago are a lot like grits."

"Oh? How's that?"

"Completely unappealing until seasoned appropriately."

Bracken chuckled, grinning with good humor. "Well played, Your Honor. Well played. I thought your angle would have been coming in different, though. Thought you were going to say that we get mixed up in all sorts of unexpected things."

Diego cleared his throat. "Speaking of getting mixed up in things, if you're in earnest about visiting the Rawling-Thom warehouse and speaking to the man in charge, I'll be the one driving you over in the cart today."

"Simon did just fine—"

"I am not sending my sixteen-year-old apprentice with you to confront a rum-runner no matter how polite you think they might be about the situation."

Bracken lifted his good hand in surrender. "No argument here, Doc."

"Good. Then finish your breakfast so I can change that dressing. If I'm going with you to inquire about *filling a graveyard plot* this afternoon, I'll need to make my rounds this morning."

Bracken scraped up the last bite of grits and set his fork down. "Well—if I die today and somebody puts you in charge of my graveyard plot, you have my permission to put 'seasoned appropriately, but not to taste' on the headstone."

Judge Hartwell didn't miss a beat. "Don't tempt me, Sheriff."

Diego sighed, but the corner of his mouth betrayed a smile as he finished his own breakfast and braced himself for an afternoon of diplomacy with Central Florida's most casually reckless sheriff.

Chapter Thirteen

Fire on the Water

Diego guided the mule to a halt near the river docks, the cart wheels crunching over shells and packed sand. He climbed down and gave the animal's neck a gentle pat, murmuring something in Spanish while Bracken eased himself from the passenger side with his good arm.

The docks stretched along the muddy Calusa River in both directions, a maze of weathered planks and pilings that reeked of fish, tar, and something else—something sweet and cloying that made Bracken's nose twitch. Warehouses lined the waterfront like crooked teeth, their tin roofs glinting dully in the afternoon sun. Men hauled crates and barrels between the buildings and a collection of small boats bobbing at the piers.

"Hell of an operation they got here," Bracken observed, adjusting his dark spectacles and taking in the bustle of activity. Workers moved with the conscientious economy of movement unique to people who knew exactly what they were supposed to be doing and preferred not to be watched while doing it.

"Stay with the cart, Doc." Bracken started toward the largest warehouse, its painted sign reading "Rawling-Thom Exports" in faded letters across the weathered siding.

"Tom."

Bracken paused and looked back. Diego had moved around to the mule's head, one hand still resting on the animal's bridle, but his dark eyes were fixed on the sheriff with an expression Bracken couldn't quite read.

"As much as I would love to avoid putting my neck that far out," Diego said quietly, "if you're going to need an extra set of hands in there, I won't do you much good back here with the mule."

Something warm and unexpected settled in Bracken's chest—gratitude mixed with the kind of surprised recognition that came when someone stepped up beside you without being asked. In Chicago, partnerships were transactions, carefully negotiated arrangements of mutual benefit. This felt different. Real.

"Doc, I—" He cleared his throat, suddenly aware of how little he'd expected anyone in this godforsaken swamp town to actually give a damn whether he lived or died. "I appreciate that. More than you know."

Diego nodded once, released the mule's bridle, and fell into step beside him. "Just promise me we're going to try talking before you start slapping people unconscious."

"Talking first is always the goal, but I make no such promises about my behavior if they decide to be unreasonable."

They approached the Rawling-Thom warehouse together, their boots echoing on the dock planks. The building loomed ahead of them, its double doors propped open to reveal stacks of crates and barrels disappearing into the shadows beyond. Men moved in and out like ants, carrying loads back and forth, just busy enough to be nondescript.

The sweet smell grew stronger as they drew closer—molasses, maybe, or something similar. But underneath it lingered something else, something that made Bracken think of the saloon on a bad night when the spittoons hadn't been emptied. Alcohol and tobacco, but as if both had been soaked in maple syrup and set on fire. Plus the fish.

"You ever notice," Bracken said conversationally as they reached the warehouse entrance, "how legitimate businesses never smell quite this interesting?"

Diego chuckled. "You ever want to smell *my* legitimate business on a bad day, see how it compares, you just let me know, *amigo*. You can help me wash out bedpans and see how interesting *that* smells."

A heavyset man emerged from the warehouse shadows, wiping his hands on a stained apron. "Help you gentlemen?"

"Looking for a man named Mercer," Bracken said, stepping closer to the entrance. The sweet molasses smell was stronger here, almost overwhelming. "Business matter."

"Mr. Mercer's in his office. Back corner." The man gestured vaguely toward the warehouse interior. "Though he might be tied up with—"

"We'll wait," Diego interrupted smoothly, moving to Bracken's left shoulder. "We're patient men."

They walked into the warehouse, their boots echoing off the high ceiling. Crates towered around them in organized stacks, each one stenciled with shipping marks and destinations. Tampa, St. Augustine, Havana—names that told stories of commerce flowing through these docks like blood through arteries.

Bracken caught sight of workers hefting barrels that seemed unusually heavy for their size, their movements careful in a way that suggested the contents were either valuable or dangerous. Maybe both.

"Sheriff Bracken?"

The voice came from behind them. They turned to see a thin man in neatly rolled shirtsleeves and an even neater vest approaching, his face pleasant but his eyes sharp as a hawk's. He moved with the fluid confidence of someone comfortable in his own domain.

"That'd be me." Bracken kept his good hand loose at his side. "You Mr. Mercer?"

"Yes. I heard you had some excitement at the Cypress House last night." The man extended his hand with a politician's smile. "Terrible business."

Bracken shook the offered hand, noting the soft palms and manicured nails. Not a man who handled his own freight. But the steel behind his dark eyes suggested he wasn't to be trifled with, all the same. "Murder is always a terrible business in my experience."

Mercer's smile never wavered, but something flickered behind his eyes—surprise, maybe, or calculation. "Strong word. I was given to understand it was a random shooting."

Bracken laughed. "A random execution-style shooting of a Pinkerton detective disguised as a mill worker so he could nose around your freight ledgers? I suppose that's possible. Stranger shots have sunk from wider angles than that." Bracken watched Mercer's face carefully. "Care to explain what a Pinkerton detective was doing documenting your payroll?"

The warehouse seemed to grow quieter around them, as if the workers had developed a sudden interest in their conversation. Diego shifted slightly, positioning himself where he could watch both Mercer and the men behind them.

"Well," Mercer said, his smile finally fading, "I suppose we should discuss this in my office."

Bracken nodded, folding his spectacles and tucking them into his vest pocket. "Office sounds civilized enough."

Mercer led them through the maze of crates to a corner office built into the warehouse structure like an afterthought, separated from the main floor by thin walls that barely muffled the sound of men hauling freight. The space felt more like a ship's cabin than a proper office—cramped, functional, with ledgers stacked on every available surface and a single window that looked out over the docks.

Mercer poured three glasses from a bottle of amber liquid, the neck wrapped in Spanish script that meant nothing to Bracken. He passed the glasses around, clearly a man accustomed to lubricating business conversations.

"Cuban rum," Mercer explained, settling behind his desk. "Figured you gentlemen might appreciate something a bit more refined than what they serve at the Cypress House."

"Never had rum before," Bracken mused, eyeing the bottle. "Always been a whiskey man."

"You'll find it has more character. Different language of heat to it."

Bracken lifted the glass and took a careful sip. The rum rolled across his tongue, burning with molasses sweet undertones, nothing at all like the sharp bite of Chicago whiskey. The finish lingered, complex and somehow smoother than anything he'd tasted in the Windy City's finest establishments a beat cop could afford.

"Well, I'll be damned." He took another sip, appreciating the craftsmanship. "That's got some stories to tell."

"The best liquor always does. One of the advantages to running an import business," Mercer said, settling back in his chair. "Access to the finer things."

Diego sipped his rum, frowning contemplatively as if he were evaluating medicine.

Mercer swirled his glass thoughtfully, studying Bracken with the careful gaze of a man sizing up a potential partner before deciding whether to shake his hand.

"Sheriff, I'll concede this is an unusual situation, and we're both standing on uncertain ground. For my own peace of mind, I'd appreciate it if we could be as frank as our professions allow."

Bracken inclined his head. "Frank keeps things tidy. So, in the interest of saving us both time—shall we admit we're talking about the same smuggling racket?"

Mercer smiled, teeth gleaming like a shark. "Sheriff, you strike me as a seasoned enough lawman to know that breaking up a business as profitable as what runs through these docks sits well beyond one very small man's reach. Allowing sleeping dogs to lie, in this instance, is much closer to the scope of work the county is paying you to do."

Diego set his glass aside, eyes shifting between them like a man watching a card game played for more than money.

Bracken took another sip of rum, letting the heat settle in his chest. "Depends on how you define 'paying,' I suppose. But sleeping dogs don't usually shoot Pinkerton detectives in saloons."

Mercer's smile thinned. "No, they don't."

Bracken leaned back, studying the man across the desk, taking a slow measured breath while he waited for the other man to take his shot at the table.

"So," Mercer said after a moment, voice smooth again, "would it be fair to say a smart officer—one who knows which fights are worth the trouble—might prefer to let certain... lesser enterprises continue undisturbed? We focus on the killing, and let commerce mind itself?"

Diego stayed silent, but Bracken could feel the doctor's tension radiating from the chair beside him. The rum sat warm in his stomach as he considered Mercer's words, rolling them around like billiard balls looking for the right angle.

The warehouse creaked around them, settling into the afternoon heat. Somewhere outside, a crane squealed as it lifted cargo from a boat, and men shouted instructions in English and Spanish.

"Truth is, Mr. Mercer, I got little desire to go kicking at foundations; sometimes the foundation's the only thing keeping the whole damn building from falling down." He gestured with his glass toward the warehouse beyond. "But I wouldn't feel I was doing my job right if I didn't catch whoever's running around town killing people."

Mercer nodded as if this was exactly the response he'd expected. "That's reasonable. Professional, even. And I can assure you, none of my men had anything to do with that detective. To be truthful, I hadn't even realized he was spying on my operation. Thought he was just another mill hand with a gambling habit."

"What about the railroad angle?" Bracken asked, leaning forward. "Morrison was tracking a link between your shipments and the land fraud John Fletcher was tracing."

Mercer's laugh held no humor. "I can't imagine what that connection would be, Sheriff, but the rest of it is politics. The politicians in Tallahassee, along with their railroad backers, think Cypress Run is their shiny new toy. They think they can muscle everyone out of the way and redraw the whole county to suit themselves." He gestured toward the window, where the half-built courthouse was just visible in the far distance. "But Tampa interests got here first, invested considerable resources. Even your brand-new courthouse has Tampa shipping companies on the construction invoices."

Diego shifted in his chair, his medical training apparently extending to reading the tension in a room. Bracken could practically feel the doctor calculating angles of escape.

"But here's the thing," Mercer continued, warming to his subject. "What's going on between Tampa and Tallahassee is a family squabble, nothing more. Rich men arguing over who gets to be richer. Hardly something to interest a very small, very underpaid county sheriff."

Bracken leaned back in his chair, twisting the rum glass to catch the lantern flame in the last dregs of the liquid. "The part that interests me is the part where two men are murdered within days of each other, one for investigating the lumber mill's involvement in your smuggling racket, the other for investigating railroad land fraud." He met Mercer's eyes. "If I didn't know better, I'd say somebody was trying to play both sides against each other."

Mercer's pleasant mask flickered like a lantern flame touched by wind, his glass paused halfway to his lips. "I'm not sure I follow."

Bracken leaned forward, tone mild. "Does the name Harlan Carter mean anything to you?"

The effect was immediate and unmistakable. Mercer's face went carefully blank, but his knuckles whitened where they gripped his glass. He set the rum down with deliberate care, as if sudden movements might give him away.

"I can't say that it does," he managed, though confidence had drained from his voice.

Bracken smiled without warmth. "Carter ran this piece of your Tampa trade before he went to State Penitentiary. You took over when he left."

Silence pressed in, broken only by dock shouts muffled through the thin walls. Bracken could almost hear the man's thoughts skidding.

Diego cleared his throat softly—a doctor warning a patient the pulse had jumped. Outside, a gull gave a single sharp cry.

"I'm afraid I have to get back to work, gentlemen," Mercer said at last, rising and smoothing his sleeves. "Freight doesn't move itself, and tide waits for no man. You can see yourselves out."

Diego stood, but Bracken lingered long enough to finish his rum. Smooth stuff—sweet enough to hide the burn. "Appreciate the hospitality," he said at last, rising. "And the education in rum. Always good to broaden one's experience."

He set the empty glass on the desk with a soft click that sounded like a period at the end of a warning.

As they stepped back into the din of the warehouse, Diego muttered, "Well, that was terrifying."

"Illuminating," Bracken corrected, mouth twitching. "Like watching a man try to shuffle cards with one hand tied. And I know exactly what that looks like."

Diego said, "Do you think—"

A heavy clatter snapped from the rafters overhead. Years of street instinct prickled through Bracken's skin, tuning out whatever the doctor was saying. The sound wasn't panic—it was *intent.*

His hand shot for Diego's sleeve, yanking the doctor sideways just as a suspended crate tore loose and smashed through the air where they'd been standing.

It hit the floor with a crack that split two barrels and sent a flood of amber liquid surging across the planks. The smell of rum rose like sweet smoke.

"*¡Carajo!*" Diego swore, scrambling upright.

Before either could move, a hanging lantern tumbled from the rafters, spilling flame. In the next heartbeat heat slammed upward in a single violent breath, turning the rum to a sheet of fire racing across the floorboards. The sound wasn't a crackle—it was a roar, a living thing bellowing for air. Men shouted and scattered.

Bracken flinched hard at the blast of heat, every nerve screaming to bolt. The scent of tar and liquor mixed until it seemed the blaze would climb inside his lungs. Smoke poured upward, clawing its way into his mouth before he could draw a full breath.

Every shout stretched thin, warped, drowned beneath the roar.

Men ran forward, throwing buckets across the blaze, their efforts chasing more choking smoke through the warehouse.

Someone screamed behind them—high, raw—and the smell that followed was worse than any gunpowder. Diego started to rise, but Bracken's fist clutched his sleeve, yanking hard. "Don't—stay down!"

While the crowd focused on the inferno, Bracken scanned the rafters. The sling was gone; his Colt was in his hand. Diego followed his gaze, trying to see what the sheriff saw.

A shadow wavered in the smoke above—a dockhand stepping out onto the catwalk, pistol flashing orange in the firelight.

Bracken sighted and fired. The shot's crack vanished inside the roar. A cry answered, the man tumbling backward through smoke and crates with the brittle crash of splintering wood.

Bracken lurched to his feet. "Get outside!"

Flames lunged up the tarred beams, snapping boards loose as they climbed. His blood turned ice-cold even as the rest of him burned.

But there was only one way to catch the fleeing shooter. He'd already lost one; he'd be damned to lose another—and he'd faced worse fires than this.

He vaulted a tipped-over crate and plunged through flame and smoke, chasing the crash and tumble of toppling cargo toward the rear of the warehouse.

The air hissed—too alive, too close.

Behind him the building cracked like kindling. Tar boiled on the beams, raining sparks. Heat hammered his back, herding him toward the dark where the wounded man crashed through stacked freight.

He burst through the rear doorway into blinding Florida sun, the fetid stink of the Calusa hitting him full in the face. Smoke and daylight collided; the change left him squinting, eyes watering, the world spinning from glare and heat.

The shooter was already twenty yards ahead, sprinting toward the far pier with his blood-slick arm clamped to his ribs. His stride was jagged but determined, weaving through stacks of lumber and coils of rope. Bracken lifted his Colt, forcing his breath steady despite the pulse hammering through his injured arm. The weight of the gun settled him; old muscle memory. He squeezed off a single round—the shot cracked sharp across the water.

The man stumbled, staggered, but didn't fall. He dove between two towers of cypress planks, vanished, then re-emerged at a skiff tied at the end of the pier, blood trailing behind like a banner.

Bracken ran. Boots pounded against sunbaked planks, the rhythm blending with the shouts from the burning warehouse and the dark slap of water below.

The rum-slick boards beneath Bracken's feet turned treacherous, shining like black glass in the sun where spilled liquor had pooled and spread. His boots slipped as he fought for purchase, arms windmilling for balance. He hit the edge of the pier just as the skiff shoved off into the murky current.

"Stop!" he barked, leveling his pistol.

The dockhand twisted, blood dark on his sleeve and the leg of his pants. His eyes were wild, his voice a rasp over the river.

"Carter's taking back what's his."

The world erupted.

The warehouse blew apart in a blinding roar, the shock wave punching through the docks like a hammer stroke. Sound vanished; air turned solid. Bracken hit the planks hard, pain blooming through his shoulder as the blast rolled over him. For one long moment there was nothing but white and a whistle in his ears.

The skiff heeled sideways. He saw the gunman lift from its deck, a dark shape flung into the air before the river swallowed him whole. The boat spun empty, spinning like a leaf on the current.

Then came the burning rain: timber, shards of tin, blackened boxes—the sky itself seemed to fall. Debris hissed into the water or clattered against the pier, each strike a small explosion. Bracken forced himself upright, shielding his head, his healing arm screaming.

Behind him the inferno howled. Heat pressed at his back like a living weight. Panic punched through the ringing in his ears. Diego.

"Doc!"

He turned toward the blaze, voice raw. The warehouse had become a single column of fire and black smoke twisting skyward.

"DOC!"

He ran—slipping, catching, running again—driven by the sound of his own voice and the rising fear that the doctor might still be inside that burning ruin.

Through the haze came a familiar figure, coughing and stumbling but mercifully alive. Diego's usually pristine shirt was black with soot, hair wild, eyes bright through the grime. He looked like a ghost dragged out of the smoke and given back his skin.

Diego shouted, "Are you out of your mind? You could've—"

"Sweet bloody Jesus, what the hell is the matter with you!" Bracken's words tumbled out in a torrent of relief and fury, his voice cracking slightly from the smoke still burning his throat.

"What do you mean, what's the matter with *me?* What's the matter with *you?"*

"I told you to get back to the cart! What in God's name did you come chasing me for?" His good hand gestured wildly as he spoke, the motion betraying just how rattled he truly was beneath the bravado.

Diego doubled over, hacking, the sound harsh in the thick heat. When he straightened, his composure was gone; anger made every word shake. "Because you ran straight into a burning warehouse after a man with a gun—*¡loco, cabrón, te vas a matar!*—with one arm that's barely fit to hold a coffee cup! Somebody has to keep you from getting yourself killed, and apparently that somebody is *me*."

Bracken stared at him, the adrenaline still singing in his veins like electricity, his chest rising and falling rapidly as he caught his breath. He was torn between overwhelming gratitude that his friend was alive and unharmed, and complete exasperation at the man's inability to follow simple, life-preserving instructions—and then the absurd thought hit him that the other man might feel the same way towards him. He started laughing: half choke, half hysteria. The dock listed beneath his boots; he wasn't sure if it was the heat or his own unsteadiness.

Behind them, the warehouse burned like judgment, smoke billowing black over the river. Bucket lines worked in vain while half the roof sagged inward.

"The man who tried to kill us," Bracken said once he found his breath. "He's in the river. Said something about Carter taking back what's his."

"Carter?" Diego's face hardened. "*Harlan Carter?*"

"Same one. Seems like our prison bird's got longer wings than anyone figured." Bracken watched the burning warehouse, pieces of the puzzle clicking into place. "Dooley said Carter pointed him at Fletcher, but how the hell's a man in prison running things this far south?"

"Maybe he's not in prison anymore."

The thought hit cold. Bracken met Diego's eyes and saw his own suspicion mirrored there. "You're talking about the prisoner leasing system."

"It makes sense. State leases prisoners out to hard labor. Everything from agricultural work to railroad construction."

"What are the damned odds of a former smuggler doing forced labor for a railroad outfit that just happens to be trying to edge out his former smuggling ring? Christ," Bracken muttered. "Ellie. She doesn't know."

Around them, dockworkers shouted in two languages; the river carried the reek of rum and wet ash. Mercer was nowhere to be seen. Another section of roof collapsed behind a wall of flame.

Diego coughed into his sleeve. "Maybe we should finish this conversation somewhere not on fire?"

Bracken slipped the Colt into his weak hand—it still ached, but it would hold. "Yeah. If Mercer's alive, he'll find me soon enough. Still—none of this is good."

Diego shot him a sideways look. "That's your professional opinion? Not good?"

Bracken tried to laugh, turned it into a cough. "Only one I've got."

They reached the cart. Diego calmed the mule with slow Spanish words, and the rough music of his voice settled Bracken's nerves more than he'd admit.

Diego grabbed his medical bag from the back of the cart. "People are injured. I'm going to see how I can help. You should wait in the—"

"I'll come help—"

"You will do no such thing. You're staying here with the cart."

"Doc—"

"Don't you 'Doc' at me. You should be on bed rest, *amigo*, so no, you're not helping and if you leave this cart for even a second, I will tell the judge you're medically unfit for duty."

"Unkind."

"Pragmatic."

"Fine. Under protest."

Diego took his bag. "Stay there. I'll be back."

Diego hurried off and Bracken climbed into the passenger seat, skin still prickling with heat, mind already working angles.

The attack felt personal—too coordinated to be random, too sloppy to be professional. Someone wanted to send a message and didn't care who burned to deliver it.

All things considered, there was only one thing that could be said for the day:

"Well, shit."

Chapter Fourteen

Husks

The cart rattled into the darkened main street like a funeral wagon, wheels grinding against dirt still warm from the day's heat. Smoke haze drifted behind them from the docks, carrying the acrid stench of burned rum and charred timber. Bracken's ears rang from the warehouse blast, everything sounding like it was coming through cotton stuffing. Diego wasn't much better—the doctor kept blinking hard and shaking his head like he was trying to clear water from his ears.

Most of the town had spilled onto the street, faces turned toward the orange glow flickering in the distance where the warehouse still burned. Women clutched shawls despite the heat, children pressed against their mothers' skirts, and men stood in small clusters, voices low with speculation. The kind of crowd that gathered when something big went wrong and nobody knew what came next.

As they approached the jailhouse, Bracken noticed the door standing ajar, lamplight flickering through the gap like a yellow eye winking in the darkness.

"Did you leave your office open?" Diego asked, his voice hoarse from smoke.

Bracken's blood went cold. He never left the door unlocked, let alone hanging open like an invitation. "No."

He was off the cart before it fully stopped, his boots hitting the dirt hard, the Colt already in his hand without conscious thought. He shouldered through the door, expecting the worst—an empty cell, maybe blood on the floor, Dooley long gone into the night.

What he found was far more awful.

"Christ almighty."

Simon lay crumpled near the desk, his left arm twisted at an unnatural angle. The boy's face was chalk white, eyes wide with shock. Beside him, Nate Harper knelt with a water pitcher, trying to help despite the fact that the entire left side of his face was purple and swollen, like someone twice his size had backhanded him across the room.

In the jail cell, Patrick Dooley sat on his cot, very much alive but shaking like a leaf in a hurricane. His knuckles were white where they gripped the cell bars.

"Sweet bloody hell." Bracken stood frozen in the doorway, his mind struggling to process the scene. His office. His prisoner. Two boys who shouldn't have been anywhere near—

Diego pushed past him, medical training overriding everything else. "*¡Dios mío!*" He dropped to his knees beside Simon, hands already moving with careful deliberation. "Simon, can you hear me? Don't try to move that arm."

"Doctor Delgado?" Simon's voice came out thin and reedy, like air leaking from a bellows. "Somebody... somebody came for the prisoner. Had a gun. Was gonna... gonna kill him."

"Easy, *niño*." Diego's fingers probed Simon's shoulder, gentle and precise. "Dislocated. Could be worse."

Bracken finally found his voice. "What happened?"

Nate looked up with his one good eye, the other swollen completely shut. "Simon and me... we were bringing Mr. Dooley his supper. Man was in here with a gun. Big man. Ugly as sin."

"He tried to protect me," Dooley called from the cell, his voice thick with something between gratitude and shame. "Both them boys did. Little one jumped the man when he saw the gun."

Bracken's gaze snapped to Nate, whose one good eye met his with stubborn defiance. "You *what?*"

"He was gonna shoot Mr. Dooley," Nate said through his split lip. "Didn't seem right."

"So you threw yourself at an armed man," Bracken said slowly.

"Worked, didn't it?"

From the cell, Dooley's rough voice cut through the tension. "Boy saved my life, Sheriff. Took that bastard's gun hand right off target."

Diego was positioning Simon's arm, ensuring that it was aligned correctly. "This is going to hurt, Simon, but I need to get your shoulder back in place."

"He got away," Simon gasped, his words tumbling together in shock-induced babble. "Ran out the back. I tried to stop him—"

"You tried to stop a gunman?" Bracken's voice pitched higher. "Christ, Simon."

"I'm sorry, Sheriff, I'm so sorry, I should have—"

"Shut *up*, Finch." Bracken growled, the words coming out rougher than he intended. "You did good. Both of you. But, *Jesus Christ...*"

Diego positioned his hands on Simon's shoulder. "On three. One... two..."

The sharp pop of bone sliding back into the socket made everyone in the room wince. Simon's scream echoed off the jail walls, then dissolved into breathless sobbing.

"There." Diego's voice held that calm authority that meant the worst was over. "Nate, bring me that cloth from the desk. We need to make a sling."

Bracken finally moved, crossing to Dooley's cell. "You see his face?"

"Not clearly. Big man, like the boy said. Wore a hat pulled low. But Sheriff..." Dooley's voice dropped to a whisper. "He knew my name. Knew exactly who I was and why I was here."

Bracken's mind was already working the angles, but every calculation led to the same pocket. Someone had wanted Dooley dead badly enough to send a killer after him. Someone who knew exactly where to find him and when the jail would be least defended. Knew when exactly the sheriff was planning to be down by the docks trying not to be burned alive.

"He say anything else?"

"Just that I'd caused enough trouble already." Dooley's laugh held no humor. "He wasn't wrong, was he."

Diego finished fashioning Simon's sling from a torn sheet, then moved to examine Nate's face. The boy sat perfectly still, trying to be brave, but Bracken could see tears leaking from his good eye.

From outside came the sound of running feet and voices calling. Word was spreading. Soon half the town would be crowding around his jailhouse, wanting answers he didn't have.

Bracken looked at the blood on his office floor, the two injured boys, the shaken prisoner who'd just escaped execution by pure chance, not knowing how the hell he could have done any different, just knowing that he should have.

Ellie's voice cut through the lamplight before she even reached the jailhouse door.

"Nate? Nathaniel Harper, where are you?"

Her footsteps quickened across the threshold, and Bracken watched her face change the moment she spotted her son. The worry lines around her eyes deepened into something harder, more dangerous.

"Sweet Lord! What happened to you?" She crossed the room in three strides, dropping to her knees beside Nate and cupping his swollen face with gentle hands.

"We were just bringing Mr. Dooley his supper, Mama." Nate's words came out thick through his split lip. "Me and Simon. But this man was here with a gun, he was gonna kill—"

"A gunman?" Ellie's voice cracked on the word. She examined Nate's bruises with clinical professionalism, but Bracken could see her hands trembling. "You were attacked by a *gunman*. In the sheriff's office. While the sheriff was where, exactly?"

The question hit him like a slap. Simple words, but loaded with every ounce of accusation a mother could muster.

Diego cleared his throat. "Ellie, we were investigating—"

"I wasn't asking you, Diego." When she finally looked up at Bracken, her eyes held enough fury to burn down half of Florida.

"Mrs. Harper—" he started.

"*Don't!*" The word cracked like a whip. "Don't you *dare* 'Mrs. Harper' me right now! He could have died! Do you understand that?" Ellie pressed a shaking hand to her mouth, sucking in a deep breath in a desperate attempt to calm herself. "My eight-year-old son could have died because some killer waltzed into your jail while *you weren't here.*"

Bracken opened his mouth, then closed it. There wasn't a defense in the world that would hold water, and they both knew it.

"Where were you, Sheriff? Where were you when two boys had to stand between a gunman and your prisoner?" Every word landed like a physical blow. Bracken had taken his share of beatings—fists, boots, billyclubs—but nothing had ever hurt quite like this. "When my son had to protect a prisoner because the man whose job it actually is was somewhere else entirely?"

Diego rose from beside Simon, voice calm. "Ellie."

She turned on him, eyes still burning with tears of rage she refused to let fall, but the doctor didn't flinch.

"I know you're scared," he said softly. "Anyone would be. But right now it's your fear talking, not reason—and the sheriff's not to blame for that."

The words didn't excuse anything—they only changed the air, angling her fury back toward what mattered: Nate.

"You think I'm overreacting? Am I really?"

"Mama, he didn't know—" Nate tried to interject.

"Hush, sweetie." Ellie's voice gentled for her son, then hardened again as she faced Bracken. "How about you, sheriff? Do you think I'm overreacting? Are you going to stand there and tell me this isn't your doing? You don't have deputies. You don't have a jailer. You don't even have a proper jail that locks from the outside. But you do have responsibilities, and one of them is making sure a man stays safe once he's locked up. But that man in there is *your* prisoner sitting in *your* jail. *Your* job. *Your* responsibility. Not my son's."

She stepped closer, and Bracken caught the scent of lavender soap mixed with something sharper—fear, anger, the particular fury of a mother whose child had been endangered.

"My boy is sitting here looking like he went ten rounds with a dockhand because he had to do your job for you. Are you going to tell me that isn't your fault?"

"We were following a lead—" Bracken started, then stopped. Even to his own ears, it sounded hollow.

"Following a lead." Ellie's laugh held no humor. "Well, I suppose we should all be grateful you were doing something better than drinking in the saloon and hustling billiards, Sheriff. While you were off following leads, an eight-year-old and a sixteen-year-old had to stand between a gunman and your jail cell because you weren't here to keep them safe."

Bracken stood perfectly still, letting every word hit him. She was right. Every furious, fear-fueled word was accurate in all the ways that mattered, and they both knew it.

"Where do you get off?" Her voice cracked on the question. "What gives you the right to put children in danger because you're too proud or too important or too whatever-the-hell-you-are to do the simple job of watching one prisoner?"

She stepped closer, close enough that he could see the tears she was fighting back.

"I trusted you. I let him look up to you, I let him think having you around meant he was safer, and this is what happens—my baby with his face smashed in."

From the cell, Dooley's voice came quiet and shame-faced. "Ma'am, if it helps any, your boy's got more courage than most grown men I've known."

"It doesn't help." Ellie didn't even look at him. "Because courage shouldn't be required of children. That's what adults are for. That's what sheriffs are for."

Bracken stood there and took it, every word a deserved slap. His arm throbbed, his ears still rang from the warehouse explosion, and his office floor was spattered with blood from two children who'd had to stand in the gap he'd left wide open.

"You're right," he said finally.

The simple admission seemed to take some of the wind out of her sails, but not the anger.

"Damn right I'm right. And if you think I'm letting Nate anywhere near this jailhouse again while you're treating it like some kind of game—"

"It's not a game to me, Mrs. Harper. It isn't." The words came out rougher than Bracken intended. "And you're right. About all of it. I should have been here."

Ellie stared at him, clearly expecting more fight, more excuses. When none came, her shoulders sagged slightly, but her voice stayed steel-sharp.

"You should remember that other people's children aren't just balls on your billiards table."

The silence that followed felt heavy enough to crush bone.

She turned back to Nate, her hands gentle as she examined his bruises. "Can you stand, baby?"

"Yes ma'am."

"Then we're going home." She helped him to his feet, one arm around his shoulders. "Diego, can you handle Simon?"

"Of course."

Ellie paused in the doorway without looking back, her voice scraped raw of emotion. "Next time you go chasing leads, Detective... get yourself a deputy. Stop leaving children to guard your cells."

The door closed behind them with a soft click that somehow sounded louder than a gunshot.

Diego exhaled through his nose—not quite pity, not quite forgiveness.

"She doesn't mean it," he said quietly. "Not like that."

Bracken didn't answer. Maybe she did.

Diego tried again, softer. "She'll be less angry tomorrow."

Bracken swallowed against the sour weight in his gut. Maybe she wouldn't.

Hours later, after the dust had settled and the last of the blood had been mopped from his office floor, Bracken stood alone in the flickering lamplight. The office felt smaller after everyone left, the silence heavier than the Florida heat, thick with the smell of blood and gunpowder and the weight of what might have been.

Bracken leaned against his desk, working his wounded arm through careful stretches—flex the fingers, rotate the wrist, test the shoulder's range of motion. The stitches pulled tight, but the arm held. It would have to—he'd need both hands for what came next.

He'd been telling himself for weeks that he could make this work. New town, clean slate, proper law enforcement in a place that needed it. But tonight had stripped that fantasy down to its bones. Two boys had nearly died covering for his mistakes, and his prisoner was a sitting duck in a jail cell that locked with a skeleton key any fool could pick.

Time to stop pretending he was running anything more than a particularly dangerous charity operation.

Bracken wrote a quick note and left it weighted underneath a coffee cup on his desk, then strapped on his shoulder harness, settling both Colts in their holsters against his ribs like old friends. The weight felt familiar, comforting—a reminder that some problems required more than wit and billiards analogies to solve. From his desk drawer, he grabbed a box of .45 ammunition, the brass clicking softly as he slipped it into his coat pockets.

He opened the gun cabinet and pulled out the Colt Lightning. The rifle had never seen much action in Chicago. Long range wasn't much use for tight alleyways and dark warehouses. But he'd practiced with it at the range just as often as he practiced with his revolvers. The slide action worked as smooth as anything—it ought to; he cleaned and oiled it more often than some men prayed. Tonight, it would have to see him through twenty miles of swamp road to the next town with a proper federal lockup.

Dooley looked up as Bracken approached the cell, keys jangling in his good hand.

"About time we took a ride, Mr. Dooley."

The lumber foreman studied Bracken's face, reading the hard set of his jaw and the deliberate way he moved. "Where we going, Sheriff?"

"Everfield Junction. Federal courthouse there has a proper jail, proper marshals." Bracken turned the key and swung the cell door open. "Can't protect you here. Figure it's time I handed you off to folks with the resources to keep a prisoner breathing until his trial."

Dooley stood slowly, studying Bracken's face in the amber light. "You really think moving me's gonna keep me alive?"

Bracken met his eyes, seeing the fear there—not of the law, but of whoever had sent a gunman to silence him permanently, whoever was smart enough to know that dead witnesses told no tales, and desperate enough to try eliminating one in broad daylight.

"Honest answer?" Bracken shouldered the rifle over his bad arm and gestured toward the door. "Can't promise it'll keep you breathing forever, Patrick. But it might buy you one more sunrise. That's more than you'll get sitting here like a carnival duck waiting for the next shooter to walk through that door."

Dooley nodded grimly. "Fair enough. Though I got to say, Sheriff, whoever wants me dead ain't gonna be particular about who gets in the way. You're taking an awful big risk."

The thought of Nate's bruised face made his jaw clench. Eight years old, standing between a killer and a prisoner because the sheriff was off playing detective. Ellie's words echoed in his head: *What gives you the right to put children in danger?*

"I'd rather take the risk myself than have someone else do it for me. Besides, staying here sure as hell isn't working out for either of us." Bracken checked his pocket watch—half past nine, with a waxing moon not quite full. Bright enough that they wouldn't need lanterns. Maybe dark enough to move without being seen, if they were careful. He opened the door, cool night air washing over them like a blessing. "Come on. Let's see if we can keep you breathing till morning at least."

The town lay quiet around them, as they stepped into the street, windows dark except for the orange glow spilling from the Cypress House. Somewhere in the distance, a gator bellowed a warning growl, the sound rolling across the water like thunder.

"Sheriff?" Dooley's voice carried a note of genuine curiosity. "Why you doing this? Could just let that gunman finish the job, save yourself a heap of trouble."

Bracken paused at the livery stable door, considering the question. "Man's gotta have a hobby," he said finally. "And apparently mine is just collecting heaps of trouble."

He knocked on the door that led into the stable master's house, hoping the man was home and wouldn't mind helping hitch up a wagon.

"Besides. I made you a promise and I intend to keep it if I can."

The morning sun had barely crested the cypress canopy when Ellie Harper made her way down Main Street, a covered basket tucked against her hip. She'd spent the better part of an hour debating whether to make the trip at all—pride warring with the uncomfortable knowledge that she'd been too harsh the night before.

Nate's bruises had looked worse by lamplight than they actually were, Diego had assured her. A split lip and a blackened eye, nothing that wouldn't heal clean. Still, the sight of her boy's battered face had stripped away every rational thought, leaving only the raw fury of a mother whose child had been hurt while under someone else's protection.

She'd said things. Sharp things that cut deep, judging by the way Bracken had taken them without a word of defense. The memory sat heavy in her chest as she approached the jailhouse, basket handle creaking softly with each step.

Inside the basket: cornbread still warm from the oven, a jar of honey, and a small bottle of Diego's willow bark tea for pain. Not an apology, exactly—she'd been right to be angry—but an acknowledgment that anger and fairness didn't always walk the same path.

Taking a deep, steadying breath, Ellie knocked at the door. "Sheriff?"

She tried the handle and found the door unlocked. Ellie pushed it open, expecting to find Bracken hunched over his desk with that morning-after look men got when they'd spent the night wrestling with whiskey and regret.

Instead, she found emptiness.

"Sheriff Bracken?" Her voice echoed off the bare walls.

No answer. She set the basket on his desk and walked toward the cells, already knowing what she'd find but needing to look anyway.

Both cells stood empty, doors hanging open. Patrick Dooley's blanket lay rumpled on the narrow cot, still holding the impression of a body that had been there recently.

Ellie returned to the front room and looked for what else was missing. The gun cabinet was empty, the rifle that had rested there yesterday nowhere to be seen. His shoulder harness with both gun holsters was gone from the peg by the door.

Bracken's desk sat neat as a pin, papers stacked with institutional precision. The kind of tidy that came from someone who expected people to come snooping and left out nothing of importance but an outward appearance. The only thing out of place was a hastily scrawled note tucked beneath a coffee cup: *"Taking Dooley to federal courthouse in Everfield Junction. Back tomorrow if all goes well. Maybe later if it doesn't. —T. Bracken."*

The words sent ice through her veins. Ellie sank into Bracken's chair, the weight of understanding settling over her like a shroud. *If all goes well.*

He'd run.

Not from the job—from the danger closing around him like quicksand and threatening the people nearest him. Smart move, really. Take the prisoner somewhere safe, let the federal marshals sort out who wanted Patrick Dooley silenced. Lead the danger elsewhere.

Twenty miles of swamp road to Everfield Junction, with a prisoner someone had already tried to kill once. In the dark, most likely, given how early they'd have needed to leave to reach the note's optimistic timeline. The man didn't even know how to ride a horse properly, and he'd taken it upon himself to transport a marked man through the most dangerous stretch of wilderness in the territory.

Half-flooded most of the year, thick with palmetto and pine. Perfect for an ambush. She'd traveled that route exactly once, years ago when Harlan was first arrested. The memory of those dark, twisting trails still gave her nightmares. Cypress trees draped in Spanish moss, creating tunnels of shadow even at midday. Countless places for armed men to wait. Ellie knew what those roads were like between here and Everfield Junction.

But Bracken didn't.

She thought of his pale face last night, his clothes singed and streaked with soot, the way he'd moved carefully to avoid jarring his injured arm.

Ellie picked up the note, reading it twice more as if the words might change. They didn't. Somewhere out there in the cypress maze, Tom Bracken was trying to atone for yesterday's failures, armed with nothing but wounded pride and whatever Chicago street sense translated to Florida swamp.

Back tomorrow if all goes well, the note said. But only if the ghost of her husband didn't catch up to him on the road—and only if the swamp didn't swallow him first.

Act Three

SECRETS IN THE DARK

CHAPTER FIFTEEN

The Word Around Town

The bell above Cotton's General Store chimed as Ellie pushed through the door, her empty basket swinging at her side. She'd come for lamp oil and coffee beans, but the cluster of voices near the pickle barrel made it clear she'd walked into something else entirely.

"—held poor Jake at gunpoint, I tell you. Made him hitch up that wagon in the dead of night like some common highwayman."

Ellie recognized the voice of Mrs. Mills, the banker's wife, whose talent for embellishment rivaled her skill at finding fault.

"That's a load of horse apples, Meredith." Jake Henley himself stood by the counter, arms crossed over his leather apron. "Nobody held me at gunpoint. Sheriff asked me to hitch a wagon together, and I did it. Man's got a prisoner to transport, that's his business. He paid Bobby to drive them both and that's the meat of it."

"Middle of the night?" Mrs. Mills's voice climbed higher. "Ran off with that murderer in tow—mark my words, we'll never see hide nor hair of either one again. Just like that Sheriff Brown, either somebody's paid him off or that Carter gang spooked him proper, and you can take that to the bank."

"Sheriff's protecting Big Dooley," said Murphy, the lumber yard worker Bracken had helped on his first afternoon in town. "Somebody tried to kill the man right here in our jail. What's he supposed to do, wait for them to finish the job?"

"Protecting a murderer while the rest of us suffer," snapped Mrs. Mills. "The docks are nothing but ash and ruin, thanks to his meddling. People are out of work, and where is our sheriff? Fled into the swamp with his tail between his legs. He got one whiff of what that Carter gang is capable of and he's running scared."

Ellie selected a tin of lamp oil from the shelf, keeping her face carefully neutral. The conversation swirled around her like smoke, each voice adding fuel to the gossip fire.

"Judge Hartwell's fit to be tied," offered Cotton from behind the counter. "Heard she's threatening a formal inquiry if Sheriff's not back in two days. Sent word to the federal marshal this morning. Can't say I blame her. Man abandons his post without so much as a by-your-leave."

"Two boys got hurt defending that prisoner," Mrs. Mills continued, her gaze sliding toward Ellie with obvious invitation. "Poor little Nate Harper with his face all beaten in, and young Simon with his arm near torn from its socket. Where was our sheriff then? Off playing detective at the docks while children fought his battles."

The tin of lamp oil felt suddenly heavy in Ellie's hands. The room had gone silent, with humidity and kerosene hanging thick in the air. Every eye in the store had turned her direction, waiting for her to join the chorus of condemnation. After all, it was her boy who'd taken the worst of it. She could feel their expectation, their hunger for her to feed the fire with her own grievances.

"Mrs. Harper," Mrs. Mills pressed, "surely you have something to say about Sheriff Bracken's conduct? Your poor Nate—"

"My poor Nate," Ellie said quietly, "defended a man who couldn't defend himself—just like his mama taught him. And Sheriff Bracken is doing his job—just like we're paying him to—taking a suspect to where he can be safe while he waits for his trial. A man is still guaranteed his day in court in this country and Sheriff Bracken is doing his best to ensure Mr. Dooley gets his."

The words came out cooler than she'd intended, but she didn't soften them. Mrs. Mills's mouth opened and closed like a landed fish. "Well. I'll say. You're mighty quick to defend him, aren't you, Ellie? Especially considering your husband's *employment*."

Ellie kept her voice steady, bolstered with sweetness and the sort of false cheer that was sharp as a paring knife. "I like to think I'm always mighty quick to point out facts rather than standing around the general store squabbling over gossip like a bunch of hens scratching at dirt."

The silence stretched taut.

Mrs. Mills's mouth compressed into a tight line of disapproval before she managed, "Well, I never—"

"No," Ellie agreed, setting coins on the counter for her purchases. "I don't expect you have."

"Sheriff Bracken's doing his job," Murphy added firmly, turning the conversation away from Mrs. Harper and back to the matter at hand. "Better than the last two we had, anyway."

The bell chimed as Ellie pushed through the door, leaving behind a store full of wide eyes and dropping jaws. But the words followed her down the street, echoing in her own head like mosquitoes—easy to ignore until one drew blood.

Ellie pushed through the clinic door, still haunted by Mrs. Mills's words. She found Diego in the clinic's back room, grinding willow bark with methodical precision. The pestle's steady rhythm against the mortar filled the silence between them, a sound as familiar as her own heartbeat after all these years working together.

"How's Simon's shoulder?" she asked, settling onto the wooden stool beside his worktable.

"Sore, but he'll live. Boy's tougher than he looks." Diego didn't pause in his grinding. "How's Nate holding up? When I checked him last night, nothing appeared broken, so the bruises should heal quickly."

Ellie nodded, watching the bark powder accumulate in fine white dust. "No, I know that. Nate's fine. I need your opinion about something else."

Diego finally stilled and met her gaze. "About what, specifically?"

"About the sheriff running off because he's afraid of Harlan."

Ellie hadn't meant to be so direct, but the speculation at the store had burrowed under her skin like a chigger.

"Mrs. Mills was holding court at Cotton's," she continued. "Half the town thinks the explosion at the docks spooked him. That he's running scared before Harlan can get to him."

Diego's eyebrows climbed toward his hairline. "Running scared? *Sheriff Bracken?*"

"That's what they're saying. That the murder attempt scared him off. That he's a coward."

A short laugh escaped Diego's lips—the kind doctors made when patients insisted their broken leg was just a bruise. "Ellie, in my experience, our sheriff runs *toward* the people shooting at him. Taking the safe option doesn't seem to sit right with that man. It's his most irritating quality."

He returned to his grinding, but his movements carried a restless energy now.

"So you don't think—"

"Sheriff Bracken's many things. Reckless, stubborn, too fond of his own wit for anyone's good. But coward?" Diego shook his head.

Through the clinic window, Ellie could see the empty sheriff's office across the street, its door hanging slightly ajar in the morning breeze. The sight made her stomach twist with an emotion she couldn't quite name.

"I was angry at him," she admitted quietly. "For not being there when Nate got hurt."

"You had every right to be. Truthfully, I was just as mad that Simon got hurt."

"But listening to those people at Cotton's, calling him a coward…" She trailed off, unable to finish the thought. "Mrs. Mills is practically holding a wake for poor, abandoned Cypress Run. She says Tom's run off for good."

"Mrs. Mills thinks her own shadow's plotting against her." Diego finally looked up, his dark eyes assessing. "What do you think?"

Ellie found herself studying her hands, noting the calluses from years of scrubbing floors and changing bandages.

"He left me a note. He didn't have to explain that he was taking Dooley to Everfield Junction; he could have just left. That's more courtesy than most men would've shown."

"But?"

She twisted her fingers. "But twenty miles through swamp country with a healing arm and someone trying to kill his prisoner? It seems… reckless."

Diego chuffed out a bitter laugh. "Reckless is a charitable word for it."

"What do you mean?"

"I'm a lot less worried about whether the gossipmongers think he's a coward and more about whether he's going to live long enough to care about it," Diego's voice was weary in the way that reminded Ellie that Diego had already patched too many gunshot wounds for one lifetime, the way that always caught her off guard when he let it slip.

Ellie felt something twist in her chest. "So, you think he's…"

"I think…" Diego looked up at the ceiling, taking a breath while he organized his thoughts. "I think that he would rather take a risk himself than let other people get hurt. Seeing the boys hurt when we got back really shook him."

"You don't think that what…" Ellie winced and looked at the jail again. "You think he would have gone even if I hadn't…"

Diego looked at Ellie with all of his attention before he resumed his grinding, the pestle's rhythm slower now.

"I honestly can't tell you how that man's head works, but I get the impression that once he decided on a right course of action, there aren't any words you could have said to talk him into or out of it. I also don't believe he's the type to abandon his post. Once he's finished his business in Everfield Junction, he'll be back, regardless of what you said to him."

"And if whoever's trying to kill Dooley catches up with them on the road?"

Diego's hands stilled completely. "Then he'll either deal with it or die trying, I imagine."

The clinical matter-of-factness in his voice made Ellie's stomach clench. She'd known death intimately—had held dying children while fevers burned them from within, had watched her own husband murder a good man for being kind to her. She had seen first-hand what bullets did to human flesh. Death was awful. Always.

But somehow the image of Tom Bracken lying still and lifeless in some cypress grove—green eyes fixed and empty, that quick grin of his gone forever—felt altogether different. It cut deeper than professional concern, sharper than mere civic duty. The thought of him shot and killed while trying to do the right thing, of him bleeding out in the wilderness while bad men jeered and congratulated themselves for breaking him... All those thoughts spun together into a knot and lodged in her throat like a fishbone she couldn't swallow or pull free.

"He asked me why I warned him about Harlan," she said quietly. "About the smuggling."

"And what did you tell him?"

"That I didn't want another good person to die."

Diego nodded slowly. "And now you're wondering if what you said to him last night about letting those boys get hurt just sent him straight into the line of fire."

Ellie rubbed at her collarbone, trying to ease the tightness in her chest. "Something like that."

The morning light slanted through the clinic's single window, illuminating dust motes that danced and settled like tiny ghosts. Outside, she could hear the normal sounds of town life—horses clopping past, children's voices, the distant ring of Jake Henley's hammer on his anvil.

"You know what I think?" Diego said finally.

"What?"

"I think you're worried about more than just his professional competence."

Ellie felt heat rise in her cheeks. "He's the sheriff, Diego. If something happens to him, the whole town suffers."

"Mmm-hmm." Diego's tone was maddeningly neutral. "I'm sure that's it."

Ellie stood abruptly, her stool scraping against the wooden floor. "I should get up to the schoolhouse. The children will be arriving soon."

"Ellie."

She paused at the doorway.

"For what it's worth," Diego said, "Sheriff Bracken's exactly the kind of *terco* who'd fight his way through hell itself to keep his word. If he said he'd be back, he'll be back."

Ellie nodded once and stepped into the bright morning heat, Diego's certainty following her like a benediction she wasn't sure she deserved. The benediction held till sundown. By dusk, the whispers chasing her through town had gone quiet, and the swamp had taken their place.

"**N**ate, time for bed."

The words came out sharper than Ellie intended. She softened her voice, smoothing a hand over her son's dark hair. "You've had enough excitement for one day."

Nate looked up from his slate, pencil hovering over half-finished arithmetic. The purple bruise around his left eye had darkened since the afternoon, making him look older somehow. Too old.

"But Mama, I ain't tired yet."

"Aren't tired," she corrected automatically. "And yes, you are. Look at you."

He was exhausted, she could tell—the way his shoulders sagged, how he kept touching his split lip with the tip of his tongue. But stubborn as his father, always pushing when he should yield.

"Can I finish my sums first?"

"No. Slate down. Now."

Something in her tone must have warned him off arguing further. Nate set his pencil aside and stood, wincing slightly as the movement pulled at what was probably a bruised rib.

"Mama?" His voice came small, uncertain. "Are you mad at me?"

The question hit her like a physical blow. "Oh, baby. No." She knelt and pulled him into a careful embrace, mindful of his injuries. "I'm not mad at you. Not even a little bit."

"Then why do you look so... angry?"

Because I nearly lost you last night. Because you threw yourself at a gunman to protect a stranger. Because you're eight years old and already braver than most grown men I know.

"I'm just tired," she said instead. "Same as you."

He nodded against her shoulder, accepting the half-truth with the easy trust of childhood. "Will Sheriff Bracken be back tomorrow?"

"I don't know, sweetheart."

"I hope he comes back soon. I want to tell him about how I jumped that man."

Ellie's chest tightened. "Nate, listen to me. What you did at the jail cell... it was very brave. But it was also very dangerous. Promise me you won't do anything like that again."

"But—"

"Promise me."

He pulled back to look at her face, reading something there that made him nod solemnly. "I promise, Mama."

"Good boy." She kissed his forehead, tasting the salt of dried tears. "Now go brush your teeth and get into your nightclothes. I'll be up to check on you in a few minutes."

After Nate disappeared up the narrow stairs, Ellie sat alone at the kitchen table, staring at the slate he'd abandoned. Half-finished sums sprawled across the gray surface—simple addition problems that would have challenged him a month ago but now seemed almost insultingly easy.

Everything seemed different now. Before tonight, her biggest worry had been whether Nate was learning his letters fast enough. Now, she couldn't stop imagining his small body flying through the air as a grown man's fist connected with his face.

She tried to banish the image by focusing on cleaning the kitchen, putting the slate away, wetting a cloth and wiping down the kitchen table.

The words she'd spoken to Sheriff Bracken echoed in her memory, each one sharp as broken glass. *You do have responsibilities—Your prisoner—Your jail—Your responsibility.* The fury had felt righteous in the moment, justified by every maternal instinct screaming for protection.

But now, in the quiet of her kitchen, doubt crept in around the edges. She'd seen Bracken's face as she'd torn into him—the way he'd stood perfectly still and taken every word without defending himself. The slump of his shoulders when she'd finished, like something inside him had broken under the weight of her accusations.

"Mama?" Nate's voice was small in the silent kitchen.

"What, baby?"

"Sheriff Bracken didn't know that man was gonna come. He was trying to catch bad people."

Ellie's hands stilled on the washcloth. "I know."

"You were awful mad at him."

The simple observation hit harder than any accusation.

She'd been furious, yes—but underneath the anger had been something more painful, something that felt too much like the fear she'd lived with when Harlan had begun staying away longer and bringing home friends that felt dangerous and more money than he could justify.

"Sometimes grown-ups say things when they're scared," she said finally. "Things that they don't quite mean in the way that they sound."

"Are you gonna tell him you're sorry?"

The question startled her. Was she? She'd been right to be angry—children shouldn't have to stand between gunmen and prisoners. But the look on the sheriff's face when she'd torn into him...

"Get some sleep, Nate."

She followed him up to the loft and tucked him into bed, smoothing the covers with the same careful attention she'd given his bruises. He was asleep within minutes, exhaustion finally claiming him despite his protests.

Alone in the main room, Ellie let herself sink into the rocking chair by the window.

The guilt she'd been holding at bay all day finally broke free, washing over her in waves that made her chest tight.

Other people's children aren't just balls on your billiards table.

She'd seen how deep those words had cut. He'd stood there and taken it, never once pointing out that he'd been following leads on the very case that had put Dooley in danger. Never mentioned that he'd been investigating the smuggling operation she'd warned him about. Never blamed her for any of it, even though her past with Harlan had made everything complicated.

What if she'd been too harsh? What if something had happened to him on that road? She'd seen the note on his desk, twenty miles through hostile territory in the dead of night with a half-crippled arm and a prisoner that her ex-husband had already tried to murder. What if Harlan's people had been waiting in the cypress shadows, and the last words Sheriff Bracken remembered her speaking to him were accusations thrown in anger and fear?

The thought settled in her stomach like a stone.

She rose and stepped onto the small porch, needing air that didn't smell like lamp oil and regret. The night sounds pressed around her—frogs calling from the cypress, the distant splash of something moving through water, the endless whisper of insects in the dark. The sky was clear, stars scattered across the black sky like scattered salt. She found herself looking up, remembering how Bracken had stopped to stare at them just a few nights ago, wonder written across his features like a child seeing fireflies for the first time.

"Makes a person feel pretty small, doesn't it," he'd said, voice soft with something that might have been longing.

The memory made her chest ache. He'd seemed so young in that moment, so far from the sardonic sheriff who deflected everything with billiards metaphors and dry humor. Just a man from the city amazed to see something he'd never known he was missing—a man still capable of being amazed by beauty, despite whatever darkness had driven him from Chicago.

Ellie's skin gradually began to prickle as she became aware of something besides the memory of the other night—a silence where there shouldn't be one.

The cicadas had stopped singing.

Ellie went still, every sense sharpening. In the Everglades, when the bugs went quiet, it meant something was moving through the darkness. Something big enough to make them nervous.

Her gaze swept the fence line, searching for whatever had spooked them. At first she saw nothing but shadows and starlight... then a figure detached itself from the dark—tall, lean, hat brim shadowing his face—but she knew that silhouette as well as her own reflection.

Harlan Carter straightened slowly, moonlight catching the edge of his smile.

"You don't look surprised to see me, Eliza."

That voice—still honey over steel, still capable of making her seventeen again. She kept her face carefully neutral.

"Should I be?"

"Most folks get a shock when their husband comes calling after three years." Harlan straightened, his movements fluid despite whatever prison had done to him. "Got out early for good behavior."

"Funny. I wouldn't have pegged you for good behavior."

His laugh was soft, dangerous. "Learned to keep my head down. Say 'yes sir' and 'no sir' like a good boy." He tilted his head, studying her. "Guess it paid off."

"How long have you been out?"

"Long enough." His gaze drifted past her to the house, where a single lamp burned in the window. "Boy asleep?"

The protective fury that blazed through her made her forget caution. "You stay away from him."

"Easy, Eliza." Harlan raised his hands in mock surrender. "I'm not here for Nate. Though I hear he's been playing sheriff's deputy these days. Got himself roughed up protecting some prisoner."

The casual knowledge in his voice made her stomach clench. He'd been watching. How long had he been in the shadows, learning their routines, their weaknesses?

"Well, you would know," she said. "You're the one who sent the man to murder him."

"You always were sharp as a tack," he said, hooking his thumbs in his belt with that casual arrogance she remembered too well. "Course, if you were really sharp, you'd have known I was never staying locked up in prison, that I'd be coming home some day. And maybe if you'd known that, you'd have been a much more faithful wife, I'm thinking."

Ellie swallowed, not letting the fear shake her voice, "If you were any kind of sharp, you'd know when you're not welcome." Her hand found the porch rail, gripping tight. "What do you want, Harlan?"

"Want?" Harlan's laugh carried soft and dangerous across the yard, the sound she'd once loved and now feared more than any gator's bellow. "I want a lot of things, I suppose. Want to see my son. Want to know why some Chicago lawdog's been sniffing around my business and why my wife's been keeping house for him."

"Sheriff Bracken boards here sometimes. Nothing more."

"Word travels fast in the swamps, Eliza. Faster than your new sheriff, seems like." Harlan's voice stayed soft, conversational, but something cold flickered behind his eyes. "And word is... you got yourself a bit of a soft spot for him. Maybe even a warm spot, too, if old Mrs. Mills is to be believed. That true, darlin'?"

The accusation hit like a slap. "He's not—"

"Not what? Not playing daddy to my boy? Not sharing your bed?" Harlan's smile sharpened. "Funny thing, though. There's also word in town that your lawman ran off last night. Left his jail cell wide open and lit out for parts unknown. Makes a man wonder if he might've proved himself... untrustworthy."

Ellie's hands clenched at her sides. "You'd know what it takes to make a man untrustworthy. Sheriff Bracken is transporting a prisoner to the federal courthouse. Standard procedure."

"In the middle of the night? Through twenty miles of swamp?" Harlan clicked his tongue with mock concern, the sound deliberate and measured. His pale blue-gray eyes glittered with something that might have been amusement if it weren't so cold. "Either he's brave or stupid. Hell, maybe both. Lot can happen on a road like that, you know. Bandits lurking in the cypress groves, gators sliding up from the water holes, accidents with wagon wheels or loose bridge planks..." He paused, letting each word settle like pebbles dropped in still water. "Man could disappear real easy between here and Everfield Junction. Vanish without so much as a ripple."

The implied threat made her stomach clench tight as a fist. Heat flashed through her chest, anger and terror warring for control. "You've always been a mean bastard, but I swear to you, if you hurt him..."

"Now, that's not fair, darlin'." Harlan's voice carried the same gentle reproach he'd once used when she'd scolded him for tracking mud through the house. "I'm just a concerned citizen, worried about public safety. Law enforcement's a dangerous profession out here in the Glades." He leaned against the fence post with fluid grace, settling in like he had all the time in the world—relaxed as a cat stretched out in warm sunshine, completely at ease with the menace he'd just delivered.

"Leave him alone, Harlan. Leave all of us alone."

"Can't do that, darlin'. See, I got responsibilities. A family to protect. A business to run." He stepped onto the first porch step, and she fought the urge to back away. "And a reputation to maintain."

"Your business and your reputation got you a cell in State Penitentiary."

"My reputation got me out again." His smile turned sharp as broken glass. "Amazing what doors open when you got the right keys. The right friends in the right places. The right leverage on the right people."

Ellie's blood went cold. If Harlan was out legitimately, it meant someone with power had arranged it. Someone who wanted him free bad enough to risk their own neck.

"What do you want?" she asked again, though part of her already knew.

"Simple thing, really." Harlan's voice dropped to a whisper that somehow carried more menace than any shout. "Your sheriff's been poking around where he shouldn't. Following trails that lead to uncomfortable places."

"You sent men after them."

"I sent men to clean up a mess." The easy charm dropped like a discarded mask. "Question is, Eliza—what are you gonna do about it?"

"I'm gonna tell you to get off my property before I wake my son up with a shotgun blast to his daddy's chest."

"Now, that's not very neighborly." Harlan's voice carried that lazy confidence she remembered from their courting days. "Besides, I think we both know you're curious about what happened on that dark road last night."

"You're lying." But even as she said it, she knew Harlan wouldn't have come here without something to show for it.

"Am I?" He reached into his coat with deliberate slowness, pulling out something that caught the moonlight.

The piece of polished wood gleamed in his palm—a billiard cue with the end snapped off—and Ellie's stomach dropped.

"Found this on the road about ten miles out. Funny thing about billiard cues—they break real clean when they hit something hard."

The sight of it broken in Harlan's hand made her knees weak.

"Where is he?"

"That's the question, isn't it?" Harlan slipped the broken cue back into his coat. "Cart overturned, one horse dead, blood on the driver's seat. But no bodies." His smile turned razor-sharp. "Makes a man wonder if they got away. Or if the man this belonged to is lying hurt somewhere in the cypress."

Ellie's mind raced. If Tom was injured, bleeding somewhere in the dark...

"What do you want, Harlan?"

"Morrison had a notebook. Names, routes, people who'd rather stay unnamed. Your sheriff took it." His voice dropped to a cajoling murmur. "You tell me where he keeps it, and I'll tell you which fork in the road my boys last saw that pretty sorrel mare heading down. Or better yet, you get your hands on it and give it to me for safekeeping. Too many people out there willing to burn things down... commit all kinds of murderous acts... just to get their hands on it."

Ellie couldn't figure out who he was trying to threaten now. He was just throwing them out to see which one caused the most damage. The only thing she could do was keep quiet.

Harlan quickly grew bored of her silence and shook his head, continuing, "But you best decide quick, Eliza. Swamp don't wait for nobody, and your sheriff's running out of time."

The cicadas remained silent, leaving only the distant sound of something moving through dark water. Somewhere out in that endless maze of cypress and saw grass, Sheriff Bracken was either dead or fighting for his life—and the man who held the answers stood grinning on her porch like the devil come calling.

Ellie met Harlan's eyes, her voice steady as stone when she finally spoke.

"Get off my property, Harlan. I got nothing to tell you, and you got nothing I want to hear."

Harlan laughed, the sound low and dripping with menace. "I'll remind you that you said that, Eliza. Tomorrow, maybe day after, when somebody finds your sheriff hanging upside down from a tree with his throat cut. I'll remind you."

It took every ounce of willpower she possessed to not duck into the kitchen and grab the shotgun. She forced herself to stay still as Harlan walked down the road, away from her house. His silhouette shrank down the road until the trees took him back. Only then did she let go of the breath she'd been holding.

Ellie stepped back inside and closed the door with hands that trembled only slightly. She turned the lock, checked it twice, then leaned her forehead against the cool wood as the weight of Harlan's words crashed over her like a falling tree. Images flashed through her mind—Tom's awe-struck smile when he'd stopped to look at the fireflies, the patient way he'd answered Nate's endless questions, the quiet determination to do his job well no matter the cost. All of it potentially snuffed out on some cypress-shadowed trail because she'd been too proud to warn him properly about what he was walking into.

Her knees gave out first. She slid down the door until she hit the floor, pressing both hands against her mouth to muffle the sob that wanted to tear free. The broken billiard cue gleamed in her memory—precision and calculation reduced to splintered wood and the aftermath of violence in Harlan's palm.

He's lying.

The thought came fierce, desperate—the only thing between her and panic. If he wasn't, if Tom lay bleeding somewhere in the dark, then nothing she did could save him. So Harlan had to be lying. Tom had to be fine, had to have outmaneuvered whatever trap Harlan had set, because the alternative was unthinkable.

He has to be lying.

She pressed her palms against the floor and forced herself upright, legs shaky but holding. In the kitchen, she lit the lamp with steady hands and pulled out her father's old Bible, the one with pages soft as cotton from handling. Her fingers found the familiar verses without conscious thought, passages she'd memorized during the long nights after Harlan's arrest when sleep wouldn't come and fear ate at her like acid.

The Lord is my shepherd.

The words felt strange in her mouth after so long silent—it had been years since she'd stopped praying with any hope that she'd be heard—but she whispered them anyway, desperate for something larger than her fear to hold onto.

He maketh me to lie down in green pastures.

She thought of Tom's wonder at the stars, the genuine delight in his voice when he'd talked about never seeing such clear skies. A man who could find beauty in a swamp night couldn't be lying dead in the cypress. Wouldn't be.

Yea, though I walk through the valley of the shadow of death.

Her voice cracked on the familiar words, but she kept going, clinging to the rhythm like a rope thrown to a drowning woman. Because if she stopped praying, if she let herself believe Harlan's poison, then Tom was already lost.

And she couldn't bear to lose another good man to the darkness that followed in her husband's wake.

The lamp flame flickered but held steady, casting dancing shadows on the kitchen walls as Ellie Harper prayed harder than she'd ever prayed in her life that Harlan Carter was still the lying bastard she'd married.

Outside, the frogs began again—cautious, tentative—as if even the swamp was waiting to see who survived till morning.

CHAPTER SIXTEEN

Bumps in the Road

The morning dragged like a broken leg through mud. Ellie arrived at the clinic with shadows under her eyes and a forced smile that fooled no one, least of all Diego. She'd spent the night pacing, checking the locks, and startling at every sound the wind made in the palmetto fronds.

"You look like hell," Diego said without preamble, glancing up from his notes. "Sleep poorly?"

"Just restless." The lie came easier than she'd expected. She clutched at her skirt, then smoothed down the fabric.

Diego set down his pen, studying her with the clinical attention he usually reserved for fever patients. "Your color's off and you've been jumping at shadows since you walked in. If I didn't know that you don't believe in them, I'd say you look like you've seen a ghost."

If only it were that simple. She forced a smile that felt like broken glass. "Too much coffee, not enough sleep. Nothing a quiet day won't cure."

Before Diego could press further, the bell above the door chimed. Simon Finch entered, cradling his injured arm against his chest but moving with more confidence than he'd shown yesterday.

"Morning, Dr. Delgado. Mrs. Harper." Simon's grin was bright despite the bruising around his shoulder. "Came to get this looked at—but honestly, it feels much better. Think I can work the soda fountain today if you need me to."

Diego gestured toward the examination table. "Let's see what we're working with before you start making promises about heavy lifting."

As Diego unwrapped Simon's bandages, the boy chattered with his usual enthusiasm. "Oh, Mrs. Harper, how's Nate doing? That was some nasty business yesterday. Nate was a great help though, got grit, through and through—stood right up to that fellow even with his face all banged up."

Ellie's throat tightened. "He's... he's healing. Children bounce back faster than adults."

"Good thing, too. I was grateful he jumped in and saved my life like he did, Mrs. Harper. Very grateful. But I think I would have felt awful if he was laid up over much for it." Simon winced as Diego rotated his shoulder.

"That's kind of you to say, Simon."

Simon kept chattering, distracting himself from Diego's examination, no doubt. "Folks are talking, you know. Mrs. Mills was in the shop this morning, going on about strangers spotted near the road to Everfield Junction. Rail men, maybe moonshiners. Hard to tell the difference sometimes."

The bottle of iodine slipped from Ellie's fingers, clattering against the counter. She caught it before it could shatter, but not before Diego shot her a sharp look.

"Strangers?" Diego asked, his hands still working on Simon's shoulder.

"That's what Jake Henley said. Spotted them yesterday evening, riding hard toward the main trail. Could be nothing, but..." Simon shrugged with his good shoulder. "Way things have been going lately, folks are jumpy about anyone they don't recognize."

Ellie gripped the counter edge until her knuckles went white.

"Speaking of which," Simon continued, "either of you heard from Sheriff Bracken? I know he left town with Mr. Dooley, but that was two days ago now. Folks are starting to wonder."

"Got a telegram from him yesterday afternoon," Diego said, testing the range of motion in Simon's arm. "After you'd left for the day, Ellie. Brief, but at least we know he made it to Everfield Junction safely. Got Dooley turned over to the federal marshals."

Relief flooded through Ellie so fast it left her dizzy. Tom was alive. Had been alive yesterday afternoon, at least. Safe enough to send a telegram.

"The telegram," she said quietly. "What exactly did it say?"

Diego studied her face with those too-perceptive eyes and handed her the thin strip of paper. "Here, you can read it for yourself."

She clutched at it like a talisman, taking a steady breath before she could focus on the type:

CYPRUN D.DLGDO -START- DLY SFE IN CUST AT EJ -STOP- BCK LTR THN EXPTD -STOP- SHF TB -ALL STOP.

It really was brief.

But it wouldn't be much longer when every word cost money. *Dooley safe in custody at Everfield Junction. Back later than expected. Sheriff T. Bracken.* As proof of life, it wasn't much, but better than nothing.

But yesterday afternoon was before Harlan had shown up on her porch with that broken billiard cue. Before he'd implied his men had already struck. The telegram could mean nothing—just proof that Tom had survived the journey there, not that he'd survive whatever trap Harlan had set on the return trip.

"Mrs. Harper?" Simon's voice seemed to come from very far away. "You feeling alright? You look sort of pale."

Ellie's mouth had flooded with saliva, and she had to swallow hard two or three times to keep the bile down as the weight of Harlan's threats crashed down at once.

"That's it." Diego's voice was sharp, his patience for argument at an end. "You're going home. Now."

"I'm fine—"

"You're not fine."

Ellie tried to argue, but her knees went shaky at just that moment, and she sat down quickly before they gave out altogether.

Diego was next to her in a heartbeat. He turned to Simon. "Can you manage the shop for a few hours?"

"Sure thing, Dr. Delgado. Shoulder feels great, honestly."

Diego helped Ellie to her feet, his grip firm but gentle. "Simon can help me with anything urgent. Go home, get some sleep. Real sleep, not whatever you managed last night. And don't come back until you can hold a bandage without dropping it."

She wanted to argue, to insist she could work through anything like she always had. But the thought of staying busy, of having her hands occupied while her mind spiraled through every terrible possibility, felt impossible.

Simon looked between them with wide, worried eyes. "Is everything all right? Did something happen to the sheriff?"

"Everything's fine," she lied, gathering her shawl with hands that wouldn't quite cooperate. "I just need some rest."

Diego's voice was heavy with disapproval, "I wish you'd tell me what has you so shaken."

My husband threatened to kill him, and there might be men in the swamp right now hunting him like an animal.

"Nothing. Just... worried about him traveling alone."

Ellie met Diego's steady gaze and saw he knew she was hiding something important, something that went beyond simple worry.

"Bracken's tougher than he looks," Diego said. "Reckless as hell, with about as much sense as God gave a goose, but tough. He'll make it back."

Ellie nodded and let herself be guided out the door, clinging to Diego's confidence like a lifeline while Harlan's laughter echoed in her memory.

They'd only just set foot outside the clinic when a commotion from down the street in front of the saloon drew both of them toward a crowd gathering in front of the doors.

Bobby Keene's freight wagon sat crosswise before the hitching rail, wheels still caked in swamp mud, the mare trembling under the traces. Fresh bullet holes were cut into the wood and Bobby was looking as white and wispish as she felt.

"Whiskey!" he called. "Somebody get me some damn whiskey before I expire up here!"

He climbed off the wagon and checked on the horse, wide-eyed and soaked with sweat. Jake Henley was there in a flash, taking the lead. "I'll get her unhitched and settled, Bobby."

The crowd pressed closer around Bobby's wagon, voices overlapping in a chorus of worry and curiosity. Jake Henley finished unhitching the trembling horse while Bobby wiped his face with a handkerchief that came away soaked with sweat. Jennifer emerged from the saloon with a bottle of whiskey, which Bobby accepted without ceremony and took a long pull.

"Christ Almighty," he gasped, then looked around apologetically. "Pardon the language, ladies. But I ain't never seen nothing like what happened out there. Has me right shaken, it does, and I ain't ashamed to admit it."

"What happened out there, Bobby?" Cotton asked, pushing through the gathering. "You look like you seen the devil himself."

"Worse. I seen the Carter boys." Bobby took another swig and steadied himself against the wagon's bullet-riddled side. "They hit us twice. Twice! First on the way to Everfield Junction, then again coming back."

Mrs. Mills pushed forward, her face bright with the hunger for gossip. "The sheriff's dead, then? I knew that man would bring trouble."

"Dead?" Bobby's laugh cracked like a whip. "Hell no, that man ain't dead. Least he wasn't when I last saw him—jumping off the back of my wagon onto one of them Carter boys like some kind of lunatic."

A murmur rippled through the crowd. Ellie found herself stepping closer despite Diego's hand on her arm, her heart hammering against her ribs.

"Tell us what you saw," Judge Hartwell's voice cut through the chatter, her expression stern.

Bobby took another deep pull from the whiskey bottle before speaking. "First ambush went smooth as silk. Must've been five or six riders waiting in the palmetto scrub."

Bobby wiped his mouth with the back of his hand. "But the sheriff, he was expecting trouble. Soon as we heard the first horse whinny, he had that rifle of his up and ready. When they came at us from the palmettos, he started picking them off neat as pins."

Simon leaned forward, eyes bright with excitement. "Did they chase you?"

"Couldn't chase what they couldn't see. Sheriff put a bullet through one of their lanterns, spooked their horses something fierce. We got clear in the confusion, slick as anything." Bobby's voice carried a note of admiration. "Got Dooley to the federal boys without any more trouble, handed him over, everything proper-like."

"But you said twice," Cotton pressed. "What happened on the way back?"

Bobby paused and started for another drink, but thought better of it. He handed the bottle back to Miss Starr with hands that were still shaking. "Much obliged, ma'am; best take this back from me now. Thought we were home free on the way back. Sheriff even joked about it, saying how easy it had been. Then the Carter boys got clever."

"How so?" Hartwell asked.

"About five miles out from town, they came at us from both sides of the trail," Bobby's face went pale at the memory. "Threw a burlap sack full of water moccasins right at the horse—near fifteen snakes spilled out over the traces, writhing and hissing. Poor Daisy went near crazy, rearing and bolting."

The crowd murmured in horror.

Ellie wrapped her shawl closer, sick with the knowledge that as horrible as a sack full of moccasins was, Harlan was capable of even far more cruelty and viciousness than that when his mind was set to it.

"Jesus," someone whispered.

"Lost control of her completely. Sheriff got thrown around something fierce. Nearly tumbled right off the wagon." Bobby's hands shook and his eyes unfocused as he recalled the scene.

"They were shooting at us while we were careening down that trail, wagon bouncing like a cork in a hurricane. Sheriff tried returning fire with his six-gun, but it wasn't much good. Horse was running full tilt, wagon bouncing over every root and rock. Hard enough to stay on, let alone aim proper." Bobby shook his head. "Carter boys were gaining on us, too. Could hear their horses getting closer."

Ellie found her voice. "How did he—what happened then?"

Bobby looked directly at her, his expression softening slightly. "Sheriff told me to keep going. Don't stop till I got to town, he said. Then he..." Bobby swallowed hard. "He jumped off the back of the wagon."

"Jumped?" Diego's voice was sharp with disbelief.

"Straight off. Landed right on one of them Carter boys, knocked him clean off his horse. Last I saw, they were rolling around in the mud, punching and clawing at each other." Bobby's voice dropped. "But there were more of them coming. I wanted to stop, to help, but the sheriff had given me an order. And poor Daisy wasn't stopping for man or beast, regardless."

The crowd fell silent. Ellie felt her heart hammering against her ribs as the world spun around her, Diego's steadying hand the only thing keeping her upright. Tom was alive when Bobby last saw him, but that had been hours ago. Wrestling in the mud with Harlan's men, outnumbered and still injured.

"How far out?" Diego asked.

"Four or five miles. Near the big cypress grove where the trail bends away from the river." Bobby looked around at the grim faces, searching for understanding or absolution. When he met Ellie's eyes, his shoulders slumped.

"Look, I know what you're all thinking. That I should have stayed and fought. But the sheriff, he looked me right in the eye when he told me to keep going. Wasn't a request. I followed his orders, just like he said."

Bobby turned to where Jake Henley was still holding Daisy's halter and he began stroking the troubled horse, soothing his own nerves as much as hers.

"You did right," Judge Hartwell said firmly. "We need to organize a search party. Every able-bodied man who can ride."

"In this heat? In broad daylight?" Cotton shook his head. "That's exactly what they're hoping for. More targets."

"How many riders were there in the second group?" Jake asked.

"Six, maybe seven. All armed, all ready for blood." Bobby's voice cracked. "Sheriff was alone out there with just his pistol and whatever he could grab off that rider he tackled."

Jake's voice was edged with grim concern, "Those Carter boys... they don't leave witnesses, Bobby. You know that."

"And they know every trail and hidey-hole in fifty miles," Cotton said. "It'd be suicide."

"Then what do you suggest?" Hartwell's voice carried a sharp edge. "Leave him out there?"

"We should wait till evening, ma'am," Jake spoke up. "If we try to find him now, men'll be dropping from heat before they hit the creek. Best give the sun time to bend west before we ride."

Diego gave Ellie a sad look before adding his voice to the mix. "Mr. Henley's right. First rule of rescue operations: don't become someone who needs rescuing too. If the sheriff is alive, the only way he stays that way is if we don't drop dead before we find him."

Mrs. Mills sniffed. "If the sheriff's fool enough to jump off a moving wagon, that's his lookout."

The words were barely out of her mouth when Ellie stepped forward, her exhaustion replaced by a cold fury that surprised even her.

"Sheriff Bracken jumped off that wagon to save Bobby's life," Ellie said, her voice carrying clearly across the street, "And he's only out there in the first place because he was trying to keep our town safe."

Mrs. Mills bristled. "I hardly think—"

"No, you don't think." Ellie's voice cut like a blade. "You just talk. That man has been shot at, threatened, and attacked twice in his first week here, and he's still out there trying to do his job. With or without the approval of the folks in this town. And now you want to just leave him out there where he could be hurt and needing our help? Because he should have known better than to put himself in harm's way to save a man's life?"

The silence that followed was broken only by the distant call of a mockingbird. Even Mrs. Mills seemed to deflate under Ellie's withering stare.

Jake cleared his throat. "We'll go out looking as soon as the sun goes down a ways, Mrs. Harper," he said quietly. "If he's alive, he'll find a way to signal. Otherwise... Well..." He didn't finish the sentence.

Ellie closed her eyes, Harlan's words echoing in her memory: *Tomorrow, maybe day after, when somebody finds your sheriff hanging upside down from a tree with his throat cut...* She'd thought he was bluffing, trying to manipulate her.

But the broken billiard cue he'd shown her, the casual certainty in his voice... the bloody memories of what Harlan had done to the last lawman who'd shown an interest in helping her—memories that still haunted her nightmares three years later... the thought of Sheriff Bracken—of Tom—tortured to death because of *her*...

"Mrs. Harper?" Simon's concerned voice broke through her spiraling thoughts. "You sure you're feeling all right?"

She opened her eyes to find the entire crowd staring at her. Somehow she'd swayed forward, gripping the side of Bobby's wagon for support.

"I'm fine," she managed.

Diego was beside her instantly, guiding her toward a nearby crate. "Deep breaths. You've had too little sleep and I'm betting you haven't eaten, either."

Bobby stepped close, hat in his hand. "For what it's worth, Mrs. Harper, that sheriff of yours fights like a wildcat. Wouldn't surprise me none if he shows up walking down Main Street come suppertime, probably with some smart remark about the mud in his boots."

Ellie pulled her shawl tighter as the crowd began to disperse. The afternoon sun felt like a predator gnawing at her shoulders—she could only imagine how much worse it was out in the open with no cover, no water, and no hope of rescue. And try as she might, she couldn't shake the image of Tom wrestling in the mud with men who wanted him dead.

CHAPTER SEVENTEEN

Bumps in the Night

By evening, the heat had broken but the worry hadn't. Diego had sent her home to rest, though rest was the last thing she managed. She watered the garden, fed the chickens, checked the latch on every window—all the small, pointless motions that kept her hands busy while her mind fixed on the road beyond Gator Creek.

The horses came up the trail just as the last light bled from the sky. Ellie's hands stilled on the dish towel, listening to the sound of hooves on packed earth. Too many horses for a search party that had left on foot, and moving with the kind of purpose that made her stomach clench.

She stepped to the front window and peered through the gap in the curtains. Six riders, maybe seven, their faces lost in shadow beneath hat brims. The lead man sat his horse like he owned everything the animal's hooves touched, and when he called out, his voice carried the smooth confidence of someone used to getting his way.

"Mrs. Harper! Got some papers here from the courthouse. Need you to come on out so we can discuss your situation."

Ellie's mouth went dry. She backed away from the window, her mind racing. No courthouse business happened after dark, and Judge Hartwell would have sent word ahead of any legal proceedings.

"What papers?" she called back, buying time while she reached for the shotgun hanging above the mantle.

"Deed transfer. Seems this property belongs to the railroad now. You got twenty minutes to gather your things and clear out, or we'll have to arrest you for trespassing."

The gun felt heavy in her hands, familiar weight from years of hunting rabbits and deterring the occasional drunk who wandered too far from town. She checked the load—both barrels ready—and grabbed the box of shells from the mantle drawer.

"I'll need to see those papers in daylight with Judge Hartwell present," she called out, moving to bolt the front door. "Come back tomorrow like civilized people."

A rough laugh answered her. "No need for all that formality, ma'am. Railroad's got authority to handle these matters directly."

Ellie's blood turned to ice water. Railroad authority didn't wear gun belts or ride in packs after sunset. She moved through the house quickly, checking window latches and drawing curtains.

"Nate," she whispered toward his bedroom. "Come here. Now."

Her son appeared in the doorway, rubbing sleep from his eyes. "Mama? What's wrong?"

"Remember the game we practiced? About hiding under my bed when strangers come calling?"

His eyes widened, suddenly alert. "Are those bad men?"

"I don't know yet. But we're going to be careful." She knelt beside him, her voice calm despite the hammering in her chest. "Go to my room. Get under the bed with the blanket. Don't come out until I say, no matter what you hear."

Nate nodded solemnly and disappeared back into the bedroom. Ellie heard the soft thump of him sliding beneath the bed frame.

Outside, the lead rider's voice turned harder. "Mrs. Harper, we're trying to be reasonable here."

"Sheriff Bracken will be back soon." Ellie positioned herself at the front window, shotgun barrel resting on the sill. The riders had spread out, flanking her house like they'd done this before. "You can discuss your papers with him."

Another laugh, this one with teeth in it. "There ain't no sheriff, ma'am. Your lawman got himself shot to pieces eight miles from here. Buzzards probably picked him clean by now. Been a real unfortunate evening for law enforcement."

Now she knew for certain. These weren't railroad men or federal marshals. They were Harlan's crew, the same ones who'd ambushed Sheriff Bracken on the trail. Her hands tightened on the shotgun stock.

She forced her voice to stay steady. "You're lying."

"Twenty minutes, Mrs. Harper," the leader said. "Clock's ticking. Harlan sends his regards, by the way. Says to tell you he's still got business to settle."

"This is my land," she called through the glass. "You want it, you'll have to come through me to get it."

The leader tipped his hat with mock courtesy. "Harlan said you'd be stubborn about it."

She heard spurs jingling as boots hit the ground. They were dismounting, spreading out around the house. Her heart hammered against her ribs, but her hands stayed steady on the gun.

The first shot shattered the window above her head in a cascade of bright splinters. Ellie threw herself flat against the floorboards, glass raining down on her back like frozen tears. The sharp fragments caught the lamplight as they fell, each piece a tiny mirror reflecting the chaos outside.

She rolled to her knees, shotgun clutched tight, and peered through the jagged frame. Muzzle flashes lit the yard like fireflies made of death, and she could see the riders spreading out, using her fence posts and the old oak for cover.

"Should've taken the offer, Mrs. Harper!" the leader called out, his voice carrying over the gunfire. "Now we got to do this the hard way!"

Ellie steadied the shotgun against the windowsill, aiming for the shadow crouched behind her water barrel. She squeezed the trigger, and the gun bucked hard against her shoulder. The shadow yelped and rolled away, clutching his leg.

More shots peppered the front of the house, splintering the door frame and punching holes through her carefully tended flower boxes. She ducked as a bullet whined through the broken window, embedding itself in the wall behind her with a solid thunk.

From the bedroom came Nate's muffled voice: "Mama!"

"Stay down!" she shouted back, sliding fresh shells into the chambers. The familiar motions steadied her hands—break the action, eject the spent shells, slip in new ones, snap it closed. Just like hunting rabbits, except these rabbits shot back.

She fired again, this time at a man trying to creep around the side of the house. The pellets scattered across the yard, and he dove behind the chicken coop, cursing loud enough for her to hear. Another movement, another blast, reload.

With a sickening drop of her stomach, Ellie realized that she would run out of shotgun shells long before the seven men with rifles and revolvers ran out of bullets.

"Nate," she called softly toward the bedroom. "Come here. Quick and quiet."

Her son appeared beside her, wide-eyed but moving in a crouch like she'd taught him. "Are we running, Mama?"

"Back door. To the barn." She grabbed his hand, the shotgun in her other. "When I say go, you run faster than you ever have in your life. Don't look back, don't stop. Get to Sunny and put a saddle on her."

"What about you?"

"I'll be right behind you." She checked the back window—no riders visible on that side yet, but they'd figure it out soon enough. "Ready?"

Nate nodded, his face pale but determined.

"Go!"

They burst through the back door together, Ellie's bare feet hitting the packed earth of her yard. A shout went up from the front of the house as someone spotted them, and she heard boots pounding around the sides of the building.

A rifle cracked, and wood splinters flew from the barn door just ahead of them. Ellie pushed Nate forward, putting herself between him and the shooters. "Keep running!"

They reached the barn as more shots rang out. Ellie spun around, raised the shotgun, and fired at the first figure to round the corner of the house. The man stumbled backward, clutching his shoulder.

"Saddle!" she barked at Nate, who was already dragging the leather toward their old mare. Sunny snorted and rolled her eyes at the gunfire, but stood steady as Nate threw the saddle blanket over her back.

Ellie broke the shotgun again, her fingers shaking as she reloaded. Another rider appeared at the barn door, rifle raised. She snapped the gun closed and fired one barrel, waiting for movement before firing the second. The man dove sideways, his shot going wide.

"Almost got it, Mama!" Nate grunted, struggling with the heavy saddle.

More shouts from outside, boots running. They were closing in, and she was down to her last handful of shells. Ellie grabbed the cinch strap and yanked it tight, her hands working by muscle memory while her eyes stayed fixed on the barn door.

The leader's voice drifted across the yard, cold and patient: "Barn's got only one way out, boys. Take your time."

Ellie pressed her back against Sunny's flank, the mare's warmth steadying her hands as she fed fresh shells into the shotgun. The voices outside had gone quiet—the kind of quiet that meant men were positioning themselves for a final rush.

"Mama." Nate's whisper barely carried over the sound of her heart hammering. "There's a loose board in the back wall. Behind the feed bin."

She glanced where he pointed. Sure enough, one of the weathered planks had warped away from its nail, leaving a gap just wide enough for a boy to squeeze through. Maybe wide enough for both of them, if they moved fast.

"Can you get Sunny through it?"

"No, but I can get to the creek path and circle back to town for help."

Ellie's throat tightened. Send her eight-year-old son alone through dark swamp while gunmen surrounded her barn? Every instinct screamed against it. But staying here meant dying here, and that helped nobody.

"You know the way? Even in the dark?"

"Yes, ma'am. Walked it a hundred times."

Boot steps scraped against the barn's front wall. They were out of time for debate.

"Go." She pressed a kiss to his forehead, tasting salt and fear. "Run like your tail's on fire. Get to Dr. Delgado, tell him what happened. Don't come back here, you understand? No matter what you hear."

Nate's eyes were too old for his face, but he nodded. He squeezed through the gap in the boards like water through a crack, disappearing into the night beyond.

The barn door exploded inward, splinters flying as rifle butts smashed the latch. Ellie raised the shotgun, both barrels aimed at the opening. The first man through wore a hat pulled low, his face lost in shadow except for the gleam of teeth in a cold smile.

She squeezed both triggers simultaneously. The double blast lit up the barn like lightning, and the man flew backward into his companions. Shouts erupted, boots scrambled, someone screamed about his ears ringing.

Ellie broke the gun, fingers flying to reload, but rough hands seized her shoulders before she could snap it closed. The shotgun clattered to the straw-covered floor as they dragged her into the yard.

The leader stepped from the shadows, hat in his hands, dark hair slicked back with pomade. "Mrs. Harper, you just made this transaction considerably more expensive."

She spat in the dirt at his feet. "Send me a bill."

His laugh was ugly, dangerous. "Oh, I will. With interest."

From somewhere in the darkness beyond the barn, a night bird called out—Ka KAW—two sharp notes that didn't belong to any creature she knew. The leader's head snapped toward the sound, his easy confidence flickering.

"What was that?"

One of his men shifted nervously. "Probably just—" Blood erupted from the back of his skull seconds before the crack of a rifle shot broke the night.

A second shot followed and the man holding Ellie fell, blood from a neck wound spraying over her dress.

Another shot. Another man down.

Now there were screams and shouts of alarm from the tree line; men she hadn't even known she'd been up against scrambling to find the unseen assailant.

The leader spun toward the treeline, his pale eyes wide with something between rage and fear. "Spread out! Find that shooter!"

His remaining men scattered like startled quail, rifles raised and swinging toward every shadow. Another shot cracked from a different position entirely, and one of them stumbled, clutching his shoulder.

Ellie rolled behind the water trough, her heart hammering as she realized what was happening. Someone was picking off Harlan's crew from the darkness, moving between shots like a ghost through the palmetto scrub.

"Three down, boss!" one of the men called out, his voice pitched high with panic. "Whoever's out there, he ain't missing!"

The leader cursed and grabbed Ellie's arm, hauling her upright as a human shield. "Show yourself or the woman dies!"

Silence stretched across the yard, thick as swamp fog. Even the crickets had gone quiet, leaving only the sound of nervous breathing and boots shifting in the dirt.

Then, from the darkness near the barn, came a voice Ellie recognized—gravelly, pained, but unmistakably alive. "Doesn't seem like a very gentlemanly thing to do, hiding yourself behind a woman like that."

Sheriff Bracken stepped into the lamplight, and every rifle in the yard swung toward him. "But I *am* from out of town; I'm sure I've got a thing or two to learn about how things are done this far south."

He stood there on the edge of the shadows like a revenant, not so much a lawman but something the swamp had chewed on and spat back out. Mud plastered him from boots to collar, streaked black with cypress rot. The swamp left its marks—scratches, blood, a coating of black peat—but couldn't quite kill the man underneath.

Tom hobbled forward slightly, one leg stiff and dragging.

The leader shoved Ellie in front of him, half-shield, half-hostage.

Tom didn't flinch. His rifle stayed steady—barrel level, eyes fixed.

"Let her go," he said quietly. "I've had a long day, and I'm in no mood to repeat myself."

The leader sneered, pressing the pistol harder against Ellie's face. "One squeeze, Sheriff. You'll never clear that trigger."

Tom's head tilted and he laughed softly, a ghost of that crooked smile back where it belonged. "Funny thing about that, I don't really have—"

The rifle cracked between one a pulse and the next.

The leader's hat flew back in a spray of blood and gunpowder smoke.

Tom had already dropped his rifle and had his Colt clear from its holster, firing as he ducked back into the shadows.

Ellie stood frozen for half a second more before the night erupted again—gunfire tearing through the yard, wood splintering, horses screaming.

"Ellie!" Tom shouted through the smoke. "Get down!"

The gunshots now came faster, his Colt revolver snapping bullets through the darkness. Tom kept moving, firing short, brutal bursts, never lingering in the same shadow twice. The return shots came less frequently as more men went down.

Ellie dropped to the ground and crawled toward the fallen shotgun near the trough, hands shaking more from disbelief than fear. Tom's silhouette flickered against the firelight—mud-soaked, blood-streaked, half-a-ghost but somehow unbroken—and she felt the breath leave her in a rush she couldn't name.

Another flash, another shot; the last of Harlan's men bolted for their horses, spurred into the dark.

Then came silence.

Only the soft hiss of settling dust and the rasp of Tom's breathing.

He half-staggered, half-fell against the water trough, revolver hanging loose in his grip. For a moment he just caught his breath and looked around the yard, scanning the tree line for more threats. After a moment, the tension in him eased and he drew a small, weary cross in the air with the barrel of his Colt and whispered, "*Pax,*" so softly, the word barely carried across the silence.

Then and only then did whatever resolve or stubborn defiance that had carried him through whatever hell he'd crawled out of drain away, leaving him slumped more heavily against the trough.

Ellie rose unsteadily, the shotgun still in her hands, and for a moment neither spoke—just the sound of gasping breaths and crickets daring to return.

"Tom! You're—" she started.

"Unsightly?" he supplied, voice hoarse, eyes bright with that familiar glint. "That'd be the word for it."

Ellie was already moving before he finished the sentence, racing across the yard to crouch by his side.

"Course, famished would be another good word." He shrugged and tilted his head slightly to see her better. "I'm liable to keel over before the pleasantries if I don't get something in my stomach."

"Good Lord, Tom—"

Up close, he looked even worse—eyes hollowed by exhaustion, streaks of swamp mud drying to gray on his skin, blood soaking through what was left of his sleeve. His head was bleeding. His leg was gouged across the thigh. If she hadn't been able to see his green eyes blinking up at her, she would have sworn he was a corpse.

"Just a few souvenirs from the trip," he rasped. "I promise it's nothing critical."

"Nate," she said suddenly, the word cracking like a whip. "He's—"

"Safe," Tom said quickly, "Spotted him on the creek path about a mile out, running toward town. Smart boy. Sent him on to fetch Doc."

Relief flooded through her so fast it left her dizzy. She'd been carrying that weight—her son alone in the dark swamp—without even realizing how much it was crushing her.

"You got any coffee left, Mrs. Harper?"

"Coffee," she said, voice cracking. "You need a doctor."

"Need both," he admitted, trying for a grin as he pulled himself painstakingly up to his feet. "But coffee first if possible. It's been a really long damned day."

His knees buckled and she caught his arm before he hit the dirt. Warm blood slicked her palm. The smell of gunpowder clung to him like a second shadow.

Ellie guided him toward the porch, his weight heavy but a burden she was grateful to shoulder. "Sit. Don't you dare fall on me now."

"Wouldn't dream of it, ma'am."

He sank onto the step with a low groan, one hand pressed to his ribs. She couldn't tell how much of the darkness on his shirt was blood and how much was swamp water. His breath came rough, but steady.

The silence that followed was almost more intense than the gunfire—just cicadas, the drip of water from the trough, and a night that pretended nothing had happened.

Ellie hovered close, her hands trembling now that the danger had passed. "You're late," she said, because anything kinder might have broken her completely.

Tom choked out a laugh. "How do you figure?"

"Your note said you'd be back yesterday."

"*If all went well,*" he corrected, a crooked smile tugging at the corner of his mouth despite the trembling in his limbs. "I believe that was how the note phrased it. I would be back yesterday if all went well. It may have escaped your notice, Mrs. Harper, but—" He drew a slow, shaky breath "—things just did not go that well."

"No," she said softly. "No, it didn't. You look like you had to crawl through a cesspool." For a heartbeat she just looked at him—his torn shirt, the mud streaked across his jaw, the pulse fluttering ragged at his throat. "But you came back anyway."

Tom's smile faltered. He reached out and pressed his fingertips to her wrist, a ghost of a touch, not quite brave enough to actually take her hand. "For what it's worth," his voice dropped to something softer than she'd ever heard from him, "I'd have crawled back through a lot worse to get here, Mrs. Harper."

The words settled between them as solid as brick and twice as heavy.

She would've said something—a retort, a comeback, anything—but the breath caught somewhere deep in her chest, tangled up with all the words she'd been wrestling with since he'd disappeared.

Whatever careful response she'd meant to give turned into something far more honest: her hand reaching out before she could stop it, fingertips brushing the stubble along his jaw, tracing the line of mud and exhaustion that mapped his face.

His eyes found hers in the lamplight spilling from the doorway, green-blue and searching, like he was trying to read something written in a language he'd never learned.

And then there was no distance left to guard, no walls left to maintain.

The kiss was clumsy at first, born of relief and desperation rather than romance. Salt and sweat and the smoky, metallic tang of gunpowder lingered between them.

Her fingers tangled in his hair, finding it damp with swamp water and something that might have been blood. His good arm came up to circle her waist, pulling her closer with a careful urgency that spoke of a man who'd spent the last two days believing he might never get the chance.

It was the kind of kiss that only happens once—when the world has just stopped ending and somehow, impossibly, two people who have squandered too many chances are both still breathing.

When they finally broke apart, he pressed his forehead to hers, both of them breathing hard in the narrow space between.

"Worth the trip, Mrs. Harper," he whispered, his voice rough with something deeper than just swamp water and gun smoke.

Ellie pulled back, her hand still resting against his cheek. The mud and blood streaked across his jaw felt real under her palm—proof he wasn't some fevered hope conjured from her worry.

"How did you—"

"Rode a horse if you can believe it."

The absurdity of the statement caught her by surprise and made her huff out an amused breath. "A horse? You rode a horse?"

"Not *well*, obviously... but... wouldn't you know it, one of those Carter boys was kind enough to leave me a horse when he died on me all of a sudden out on the road, and I figured it was too kind a gift to go to waste, so I got on and stayed on. Horse led me this way a bit. Got close enough to hear gunshots and thought

I'd move faster on foot, so I got off and tied him up a few hundred yards back that way—"

"Tom. You're rambling a bit." Ellie studied his face in the lamplight, cataloging the new lines etched around his eyes, the way exhaustion had settled into his shoulders like a weight he couldn't shake off. "How bad are you hurt?"

"Bad enough that I probably shouldn't have tried riding a horse." Tom shifted against the porch step, wincing as the movement pulled at something tender. "Doc's going to have some choice words about my medical compliance."

"He's going to have choice words about a lot of things." She glanced toward the bodies scattered across her yard, already calculating how much explaining this would require. "Starting with why there's a small battlefield in my front garden."

"Well, when you put it like that, it does sound a bit excessive." His grin flickered, weary but genuine. "Though in my defense, they started it."

The sound of hoofbeats carried across the night air—multiple riders approaching fast. Ellie tensed, but Tom's hand found hers, steady despite the tremor of exhaustion running through him.

"That'll be Doc and the cavalry," he said, though his free hand still rested near his holster.

Ellie laughed. "Nate probably painted quite the picture."

Sure enough, Diego's voice cut through the darkness, sharp with medical authority and barely contained panic. "Ellie! Where are you?"

"Here!" she called back, not moving from Tom's side. "We're both here!"

Diego materialized in the lamplight like an avenging angel in a medical coat, Nate close behind him and Judge Hartwell bringing up the rear with what looked like half the town's men trailing in her wake.

"*Madre de Dios.*" Diego took one look at the sheriff and immediately shifted into professional mode. "What did you do to yourself now?"

"Nothing a little whiskey won't cure," Tom replied, though he didn't resist when Diego knelt beside him and began checking him over.

Hartwell surveyed the carnage with the cool detachment of someone trying not to be affected by the bloodier side of law enforcement. "How many?"

"Seven down, maybe three got away. Plus four on the road from the first ambush. And two the second time on the way back." Tom ran a trembling hand through his hair, shaking loose clumps of dirt and mud. "Christ. I thought the backside of the Stockyards was a rough beat, but we'd see two, maybe three bodies a week at the *worst*. This is..." He gestured at the carnage, almost too exhausted to move his arm that far. "Jesus, that's a lot of bodies in two days." His face went suddenly white and he lurched to his feet, dragging himself off Ellie's porch and onto the grass before he started retching.

Diego set his medical bag down with a sigh and crouched beside Tom, checking for fresh wounds. "How many times did you get shot this trip?"

"Define 'shot,'" Tom mumbled, wiping his mouth with a shaking hand.

"Bullets came close enough to entering your body that they drew blood," Diego said.

"Once. Maybe twice. Hard to tell with all the mud." Tom straightened slowly, his face still pale but steadying. Diego pressed the back of his hand to Tom's forehead, checking for fever, then took hold of his wrist to check his pulse—rapid but steady—while his eyes cataloged the damage visible in the lamplight. Tom let him work, reassuring him softly, "Nothing vital, I promise."

"Vital or not, you're still suffering from blood loss and exhaustion," Diego muttered darkly, his voice carrying the worn exasperation reserved for patients who treated their bodies like borrowed equipment. "And infection kills just as easily as an artery shot. When's the last time you ate?"

"Uhh... breakfast...?"

"Which day?"

"Erm. Hmm." Tom mumbled quietly with a sheepish expression, "Day the warehouse blew up...?"

"*Jesús, este hombre... Mi paciente de los infiernos.* Two days, Tom? Two days?" Diego finished his quick examination and shook his head. "*Dios, dame paciencia.* Bed. Now. And if you argue with me this time, I'll have Judge Hartwell write a court order."

"Wouldn't dream of it, Doc." Tom's grin flickered weakly. "I know when I'm beaten."

Diego looked up at Ellie, letting the question stay unasked, but she was already moving, clearing a path to her front door. "Nate, fetch water from the well," she said. "We need to get him cleaned up before we can get him into bed."

"Yes, Mama!"

Diego slipped his arm under Tom's shoulders, supporting his weight as another wave of nausea hit. "Easy, Tom. Just breathe."

"Sorry," Tom gasped between heaves. "Not very sheriff-like, is it?"

"You've lost enough blood to float a small boat, and you're apologizing for being human?" But Diego's voice carried warmth beneath the professional briskness. "Just shut up and let me do my job."

Judge Hartwell surveyed the bodies scattered across Ellie's yard, tallying the political damage. The other men that had ridden up with her had already begun collecting them to lay out. "Did they say why they were here?"

Ellie shook her head, "They said something about railroad papers and eviction notices. I think they had some sort of forged land deeds saying the railroad owned my property. They said the... They said the sheriff was dead."

"Reports of my death were greatly exaggerated, just for the record," Tom spoke quickly, his words urgent even if his voice was weak. "Don't want the county thinking they don't have to pay me if I'm slightly deceased..."

Diego's voice carried all the humor of a tombstone, "One more joke, just one, and I swear by all that is holy, I will gag you."

Judge Hartwell shook her head. "How many witnesses to this... engagement?"

"Just me and my son," Ellie said, helping Diego guide Tom toward the porch steps. "And the survivors, assuming they're fool enough to talk."

"They won't be," Tom managed, his voice steadier now that his stomach had emptied. "I don't imagine Harlan Carter allows his crew to advertise failures."

Hartwell's eyes sharpened. "Harlan Carter? He's supposed to be incarcerated. A prisoner of the state."

"Not anymore, apparently." Tom leaned heavily against the door frame, his face pale but determined. "Got confirmation by telegram while I was in Everfield Junction. Question is, Judge—what are we planning to do about it?"

"We?" Hartwell asked.

"Yeah. We. I keep trying this 'lone sheriff out in the wilderness' thing and it keeps biting off pieces of me and breaking others. I'm gonna need a bank loan if I rack up any more doctor's bills. So, yeah, what are *we* going to do about it?"

Judge Hartwell took a slow breath and let it out. "I imagine the first step should be to discuss it over breakfast. Would you like me to meet you here at Mrs. Harper's or do you plan on sleeping down at the clinic?"

Ellie spoke quickly. "He's staying here tonight."

Judge Hartwell nodded. "Then I'll be here at eight."

Before Diego and Ellie could get him inside, Tom stopped dead in his tracks. "My horse. I have a horse, now. I left him tied up that way."

Bobby Keene, one of the men who had ridden up with Diego and the judge, called out. "I'll fetch him for you, Sheriff. Don't you worry none."

"Oh, good. Thank you." With that, his strength drained completely and Diego and Ellie ended up carrying him the rest of the way inside. "Never had a horse before."

Ellie sighed, exhaustion tugging at her as she looked around the living room, the broken glass, and the things that had been destroyed by gunfire.

He moaned sadly, "You're getting my muddy boots all over your floor. And you told me not to bleed on anything."

"You let me worry about my floors, Tom." Ellie said, voice soft. "Just close your eyes and rest for a bit, we'll sort you out."

"Would really love some coffee..." he muttered, but was out cold and dead to the world long before anyone could have gotten him some.

Chapter Eighteen

Fever Dreams

The morning sun painted Ellie's kitchen golden, though bullet holes in the windows kept reminding everyone of the previous night's violence. Judge Hartwell arrived promptly at eight, accompanied by a petite woman carrying a woven basket that smelled of cinnamon and coffee.

"Mrs. Harper, thank you for hosting this morning," Hartwell greeted with uncharacteristic warmth. "Mrs. Delgado insisted on bringing breakfast."

Julietta stepped forward with a gentle smile, her dark eyes taking in the damage to Ellie's home without comment. "Judge Hartwell told me what happened. I thought you might need some proper food after such a terrible night."

"That's very kind." Ellie wiped her hands on her apron, suddenly conscious of her disheveled appearance. She'd barely slept, spending most of the night checking on Tom and cleaning up broken glass.

Diego emerged from the guest room, looking as tired as Ellie felt. His shirt was wrinkled, sleeves rolled to his elbows, and dark circles shadowed his eyes. His face brightened immediately upon seeing his wife.

Julietta set down her basket and immediately pulled her husband into her arms. "Ay, *mi amor*—you've worked yourself half to death again."

"Long night," Diego murmured against her shoulder, allowing himself this moment of weakness.

"Then you need proper food." Julietta touched his cheek with gentle fingers. "And coffee. Real coffee, not that swamp water you drink at the clinic."

Diego caught her hand and pressed it to his lips. "The girls?"

"Carmen is watching her sisters. They're fine." She squeezed his fingers. "How is your patient?"

Diego reluctantly pulled away from his wife's embrace, though his hand lingered on her arm.

"Alive, which is more than he deserves after yesterday's performance. Nothing immediately life-threatening, but he's running on fool's luck and bad decisions." Diego hovered nearby as Julietta unwrapped the basket on the kitchen table, releasing the aroma of toasted butter, caramelized sugar, and strong coffee.

Julietta plucked two tins from the basket and went straight to the oven to heat them up properly. "No good breakfast can start without *café con leche*. Just the thing to restore the spirits after a rough night."

Judge Hartwell took a place at the table. "Nothing incapacitating, I hope?"

"Three new bullet grazes. One nicked through his thigh, thankfully missed the artery. Another across his ribs—shallow, but it'll hurt like hell for weeks. Third one barely kissed his shoulder, more of a burn than anything." Diego gratefully accepted a cup of coffee from his wife and paused to sip appreciatively. "The fever worries me more than the wounds."

"Fever?" Julietta asked, passing around the rest of the coffee.

"Started around midnight. Not unexpected, considering what his body's been through. Two days of stress, God knows how little sleep, dehydration, blood loss, then yesterday's excitement." Diego's voice carried the weary patience of a man who'd explained medical conditions to worried families countless times. "His body's fighting infection and exhaustion simultaneously."

Julietta ladled beans onto plates while Ellie sliced the bread. "He'll recover, though?"

"*Sí*, but only if I tie him to that bed for the next week." Diego accepted a plate from his wife. "The man thinks he's made of cast iron and treats himself accordingly."

From the guest room came the sound of movement, followed by a muffled curse. Diego sighed and started toward the door, but Tom's voice stopped him.

"I can hear you talking about me out there..."

"Then you heard the part about staying in bed," Diego called back.

"Close proximity good enough?" Another muffled thump from behind the door.

"No, it's not! Staying *near* the bed is not at all the same as staying *in* the bed. Staying in bed means lying down, horizontally, flat on your back, blankets up to your chin—*Maldita sea*, Thomas!"

"Language, Diego."

"Must really be in trouble, now." Tom leaned heavily against the door frame, wearing only his undershirt and trousers. His face was flushed with fever, and he swayed slightly on his feet. "Father Patrick only called me Thomas when I'd about driven him to take the Lord's name in vain. Morning, folks, Judge Hartwell. And you must be Mrs. Delgado."

Julietta's eyebrows rose as she took in his appearance. "*Dios mío,* you look terrible."

"Face I was born with, unfortunately." Tom managed a weak grin. "Doc's told me I've been monopolizing his time, keeping him away from home. Figure I owe you an apology for that, Mrs. Delgado."

"My husband explained everything—that he had a hopeless gringo who needed his attention more than I did. I can see he wasn't telling me tales." Julietta's smile was warm despite her words. She stepped closer, the back of her hand brushing his cheek as if to test a child's fever. He tried to ignore how his eyes drifted shut, how he leaned into her touch like a half-tamed house cat craving affection.

"Ay, *pobrecito.*" Her tone softened, then sharpened again. "Sit down before you fall down, Sheriff—you're making my husband nervous."

Tom shuffled to the table and lowered himself carefully into a chair. The simple movement left him breathing hard. "Sorry about the lack of proper dress, by the way—my shirt seems to have disappeared."

Ellie shook her head. "Between the bullet holes, the blood stains, and the swamp peat, that shirt isn't worth saving for fabric scraps. You're lucky I was able to wash your trousers."

"You aren't in any better condition than the shirt was, by the way," Diego said pointedly. "Which is why you should be in bed."

"Can't conduct sheriff business from a sickbed." Tom accepted a plate of food from Ellie. "People start thinking you're weak."

Judge Hartwell shook her head. "Sheriff Bracken, you single-handedly fought off several armed men yesterday. I don't think anyone's questioning your stamina."

"Only the people who watched me throw up afterwards," Tom corrected, then winced as he shifted in his chair.

Ellie poured him coffee, noting how his hands trembled slightly as he reached for the cup. Tom took a careful sip, then looked at the food with genuine surprise. "This is incredible, Mrs. Delgado. Thank you."

"*De nada.* Now eat. You're too skinny."

Diego leaned back in his chair, watching Tom struggle with the simple act of eating breakfast. "Judge Hartwell, I need to be clear about something. He's not dying, but he's not fit for duty either. That fever's going to get worse before it gets better."

"How much worse?" Hartwell asked.

"Probably delirious by tonight. Definitely bedridden for at least three days, maybe a week." Diego's tone brooked no argument. "And that's if infection doesn't set in."

"I'm going to feel awful whether I'm being useful or not." Tom lowered his fork. "I may as well be useful. I can work with a fever."

"No." Three voices said it simultaneously.

"Tom," Ellie said gently, "you can barely sit upright."

"I'm sitting upright right now."

"You're listing to port like a damaged ship," Judge Hartwell observed dryly.

Tom glanced down at himself and realized she was right—the table was supporting a lot more of him than he'd originally given it credit for. "Listing to port, but still afloat. I'll take that as a win."

When nobody at the table seemed to agree with him, he sighed and slumped a little more solidly against the table. "Alright, so it's a pathetic state of affairs, but it's what I've got to work with."

"What you've got is doctor's orders to rest." Diego's voice carried the authority of someone accustomed to being obeyed. "And a doctor's wife who's very good at tying knots if you make this difficult."

Julietta smiled sweetly. "Very good knots, Sheriff. My *abuela* taught me."

Tom looked around the table at four determined faces and recognized defeat. "Fine. I'll be good. But if Carter burns down the courthouse while I'm napping, I'm not taking the blame for it."

Judge Hartwell raised her coffee cup in a mock toast. "Deal. Now eat your breakfast before you pass out in it."

It took all his concentration, but he was able to finish roughly half his food before his fork clattered to the plate, his hand trembling too badly to continue. He stared at the offending utensil as if it had personally betrayed him.

Ellie rose and moved behind Tom's chair, pressing the back of her hand to his forehead. The heat radiating from his skin made her frown. "Diego, he's burning up."

"I know." Diego stood as well, his expression grim. "Tom, you need to get back to bed, now."

"In a minute." Tom's words came slower now, each one requiring visible effort. "Need to tell you about Carter first. What I learned."

"It can wait," Ellie said firmly.

"No, it can't." Tom turned in his chair to look at her, his fever-bright eyes struggling to focus. "Ellie, your husband didn't just escape from state custody. He had help. Inside help."

Judge Hartwell leaned forward. "What kind of help?"

"The kind that comes with badges and legal papers." Tom's voice carried a harsh rasp. "Someone in the state government signed his release papers."

The kitchen fell silent except for the distant buzz of insects through the bullet-riddled windows.

"That's impossible," Hartwell said finally. "I would have been notified of any prisoner release."

"Would you?" Tom fixed her with a stare that seemed more lucid than his physical condition suggested. "Or would someone with more authority than a county judge simply make it happen?"

Julietta glanced between her husband and the sheriff. "What does this mean?"

Diego gave her a troubled look. "It means Harlan Carter isn't just an escaped convict causing trouble." He looked at Hartwell. "He's got official protection from someone in Tallahassee or Jacksonville. Someone who wants whatever Detective Morrison was investigating to stay buried."

Tom shook his head slowly, the movement clearly costing him. "Not buried. In their own pocket. Morrison was investigating the smuggling racket that operates out of Tampa. His notebook has names, supply routes, all kinds of information that a big public persona at the head of a smuggling organization wouldn't want having closely scrutinized."

Ellie nodded, only just biting her tongue in time to keep from admitting out loud that Harlan had visited her in person to ask for that notebook specifically, that he'd tried to make her trade it in exchange for Tom's life. She wasn't ready to admit any of those things to anyone yet. Especially not the fact that if Tom had been at Harlan's mercy that night, her refusal to cooperate would have cost him his life.

Tom reached for his coffee with both hands, taking a heavy sip before continuing. "Short story long, if the railroad bigwigs were to get their hands on this notebook, they could use it to blackmail the Tampa interests into backing down."

"Blackmail?" Judge Hartwell leaned forward.

Diego raised his eyebrows, mulling it over. "It makes sense. If this smuggling ring is the only entity with the money and the clout to really stand in the way of the railroad's land grab operation, having a way to force them down... well, it's valuable enough to kill over."

Ellie asked, "I don't understand Harlan's role in this. He worked for Tampa, he ran the smuggling ring through Cypress Run for years before he was sent to the State Penitentiary. If the railroad and the government are connected, why would the government release one of Tampa's biggest assets from prison? Wouldn't they want to keep him locked up?"

Tom blinked at the question, concentrating on the words before speaking slowly. "My guess is that Carter wasn't happy that his boss in Tampa allowed him to sit in prison for so long. Might have been only too happy to use his inside information to burn it all down. Which means Carter isn't just the muscle. He's got his own separate agenda from whoever else is pulling his strings."

"Who?" Ellie asked, though part of her dreaded the answer. "Who would go to that much trouble?"

"Don't know yet." Tom's eyes were beginning to lose focus again. "But whoever it is, they've got power. Enough to turn a convicted outlaw into a free man overnight."

Judge Hartwell shook her head. "I need to send some telegrams. If what you're saying is true, then half the administration could be compromised."

"Judge Hartwell," Tom said softly. "Be careful who you trust with those telegrams. Telegraph operators can be bought—same as anyone else."

Hartwell looked at him, really looked, her hard gaze taking in every weary line, every angle of his posture that hinted at the exhaustion he was holding at bay. She nodded firmly. "Noted. You've done good work, Sheriff Bracken."

Tom nodded slowly, evidently taking that as the permission he needed to stand down. He slumped forward, resting his forehead against the cool table surface. "Sorry about this, folks. Think I just need a moment."

"That's enough," Diego said, rising from his chair. "Back to bed before you fall over."

"I'm fine, just give me a minute."

"Sheriff." Julietta's voice carried the authority of someone accustomed to managing stubborn men. "My husband is a very good doctor, but he becomes unreasonable when patients ignore his orders. For all our sake, please listen to him."

Tom attempted to stand, made it halfway upright, then sat back down hard. "Christ. This is embarrassing."

"No more embarrassing than passing out face-first on your breakfast plate," Ellie observed, moving to his side. "Come on. Let me help."

"I don't need—"

"You're shaking like a newborn colt." Ellie's tone carried no sympathy. "And you're about as steady on your feet."

Tom looked around the table at four expectant faces and sighed. "Fine."

Ellie slipped her arm around Tom's waist as he struggled to his feet. He leaned heavily against her, his skin burning with fever even through his undershirt.

"Easy," she murmured as they made their way slowly toward the guest room. "One step at a time."

They reached the bedroom doorway where Tom paused, swaying slightly.

"This is humiliating," Tom muttered, his voice barely audible.

"This is smart. There's a difference."

Ellie guided him to the bed.

Tom's hand found her wrist, his grip weak but insistent. "Mrs. Harper, about last night—"

"Don't." Her voice was quiet but firm. "Not now. You're too sick to think straight."

"I'm sick, not senile." He met her eyes, his own bright with fever but surprisingly focused. "What happened between us—"

"Was adrenaline and fear and relief that you weren't dead." Ellie kept her tone carefully neutral. "Nothing more."

"Would you look at me, please?"

She did, reluctantly.

"Maybe it *was* relief," he said quietly. "But it wasn't adrenaline. And it sure as hell wasn't fear. Hell, I'm more afraid right this moment of you telling me it didn't mean anything than I ever was of getting shot last night."

Ellie felt the weight of his words settle into the space between them, growing heavier the longer they waited for an answer she couldn't give—not with Judge Hartwell's voice carrying from the kitchen, not with his skin burning under her touch, not with everything still raw and uncertain between them.

"Tom—"

"I know. Wrong time, wrong place, wrong everything." His grip on her wrist loosened, fingers sliding away. "Wouldn't be me if it was convenient."

Heat flooded Ellie's cheeks, and she busied herself straightening his pillow. "You need to rest."

"Undoubtedly."

From the kitchen came the sound of chairs scraping and Judge Hartwell's voice rising. "...need to discuss...federal marshals are expecting...next move..."

"Go," Tom said quietly, still watching Ellie's face. "Sounds like grown-up business out there."

Ellie helped him ease back against the pillows, noting how his breathing hitched with even that small movement. "Try to sleep. The fever will break easier if you rest."

"Ellie."

She paused at the doorway, not turning around.

"It wasn't nothing, Ellie. Whatever else it was, it wasn't nothing."

Her breath caught, but before she could respond, he exhaled deeply and his eyes fluttered closed—sleep had claimed him again.

Ellie stood frozen for a moment, watching his chest rise and fall with the uneven rhythm of illness.

From the kitchen came the murmur of voices, their conversation a distant buzz against the sudden quiet of the bedroom.

She pulled the quilt up to Tom's chin, her fingers brushing his burning forehead. He didn't stir.

"Stubborn fool," she whispered, but her voice carried no real reproach.

In sleep, the lines of pain and exhaustion softened, revealing glimpses of the man beneath the badge—younger somehow, vulnerable in ways his waking swagger never allowed. Her thumb traced along his temple where auburn hair stuck damply to fevered skin.

It took a tremendous effort, but she left him sleeping there and pulled the door closed behind her with careful deliberation, cutting herself off from the temptation of holding his hand and watching him as he slept.

In the kitchen, Judge Hartwell was spreading papers across the table while Diego refilled coffee cups. "How is he?" the judge asked without looking up.

"Asleep already. Stubborn as a mule and twice as ornery," Ellie replied, settling back into her chair. "But he'll live. For now."

"Good. Because we have work to do." Hartwell tapped one of the documents with her finger. "These papers were found on one of the men who attacked your property last night. They confirm what Sheriff Bracken said—that Harlan Carter has been operating freely while we assumed he was safely locked away. Assuming that he was released at the same time this prison transfer occurred, he's been out walking free now for four weeks."

Diego frowned. "Four weeks? That's more than enough time to plan everything we've seen—the warehouse fire, the murders—all coordinated."

"It's more than enough time to plan things we haven't seen, as well." Hartwell's expression was grim.

From the guest room came the sound of restless movement, followed by Tom's voice, muffled but audible: "...need to stop...fire's too hot...son of a bitch..."

Judge Hartwell raised an eyebrow. "Is he talking to someone?"

"Fever dreams," Diego said matter-of-factly. "They'll get worse before they get better."

Ellie stared at the closed bedroom door, remembering the intensity in Tom's fevered eyes when he'd insisted their kiss had meant something to him. The problem was, she was beginning to suspect it meant something to her, too.

——— ★✹★ ———

By two o'clock, the fever had Tom firmly in its grip.

Ellie pressed a damp cloth to his forehead as he mumbled about Chicago aldermen hiding in the cypress trees. His skin burned hot, like an iron stove just after the fire had gone out, and when she tried to get him to drink water, he pushed the cup away with surprising strength.

"The billiard table's crooked," he muttered, eyes closed but restless. "Someone's been moving the rails. Can't make a straight shot when the rails keep shifting."

"Tom, you're safe. You're at my house." Ellie wrung out the cloth in cool water, then placed it across his burning forehead again. "No one's moving anything."

"Have to find Morrison's killer. Can't let them get away with..." His voice trailed off into incoherent mumbling about survey stakes and crooked cops.

Diego had warned her the fever might worsen before it broke. The human body fighting infection and exhaustion simultaneously, he'd explained, sometimes took detours through strange territory. But watching Tom wrestle with phantoms was harder than she'd expected.

"Ellie?" Tom's eyes opened, unfocused but seeking. "That you?"

"I'm right here."

"Good. Can't trust the others. They're all on the pad." His hand found hers, gripping with fevered intensity. "Everyone's got an angle. Even the gators."

She let him hold her hand, feeling the heat radiating from his palm. "What about me? Do I have an angle?"

"You..." He studied her face with the earnest confusion of a man trying to solve a puzzle with half the pieces missing. "You've got freckles. Like stars. Chicago doesn't have stars."

Despite everything, Ellie smiled. "No, I suppose it doesn't."

"Don't let them move the stars, Ellie. Promise me." His grip tightened. "Once they start moving the stars, you can't trust anything."

"I promise."

He seemed satisfied with that answer and drifted back into restless sleep, muttering about piano keys that wouldn't stay in tune and card games where the deck kept changing hands.

Around four, he sat bolt upright, eyes wide with panic.

"Where's my rifle? They took my rifle!" He tried to swing his legs out of bed, but Ellie caught his shoulders.

"Tom, stop. Your rifle's safe. You're safe."

"Can't protect anyone without my rifle. The boys—where are the boys? Simon and Nate, they shouldn't be at the jail. Too dangerous." He fought against her gentle pressure, his injured body moving with the desperate strength that sometimes accompanied high fevers. "Someone's coming for Dooley. They'll hurt the boys."

"The boys are fine. Nate's at school, Simon's at the apothecary. Dooley's with the federal marshals." She spoke slowly, clearly, the way she would to calm a frightened child. "Everyone's safe."

Tom's eyes searched her face, trying to separate reality from fevered imaginings. "You sure?"

"I'm sure."

He slumped back against the pillows, exhausted by the brief struggle. "Feels like I'm losing pieces. Like someone's stealing parts of the picture while I'm not looking."

Ellie smoothed the damp hair from his forehead. "Fever does that. It'll pass."

"What if it doesn't? What if I can't put the pieces back together?" His voice carried a vulnerability she'd never heard before, the fear of a man who relied on his sharp mind suddenly finding it unreliable.

"Then I'll help you find them."

Tom studied her face for a long moment, some of the confusion clearing. "Why would you do that?"

The question was too heavy for the warm afternoon air. Outside, a mockingbird ran through its repertoire of stolen songs.

"Because you and I both need to stop expecting you can do everything alone, Tom. And because I don't want to watch you trying anymore," Ellie said quietly. She swallowed and continued, her voice carrying the weight of a promise she'd broken once already, "Because I told you I'd be in your corner, believing in you. Remember?"

Tom's fevered gaze struggled to focus on her face, fragments of memory surfacing through the haze like debris from a shipwreck. "You said... in my corner. You'd tell Nate to get back on the horse after he fell, but you told me..." His voice cracked with confusion and rising panic. "You said I shouldn't try. You said I would die if I rode a horse before my arm healed, and I rode one anyway." The words tumbled out faster now, fear sharpening his tone. "Oh, Christ... am I going to die? Is that why you're here? Are you watching me die?"

"No." Ellie's voice cut through his fevered panic like a clean blade, sharp enough to slice through the delirium clouding his thoughts. Her hand found his uninjured shoulder, gripping it with steady strength. "You're not going to die from a fever, Tom Bracken. I won't let you."

She pressed the cool cloth more firmly against his forehead, her touch steady and sure. "You rode that horse because you're stubborn as a swamp weed, not because you're dying. The fever's making you confused."

Tom blinked up at her, trying to focus through the haze. "But the horse... I fell off the horse. You said—"

"I said you'd get yourself killed if you rode before your arm healed properly. And you nearly did." Her hazel eyes held his, direct and uncompromising. "But nearly isn't the same as dead. You're too ornery to die from a little fever."

"Little fever?" He managed a weak laugh. "Feels like my brain's been dunked in Cuban rum. Burns really hot when you light it on fire, did you know that? But it's good to drink. Could get real drunk off Cuban rum."

"Well, that would explain why you're making less sense than usual."

The familiar bite in her voice somehow grounded him more than any gentle reassurance could have. Tom's breathing steadied slightly, the panic receding as her calm certainty anchored him to the present moment.

"Stay with me?" The words startled her, raw and unguarded.

Ellie's expression softened, just a fraction. "Where else would I go?"

Outside, the mockingbird had moved on to imitating a cardinal's call, but something in the surrounding silence felt different now—watchful.

"I meant what I said, you know... when you kissed me." His voice was rough with fever and something deeper. "Every word that came out of my mouth, and all the ones that got stuck. I meant every damn one of them."

Ellie's hand stilled against his forehead. "What words got stuck?"

Tom's green eyes, glassy with fever but startlingly direct, found hers in the lamplight. "That you make me want to keep trying." The admission came out quiet, like a confession he'd been carrying too long. "When everything's gone to hell—when the job's impossible and everyone wants me gone and I'm about as useful as a Chicago cop in a Florida swamp—I think about how it'd look in your eyes if I just gave up. And that hurts worse than all the rest put together."

He swallowed hard, his Adam's apple working against the column of his throat. "Disappointing you... Christ, Ellie, I don't like how it feels when I keep disappointing you."

The words were too honest, stripped of his usual wit by fever and exhaustion. Outside, even the mockingbird had fallen silent.

Ellie felt something shift in her chest—not the flutter of attraction she'd been fighting, but something deeper and more dangerous, a door she'd kept bolted shut for three years creaking open despite her better judgment. The raw earnestness in his fevered confession cut through every defense she'd built since Harlan's betrayal.

She'd forgotten what it felt like to matter to someone beyond duty and necessity. That reminder—the crack in her wall—left her feeling more exposed than she'd like.

"Tom..." she began, then stopped, unsure what words could possibly follow such a confession. Anything she could say felt liable to betray the truth she'd been avoiding: she cared about this stubborn, reckless man far more than was safe.

He was watching her, waiting for her to either pull away or step closer to the sinkhole they'd been circling since the night he'd stumbled into her life with an alligator clamped on his arm and Chicago swagger.

"I meant what I didn't say, too," she whispered, her voice barely audible. Her fingers found the edge of his blanket, smoothing it with a tenderness that had nothing to do with nursing and everything to do with needing something to occupy her hands. "But I'm not going to tell you what that is until you're well enough to remember it. Until you're clearheaded enough to know what it means when I say it."

The words felt like a promise and a threat all at once, spoken to a man who might not even hear them past the fever's grip. She could see him fighting to stay present, those green-blue eyes trying to focus on her face as if memorizing it, but exhaustion was already pulling him under like quicksand.

Tom's gaze held hers for another long heartbeat, his lips parting as if he might try to respond, might push through the haze to ask what she meant. But then his eyelids fluttered closed, and he drifted back into the restless, turning sleep that had claimed him on and off since the fever spiked.

Ellie remained perfectly still beside him, watching the rise and fall of his chest, and wondered if he'd remember any of this when the fever finally broke—wondered if she wanted him to, or if some confessions were safer left buried in the shadows between sleep and waking.

Chapter Nineteen

Wounds Left to Fester

The fever dreams came in waves, carrying Tom through a maze of Chicago alleys that bled into Florida swampland without warning. Ellie pressed another cool cloth to his burning forehead, watching his eyes dart beneath closed lids as he thrashed against the sheets and muttered fragments of half-formed thoughts.

"Clayborne... Can't see it... right there on the page but I can't..." His voice was thick with delirium, words slurring together. "Carter stopped him before he found the connection..."

Ellie leaned forward, trying to make sense of his ramblings. But Tom's fevered mind was jumping between memories, weaving threads that might be crucial or might be nothing more than illness talking.

"Ellie? The notebook—where's the notebook?"

"Shh." She pressed the cool cloth to his forehead. "You're safe. The notebook's safe."

"The notebook... it's all there, but I can't..." Tom's hand clutched at the blanket, knuckles white. "Morrison saw it. Why Carter got released. Who signed the papers..."

His breathing grew more labored, and Ellie dabbed at the sweat beading on his temple. The fever had spiked again near midnight, turning him restless and incoherent. She'd been by his side for hours, watching him fight battles that existed only in the fevered landscape of his mind.

"Railroad... courthouse... Edwin runs it all... he's moving the rails." Tom's eyes snapped open suddenly, unfocused but intense. "He's moving the rails to get to me. He wants me dead, Ellie... He won't stop haunting me till I'm dead."

"Shh." Ellie's voice was gentle but firm. "You're safe. You're here with me."

But Tom wasn't hearing her. He was trapped somewhere between a Chicago card game and a Florida swamp, chasing connections that danced just beyond his grasp.

"Need to find the link. Clayborne to the railroad to Carter's release. All connected. Has to be." His voice cracked with frustration. "It's right there in the notebook, but I can't see it. Can't make the pieces…"

He trailed off, his breathing evening out as the fever momentarily released its grip. Ellie watched his face relax slightly, hoping this meant the worst was passing. She'd been through fever vigils before—with Nate when he was younger, with patients at the clinic—but never had she felt so invested in the outcome. Never had someone's delirium revealed fragments of a puzzle that might determine whether they lived or died.

"His son," Tom whispered, so quiet she almost missed it. "Christ, his son. That's why… that's why everything moved… it's all my fault… everything's all my fault." His voice was plaintive, like a lost child's.

"Hush, nothing's your fault. It's just the fever talking."

The fever took him again, pulling him back under its influence like a gator in a death roll. He muttered about billiard tables and train schedules, about Morrison's neat handwriting and blood on courthouse steps. Ellie held vigil through it all, changing cool cloths and monitoring his breathing, praying silently that his strength would outlast the illness.

Near dawn, his fever finally crested. The wild muttering gave way to deep, exhausted breathing, and when Ellie touched his forehead, she found cool skin instead of burning heat. She sagged back in her chair, allowing herself a moment of relief.

She meant to stay awake, to keep watching over him, but the chair was comfortable and the worst danger had passed. Her eyelids grew heavy as the first pale light of morning crept through the window. Just for a moment, she told herself. Just until she was sure he was stable. Ellie pulled a quilt around her shoulders and let her eyes drift closed, one hand resting protectively on Tom's arm.

She woke to silence—the particular kind of quiet that meant something had changed. Pale morning light filtered through the window, and Tom lay still beside her, his breathing steady and natural for the first time in hours. The fever had broken completely, leaving him in a deep, healing sleep.

But that wasn't what had woken her. Some instinct, honed by three years of single motherhood in frontier Florida, had pulled her from sleep with the certainty that something was wrong. She sat perfectly still, listening for whatever had triggered the alarm in her sleeping mind.

Tom was still sleeping, his breathing steady and natural. Someone had tucked a small brown stuffed bear under his arm—Nate's old companion that usually lived on the boy's shelf. Her son must have crept in while she dozed, worried enough about the sheriff to share his most prized possession.

The sight of that ratty bear nestled against Tom's side made something fierce and protective flare in her chest. This stubborn, reckless man had nearly died protecting her family, and now her eight-year-old son was trying to return the favor with the only comfort he had to offer.

She rose quietly, working the kinks out of her spine. Tom didn't stir, lost in the deep sleep of recovery. But his fevered words echoed in her mind: the notebook's the key. Morrison figured it out before they killed him.

While Tom possessed Morrison's notebook, people would keep trying to kill him. And by extension, they'd keep threatening anyone close to him.

Including Nate.

Injured and sick as he was, Tom wouldn't be able to defend himself. And Ellie couldn't keep all of them safe by herself, not if Harlan's men came for them again.

Her thoughts circled back around and around: Tom and Nate were both in danger while Tom had that notebook and Tom couldn't keep them safe while he was sick.

Ellie rose quietly from her chair, moving with the practiced silence of a mother accustomed to not waking sleeping children. She'd made her decision somewhere in the space between Tom's delirium and her own exhausted slumber.

The notebook had to go.

Not destroyed—the evidence it contained might be the only thing that could bring justice for Morrison's death and stop Harlan's operation—but removed from her home, from her son's vicinity, from Tom's protective but ultimately vulnerable care.

She found Tom's vest in the corner where Diego had set his belongings. It didn't take long to locate Morrison's leather-bound notebook wrapped in oil cloth and tucked into an inside pocket. The pages were filled with neat handwriting documenting payments, dates, and coded references that Tom's fevered mind had been trying to decipher. Whatever connections there were between Harlan's release, the railroad corruption, and Morrison's murder—it was all here, waiting for someone with the authority and resources to act on it.

Ellie slipped the notebook into her coat pocket and returned to Tom's bedside. He looked younger in sleep, the lines of pain and exhaustion smoothed from his face. The bear tucked against his arm made him seem almost boyish, despite the stubble and the bandages.

"I'll be back soon," she whispered, leaning down to press a gentle kiss to his forehead. His skin was cool and dry, the fever truly gone.

Tom stirred slightly at her touch, his eyes fluttering open just enough to register her presence without fully waking.

"Ellie?" His voice was hoarse but lucid.

"Sleep," she murmured. "You're going to be fine."

He made a sound that might have been acknowledgement, already drifting back toward healing rest. Ellie waited until his breathing deepened again, then slipped quietly from the room and out of the house, Morrison's notebook a weight in her pocket and a dangerous certainty in her heart.

The burned skeleton of the Rawling-Thom warehouse still smoldered in patches, sending wisps of choking smoke across the docks. Ellie picked her way through the debris field, her boots crunching on charred wood and broken glass. Stevedores labored around the wreckage, river men accustomed to lifting freight now picking through the debris and salvaging what they could from the explosion that had nearly killed Tom and Diego five days prior.

"Looking for someone?" A man in a soot-stained shirt blocked her path.

"The person in charge."

He studied her face with careful attention, a man paid to remember troublemakers, then grunted, "Wait here."

Ellie stood among the ash and twisted metal, breathing the acrid smell of burned wood and spilled rum. The notebook seemed to pulse against her ribs with each heartbeat. Around her, men loaded salvaged goods onto wagons, their voices low and cautious.

"Mrs. Carter." The voice came from behind her, smooth as aged whiskey.

She turned to find a lean man in an expensive suit that somehow remained crisp despite the destruction surrounding them. His dark eyes reminded her uncomfortably of a shark; this was a man accustomed to solving problems permanently.

"Harper," she corrected. "It's Harper now."

"Of course. My apologies." Mercer's smile never reached his eyes. "Though given recent events, I find myself curious about your family loyalties."

"I didn't come here to discuss my marriage."

"No?" He gestured toward the ruins. "Your husband torched my warehouse not long ago. Put three of my men in the ground and cost me a cargo shipment worth more than this entire town. My associates in Tampa are... displeased."

Ellie's hand tightened around the notebook through her coat. "Harlan's not my concern anymore."

"Yet, here you are." Mercer stepped closer, and she caught the scent of expensive cologne failing to mask the smell of smoke and violence that clung to him. "The ex-wife of the man who tried to have me killed, standing in the ashes of my livelihood. You'll forgive me if I question the coincidence."

"I have something you want."

"Do you?" he asked with lazy interest, a cat toying with wounded prey. "Because at the moment, Mrs. Harper, I'm having difficulty thinking of a good reason why I shouldn't use your body to send a message back to Mr. Carter. Maybe do a few choice things to it before I do. A reminder of what happens when people interfere with my business arrangements."

The dock workers had stopped their salvage efforts, though they pretended to stay busy. Ellie felt their attention like a physical weight, recognized the stillness that preceded violence. Her mouth went dry, but she forced her voice steady.

"Because what I have will solve your Tampa problem."

Mercer's expression didn't change, the pleasant mask not drifting an inch, but something shifted in his posture. "Explain."

"Detective Morrison's notebook." His eyes flickered at the name and Ellie stood a little taller. "The one Carter's people killed him for. The one that documents every payment, every route, every contact in your operation. Including the names of the people who helped Harlan escape prison."

"An interesting artifact, if true."

"The railroad wants it to blackmail your Tampa connections. Harlan wants it to protect his own operation. But you?" Ellie pulled the leather-bound book from her coat, holding it where he could see it. "You want it destroyed before it destroys you."

Mercer stared at the notebook, and for the first time, his composed mask slipped enough to reveal the dangerous man beneath, the one that matched his eyes. "What do you want for it?"

"My family left alone. Harlan's men away from my property. And safe passage out of your..." She didn't know what Tom would call it. "...out of your place of business here."

Mercer chuckled dryly at her stumble, then asked "That's all?" Suspicion colored his voice. "No money? No threats? No demands for revenge?"

"I want my son to grow up without looking over his shoulder." Ellie met his gaze directly. "Harlan made his choices. I'm making mine."

The silence stretched between them, broken only by the lap of water against the dock and the distant cry of gulls. Mercer studied her face as if reading a contract written in blood.

"You realize," he said finally, "that once I have that notebook, nothing stops me from killing you anyway."

"Except good business sense. You need this problem to go away quietly, not turn into a bigger mess. And you still need to deal with Harlan, whether I'm dead or not." Ellie's voice remained steady despite the fear crawling up her spine. "And because Tom thought there was something about you or your place in your organization that was worthy of respect. If you were really just a cold-blooded killer, I don't think he would have bothered to come talk to you the other day."

"Tom, is it?" Mercer's smile returned, sharper this time. "You're either very brave or very stupid, Mrs. Harper."

"I'm a mother protecting her child." She held the notebook steady between them. "Which makes me the most dangerous thing in this swamp."

"Is that all?" Mercer tilted his head and laughed, looking over at his burned warehouse. "He doesn't know you have this, does he? Bracken, I mean. He certainly doesn't know you're handing it over to me."

Ellie was quiet for a moment before admitting softly, "No."

"I doubt he's going to thank you when he finds out."

"I think I'd rather he be alive and angry than dead and clutching to his principles."

When Mercer finally looked back at her, something like respect flickered behind his smile. "And if I do take this notebook off your hands. What exactly do you expect of me? I'd like to know the exact terms before I agree to them."

"I just want my family safe."

"Awfully vague wording, Mrs. Harper."

Ellie met his gaze until the corners of his smile began to widen in amusement, the first truly genuine expression she'd seen from him.

"How you make sure of it is your concern," she said, finally. "Just see that it's done."

Mercer studied her for a long moment, head tilted as if testing the weight of her conscience. Then he reached out and took the notebook from her hand, slow and deliberate, like accepting an oath.

"And Sheriff Bracken?"

"Without that book, he's not your problem," she said. "He stays out of this."

Mercer's brows lifted, a predator's smile touching his mouth. "You sound certain. Are you so sure *he's* not a threat to your family too?"

"Sheriff Bracken doesn't belong in this arrangement," she said evenly. "I'd like him kept clear of it—if you please."

"Very well." The charm was back, his amusement forefront. "Always a pleasure to bargain with a lady who knows her boundaries." He slipped the book inside his coat. "I'll see to your... security."

"I don't want to hear about it," she said. And she turned before he could say anything more, before her resolve could crack, or her fear betray her.

The breeze off the river carried smoke and salt, and the smell followed her up the dock no matter how fast she walked. Each step away felt heavier, as if the river itself meant to drag her back and ask what she'd just agreed to.

By the time she reached the road, the sound of men's voices rose again behind her—low, purposeful, sealing a bargain she didn't want to hear.

She kept walking.

She told herself her boy would sleep sound tonight, and that was all that mattered.

But the ache in her stomach said someone else wouldn't.

The rain had started as a whisper against the leaves, but by the time Ellie reached her front porch, it drummed against the tin roof like bullets. Water streamed from her hair and pooled at her feet as she pushed through the door, shivering despite the humid warmth.

"Ellie?"

She startled, hand flying to her chest. Diego sat at her kitchen table, a steaming cup of coffee before him and concern etched across his weathered features.

"Diego. I—" She pushed wet strands from her face, suddenly aware of how she must look—soaked through, pale, with guilt written across her face like ink bleeding in rain.

"*Dios mío,* Ellie. You look like you swam home." He rose, already reaching for a dish towel.

"What are you doing here?" The words came out sharper than she intended. "Is Tom worse? Did something happen?"

"No, no. He's still sleeping peacefully. Fever's completely broken." Diego handed her the towel, studying her face with the same careful attention he gave patients. "Where were you? I wouldn't send a dog out in this weather."

Heat crept up her neck despite the chill. The weight of the notebook—now gone, handed over to a man who smiled like a shark—pressed against her memory. Ellie's mind raced through possible explanations—visiting a friend, checking the schoolhouse, running errands—but each felt flimsy as wet paper.

"Just... errands." She turned away, busying herself with hanging her soaked shawl on a peg. "Nothing that couldn't wait, as it turns out."

"An errand." Diego's tone suggested he wasn't buying it. "In a thunderstorm."

"You said you had news?" She changed the subject with the determination of a woman steering a conversation away from dangerous waters.

Diego hesitated, clearly wanting to press further, but finally gestured toward a stack of newspapers on the table. "I didn't say anything of the sort, but actually, yes—I do have news. Do you remember the day Tom arrived? When Judge Hartwell made those comments about his background? All those hints about his complications in Chicago?"

"Hard to forget." Ellie poured herself coffee with hands that trembled slightly. "She made it sound like he was evicted from the whole state of Illinois."

Diego reached into his medical bag and withdrew a bundle wrapped in brown paper. "I thought it prudent at the time to send away for some newspapers. Find out exactly what we were getting into with our new law enforcement."

"Diego—"

"They only arrived today." He unwrapped the bundle, revealing several folded newspapers, their headlines stark in black ink. "I thought you might help me go through them. Two pairs of eyes, you know."

Diego spread the newspapers across the table—the *Chicago Daily Tribune*, the *Inter Ocean*, the *Chicago Herald*. Their datelines stretched over several weeks, but the headlines told the same grim story: **POLICE DETECTIVE CLAIMS SELF-DEFENSE IN CARD GAME GONE WRONG.** Another: **SENATOR CLAYBORNE DEMANDS JUSTICE.**

Ellie's stomach clenched. After what she'd just done—handing over evidence that could protect Tom to a man who might well want him dead—the last thing she wanted was to learn more about the dangers already following him.

"Diego, I'm not sure I want to—"

"Whatever happened in Chicago was serious enough to get him exiled here." Diego spread the papers across her kitchen table like evidence at a trial. "Whatever's happening now—with the railroad, Harlan, all of it—it's serious too."

Diego looked up at her, his physician's eyes missing nothing. "It could be a coincidence, but two serious things happening at almost exactly the same time?

In this county? In *our* town? Don't you think we deserve to know what we're dealing with? Especially now, with everything that's happened?"

Rain hammered against the windows. Ellie thought of Morrison's notebook, now in Mercer's hands. Of the bargain she'd struck. Of all the secrets that seemed to multiply like kudzu vines. And here they were casually talking about raking all of Tom's secrets into the daylight without his permission. The thought made her sick.

"I don't want to know," she said quietly, but it wasn't the knowing that was the problem; it was the guilt. It was the thought of digging into his past without his knowledge, as if betraying that one little piece of trust was too much to add to the deeper, more personal betrayal she had already committed.

"Ellie, if Tom's in danger because of something that happened in Chicago—"

"Then maybe it's not our business." The words tasted as bitter as burnt coffee. "Maybe if it was something we needed to know, he'd have told us about it already."

Diego studied her with those dark, searching eyes that missed nothing. "This isn't like you. You're the one who always wants to know exactly what we're dealing with. Remember when that fever broke out two summers ago? You read every medical journal I had until you understood the symptoms better than I did."

The storm lashed at the windows with renewed force. Somewhere in the back room, Tom slept peacefully, unaware that his past was spread across her kitchen table in black and white headlines—and that his future might have just been bargained away by the woman who claimed to care about him.

The silence stretched between them, broken only by thunder rolling across the swamp. Diego folded the newspapers slowly, his movements deliberate.

"You know," he said finally, "in my experience, secrets have a way of surfacing whether we want them to stay buried or not. Like bodies in the creek."

Outside, lightning split the sky, illuminating the rain-soaked world in stark, unforgiving detail.

Ellie stared at the folded newspapers, water still dripping from her hair onto the kitchen floor. Something nagged at the edge of her memory—fragments of Tom's fevered rambling from the night before, half-coherent mutters about Chicago and someone named...

"Wait." She looked up at Diego. "Tom mentioned that name during his fever. Clayborne. He kept saying something about Edwin wanting him dead."

Diego's eyebrows rose. "Edwin Clayborne? That would be the senator mentioned here." He unfolded one of the papers, scanning the headlines. "Senator Edwin Clayborne's son was the one who died in the saloon shooting."

"What did the article say about Tom's investigation?"

Diego unfolded the *Chicago Tribune* dated six weeks prior, scanning the headlines until he found the right article. "Here. '*Police Detective Dismissed After Controversial Investigation.*'" He cleared his throat and began reading aloud.

"'*Police Lieutenant Thomas Bracken, formerly of the Detective Division at the 12th Precinct, was quietly dismissed from the Chicago Police Department following an incident involving Jeffrey Clayborne, son of United States Senator Edwin Clayborne. The younger Clayborne was shot and killed during what witnesses describe as a card game dispute at McMurphy's Saloon on Halsted Street.*'"

Ellie leaned forward, her hands clasped tight around her coffee cup.

"'*According to police reports, Detective Bracken claimed self-defense after Clayborne drew his weapon first during an argument over the game. However, sources close to the investigation suggest Detective Bracken had been pursuing an unauthorized investigation into a series of unsolved murders involving local immigrant children, despite direct orders from his superiors to cease the inquiry.*'"

"Children?" Ellie's voice barely rose above a whisper.

Diego continued reading. "'*The investigation was officially closed mere days before the saloon incident, with Police Chief Killigan citing insufficient evidence. Detective Bracken's continued interest in the matter allegedly led to mounting tensions with the Clayborne family, who wielded considerable political influence in the district.*'"

Thunder rumbled overhead, closer now. Ellie felt something cold settling in her stomach as the pieces began forming a picture she didn't want to see.

"'*While no charges were filed against Detective Bracken due to multiple witness accounts supporting his claim of self-defense, Senator Clayborne has publicly stated that justice must be served, but has agreed to forgo prosecution in exchange for Detective Bracken's dismissal from the police force. City officials declined to comment on rumors that Detective Bracken had questioned Jeffrey Clayborne regarding the unsolved murders before the fatal confrontation.*'"

Diego set the paper down, his dark eyes troubled. "Ellie, if Tom was investigating child murders and the senator's son was involved—"

"Then Tom didn't just kill a man in self-defense." Ellie's words came out steady despite the tremor in her hands. "He killed a child murderer."

Diego nodded, drumming his fingers on his coffee cup. "If he had evidence connecting Jeffrey Clayborne to crimes against children, a public trial against Tom would have exposed that. The senator may have decided protecting his son's reputation was more important than seeking justice for his death. That'd explain the sudden change of heart in seeking his dismissal from the force instead of a murder trial."

"Diego," Ellie said quietly, "what if Tom came to Florida not just because Chicago needed him gone, but because someone wanted him somewhere they could control him? Someone with enough political reach to destroy Tom's career and send him to the most godforsaken assignment in the country?"

"Where he'd be vulnerable. Isolated. Easy to eliminate if needed."

The coffee had gone sour on her tongue. "Edwin Clayborne didn't just want Tom gone from Chicago. He wanted him somewhere he could be dealt with permanently. Tom walked into a trap the moment he stepped off that train." Ellie's hands shook as she folded the newspaper. "And everyone he's met since—Judge Hartwell, the railroad men, even Harlan's people—they could all be part of it."

A soft sound from the back room made them both freeze. Tom's voice, thick with sleep but coherent: "Ellie? Everything all right out there?"

She startled, nearly spilling her coffee, then called, "Fine, Tom. Just Diego checking on you. Go back to sleep." She looked at Diego, who was already folding the newspapers back up and tucking them into his medical bag. "What do we tell him?"

"Nothing. Not yet." Diego's voice carried the authority of a man used to making life-and-death decisions. "He's still recovering. And besides—"

A floorboard creaked.

Ellie turned. Tom stood in the doorway, one hand braced against the frame for balance, the other resting against his ribs. The lamplight caught on the hollows under his eyes, shadows deepened by the fever that had only just released its hold.

For a moment no one spoke. The rain filled the silence, hard and steady against the roof. Then his gaze dropped to the table—the open newspapers still creased between Diego's fingers, Ellie's pale face caught mid-guilt.

"You were reading about me?" His voice was hoarse, still raw from the fever, but clear enough to cut through the storm.

Ellie's breath caught. The folded edge of one headline—**SENATOR'S SON DIES IN SALOON SHOOTING**—stared up at her like an accusation.

"Tom," she started, too quickly, "you shouldn't—"

"Don't stop on my account. Just came out to get a glass of water." He sounded tired, the humor thin as a blade. His eyes flicked between them, weighing more than she wanted him to see.

Ellie hurried to get a clean cup and fill it from the pitcher. She handed it to him and he took it without meeting her eyes.

"Thanks."

"Tom—"

He shook his head, cutting her off. "Anything interesting in that rag?"

"Nothing to concern you right now." Diego stepped forward, his physician-calm masking his unease. "You need rest. We'll talk when you're steadier on your feet."

But Tom only looked at Ellie—not angry yet, not even suspicious, just *measuring*. A lawman's instinct searching the room for what wasn't being said.

Thunder rolled low across the swamp, rumbling long after the words had died. After a moment he nodded once, slow. "Right. When I'm steadier."

He finished the water and set the cup on the table, then turned back toward the hallway, his footing uncertain but his silence sharpened to a point. Diego exhaled. Ellie stayed frozen, staring at the damp floorboards where his bare footprints faded away in the lamplight.

Outside, the rain eased to a whisper again, and the sound of it was worse than the thunder—too soft, too knowing.

CHAPTER TWENTY

Out in the Open

Tom woke to the peculiar stillness that follows illness—his mind trundling along the path back to clarity, his body feeling like it had been dragged behind a wagon through twenty miles of swamp. Which, he reflected grimly, wasn't far from the truth.

He tested his range of motion with the methodical patience of a man who'd learned the hard way that wishful thinking didn't heal bullet wounds. His left shoulder screamed when he rolled it, his ribs felt like someone had used them for billiard practice, and his left arm—the one the gator had introduced itself to—throbbed with a dull, persistent ache. But nothing was broken. Nothing was bleeding fresh. He'd live to disappoint people another day.

Sitting up slowly, he took inventory of his situation with the same dispassionate attention he'd once given crime scenes. No coat—probably ruined anyway. No shirt—likely torn to shreds. His vest was folded neat on the chair beside the bed, his gun harness hanging from the bedpost like a leather scarecrow. His Lightning leaned against the corner, and both Colts rested in their holsters, oil-dark and patient. He wasn't certain where the bear had come from, but it seemed important. He squeezed it close briefly before setting it carefully aside.

The room smelled of willow bark and carbolic soap, with an undertone of something sweeter—cornbread, maybe, or honey. Ellie's touch, making even a sickroom feel like something more than a place to wait for death.

He reached for his vest, fingers finding the inside pocket by habit. The small collection of dollar bills was still safety-pinned to the lining—not much, but enough to keep him in meals and ammunition for a week or two. Old Chicago instincts died hard; never keep all your money in one place, and never trust anyone who knew where you kept it.

But the notebook was gone.

Tom's hand went still against the empty pocket. Detective Morrison's notebook—the one that had gotten the man killed and made Tom himself a target for every two-bit gunslinger between here and Tampa. The notebook that connected Harlan Carter to a land grab scheme as well as a smuggling operation worth more than most men saw in a lifetime. The notebook that had shown the tenuous connection between everything going on here in Cypress Run to a powerful man that wanted Tom dead.

Gone.

He checked the other pockets methodically, though he already knew what he'd find. Nothing. Someone had lifted it clean while he'd been burning with fever, talking out of his head about aldermen and billiard tables and God knew what else.

The hurt that settled in his chest had nothing to do with bullet grazes or gator bites. Someone in this house—someone who'd nursed him through the worst of it, who'd sat beside his bed and held cool cloths to his forehead—had robbed him while he was helpless.

But he wasn't going to jump to conclusions. He was going to gather facts and act accordingly, same as he would with any other crime. The evidence was clear enough: the notebook had been in his vest before the fever had made him incoherent. Now it wasn't. Either Ellie had taken it, or Diego had, or someone else had been in this room while he was unconscious.

The smart money was on Ellie. She'd known about her husband's connection to the smuggling ring. She'd heard him talk enough about Morrison's notes to understand what they meant. And she'd made it clear that her son's safety came before anything else—including justice for a dead Pinkerton detective.

Tom couldn't even say he blamed her for it. He just wished it didn't feel like he'd swallowed broken glass that got stuck behind his rib cage.

Tom stood, stretching slowly, careful of the new scrapes. Part of him wanted to pull his boots on and walk back to town, to lick his wounds in the relative privacy of his jail cell. But the rational part of him knew that walking a mile into town mere hours after breaking a fever while wearing nothing but an undershirt and a muddy vest would be a peculiar choice, all things considered.

He could hear them through the wall. From the kitchen came the faint clink of crockery and the low murmur of voices. Ellie's tone—steady, domestic, careful. Diego's deeper reply, impossible to catch through the thin wall.

They were talking about something. The rhythm wasn't casual. For a moment, Tom wanted nothing more than to lay back in bed, to close his eyes and ignore the world. Maybe if he was lucky, the fever would return and he could just detach himself from reality for a bit.

Maybe he could tell the good doctor the pain was too much and beg for some laudanum. A bottle of whiskey. Anything to make the sick feeling under his ribs just stop for a few minutes. Christ, he hadn't known a man's *heart* could feel nauseous. He wished he still didn't.

But putting off talking to people wasn't going to make things easier. He took a deep breath and pushed open the door, slipping silently into the front room of Ellie's house.

He crossed the hall slow enough that the floor didn't creak. The smell met him first—coffee and woodsmoke—and underneath it, rain still steaming off the clay around the porch. He stopped just short of the doorway.

They were at the table, hands wrapped around mugs. Diego looked like he hadn't slept; Ellie looked like she'd been trying not to. Her hair was half-dried and frizzed from the humidity, the lamplight catching in damp strands at her temples. There were no newspapers on the table now. Too clear, too tidy.

Cleaned up, he thought. Fast.

He let the moment draw tight before saying, "Smells peaceful out here."

Ellie jumped. Diego didn't.

"You shouldn't be moving around," she said, her tone too light.

"Seems I shouldn't be doing a lot of things lately." He reached for a cup, poured the coffee slow and careful. "Feels like I slept through most of the storm."

"You needed the rest." Diego's voice was even, but his gaze tracked every motion.

Tom nodded, took a sip—lukewarm, bitter, still mana to an addict—then drained half of it before refilling it and sitting down at the table. "Appreciate the vigilance. House in one piece, nobody shot, all our paperwork where it *ought* to be. Good state of affairs to wake up to."

Ellie froze for the smallest breath. That was enough.

Tom didn't press. Not yet.

He twisted the coffee cup in his hands. "I don't suppose anyone might be feeling charitable, willing to run by my office for me? I seem to be missing some things."

Ellie flinched and Tom closed his eyes, wishing he hadn't seen it.

"Oh?" she asked.

"A shirt, for one thing. I couldn't help but notice mine didn't survive the night. I imagine I'd get an awful lot of looks if I tried to stroll through town like this. Maybe not from you and Judge Hartwell, seeing as you two have made a habit of seeing me at my worst. But poor Mrs. Mills is liable to have a conniption."

The humor came easily, but Tom knew it didn't reach his eyes. Chatter. Deflect. Hide beneath a suit of armor pieced together from words. Easy.

Diego set his coffee cup down with deliberate care. "I'll get you a shirt."

"Appreciate it, Doc. They're in the filing cabinet. Under 'S' for shirt." Tom's voice carried the same forced lightness Ellie recognized from their first meeting—when he'd tried to maintain his composure while bleeding all over Diego's examination table. "Maybe you could grab my gun cleaning kit while you're at it? Swamp water's just as hard on gun barrels as it is on gunshot wounds, I imagine."

"Tom." Diego's tone carried the patience of three children's worth of experience fighting against the unreasonable. "We need to talk."

"Do we?" Tom leaned back in his chair, and Ellie caught the careful way he held himself—ready to bolt if needed. "Because it feels like we already covered the important bits. I'm alive, the fever broke, and I'm standing upright against medical advice. Seems like a successful night's work to me."

Ellie watched the two men size each other up across her kitchen table. Diego's expression held the same studied neutrality he wore when delivering bad news to families. Tom's smile had sharpened to something that would cut glass.

"There were newspapers," Diego said finally.

"Were there?" Tom's fingers drummed against the side of his coffee cup. "You know it's funny, but now that you mention it, I don't think I'm feeling entirely well just yet. Think I'm gonna go lie back down and wait to feel *steadier*."

He stood and turned his back on the kitchen.

Diego couldn't help but see the stiffness in Tom's shoulders as he turned away—a tell far too controlled and deliberate to be caused by physical pain—and something in the gravity of that movement made him speak before he could think better of it.

"Tom. Wait."

The sheriff paused in the doorway but didn't turn around.

"I was wrong to brush you off when you caught us reading those papers." Diego set his coffee cup down with more force than necessary. "You deserved better than that. We both know you saw right through us, and I should have owned up to it instead of treating you like you were still half-delirious from fever."

Tom's head tilted slightly, like he was listening to something Diego couldn't hear. The silence stretched long enough for Diego to have earned his entire medical degree twice over again. And Diego let it continue because it wasn't his silence to break.

"Appreciate that, Doc," Tom said finally.

"Do you?" Diego leaned forward. "Because you're standing there like a man ready to bolt, and I don't blame you for it. But I wish you would tell me you're angry, so I can start making amends."

Tom finally turned, his expression unreadable. "Doc. You pulled a gator tooth out of me, stitched me up more times than I can count, sat up half the night making sure I didn't die of fever, and your wife brought me breakfast. Far as I'm concerned, you've earned the right to read whatever newspapers you damn well please."

"Even when they're about you?"

"Especially then." Tom moved back into the kitchen, settling gingerly into the chair across from Diego. "Most of what gets printed about me tends to be more fiction than fact anyway, so I'm not sure what you're hoping to learn."

Ellie remained quiet, her hands wrapped around her coffee mug like it was the only solid thing in the world. Diego noticed the way she avoided looking directly at either of them.

"Tom, what really happened in Chicago?"

The sheriff's face went carefully blank. "I'm contractually obligated to never speak about what happened in Chicago."

The phrase came out smooth as silk, practiced as a prayer. Diego recognized the tone—the same one Tom had used with Judge Hartwell the night the Pinkerton was murdered. Professional deflection, polished to a mirror shine.

Diego studied the younger man's face, noting the tension around his eyes, the way his fingers drummed once against the table before going still. "Contractual obligation," Diego said slowly. "That's lawyer talk."

"Sometimes lawyer talk is the only kind that keeps you breathing. But you know me. I don't try to hide who I am, not really. And the two of you are the closest thing I've had to friends since..."

Tom sighed, shaking his head, his voice carrying a note of something that might have bordered on hope or prayer. "You *know* me, Doc. And you're a smart man. I'm sure you can follow the chess pieces across the board and see how the game played out. Whatever you're thinking happened is probably closer to the truth than a lot of other people bother to get."

Diego absorbed this, thinking of the newspaper headlines they'd read: "Senator's Son Dies in Saloon Shooting." Tom investigating child murders. A shooting ruled self-defense that somehow ended with him being shipped off to the furthest corner of the Florida frontier.

But he also thought of Tom saving a man from a beating by challenging an angry cowhand to a game of pool. Of him subduing a violent man twice his size despite a crippling injury, then restraining him with shoelaces to haul him in alive.

He thought of Tom announcing his intention to visit the leader of a smuggling ring because it was the *polite* thing to do—and standing on the dock ready to walk into danger alone because he wouldn't ask anyone else to risk it.

All were moments when drawing his Colt might've been simpler. Yet the gun had stayed in its holster.

He thought, too, of Tom sneaking a confessed murderer out of town in the dead of night because it was the only way to keep the man alive long enough to stand trial. Because it was *right*.

Something settled in Diego's chest as he watched the sheriff's face—not relief exactly, but recognition. That careful posture, the practiced deflection, the hint of something raw beneath the polish.

Diego nodded once. "I think that what happened in Chicago... is that you did the right thing—even though it was dangerous—and it cost you more than most men would be willing to pay."

Tom exhaled a breath Diego hadn't realized he'd been holding—the relief now obvious when the tension hadn't been, one more piece of evidence that this was a man who'd learned to carry weight without letting it show.

Diego continued, quietly, "A guilty man who wasn't going to face justice. You provoked him—knowing how he'd react, knowing exactly what would happen."

"Contractually obligated to neither confirm or deny whether the man was guilty or not, but you're free to assume whatever you wish to."

There it all was, laid out in that kitchen neat as a picture. Diego understood now why a born-and-bred city detective had been shipped to the furthest corner of civilization. And he understood why Judge Hartwell had been warned—or instructed even—to treat him like a loaded gun that might go off at any moment: a senator's grief didn't just magically heal itself; it festered, growing like a cancer until it destroyed what it wanted.

"I'm guessing your continued employment in law enforcement combined with your relocation outside of Illinois were both a part of some sort of com promise... Hence the contractual obligation to keep quiet," Diego observed.

"Hence a lot of things." Tom's fingers resumed their slow drum against the table. He tried to smile, but it failed halfway. "Legally, what I did was self-defense. I went to confession after—tried to square it upstairs—but turns out *premeditated* self-defense isn't a very good excuse; Father told me it doesn't count when you schedule the appointment."

He gave a small shrug. "And I can't make myself be sorry for it."

Diego went still—hands paused over his coffee, breath held. The meaning of those words stretched between them: *not sorry* meant *not forgiven*. A Catholic didn't need doctrine to hear the tolling of that bell.

"Oh, Tom…" he murmured, half sorrow, half resignation.

"What happened in Chicago, and how it happened," Tom said, voice steady as a surgeon's hand, "that's not nearly as important as *why* it happened—or what came after."

Diego noticed Tom's fingers had gone still again: whatever was coming next mattered.

"I get to sleep a little easier knowing a handful of families got some sort of closure." Tom's gaze drifted toward the window, where morning light filtered through Spanish moss. "And an untold number of families will never have to go through that pain."

The words carried weight—not the theatrical gravity he usually wrapped around his stories, but a quieter kind Diego recognized: the satisfaction of cutting out something rotten, even when the surgery left scars.

"That's worth something," Diego said.

"Worth quite a bit, actually." Tom's mouth quirked upward, but the humor never reached his eyes. "In exchange, I just have to live with Senator Clayborne wanting his own version of justice. Small enough price to pay, when you do the math."

"But that's not the only price you paid."

Tom met Diego's eyes, throat tight, and shook his head.

Ellie shifted in her chair, hands tightening around her coffee mug. She'd been too quiet, letting the two men dance around truths while she sat frozen at her own table.

"Tom," Diego said carefully, "how much danger are you in?"

"Aside from being damned to hell?" The sheriff's smile finally reached his eyes, though it offered no comfort.

Diego's mouth twitched—not quite amusement, not quite pity. "That's not the kind of danger I can treat, Sheriff."

"In that case, more than I'm comfortable with, but less than I probably should be, all things considered." The humor drained away as quickly as it came, leaving the brittle half-smile that seemed to survive on habit alone. "Jokes aside, I can't really tell you how *much* danger I'm in, Doc. A lot of that depends on information I don't have access to at the moment."

Diego saw how the words stretched between Tom and Ellie like a tightrope ready to snap. Tom's precisely chosen words carried hidden barbs of accusation wrapped in silk politeness—the kind of verbal footwork that would make a Chicago politician proud.

Ellie's coffee mug trembled against the table as she set it down.

"Tom," she said, her voice carefully steady. "There's something I need to tell you."

The sheriff's expression didn't change, but Diego caught the way his shoulders squared—a man bracing for impact. "I figured there might be."

Ellie's hands folded in her lap, knuckles white against her dark skirt. "Morrison's notebook. The one from your vest. I took it."

Tom nodded once, slow and deliberate. "I know."

"You... know?"

"Ellie, I've been robbed by professionals in Chicago alleys who at least had the courtesy to leave my dignity intact." Tom's voice held no heat, just the flat certainty of mathematics. "Either you took it, or Doc did. Nate could have, I suppose. Or someone else walked through that bedroom while I was burning with fever. Got a theory on which one makes the most sense?"

Diego found himself oddly proud of the younger man's restraint. No accusations, no wounded pride—just facts laid out like cards on a table.

"Where is it now?" Tom asked.

Ellie couldn't meet his gaze directly, but she could at least hold her chin up. "Gone. And it's going to stay that way."

The silence stretched long enough to settle into the room like an unwelcome guest.

"Gone," Tom repeated finally, his voice flat. Simply repeating facts. "And it's going to stay that way."

"Yes."

"Because you traded it to Mercer." Not a question. Tom leaned back in his chair, slow and careful, testing how much weight his broken ribs could bear the same as he was testing how much water his theory could hold.

Ellie's chin lifted. "You don't know what you're talking about."

"Really?" Tom's fingers drummed once against the table before going still. His gaze locked onto the curtains that hung by the kitchen window. "Let me paint you a picture, Mrs. Harper. You wake up this morning, take a look at a notebook full of evidence that could put your husband back in prison for the rest of his natural life. Maybe get him hanged, depending on what a federal judge thinks about Detective Morrison's murder."

Diego found himself holding his breath as Tom's voice remained level, almost conversational. Ellie turned away, her hands tightening around her coffee cup.

"So, you take a walk down to the docks. Have yourself a chat with the one man who wants that evidence more than anyone else breathing: the smuggler whose entire operation just got burned to the waterline. And you make a deal."

Ellie's coffee cup trembled against the table, but her voice stayed steady. "You're fishing."

"Am I? Then tell me I'm wrong." Tom's smile held no warmth, and he stared into the cold liquid at the bottom of his coffee cup like it held all the answers he was looking for. "I know you wouldn't give it to the railroad men and sell out the whole town. If you'd been willing to give it to your husband, I wouldn't have stumbled into that little lover's tiff of a gunfight the other day where a half dozen of his men ended up dead. Mercer's the only angle that makes sense from where I'm sitting, but if I'm wrong, and you *didn't* steal from me to keep your husband safe, then please, by all means, say so."

He looked up and met her eyes for the first time since sitting down. "I'm begging you, Ellie: tell me I'm wrong."

Ellie swallowed, held his gaze as long as she could, and plunged off the edge. "You *are* wrong. About one thing, at least."

Tom raised his eyebrows, waiting for clarification.

"I didn't do it to save *Harlan's* life, you stupid ass." With that, she rose and walked steadily to her bedroom, shutting herself away before she could shatter to pieces. The door closed behind her, soft but final.

Tom sat motionless, the echo of her words still hanging between them. The sun had set, leaving the kitchen looking colder and grayer than it had minutes ago.

Outside, the swamp was waking to dusk—frogs, wind, a crow someplace far off.

He rubbed a hand over his face and let out a breath.

"Well," he said softly. "Shit."

Diego whistled low. "I think I'll pick up a bottle of whiskey when I stop to get your shirt. Medicinal purposes." He rose himself and gave Tom a soft pat on the shoulder as he passed. "Good luck, *amigo.*"

"Thanks."

Tom sat at the table alone, long after Diego had left, watching the shadows grow longer. It was that hour of the day when the sun was still trying to cling to something before the darkness creeped in to swallow everything whole. The sun was losing.

With one last look at the bedroom door that Ellie had disappeared behind, he rose and grabbed the coffee pot, taking it with him to his own room.

Act Four

THE LONG ARM OF POLITICS

CHAPTER TWENTY-ONE

Inquiry

Judge Margaret Hartwell set her fountain pen aside when the Western Union envelope arrived bearing the State Government seal—always either good news about courthouse funding or very bad news about everything else.

She tore it open with the vicious determination she tackled all unpleasant correspondence with.

FROM COMMITTEE ON INTERNAL IMPROVEMENTS. INQUIRY CONVENED. REPORT REQUESTED ON RECENT INCIDENTS IN CYPRESS RUN. SUBMIT WRITTEN ACCOUNT WITHIN 48 HOURS REGARDING ALL CRIMINAL ACTIVITY OVER PAST 7 DAYS.

"Pompous bureaucrats," she muttered, already composing her reply in her head. Another committee, another round of government oversight stepping on her jurisdiction. She'd handled such inquiries before—railroad investors nervous about their money, Tampa businessmen worried about shipping delays.

But as she read the telegram a second time, certain phrases began to stand out like ink stains on white cloth.

COMMITTEE EXPECTS DELINEATION OF RESPONSIBILITY BETWEEN THE OFFICE OF THE SHERIFF AND THIS COURT.

She paused, pen hovering over her notes. That wasn't standard language for a routine inquiry. That was the careful phrasing of officials already sharpening their knives.

Her eyes found the next line.

SHOULD THIS OFFICE FAIL TO PROVIDE SATISFACTORY CLARIFICATION, OVERSIGHT WILL ASSUME DIRECT CONTROL.

The pen slipped from her fingers and clattered against the desktop.

Hartwell leaned back in her chair, the telegram suddenly feeling heavier than a gavel in her hands. She'd been in politics long enough to recognize a carefully worded threat when she saw one. Someone wasn't just asking for information—they were offering her a way out.

She pulled a file out of her desk—the one labeled 'Personnel - Bracken, Thomas'—and pulled out the pair of letters that she'd received from Chicago just days before the new sheriff's arrival. She already had the contents memorized, but one more glance over could only help.

After she'd read through them both again—twice—she turned to her notes, spread across the desk like evidence at a crime scene.

Seven days.

Only seven days since Thomas Bracken had stepped off that train with his inappropriate wool suit and his billiard cue case. She picked up her pen and pulled over a clean sheet of paper and began writing.

Day one*: John Fletcher, railroad surveyor, found murdered at Gator Creek. Bracken nearly killed by alligator during the investigation.*

Day two*: Bracken arrested Patrick Dooley for Fletcher murder after confrontation at lumber camp. (follow up: what in the world is a slap nap? more info needed)*

Day three*: Detective Morrison shot dead in The Cypress House saloon. 2 injured. Shooter escaped.*

Day four*: Rawling-Thom warehouse destroyed, explosion visible from town, body count 3, plus 1 unknown arsonist. Jailhouse attacked, two children injured defending prisoner.*

Day five*: Bracken transported prisoner to Everfield Junction to await trial. Multiple attacks on Sheriff's transport, body count 6 (unverified).*

Day six*: Harlan Carter's men killed in firefight at Ellie Harper's property, body count 7.*

Day seven*: Blessedly quiet, suspect because Bracken too injured to leave bed.*

Day eight*: Committee of Inquiry's telegram.*

Hartwell stared at the list, her coffee growing cold as the implications settled like sediment in her mind. It was an awful lot of violence to have descended on one small town in the space of a week. More blood than Cypress Run had seen in the previous five years combined.

She wasn't unkind enough to imagine any of it was Bracken's *fault*. The railroad survey fraud, the smuggling operation, Harlan Carter's prison release—those wheels had been turning long before the new sheriff arrived. But she couldn't convince herself that it hadn't all erupted *because* of him. Like a man walking into a room full of gunpowder with a lit cigar, unaware of what he was about to ignite.

The telegram's timing bothered her most. News traveled slow in the counties, especially between remote towns. There was no conceivable way the politicians in Tallahassee could have already received word of this week's events through normal channels. Which meant someone had sent word directly.

Or someone knew that things were going to happen before they actually had.

Someone who had both local access and political reach—and who had assembled a committee and drafted this inquiry before the first shot was even fired.

Hartwell rose and walked to her window, looking out at the half-finished courthouse where Bracken had chased Morrison's killer through the timber framework. The building stood like a promise half-kept, all raw wood and ambitious plans.

Much like Bracken himself.

She could almost see the committee's logic. Send an inexperienced sheriff to a troubled town, wait for the inevitable explosion, then use the chaos to justify intervention. Clean up the local corruption while removing an inconvenient lawman who'd already proved troublesome in Chicago.

Two birds, one carefully aimed stone.

The question was whether she wanted to be the stone.

Hartwell returned to her desk and picked up her pen. She had forty-eight hours to decide whether to throw Thomas Bracken to the wolves or risk her own career defending a man who'd brought nothing but gunfire and complications to her jurisdiction.

She looked again at her notes. Seven days of chaos, yes; but also seven days of results. Fletcher's killer in custody. Morrison's murderer identified. The smuggling operation exposed. Harlan Carter's gang reduced, even if not eliminated.

Messy, violent, unorthodox results—but results, nonetheless.

The kind of justice that looked terrible in committee reports but felt right in the bones of a woman who'd spent too many years watching corruption hide behind procedure.

Margaret Hartwell closed her eyes and took a deep, slow breath, then reached for a fresh sheet of paper.

She had just finished her draft when Dr. Delgado entered her office looking almost rougher than the Sheriff had when last she'd seen him.

"Doctor, just the man I wanted to see."

Diego sighed. "Mind if I go first?"

Hartwell took in the weariness. The man had clearly been working nonstop, and it was a small enough courtesy. She gestured for him to proceed.

"I have the written reports for the seven men who died on Mrs. Harper's homestead. My hand started cramping by the sixth, so I hope you'll forgive the penmanship, but they're all accurate. All they need is Sheriff Bracken's signed statement and they're ready to be filed. I'm also requisitioning funds to pay laborers to help with the burial."

"More county funds, doctor?"

"I have seven bodies piled in the jail with all the ice I could get my hands on, but that's only going to keep them for a very, very short amount of time. Believe me when I say this is a problem that's best dealt with sooner rather than later."

Hartwell nodded. "Very well. I'll also add compensation for the ice."

"It'd be appreciated."

"Anything else?"

Diego blinked at her. "That isn't enough?"

Judge Hartwell almost cracked a smile. "Has Sheriff Bracken recovered?"

"Recovered?" Diego laughed. "In what context? Physically, emotionally? Psychologically?"

"I'm asking for your medical opinion, Dr. Delgado. I need to know if he's capable of appearing before me in an official capacity."

"Oh." Diego looked at her. He glanced toward the door, then back at the judge. "If you're asking whether he's physically able to stand upright and speak coherently, then yes—he's recovered enough for that. But whatever you're planning to put him through, I'd recommend keeping it short."

"Do you think he's competent enough to defend himself at an official inquiry?"

Diego's eyebrows rose. "That's a hell of a question."

"It's the question I need answered."

Diego studied her for a long moment, the way he might examine a patient presenting with symptoms that didn't quite add up. "Judge Hartwell, are you asking me if Sheriff Bracken is mentally competent to *stand trial*?"

Hartwell considered this. Through her window, she could see the afternoon bustle of Main Street—merchants managing their shops, children chasing chickens, the ordinary rhythm of a town that had no idea it was about to be dissected by a committee. "I'm asking if he's well enough to handle whatever's coming next."

Diego settled into the chair across from her desk. He rolled his neck, trying to ease the tension, but too many sleepless nights made that difficult to do. "Physically, he's healing faster than he has any right to. The fever broke, wounds are closing without infection. Man's tougher than gator skin."

Hartwell waited.

"Whatever official capacity you're planning, he'll find a way to handle it." Diego leaned forward. "Whether you want him sharp enough to handle it well, or desperate enough to burn everything down on his way out—that's probably the more useful question to ask yourself."

Hartwell felt the telegram crinkle in her grip. In other circumstances, she might have been tempted to laugh.

"I'm already asking myself that, Doctor," Hartwell said, picking up the telegram and handing it to Diego. "I received this today."

Diego read the telegram twice, his expression darkening with each line.

"Forty-eight hours," he said finally. "*Jesucristo.*"

Diego read the telegram a third time, as if the words might rearrange themselves into something less damning; they didn't.

"Forty-eight hours to what, exactly?" he asked, though the careful bureaucratic language made the answer clear enough.

"To decide whether I throw Sheriff Bracken to the wolves or risk having them tear apart everything we've built here." Hartwell took the telegram back, folding it delicately. "The committee wants a scapegoat for this week's violence. They're offering me a choice: give them Bracken's head on a platter, or watch them dismantle my entire jurisdiction."

For a moment, Hartwell felt the old familiar pull in her gut—the reminder that her authority had never been as ironclad as people assumed. Appointed during the chaotic Reconstruction years, grandfathered in by technicality more than statute, she'd spent her entire career pretending that the foundation beneath her feet was bedrock, not shifting political sand. A woman on the bench didn't get second chances. She barely got first ones.

Diego rubbed his temples where a headache had been building since dawn. "And if you choose to give them Tom?"

"Then I write a report explaining how an inexperienced sheriff from Chicago turned a minor survey dispute into a week-long bloodbath. How his reckless methods endangered civilians and destabilized the entire county." Hartwell's voice carried no emotion, the tone of a judge reading a verdict. "The committee removes him, assigns a federal marshal to restore order, and I keep my courthouse."

"Removes him," Diego repeated. "And files charges against him, I gather."

"In all likelihood—misfeasance in office, reckless homicide, destruction of property, conduct unbecoming a county official. Whatever else they care to add on."

"*Santo cielo...* And if you don't?" he asked hopefully.

"Then I write a different report. One explaining how corruption in the administration allowed a convicted outlaw to escape prison and orchestrate a conspiracy involving railroad fraud, smuggling operations, and multiple murders."

She tapped the telegram against her desk. "Then hopefully the committee finds itself too busy conducting their own investigation into *those* allegations, starting with everyone who had access to Harlan Carter's release papers."

Diego let out a slow whistle. "That's a hell of a gamble, Judge."

"Sheriff Bracken isn't the only one who knows how to read a rigged deck, Doctor." Hartwell opened Bracken's personnel file. She hesitated only a moment before sliding the folder across the desk. "Here. Two letters. One they meant me to see—and one they did not."

Diego unfolded the top page, the paper crisp and formal, the signature bold at the bottom: Chief Raymond Killigan, Chicago Metropolitan Police. He read through it quickly, his brain automatically picking out phrases that, true or not, weren't the sort of things one would say to an employee's new boss if the intention was for them to do well in their new position.

...inclined to act independently of supervision... fundamentally unfit for any position demanding coordination, restraint, or adherence to superior authority... disaster that followed in his wake... temperamentally unsuited to disciplined serv ice...

"Well," he said eventually, setting the letter down carefully. "This is quite instructive. Though I suspect Chief Killigan reveals as much about himself as he does about our sheriff."

"You think so?"

Diego took his spectacles off and cleaned the lenses with a pocket kerchief. "Certainly. The part that truly catches my attention is what the man doesn't say. No mention of corruption charges. No suggestion that Bracken was dishonest or brutal or incompetent—just 'unreliable' and 'insubordinate.' For a Chicago police chief to complain that an officer won't follow orders..." Diego shrugged. "I would be curious to know what those orders were that he wouldn't follow."

"Indeed. That, of course, is the officially sanctioned letter," Hartwell said. "Now the one the Chief didn't intend for me to receive."

She pulled a thinner sheet from the envelope, the paper smudged in the corners. Ink scrawl covered the margins, a clerk's pencil note still visible along the side: *Dictated 08/01/83, tighten it for the record, make me sound civil.*

Diego read, slow and quiet:

Bracken is brilliant in the way a lightning strike is brilliant—spectacular, unpredictable, and usually followed by the smell of something burning. For every case he solved, he started two new ones with his mouth. Clever, restless, contemptuous of every rule that ever kept a man alive in my command. He called procedure a crutch for the morally crippled and obeyed orders only when they happened to match his own ideas of justice—which was rarely, and never quietly...

"*Mierda*. This is—"

"Keep reading."

Diego skimmed lower.

...Yes, I kept him out of a cell. I traded years of political capital to turn a murder into a transfer. I bought him exile instead of a noose—and he never even looked back long enough to understand the cost. You asked whether he's fit for duty. He isn't. He's fit for crusades, for martyrdom, for burning down anything that smells of compromise.

Every paragraph was more damning than the last, until finally:

He's a hero in his own mind, and that's the worst kind of criminal we breed—one who's deluded himself into believing that adherence to the law is optional so long as his own sense of justice is sufficiently catered to.

When he reached the end, Diego set the paper down even more slowly than the first, staring at it as if close enough scrutiny could summon the man from the pages to answer for himself. The silence lingered while Diego sorted through the narratives he'd collected and could now piece together.

"It explains some things. I can see why you might have been inclined to think the worst of him when he arrived here."

"And can you also see why his behavior hasn't helped to disabuse any of the opinions they wanted me to have?"

Diego folded his arms in front of his chest. "It seems to me, you don't need me to tell you if Tom Bracken is capable of doing his job. You want me to tell you if he's worth saving."

"Is he?"

"I can't tell you that, Judge Hartwell, I'm sorry. What I can tell you is that in my experience, the true character of a man comes out in the worst situations. It's easy to be a good man when it costs nothing. But when it costs everything?" Diego shrugged, the gesture closing his argument better than his words could.

"You're suggesting that the incident that ended Bracken's career—he knew what the consequences would be and chose his course of action anyway?"

"Tom was careful not to violate the terms of whatever contract he was made to sign, but he allowed me enough to read between the lines. I don't wish to betray his confidence, but knowing what he did and what it cost, I would consider him a good and moral man."

"Thank you, Doctor. That speaks volumes." Hartwell sighed and tapped the second letter. "I had thought, at first, that the clerk who included that draft with the letter had intended to do me a service, to warn me of the sort of man I would be responsible for. But I'm starting to wonder. It made certain I was looking for flaws before the man even stepped off the train. Every word I've witnessed since, every fight, every body, has fit too neatly into the frame they built for me."

"You think the person who included it meant you to see it that way."

"Oh, I'm sure of it." Hartwell leaned back, weighing the telegram now folded in her hand. "And now this—" she lifted it slightly "—inviting me to cut him loose and climb the ladder without a stain on my record. A lifeline thrown to someone teetering overboard—if only she'll let go of the man pulling her down."

Diego studied her a long moment. "Are you sure the lifeline wasn't thrown by the same pair of hands that pushed our sheriff over the edge first?"

"That's the problem—I'm almost certain it was."

"And will you?" Diego asked. "Cut him loose?"

Hartwell's gaze drifted to the half-built courthouse framed in her window. The silence stretched between them, filled with the distant sound of hammers from the courthouse construction and the ever-present buzz of insects that never seemed to rest in this part of the world.

"I suppose that depends, doesn't it?" Hartwell took the two letters and folded them neatly back into Bracken's personnel folder. "On whether the person who set this in motion has misjudged my character as much as they've mislabeled Sheriff Bracken's."

The truly terrifying part was that Hartwell wasn't certain she knew the answer either. And she had less than forty-eight hours to figure it out.

Chapter Twenty-Two

A Town Meeting

The church hall buzzed with more bodies than it had seen since Christmas service the year before. Judge Margaret Hartwell surveyed the packed room from behind the makeshift podium, noting faces that never graced regular town meetings: ranchers from the outlying homesteads, railroad workers still smelling of creosote and sweat, even Mrs. Wyatt from the boarding house who usually claimed her rheumatism kept her home after dark.

Every seat was filled. Men leaned against the walls, arms crossed, while women clutched shawls despite the humid evening air. The usual suspects occupied their regular spots—Cotton and his wife in the front row, Jake Henley with his blacksmith's hands folded in his lap, Simon Finch scribbling notes in a corner—but tonight they were outnumbered by people who'd apparently decided this meeting concerned them directly.

Hartwell rapped her gavel against the wooden podium.

"This meeting of the Cypress Run Town Council will come to order."

The chatter died to a restless murmur, like water settling after a stone's been thrown.

"First item on tonight's agenda concerns progress on municipal improvements. The courthouse foundation work proceeds on schedule despite recent setbacks. We expect to resume full construction within the week. Railroad surveying has resumed following resolution of the boundary disputes that—"

"What about the murders?"

Mrs. Mills's voice cut through the formal proceedings like an axe through kindling. The woman stood in the third row, her weathered face set in hard lines.

"The agenda clearly states—"

"Seven people are dead, Judge." Cotton's voice carried the weight of a man who'd been tallying the cost. "My customers are asking whether it's safe to come to town. The railroad boys are talking about pulling their crews back to Everfield Junction until things settle down."

A rumble of agreement rolled through the crowd. Someone in the back called out, "What about the saloon shooting?"

"And the warehouse fire!"

Hartwell raised her gavel but didn't bring it down. The voices overlapped, building into a crescendo of grievances and fears that had been simmering all week.

Judge Hartwell let the storm blow itself out, watching faces in the lamplight. Fear, anger, frustration—the raw emotions of people who'd watched their quiet town transform into something they no longer recognized. When the voices finally quieted, she set down her gavel.

"You want answers about the violence."

"Damn right we do." Jake Henley's voice carried the blunt authority of a man used to shaping metal with his hands. "Week ago, biggest problem in this town was whether the river would flood come hurricane season. Now we got shootouts in the street and bodies floating downstream."

"The sheriff—" Simon began from his corner.

"The sheriff," Mrs. Mills interrupted, "has been here one week. One week, and we've had more bloodshed than we've seen in near a decade."

Murmurs rippled through the crowd. Hartwell watched the tide of opinion shift, measuring the temperature of the room like a politician weighing votes. These weren't the usual council meeting complaints about road repairs or tax assessments. This was fear talking.

"Sheriff Bracken inherited a situation that was already—"

"Sheriff Bracken shot up half the countryside chasing shadows," called out a voice from the middle of the room.

"Those weren't shadows that attacked Bobby Keene's wagon."

"How do we know? Man shows up covered in blood claiming he fought off bandits, but where's the proof?"

The crowd grew louder, voices overlapping in a cacophony of suspicion and anger. Someone mentioned Chicago. Someone else brought up the warehouse explosion. A third voice demanded to know why a county sheriff was sleeping in jail cells like a vagrant.

Hartwell raised her gavel again, but the room had found its rhythm now, feeding on shared anxiety and the peculiar satisfaction of having someone to blame for forces beyond their control.

Nobody noticed the door creak open at the back of the hall or the man who slipped unobtrusively through it.

Sheriff Tom Bracken stood in the doorway for a moment, surveying the sea of backs and bonnets before him. His hair was washed and combed neat as Sunday service, face freshly shaved, the blue jacquard vest and tie giving him the polished look of a man who'd just stepped out of a tailor's advertisement in a city paper, even if the evidence of his injuries spoiled the effect some. The thin white bandage wrapped around his temple caught the lamplight, and his left arm rested in its sling, crisp white against the blue of his vest. A wooden crutch supported his right side—though he leaned on it more for effect than necessity, favoring the leg that still bore a bullet graze along the thigh.

He picked his way through the crowd, each deliberate step tapping the crutch against the wooden floor as he navigated between chairs and standing bodies. A few heads turned as he passed, voices faltering mid-complaint.

Awareness rippled outward like rings in still water. Conversations died in patches—here a cluster of railroad workers falling silent, there a group of ranchers turning to stare.

Bracken continued his measured progress toward the front, nodding politely to familiar faces. Cotton's wife gripped her husband's arm. Jake Henley straightened in his chair. Simon Finch's pencil stopped scratching across his notebook.

By the time Bracken reached the front of the room, even Mrs. Mills had run out of steam. The hall fell quiet as a tomb; two dozen pairs of eyes fixed on the sheriff as he positioned himself beside Judge Hartwell's makeshift podium. He planted the crutch beside him and eased his shoulder back, straightening his vest with his free hand.

The silence stretched taut as a bowstring.

"Evening, folks." Bracken's voice carried easily through the hushed room. "Sorry I'm late. Turns out fighting off fever plays hell with a man's sense of time, and I seem to have misplaced my pocket watch somewhere between the swamp and my sickbed."

A nervous chuckle escaped from someone in the back row, quickly stifled.

Bracken's green eyes swept the crowd, taking in every face with the same attention he'd paid to crime scenes and poker tables. When his gaze found Mrs. Mills, he offered her a slight nod of acknowledgement.

"I understand folks have some concerns about recent events in our fair town." He let his balance settle on his good leg and rested his hand on the podium's edge. "I'd be happy to address them all, if you'd kindly agree to keep them to one at a time. My head's still a bit tender from bouncing off the ground as it did when I jumped off the back of Mr. Keene's wagon and I find I currently follow conversations better when they don't all happen at once."

He smiled then—not the sardonic smirk that usually played at the corners of his mouth, but the charming smile that convinced people they wanted to be kinder than they necessarily had to be.

The hall remained silent as a church between hymns, waiting to see who would be brave enough to speak first.

"Mrs. Mills, why don't you start?" Bracken asked gently. "I seem to recall hearing that your opinion is closely regarded in these parts."

Mrs. Mills straightened her shoulders, jaw set like a woman preparing to deliver an ultimatum to the devil himself. The feathers on her hat trembled with barely contained indignation.

"Seven people dead, Sheriff Bracken. Seven. In one week." Her voice carried the cadence of someone who'd rehearsed this speech. "John Fletcher, that man in the saloon, three men at the docks, two more at the Harper place. All since you arrived."

Bracken nodded gravely, as if she'd just informed him that water was wet.

"That's a fair concern, Mrs. Mills. Though I'm afraid I will have to point out that your accounting is slightly mistaken. First, I'd like to mention that Detective Morrison was already investigating criminal activity before I set foot in Cypress Run, and Mr. Fletcher's killer confessed to strangling him over boundary stakes that someone else had been moving for weeks."

"That doesn't change the fact they were only killed after you arrived," Mrs. Mills snapped. "And the three men who died in the explosion were killed during your time in office as well."

"That is very true," Bracken agreed amicably, drumming his fingers against the handle of the crutch. "The deaths that occurred at the dock were tragic. Of course they were. But I have to correct your count and confirm that it was four men who died there: three of Mr. Mercer's employees as well as the saboteur that started the fire. I did pursue the man with the intent of bringing him to face justice, but the explosion knocked his body into the river where it became impossible to recover."

One person spoke up from the back, "What about the fire at the warehouse? What caused the explosion?"

"The fire and the explosion were both the unfortunate consequences of an arsonist setting fire to shipments of illegally imported Cuban rum and crates of what I believe were smuggled arms and munitions. Rum—while surprisingly enjoyable—happens to be highly flammable and combined with gunpowder..." Bracken shrugged one shoulder, rolling it in a stretch as he did. "A very explosive combination. What happened is tragic, but the physical dangers of the cargo itself, as well as those of sabotage from rival organizations, are risks that smugglers and rum-runners accept when they choose to operate outside the boundary of the law."

Mrs. Mills's eyes narrowed, calculating the arithmetic of blame with the glee of a banker foreclosing on a mortgage. "And the Harper place? Two men dead in that poor woman's yard because you brought trouble to her door."

"Again, I feel an obligation to correct your arithmetic, Mrs. Mills." Bracken's voice stayed level, but something sharper entered his tone. "It was seven men, not two, who unfortunately lost their lives in Mrs. Harper's yard, each of them a member of Harlan Carter's gang—the same gang I'm given to understand shot up the Sheriff's Office and ran your last sheriff out of town... Sheriff Brown, was it? Three more of their gang retreated after being injured or deciding that discretion was the better part of valor. Those men targeted Mrs. Harper because criminal interests in the area thought they could use violence and terror to achieve their ends, whatever those may be."

Bracken took a breath, looking out across the crowd, meeting people's eyes directly for brief moments before moving his gaze to the next person. "Normally, I would consider it my professional duty to bring criminals in alive to face justice as they should. I hope that my conduct in the Fletcher case—as well as any future cases that come along—will allay any doubts that that is indeed the truth. But injured and outnumbered ten to one, I hope you can grant me a little grace in my decision to defend Mrs. Harper and her son with lethal force. You have my word—every person who died in that yard came there intending to kill a mother and her eight-year-old boy and I acted according to my best judgment at the time."

The crowd shifted in their seats, some nodding slowly, others exchanging glances that suggested Mrs. Mills might have picked the wrong fight. But the banker's wife wasn't finished.

"That's all very convenient, Sheriff, but what about the fact that none of this violence started until you arrived?" Her voice carried the sharp edge of determination. She was accustomed to getting the last word in every argument and wasn't about to let her streak be broken. "We had peace in this town before Chicago sent us their problems."

Bracken's smile didn't waver, but something cooler entered his eyes—he'd heard this particular song played in different keys across half the saloons in Illinois.

"Ma'am, I appreciate your concern for the town's welfare. Truly. But I have to wonder—when you say 'peace,' are you referring to the criminal operation that's been smuggling illegal goods through your docks? The boundary fraud that threatens to steal land directly from homesteaders? Or maybe the way two good men were murdered for asking too many questions about both?"

Mrs. Mills's mouth opened, then closed without sound.

"Because if that's what passes for peace in Cypress Run," Bracken continued, as casual as if he were discussing the weather, "then I'm afraid I'm going to have to continue to disappoint you. That kind of peace tends to end badly for folks who aren't getting their cut. And that's exactly the sort of peace that I refuse to tolerate."

The silence that followed was the kind normally reserved for graveyards at midnight, the kind that had teeth.

Cotton cleared his throat, the sound cutting through the charged silence like a handsaw biting pine. His weathered hands fidgeted with the brim of his hat as he glanced between Mrs. Mills's flushed face and Bracken's steady gaze.

"Sheriff," he began, as careful as a man testing ice over a creek, "folks aren't questioning your intentions, exactly. It's just... well, some of us are wondering if maybe there's a different way to handle things, a way that doesn't involve quite so much shooting."

Bracken drew a slow breath through his nose, studying Cotton with the same attention he'd give a tricky bank shot, patience coiling behind the polite tone of his voice. "What kind of different way did you have in mind, Mr. Cotton?"

"Maybe... talking to these criminal types before the bullets start flying? Working out some kind of arrangement that keeps the peace without turning Main Street into a battlefield?"

A few murmurs of agreement rippled through the crowd. Mrs. Mills nodded vigorously, her feathers bobbing like a rooster's comb.

"Talking?" Bracken's smile widened. "That's certainly one approach to law enforcement, absolutely. One I happen to believe in, as a matter of fact."

Bracken limped forward a step. "Mr. Hendricks," he called out, his voice carrying easily through the hushed room. "You're standing right there by the wall. Mind stepping forward a moment?"

The cattleman pushed off from where he'd been leaning, his weathered face uncertain as he moved into the lamplight. The crowd parted slightly, giving him space while keeping their eyes fixed on both men.

"Evening, Sheriff," Hendricks said, touching the brim of his hat with grudging respect.

"Evening. Now, I was wondering if you would mind terribly telling these folks about our first meeting at the saloon. When you and your boys were having that discussion with Mr. Murphy about his gambling debts?" Bracken's tone stayed conversational, almost friendly. "Do you remember me suggesting, at any point during that conversation, that we settle the matter with violence?"

Hendricks glanced around the room, clearly wishing he were anywhere else. "No, sir, you didn't."

"Do you remember what I suggested instead?"

"A game of eight-ball." The admission came reluctantly. "Winner takes all."

"And after I won, what happened to you and your boys?"

Hendricks shifted his weight, his voice growing quieter. "You... you bought us each a drink. Said it had been a good game."

"Now, I'll confess it might have been a little on the unfair side, challenging you out of the blue like that when you didn't know quite what you were getting into... but on the whole do you think that was an unreasonable exchange between us?"

Hendricks shook his head, voice a little firmer. "No, sir."

"Thank you, Mr. Hendricks. And I wasn't lying; it *was* a good game. In fact, I'd be happy to offer you a rematch just as soon as this arm of mine heals enough that Doc won't hunt me down and blister my ears for it."

Hendricks touched the brim of his hat again. A few chuckles, a few murmurs rippled through the crowd. Mrs. Mills's mouth tightened into a thin line.

Bracken nodded his thanks and let his gaze drift across the room until it settled on another face. "Now, I see we've got some lumber boys here tonight. Any of you fellows work for Mr. Jennings?"

A weathered man near the back raised his hand slowly. "I was there when you came for Big Dooley, Sheriff."

"Perfect. Come on up here." Bracken waited as the man worked his way through the crowd. "Tell everyone your name."

"Will Roberts, sir."

"Mr. Roberts, when I arrived at your camp to arrest Mr. Dooley, did I start the conversation by drawing my weapon?"

"No, sir." Roberts's voice was clear and steady. "You walked right up and asked to talk to him peaceful-like."

"How long did we talk before things got heated?"

"Good five minutes or more. You kept trying to get him to come willing. Kept calling him 'mister' and asking polite."

"When did I reach for my gun?"

Roberts glanced around the room, then back at Bracken. "You didn't, Sheriff. Never touched it, not once. Even when Dooley said he wasn't getting arrested by a one-armed weakling and charged you like a bull, you just... well, you used your hand."

"My hand?"

"Yes, sir. That slapping trick. Never saw anything like it. Put him down clean as you please, then tied him up all proper like. Told us all you were arresting him under suspicion of murder and asked if any of us had objections."

"Would you say I was overly violent with Mr. Dooley?"

"No, Sheriff. In fact, I don't see how you could have been less violent if you tried, least not without lying down in the mud and letting him up and pummel you to death. Don't reckon that's a reasonable way to get any law enforcing done, though."

Bracken smiled, the expression warm enough to melt butter. "Thank you, Mr. Roberts."

He waited until both men had returned to their places before continuing, his voice carrying the patient cadence of a teacher explaining simple arithmetic to schoolchildren.

"Talking, Mr. Cotton, is exactly what I do. Every single time. Now, I seem to recall you suggesting I make some sort of arrangements with these criminal types. And I hope you'll forgive me for putting you on the spot, but I'd like to ask you, sir, just what sort of arrangement would you find appropriate? With these violent criminal types who shoot up Main Street and set buildings on fire, who send executioners to murder lawmen in saloons and prisoners in jail cells, or send gangs of armed thugs to terrorize women and children?"

Bracken was quiet for a moment, giving the question a good chance to breathe, before he continued, "If you can stand there and tell me with perfect honesty that you think that my asking them politely to stop committing crimes will get the job done, I might just be willing to give it a try."

Cotton's face flushed red as a ripe tomato, his weathered hands gripping his hat brim so tight the fabric creaked. The silence stretched between them, every person in the hall holding their breath as they waited to see if the storekeeper would take up Bracken's challenge.

"I... well, Sheriff, I just meant..." Cotton's voice faltered, the words dying in his throat as he stared into Bracken's steady green eyes.

Mrs. Mills shifted in her seat, her mouth opening as if to speak, then closing again when she caught sight of the expressions on her neighbors' faces. The tide had turned, and even she seemed to sense it.

Bracken nodded, a worn kindness flickering at the corners of his smile. "As I said, Mr. Cotton, I hope you can forgive me for putting you on the spot like that. It's not a question that has a neat answer, and I know that better than anyone. Far as I can tell," Bracken continued, easing off the crutch a little and drawing himself up taller, "talking only works when both parties are interested in hearing what the other fellow has to say. And when they respect the other fellow enough to listen when they say it."

His gaze swept the room, his smile steady. "A wise person told me my first day here that respect has to be earned, out this way; it's not just granted to every fool who comes along and demands it because some bureaucrat with a rubber stamp was foolish enough to appoint him." Bracken's eyes searched the crowd until he found Ellie, standing unobtrusively by the door where she'd been since Bracken had made his entrance. "I understand that it takes time and steady action to earn respect the proper way and I hope to keep earning yours for a long time coming."

The room remained silent as a tomb, waiting to see who would be fool enough to argue with that particular brand of frontier logic.

Bracken let the silence hold for another moment, watching faces in the lamplight. Some folks looked convinced, others still carried the stubborn set of people who'd already made up their minds. Mrs. Mills sat rigid as a church pew, her feathers trembling with barely contained indignation.

The sound of floorboards creaked softly as he braced the crutch and leaned forward a fraction. "Now, if anyone has specific concerns about how I've handled particular situations, I'm happy to discuss them. But I would ask that we stick to facts rather than speculation. Facts have a way of staying put when you examine them, whereas rumors tend to scatter like startled rats the moment you get too close."

A few nervous chuckles rippled through the crowd. Simon Finch scribbled frantically in his notebook, trying to capture every word.

"Sheriff," called out a voice from the middle of the room, "what about the future? How do we know this violence won't continue?"

Bracken's smile never wavered.

"Well, sir, I can't promise you peace. Peace is something honest folks have to build together, one conversation at a time. But, I can promise you this—as long as I'm wearing this badge, the law in Cypress Run won't be for sale. And it certainly won't tuck its tail and run for Tampa at the first whiff of gun smoke."

Judge Hartwell watched the crowd absorb Bracken's words, measuring the shift in atmosphere like a politician counting votes. The banker's wife had retreated into stony silence, her feathers wilted and her mouth pressed into a thin line of defeat. Even Cotton seemed to have found something fascinating about his boot leather, unwilling to meet anyone's eyes after his suggestion had been so thoroughly dissected.

"Are there any other concerns for the sheriff to address?" Hartwell asked, her voice carrying the crisp authority of a gavel striking wood.

The silence stretched long enough for a cricket to chirp somewhere in the rafters. Mrs. Mills shifted in her seat but said nothing. A few people exchanged glances, but nobody seemed eager to follow Cotton's example.

"Very well then." Hartwell straightened the papers on her makeshift podium. "Moving on to the next item—"

Hartwell watched Bracken move over to the wall and ease himself against it, using it and the crutch in conjunction to prop himself up while he dropped into a semi-trance-like state that Hartwell recognized from her own profession, the one used by law students listening to long legal briefs where the jargon and the spoken words didn't matter nearly as much as staying awake until the end.

She'd seen politicians work crowds before, watched them cajole, and threaten, and promise their way through hostile rooms. But Bracken had done something different entirely. He'd simply told the truth, then stood there while it did the heavy lifting. No grand speeches, no appeals to higher principles—just cold facts delivered with that peculiar blend of charm and steel that made people forget they'd come here looking for someone to blame.

Hartwell turned back to her agenda, but her thoughts remained on the lean figure propped against the wall. Bracken had bought himself breathing room tonight, perhaps even genuine support. But political theater was a temporary solution to a permanent problem—and the telegram from the state government still sat in her desk drawer, demanding answers she wasn't sure she wanted to give.

The crowd dispersed into the muggy night, voices drifting through the courthouse windows as folks headed home to their suppers and their gossip. Bracken remained propped against the wall, watching the last stragglers file out while Judge Hartwell shuffled her papers.

When most of the townsfolk had left the room, she turned to him and said quietly, "That was well done, Sheriff."

Bracken smiled. "That's why you keep bringing me breakfast, I imagine."

Her lips twitched into what could almost have passed for a smile. "Indeed." She finished gathering her papers and left the room, heels clicking rhythmically against the wooden floor.

Diego approached him as the room continued to empty, medical bag in hand and that familiar expression of professional concern creasing his forehead.

"Thanks for the heads up about tonight," Bracken said, giving the crutch a casual half turn as he continued leaning against the wall. "I hadn't realized it was Thursday already, or that my head would be on the chopping block."

"Happy to help." Diego's mouth quirked upward at one corner. "Though I suspect you'd have figured it out when you saw the torches and pitchforks."

"You're a good friend, Doc." Bracken shifted his weight, wincing as his injured leg reminded him why standing for extended periods of time wasn't advisable.

"Better at it than you are," Diego agreed amiably.

Bracken chuckled and gave Diego a mischievous smirk. "Just out of curiosity, though... You wanna tell me why my jail cell's been turned into a body locker?"

Diego's expression flattened and he raised an eyebrow. "Not unless you want me to start listing *my* grievances."

Bracken laughed and held up his free hand in surrender. "Message received; question withdrawn. You're still a good friend, even if you did cover my jail in quicklime and corpse juice. Needed to give the floors a good cleaning anyways."

Ellie approached as the last townspeople drifted out, her footsteps quiet on the wooden floor. Diego glanced between her and Bracken, then cleared his throat.

"I should check on the supplies I left at the clinic," he said, gathering his medical bag. "Make sure everything's properly secured for the night."

Bracken watched him go, noting the way Diego's shoulders straightened as he made his exit. The man had a gift for reading rooms and knowing when to disappear.

"Thank you," Bracken said once they were alone, adjusting his stance in an attempt to ease discomfort that wasn't entirely physical. "For helping me get ready tonight. For getting me down here."

"It was nothing."

"No, it wasn't nothing." He studied her face in the lamplight, noting the way she held herself—straight-backed but tired, like she'd been carrying something heavy all day. "You helping me when I ask—and even when I don't—that means something."

Ellie's expression softened slightly. "Well... Thank you for asking me to help. That means something, too."

Bracken smiled, but it came out sadder than he'd intended, and he looked away toward the empty chairs where an hour ago half the town had been calling for his head. The victory felt hollow somehow, like winning a hand of poker with cards you'd rather not be holding.

"Tom, about the notebook—I need to apologize for—"

"Don't." He cut her off gently, still not meeting her eyes. "I just don't have it in me to focus on that right now, Mrs. Harper. There's too much else happening."

She went quiet, and when he finally looked back at her, he could see the hurt flickering behind her careful composure. Christ, he hated seeing her upset. Made his chest feel tight in a way that had nothing to do with his injuries.

"Look," he said, shifting his weight on the crutch and trying to find words that wouldn't make things worse. "The notebook's a ball already in a pocket, you understand? No matter what we do now, we can't fish it out and put it back in play again."

Ellie frowned. "Tom—"

"But the game's still going," he continued, warming to the analogy despite himself. "There's a whole table full of balls still in play, and it makes no damn sense to miss every other shot in the game just because one ball didn't go where I wanted it to."

She was quiet for a long moment, studying his face with those sharp hazel eyes that seemed to see straight through his attempts at deflection.

"Thomas Bracken, did you just compare our relationship to a billiards game?" she asked finally.

Bracken felt heat crawl up his neck despite the cool evening air drifting through the courthouse windows. He'd walked into that one like a drunk stumbling into a lamppost.

"That's not what I—" He stopped, shook his head with a rueful laugh.

"Well?" She crossed her arms, but there was something almost playful in her expression now. "Did you?"

He reached down and massaged his thigh, soothing the ache and buying himself a moment to think.

"Look," he said finally, "I'm not good at this part. The talking about feelings part. Back in Chicago, if you liked somebody, you bought them a drink and hoped they didn't shoot you when they tried to rob you blind in the morning. But this? Here..." He gestured vaguely at the empty building around them. "Here I keep stepping in gator holes, literal and otherwise."

Ellie's smile was small but genuine. "Tom."

"Yeah?"

"You didn't answer my question."

Bracken looked at her standing there in the lamplight, patient as sunrise, waiting for him to stop being clever and start being honest.

"No," he said quietly. "I wasn't comparing our relationship to a billiards game. But I might have been comparing my *courtship* of you to a billiards game...?"

Ellie's eyebrows rose, and for a moment the lamplight caught something in her expression that might have been amusement—or maybe just exhaustion finally catching up with her.

"Your courtship," she repeated, testing the word like she wasn't sure it belonged in her mouth. "Is *that* what we're calling it?"

Bracken felt his face warm again. The woman had a gift for making him feel like he was stumbling through conversations in the dark, always one step behind whatever she was actually thinking. But he tilted his head with that crooked smile that somehow looked both innocent and troublemaking, and asked, "Is that not the word for it down south?"

Ellie's mouth twitched at the corners despite herself. "Depends. Up north, do you go courting a woman by bleeding on her every time you see her?"

"It seems to be working for me so far." His grin widened. "Even got you to kiss me once."

"That wasn't—" Ellie started, heat flashing in her cheeks.

"It was a very nice kiss, Mrs. Harper."

She crossed her arms tighter, fixing him with that look she usually reserved for Nate when he tracked mud through the house. "It wasn't even a good one."

"Best damn one I ever had."

The simple honesty in his voice caught her off guard, made something flutter in her chest that she'd thought she'd buried years ago. But she recovered quickly, raising an eyebrow with the kind of skeptical expression that could wither weeds.

"Then you clearly don't have a lot of experience, if *that's* what you call the best."

Bracken's eyes lit up with mischief, and he shifted his weight on the crutch, moving just close enough that she could smell the faintest trace of gun oil and big-city cologne—the scent that seemed to ghost around him on the rare occasions when he wasn't soaked through with swamp water, blood, and bad decisions.

"Maybe you could educate me?"

The question hung between them in the lamplight, soft and dangerous. Ellie felt her breath catch, her pulse jumping in a way that made her glad the hall had emptied out because she was fairly certain her face was giving away every thought she'd been trying not to think.

She looked at him standing there—bandaged, bruised, barely upright, but still managing to look at her like she was the only thing in the room worth seeing. The man was nothing but trouble, she thought, pure and simple. He'd brought chaos to their quiet town, turned her life upside down in ways she was still trying to understand.

And he was asking her to kiss him again like it was the most natural thing in the world.

"You're very presumptuous," she said finally, but her voice came out softer than she'd intended.

"I've been called worse."

"I'll bet you have."

He chuckled, low and warm. "Come on, Mrs. Harper. Take pity on a wounded man who's clearly been deprived of a proper education."

Ellie shook her head, fighting the smile that wanted to break across her face. "Tom Bracken, you are—"

"Charming?"

"Insufferable."

"That too." He said softly. "But I'm not hearing a refusal yet, so..."

The flutter in her chest was getting harder to ignore, and she found herself taking a half-step closer despite every sensible thought in her head telling her this was a terrible idea.

But then he reached out with his free hand, fingertips brushing against her wrist with the kind of gentleness that suggested he knew exactly how fragile the moment was.

"Ellie," he said quietly, and hearing her name in his voice like that—no teasing, no jokes, just her name spoken like something precious—made her forget every reason she'd been telling herself this couldn't happen.

She looked up at him, noting the way the lamplight caught the auburn in his hair, the laugh lines around his eyes that had deepened since he'd arrived in Cypress Run. He was watching her with an expression she'd never seen before—hopeful and uncertain in equal measure, like a man who'd spent so long expecting disappointment that good things still surprised him.

"This is a bad idea," she whispered.

"Probably."

"You're injured."

"I'll manage."

"Someone could walk in."

"Door's closed."

She was running out of protests, and they both knew it. The space between them felt charged, like the air before a summer storm.

"One kiss," she said finally, the words barely audible. "In the interest of making sure you have a proper education."

Tom's smile was soft and genuine this time, no trace of his usual smirk. "Yes, ma'am."

When she rose up on her toes to meet him, the walls seemed to hold their breath.

The kiss was softer than their first—deliberate where that one had been desperate, tender where it had been fierce. This one was everything a first kiss should have been. Ellie's hand found the front of his shirt, steadying both of them as Tom leaned into her, the crutch forgotten against his side. When they broke apart, her cheeks were flushed, and his breathing had gone uneven.

"Well," Tom said quietly, his voice shakier than usual. "You're absolutely right. That was considerably better than the first one."

Ellie's laugh was breathless, surprised. "You're impossible."

"So I've been told." He brushed a strand of hair from her face with his free hand. "Grateful for the lesson, though. You're a very good teacher, Mrs. Harper."

He leaned in to kiss her again and Ellie wrapped her arms around his neck, telling him with her lips, her hands, and her body what her words always seemed to fail at. She could taste the faint sweetness of the coffee he'd had earlier, could feel the slight tremor in his hand where it cupped her cheek. When she finally ended the kiss and pulled back to look at him, Tom's eyes stayed closed for a moment longer, like he was trying to concentrate on something.

"Better?" she whispered.

"Much." His voice was quiet, as if too much sound would break this moment between them. "Though I'm starting to think your teaching methods might bring that fever back again."

Ellie laughed softly, stepping back before the warmth in her chest could convince her to do something even more foolish. "I think you'll be fine. You're tougher than you look."

"Why, Mrs. Harper, are you saying I look *fragile*? What part of my appearance presents *that* notion?"

The absurdity of his statement coupled with his expression of injured dignity made her giggle. She shook her head, already missing the closeness but knowing they'd pushed their luck far enough for one evening. The town hall felt too quiet suddenly, too isolated, and she was acutely aware that they were alone in a building where half the town had been assembled just minutes ago.

"We should get you home so you can get some rest," she said, smoothing her skirts with hands that weren't quite steady. "Doctor's orders."

Bracken nodded solemnly. "Yes, ma'am. Though I should probably mention—I'm really not very good at following doctor's orders."

The heat in his voice made her pulse jump again, but before she could respond, footsteps echoed on the steps outside, sharp and deliberate. They sprang apart like guilty children as the door swung open, Judge Hartwell's silhouette filling the frame.

"Sheriff," Hartwell said, her voice carrying that particular edge that meant trouble. "I hate to break up a moment, but we need to talk. Now."

Tom cleared his throat, "Your Honor, what—?"

"This was on my desk." Hartwell handed him a telegram. Tom read over it, his eyebrows scrunching together in confusion. "The Committee of Inquiry is sending a delegate in person to investigate our effectiveness as a municipal seat. He intends to evaluate your conduct and mine. And he arrives tomorrow morning."

Chapter Twenty-Three

The Hatchet Man

J udge Hartwell paced the length of the town hall, heels clicking sharp as a gavel. Her silver-blonde hair had come loose from its usual perfect arrangement; each time she brushed it back, irritation flashed brighter.

"Twelve hours," she muttered, turning at the wall to pace back the other direction. "Twelve hours to prepare for a delegate who's going to walk into this—" she gestured around the modest church annex building, "—and decide whether Cypress Run deserves to remain a municipal seat or if this district constitutes an administrative liability."

"Judge," Ellie said gently, "surely it won't be—"

"It's going to be a disaster." Hartwell's voice rose with each word. "An absolute, unmitigated disaster. Twelve deaths in one week, not including however many you gunned down on the road. Gunfights in the saloon. A warehouse burned to the foundation. A murder attempt in our very own jail, for God's sake!"

Tom leaned more heavily on his crutch, his bandaged arm aching from the evening's exertions. "Your Honor, I know it looks bad, but—"

"Looks bad?" Hartwell whirled on him. "Sheriff, do you have any conception of what a county audit means? This isn't some bureaucrat checking our arithmetic. This is a political execution. Someone in Tallahassee wants us gone, and they're sending their executioner to find justification."

"Ah..." Tom nodded slowly. "Your first audit. Explains it."

The temperature in the room seemed to drop ten degrees. Hartwell's eyes narrowed to steel-gray slits.

"Excuse me?"

"Nothing, Your Honor. Just that back in Chicago—"

"This is not *Chicago,* Sheriff Bracken! This is a frontier county trying to prove it can govern itself, and right now we look like the Wild West's most violent circus act!"

Ellie stepped between them before Tom could respond. "What do we need to do?"

Hartwell resumed her pacing, her mind clearly racing. "Appearance. Respectability. We need to *look* like a legitimate seat of government, not some backwater settlement that can't maintain order." She stopped mid-stride. "My office. I don't even have a proper, permanent office. How is that going to look when he arrives? 'Oh yes, here's where I conduct county business—in the church Sunday school room.'"

"That's easily fixed," Ellie said. "We could set up a temporary office in the Sheriff's building. A combined operation. Show you're working together, present a united front."

Hartwell's expression brightened for exactly three seconds before Tom winced and held up his hand.

"Actually... that's not such a good idea."

"What?"

"Why?"

Tom glanced between Ellie and Judge Hartwell. "Well, the united front part is solid gold. I'm all for that. But the Sheriff's office isn't exactly... Well, it's not much to write home about on the best of days. And since Doc's been using the jail cell as a body locker..." He gestured vaguely toward the door. "Let's just say stuff seeps into the floorboards no matter how careful you are. Even if those bodies were all buried immediately, there's no way that stench is going away any time soon."

Hartwell's face went pale. "Oh, God."

"It's not that bad," Ellie offered weakly.

"It's definitely that bad," Tom confirmed. He cocked a grin at her. "Maybe not to a tough as nails frontier nurse with grit in her veins, but to a pencil pusher from the city? Very bad."

Hartwell sank into one of the wooden chairs, her head in her hands. "We're doomed. Absolutely doomed."

Tom was quiet for a moment, tapping his crutch against the floor as he thought. Then his face brightened with the kind of expression that usually preceded either brilliance or catastrophe.

"Unless..."

"Unless what?" Hartwell looked up hopefully.

"What if it had already been a joint office? Before it had to be closed for public safety reasons?"

Ellie frowned. "What do you mean?"

"Structural damage. Renovation. Some kind of legitimate reason why we had to temporarily relocate to the church annex building." Tom's voice gained momentum as the idea took shape. "It's not that we don't have proper facilities—it's that our proper facilities are undergoing necessary repairs."

Hartwell sat up straighter. "That... could actually work."

"Course it could work," Tom said with his familiar smirk. "Judge Hartwell, I may not know how to ride a horse or eat an orange, but I know plenty about how to make a precinct look spit-polished and respectable when the brass swoops in. And I have just as much interest in our delegate walking away with a good impression as you do. Let me help you make this work."

For the first time since reading the telegram, Judge Hartwell was able to take a deep breath.

"Alright, Sheriff. How do we make ourselves look presentable?"

Tom studied the judge's anxious face, then glanced around the modest church annex that served as their temporary courthouse. His mind was already working angles, mapping out the problem like chalk lines on green felt.

"First thing we need is to close the Sheriff's Office—officially—and for that, we need documentation," he said, shifting his weight off his injured leg. "Something official-looking that explains why we're operating out of the church. Water damage, maybe? Structural concerns after the recent... excitement?"

"The jailhouse did take considerable damage during the last sheriff's tenure," Ellie offered. "Bullet holes, broken windows, blood—"

"Perfect." Tom's grin was sharp as a cue tip. "Judge, you write up a formal notice about emergency relocation due to structural damage and public safety concerns. Make it sound like responsible government decision-making, not desperation."

Hartwell was already reaching for paper. "Yes, that could work. What else?"

"Next we need to set the scene. A map of the county we can pin to the wall, at least one filing cabinet, a bookshelf. If you can get some muscle to shift it, I've got some of that furniture in my office."

"I can help with that," Ellie said. "And we should set up proper desks, files arranged neatly. Make this space look the part."

"Good. Next comes the hard part." Tom's expression grew serious. "If someone's sending a hatchet man to catch us by surprise, it means they've already got a narrative prepared—they know what ammunition they're looking for."

He shifted his weight, the words gathering rhythm. "We need to figure out what story the boss up top wants to hear, so we can make sure *our* paperwork tells a better one. For instance—an arsonist sabotaging a rival smuggler's illegal goods, ending in an explosion? Sort of headline that makes the scandal sheets sing, and exactly the kind of flashy thing a hatchet job feeds on."

He tapped the table for emphasis. "But rewrite it as *a fire broke out in a warehouse, owner fined for improper storage of flammable goods*—boring as hell, nobody looks twice. Once we've guessed which cases he'll dig into, we prep those files until they read cleaner than a hymnbook."

Hartwell looked up from her writing. "How do we go about doing that?"

"Well, for starters, he's going to want an account of all the violent crimes committed in the last month or two. I can write up my reports for this week, but I'm going to need somebody to help me fill in the blanks from before my arrival. We get all those reports ironclad and copied in triplicate. Shows even though there's violence, we take it seriously and handle it accordingly. And three copies of anything gives these auditor boys the warm tickles something fierce."

Hartwell looked at her list. "This is a lot."

"It'll go quick once we get started." Tom limped toward the wall and propped himself against it with a soft groan. "There's one more thing we have to sort out."

"What's that?"

"We gotta decide on a bone to throw away."

"Excuse me?" she asked.

"No place is perfect. Everyone knows it. You make it look too perfect and an auditor's likely to start chewing at things like a dog with a bone. You make sure something is out of place, and he gets to feel like he did a good job finding the bone you left out for him instead of the ones you don't want him chewing on."

Ellie frowned, studying Tom's expression. "What kind of bone?"

"Something harmless but sloppy." Tom shifted his weight again, putting all of it on his good leg. "Back in Chicago, we'd leave a bottle of whiskey sitting out in plain sight in the evidence locker. Every inspector would write it up like they'd uncovered the crime of the century, and meanwhile they'd miss the real problems we'd swept into a closet."

Judge Hartwell looked up from her notes, a calculating gleam in her steel-gray eyes. "That's... surprisingly devious."

"Course it's devious. Politics is just poker with more players and worse consequences." Tom grinned. "Game isn't always decided by who has the better hand."

"We'll need to work through the night," Hartwell said, already mentally cataloging tasks. "Files organized, reports written, office space transformed. Ellie, can you help us move furniture?"

"I can do more than that. I can make sure this place looks like a real courthouse instead of a Sunday school room."

Tom nodded approvingly. "There's the spirit. Any other troops we can call in? I know Doc's been working himself to sand with all the coroner's reports I've made him write this week, so I'd rather not bother him tonight if we can avoid it."

"Simon," Ellie said suddenly. "He'd help. And he knows where everything is stored around town."

"Perfect." Tom nodded. "Kid's got energy to burn. And he's already been shot at once this week, so I'd say he's earned his stripes."

Hartwell looked up from her growing list of tasks. "What about Mrs. Delgado? Julietta has an eye for making spaces look proper."

"Good thinking. And Jake from the blacksmith shop seems to have a sense of civic responsibility. We get enough hands working, we can have this place looking like the county capitol by sunrise." Tom shifted his crutch to his other hand. "Ah, Christ, I gotta sit down." He hobbled to a chair in front of the table and collapsed into it with a thump, clutching his thigh.

Ellie hurried forward to check on him. "Tom, you should be resting; you're going to bring your fever back if—"

"Just been standing too long is all. Bring me a ream of paper and a bottle of ink and I won't move an inch further from the chair than necessary. I'll have my hands full writing reports until my fingers fall off."

"Tom."

He smiled tiredly. "I'm fine, Mrs. Harper, really. Cup or ten of coffee and I'll be right as rain, I promise."

Ellie breathed out a frustrated sigh. "If you set your recovery back, don't think I won't be rubbing your nose in it."

"Gleefully, I'm sure."

Ellie shook her head and wrapped her shawl around her shoulders, already moving toward the door. "I'll fetch Simon and see about getting some of the other women to help. Mrs. Henderson told me she just replaced her curtains, maybe she hasn't gotten rid of the old ones yet. And Agnes from the boarding house has furniture we could borrow."

"Mrs. Harper," Hartwell called after her. "Thank you. Truly."

Ellie paused in the doorway. "Save the thanks until we see if this works, Judge."

She tightened her shawl and went out into the humid dark, her voice already calling names down the street.

After Ellie left, Tom and Judge Hartwell sat in the quiet church annex, the weight of the coming dawn pressing down like humidity before a storm. Tom rubbed his eyes with his good hand, then picked up a pen and pulled a stack of blank paper toward himself.

"Alright, Your Honor. Let's make ourselves look respectable."

Hartwell organized her notes, her earlier panic crystallizing into focused determination. "We'll start with the incident reports. I need everything documented, timestamped, and filed properly."

"Yes, ma'am." Tom began writing, his penmanship surprisingly neat despite his exhaustion.

"Sheriff, is this going to work?"

"Only if you think positively."

"I'm not sure I know how to do that."

He paused, considering. "Then I guess I'll do my best to think positively enough for the both of us."

Tom kept writing, his pen scratching steadily across the paper, while outside, the first hints of activity stirred as Ellie's voice carried through the night air, already rallying volunteers.

By the time the bells rang the nine o clock hour, the church annex bore little resemblance to its former self—borrowed furniture arranged in a way that glowed with clerical polish, case files stacked in neat towers, even proper curtains hung to soften the raw wooden walls.

The women of Cypress Run had worked miracles with fabric and determination, transforming a Sunday school room into something that might pass for governmental dignity.

Judge Margaret Hartwell surveyed the makeshift courthouse with exhausted satisfaction.

Sheriff Bracken remained face-down on his desk, pen still clutched in his writing hand, a half-finished bit of set dressing that they probably didn't strictly need serving as his pillow.

He'd been that way for nearly an hour, insisting he was merely "resting his eyes" whenever she'd checked on him. She'd attempted to shift him to a more comfortable position, but he'd mumbled something about being "perfectly awake" and refused to release the pen.

The sound of carriage wheels on packed earth drew her attention to the window.

Through the glass, she watched a sleek black conveyance roll to a stop, dust settling around its polished sides like accusations.

"Showtime, Sheriff." She placed her hand on Bracken's shoulder, applying gentle pressure.

He stirred, blinking owlishly at the paper stuck to his cheek. "Not sleeping. Just thinking with my eyes closed."

"Naturally. Our auditor friend has arrived."

Bracken peeled the report from his face and straightened in his chair, wincing as his injured arm protested. He managed to smooth his hair with his good hand and arrange his features into something approaching professional composure just as footsteps approached the door.

The auditor entered with a measured stride, his quick eyes, accustomed to finding fault, already darting around the room. Thin as a buggy whip, he carried the pallor of indoor work and city living. His immaculate suit bore the fine layer of travel dust that marked him as distinctly not from around here, and he clutched a leather folio like a weapon.

His eyes swept the transformed space with the precise distaste of a judge examining evidence of a crime.

"Judge Hartwell. Winston Price, at your service." Price's greeting carried the correct amount of professional courtesy. "I trust you received our telegram regarding this inquiry."

"Indeed, Mr. Price. Welcome to Cypress Run." Hartwell stepped forward, her judicial bearing at full authority. "May I present Sheriff Thomas Bracken."

Price's gaze shifted to Bracken, taking in the sling, the bandage around his forehead, the crutch leaning close by—the general appearance of a man who'd recently been through a war. His expression suggested he'd found exactly what he'd expected to find.

"Sheriff Bracken." The title emerged with obvious distaste. "I do hope your injury doesn't impair your performance of official duties."

Bracken rose carefully from his chair, managing a sardonic smile despite his obvious discomfort. "Well, Mr. Price, at least it's not my writing arm that got chewed up. Otherwise, you'd have a hell of a time reading my reports."

Price's lips tightened. "Yes. Your reports. That's precisely what we're here to discuss."

He opened his folio with ceremonial gravitas, pulling out a sheaf of papers that rustled like dried leaves. "Committee on Internal Improvements has received... concerning correspondence regarding recent events in this jurisdiction."

Hartwell felt the familiar steel settle in her spine. "I trust you'll find our documentation thorough and our procedures entirely within county guidelines."

"We shall see, Judge Hartwell. We shall indeed see."

Price's gaze returned to Bracken, who remained standing despite the obvious strain.

"I see no reason to waste much time on pleasantries. Let's discuss your case management, shall we? Two homicides, only one arrest, twelve fatalities in total this week alone. Does that strike you as... disproportionate for a township of four hundred souls?

"We are actively working to reverse the trend and provide more arrests with fewer fatalities—but I have only been in office a week. Takes time to settle into any new job." Bracken's voice carried the easy confidence of a man explaining billiards to a child.

"Right. And how are you settling, Mr. Bracken? You previously served as law enforcement in—Chicago, was it? A sizable adjustment."

Bracken tilted his head. "I'm sure you're aware of the size of the adjustment, Mr. Price. Got a bit of a Springfield accent to you, if I'm not mistaken. Florida's a long way from Illinois, isn't it?"

Price grimaced, but didn't comment on the observation.

Bracken continued, "Anyway, the paperwork's all square. I have my case reports ready for you to peruse at your leisure." He slid a neat stack of folders across the table in Price's direction. "Feel free to have a seat if you'd like."

"I believe I will, thank you." Price took the seat the sheriff had occupied the entire night.

Bracken hobbled over to the side table where some kind soul had left a warm kettle full of coffee and a plate of golden baked pastries.

Hartwell found herself momentarily distracted from the man picking through their carefully prepared documentation by the sight of the sheriff examining the breakfast offerings with the cautious intensity of a munitions expert. He glanced around the makeshift courthouse like a child checking for disapproving adults, then gingerly selected one of the golden pastries from Mrs. Delgado's plate.

His first bite was cautious—a tiny nibble from one corner. Hartwell watched his expression shift from suspicious to mildly surprised. He tilted his head, apparently conducting some internal debate about the taste. Emboldened, he took a proper bite.

The transformation was immediate and startling. Bracken's eyes rolled back so far only the whites showed, and he pressed his injured hand against his mouth to muffle what sounded suspiciously like a groan of pure pleasure.

Hartwell bit back a smile as the sheriff's knees actually buckled slightly. The man was having what could only be described as a religious experience with a breakfast pastry.

Price's papers rustled behind them, but Hartwell remained transfixed by Bracken's obvious struggle for composure. The sheriff stood frozen, pastry halfway to his mouth, looking as if he'd accidentally bitten into paradise and wasn't quite sure how to process the experience.

"Sheriff," she said quietly, moving to his side. "Do you need to step outside for a moment?"

Bracken startled, blinking rapidly as if emerging from a trance. He shook his head, though his hand remained protectively cupped around the half-eaten pastry.

"What—" His voice came out as a croak. He cleared his throat and tried again. "What exactly am I eating here?"

"Mrs. Delgado called them *pastelitos*. The filling is guava and cheese." Hartwell kept her voice low, aware of Price's presence behind them. "I asked her to provide breakfast this morning. Seemed only fair, considering how hard you worked through the night."

Bracken mumbled something that might have been thanks, though his attention was already focused on devouring the remainder of the pastry with impressive speed. He closed his eyes again as he chewed, savoring each bite like a man who'd discovered treasure.

"I didn't know fruit pies could taste like this," he said finally, carefully brushing crumbs from his fingers.

"They're not exactly pies—"

"Whatever they are, they're about the finest thing I've put in my mouth since leaving Chicago." He glanced toward the plate with obvious longing, then forced himself to step back. "Probably shouldn't demolish the entire breakfast before our guest finishes reading."

Price cleared his throat pointedly from his position at the desk. "Sheriff Bracken, if you could spare a moment from your... refreshments, I have several questions regarding your incident reports."

Bracken straightened, wiping crumbs from his mouth with the back of his good hand. The brief moment of wonder was quickly replaced by his usual sardonic composure, though Hartwell noticed he managed to palm another pastry with impressive sleight of hand.

"Let's begin with the matter of seven fatalities at a single homestead. That seems... excessive for a domestic quarrel."

"Well, I certainly agree that it would be excessive—if this had been a domestic quarrel." Bracken's voice carried that familiar note of barely restrained sarcasm. "I think you'll find if you read my written account, I arrived mid-conflict. Ten armed men were attempting to evict a single mother and her young child from their homestead using illegally forged land deeds, which are recorded as evidentiary exhibits A, B, and C and included in the back of the file."

Bracken continued, "When I arrived on the scene, matters had already progressed to lethal violence. The armed men had begun shooting at the house, breaking two windows and causing excessive damage to the property, and lethally endangering the mother and child. I requested that the men cease their activity and remove themselves from the premises. They opened fire on me, at which point I engaged with lethal force. It wasn't until the seventh casualty that the surviving violent perpetrators chose to retreat. All of this is documented in my written report and there are witness statements from both Eliza Harper and Nathaniel Harper."

Bracken cleared his throat. "Now, what precisely was your question?"

Hartwell watched Price's composure crack slightly as he processed Bracken's methodical dismantling of his accusation. The auditor's pen hovered over his notepad, clearly searching for some angle of attack that wouldn't make him appear incompetent for failing to read the actual report.

"I see." Price's voice was all strained politeness. "And these... forged deeds. You're certain of their illegitimacy?"

"Checked the county land office records myself yesterday evening." Bracken's tone remained helpful, though Hartwell caught the glint of satisfaction in his eyes. "Amazing how much clearer these things become when you actually compare the paperwork to the official filings."

Price flipped through several more pages with increasing agitation. "Your methods seem... unorthodox, Sheriff. This report mentions you commandeered a civilian cart rather than pursuing suspects on horseback."

Hartwell watched Bracken's face shift through several shades of confusion as he blinked at the auditor's question. For a moment, the sheriff looked genuinely puzzled, his brow furrowing as he parsed the wording.

"Commandeered?" Bracken repeated slowly, then understanding dawned across his features. "Oh, you mean the cart to the railroad camp."

He moved to the filing cabinet, muttering under his breath, "Wouldn't have pegged that one." The metal drawer squealed in protest as he pulled it open, rifling through papers with his good hand until he found what he sought.

"Here we are." Bracken extracted a thin folder marked 'PERSONNEL - BRACKEN, THOMAS' and flipped it open on the desk in front of Price. "Dr. Delgado's official medical assessment and work restrictions, filed with Judge Hartwell three days ago."

Hartwell leaned forward, recognizing Diego's precise handwriting on the letterhead. She remembered receiving the document, though she hadn't expected it to become evidence in their favor.

Price scanned the paper, his expression growing increasingly strained. Bracken waited with obvious satisfaction, rocking slightly on his heels despite the discomfort the motion clearly caused.

"As you can see," Bracken continued conversationally, "Dr. Delgado specifically requested that Judge Hartwell place me on full administrative leave if I attempted to ride a horse before receiving medical clearance. The cart wasn't commandeered—it was prescribed."

He turned a page in the folder, revealing another document. "And here's the requisition form I filed requesting civilian transportation assistance, properly signed and dated. Young Simon Finch volunteered his services as driver, also documented."

Hartwell suppressed a smile as Price's pen trembled slightly over his notepad. The careful adherence to medical protocol was clearly not what Mr. Price had been expecting to find here.

"I see," Price managed, his voice tight with frustration. "And this... injury that required such restrictions?"

"Alligator bite received in the line of duty while investigating the Fletcher homicide. I was in the process of retrieving the corpse of the murder victim from where it had been disposed when the alligator attacked," Bracken's tone remained perfectly professional. "Dr. Delgado's report includes a rather graphic and detailed description of the wounds and the treatment, if you'd like to review them. Fair warning—it's not a particularly appetizing account, especially so close to breakfast. I can tell you, as one Northerner to another, I do not recommend getting yourself bitten by an alligator. Did you know, those things carry so much bacteria in their mouths that most folks that lose limbs to gator bites—it's cause of their flesh rotting away, not the gator actually ripping it off that does it."

Price's complexion had taken on a distinctly greenish tinge. He shuffled through the remaining papers with obvious reluctance, clearly searching for safer ground to attack.

Hartwell found herself grudgingly impressed. Whatever else could be said about Thomas Bracken, the man understood the value of proper documentation when political wolves came calling.

Price turned another page with the deliberate care of a man defusing explosives, his confidence visibly eroding with each neatly documented procedure. Hartwell found herself experiencing an unexpected surge of civic pride—whatever chaos had engulfed Cypress Run, they'd at least managed to make their paperwork pristine.

"Your arrest of Patrick Dooley appears to have been... precipitous," Price ventured, seizing on what he apparently considered safer ground. "A single witness statement hardly constitutes sufficient evidence for murder charges."

Bracken's eyebrows rose with genuine surprise. "Single witness? Mr. Price, I'm not sure which file you're reading, but my arrest of Patrick Dooley was based on physical evidence, a full confession, and corroborating testimony from six lumber mill workers."

He reached across the desk, flipping to a section marked with red tabs. "Dooley confessed to strangling John Fletcher during a boundary dispute. His confession is documented here, witnessed by Dr. Delgado. The physical evidence—skin under Fletcher's fingernails, fresh scratches on Dooley's neck and hands—is catalogued with photographic plates courtesy of young Simon Finch's camera work. Those photographs are recorded as evidentiary exhibits A and B, by the way."

Hartwell watched Price's face cycle through several shades of frustration as he absorbed this information. The committee's auditor had clearly arrived expecting to find a frontier cowboy with loose trigger discipline, not a methodical investigator who documented evidence like a federal marshal.

"Furthermore," Bracken continued, settling into his explanation with obvious satisfaction, "Dooley's coworkers confirmed he returned to camp late the night Fletcher disappeared, covered in mud and bearing fresh injuries consistent with a physical altercation. All of this testimony is recorded and signed."

Price's pen scratched frantically across his notepad, clearly trying to find some angle of attack that wouldn't make him appear incompetent. "And yet you released the prisoner into federal custody rather than maintaining local jurisdiction. Some might consider that an... an abdication of responsibility."

Bracken's expression shifted, humor fading into something sharper. "Someone attempted to assassinate my prisoner while he was in my custody, Mr. Price. As much as I wish it was otherwise, a single man is incapable of providing round-the-clock guard to a prisoner while also attending to his other professional duties in the jurisdiction. When it became clear that Mr. Dooley was in danger—and that the danger likely extended to other civilians nearby—transferring Mr. Dooley to a facility with more personnel available to ensure his safety seemed like an execution of my responsibility rather than abdication of it."

The temperature in the makeshift courthouse seemed to drop several degrees. Hartwell realized she was witnessing something she'd rarely seen from Bracken—genuine anger without the protective coating of sarcasm.

"Unless the Committee on Internal Improvement's position is that I should have allowed a prisoner in my custody to be left vulnerable and defenseless when I had prior knowledge of an imminent threat to his safety?" Bracken's voice remained level, but steel ran beneath each word. "Because that strikes me as a dereliction of duty owed to a man in custody and exactly the kind of behavior that *should* warrant an inquiry."

Price's Adam's apple bobbed as he swallowed hard, apparently realizing he'd stumbled into territory where his criticism might backfire disastrously.

Hartwell suppressed a smile, recognizing the moment when a predator discovered it had cornered something with sharper teeth.

Price shifted in his chair with the restless energy of a man trying to regain his footing after the ground had been knocked out from under him. "I wonder if I might trouble you for a cup of coffee, Sheriff? This heat is rather oppressive for someone unaccustomed to the climate."

"Of course." Bracken's smile carried its usual hint of mockery, though Hartwell caught the way his shoulders sagged slightly as he pushed himself up from the desk. "Fresh pot's right over there."

She watched him hobble toward the side table, his injured arm held close to his body, each step requiring visible effort. When their eyes met across the room, he offered her a weary sigh that spoke volumes about auditors, political theater, and the general absurdity of performing competence while running on fumes and Cuban pastries.

He pulled himself together, though, compartmentalizing the pain like it was a profession. He carefully poured coffee with his good hand while Price shuffled through papers with renewed enthusiasm.

"Ah!" Price's voice carried a note of restrained triumph that made Hartwell's stomach clench. "Now this is interesting."

She moved closer as Price held up two documents, comparing them with the satisfaction of a cat discovering cream. "Your seizure of illegally imported Cuban rum, Sheriff. Your incident report states twelve bottles confiscated at the docks, but your evidence log lists only eleven."

Bracken returned with the coffee, setting it carefully beside Price's elbow. "What's that now?"

"A discrepancy in your documentation." Price's thin lips curved into something resembling a smile. "I'd like to examine your physical evidence storage, if you please."

Hartwell's jaw tightened as she led them to the church closet they'd converted into evidence storage. The space smelled of old hymnals and lamp oil, shelves lined with carefully labeled items from various cases. Price counted the rum bottles with obvious relish—eleven, exactly as the evidence log stated.

"Well, Sheriff?" Price's pen hovered over his notepad like a weapon. "Care to explain this discrepancy?"

Bracken examined the bottles with puzzlement etched into the lines on his face, his brow furrowing as he processed the numbers. "I must have miscounted during the seizure. Simple clerical error."

His voice carried none of its usual sardonic edge—just the flat admission of a tired man acknowledging human fallibility.

Hartwell watched Price's pen scratch triumphantly across his notepad, clearly savoring his discovery of the missing rum bottle like a prospector finding gold. The man had finally located something he could sink his teeth into—one discrepancy in an otherwise pristine collection of documentation.

"A simple clerical error," she said firmly, stepping beside Bracken. "Hardly grounds for questioning the sheriff's competence."

"Perhaps not." Price's smile a satisfied gleam; he'd found his angle of attack. "But it does raise questions about attention to detail. Standards of evidence handling. The kind of... oversight that federal administration takes quite seriously."

Bracken's jaw tightened almost imperceptibly, though his voice remained level. "Mr. Price, I've been sheriff for exactly one week. In that time, I've solved two murders, impeded a smuggling operation, and transferred one dangerous prisoner to federal custody without losing him to assassination. If you mean to hang me for miscounting liquor bottles while bleeding from gator bites, that's your prerogative. But I'm not sure how that would look in your report."

Price's pen hovered over his notepad like a sword waiting to fall.

Hartwell stepped forward, her judicial bearing crystallizing into something sharp and predatory. The hatchet man had overplayed his hand, and she intended to make him understand exactly how badly he'd miscalculated.

"Mr. Price." Her voice carried the measured authority of a gavel striking wood. "Out of all the misconduct you expected to find here, this is what you've settled on? One number on one page, filed on exactly the *same day* as the medical report detailing the physical injury that Sheriff Bracken sustained in the line of duty two days earlier?"

She gestured toward the evidence closet, her tone sharpening with each word. "The only person who would see that as evidence of incompetence—rather than evidence of an otherwise diligent man's human fallibility—is someone who arrived here with orders to find fault wherever he could and prepared to destroy a good man's reputation."

Price's pen had stopped moving entirely, his face cycling through shades of unease as Hartwell continued her methodical dismantling.

"Any reasonable person presented with this collection of evidence is going to look at any negative report you write and immediately know that something doesn't add up." Her smile carried the cold satisfaction of a predator cornering prey. "And when they look into it, they're going to find far more than a 'one' where a 'two' should be."

She stepped closer, her voice dropping to a conversational level that somehow managed to sound more threatening than if she'd shouted. "They're going to find a federal auditor who traveled here with a predetermined conclusion, ignored overwhelming evidence of competent police work, and fixated on a single clerical error made by an injured man continuing to do his job despite a life-threatening injury and a medical doctor's documented recommendation for bed rest."

Price swallowed hard, clearly recognizing that his hunting expedition had turned and he was now the prey.

"They're going to wonder," Hartwell continued with the quiet menace of a predator moving in for the kill, "who sent you here with such specific instructions—who wanted to discredit Sheriff Bracken badly enough to waste government resources on this charade. And when those questions start getting asked in the right circles...?"

She let the implication hang in the humid air like Spanish moss.

"Do you understand exactly what I'm saying, Mr. Price?"

Price's pen trembled against his notepad, the authority he'd arrived with evaporating like morning mist under Hartwell's surgical dismantling. She watched him absorb the full implications of her words—the carefully constructed trap he'd walked into, the political quicksand now sucking at his ankles.

"I believe," he said finally, his voice stripped of its earlier smugness, "that perhaps I was... overzealous in my interpretation of certain administrative irregularities."

"I do believe you were, Mr. Price. I trust your report will reflect the... *complete* picture of Sheriff Bracken's conduct?" Her tone carried the weight of a gavel striking final judgment.

Price nodded face pinched and shoulders sagging with defeat as though he'd just discovered his ammunition was loaded with blanks. "Naturally, Judge Hartwell. The federal administration values thoroughness and accuracy above all else."

Hartwell allowed herself a thin smile. The government vulture had been properly caged.

Behind them, Bracken remained quiet and still beside the evidence shelf, though she caught the subtle relaxation in his shoulders and the bulging of one cheek that suggested he'd found an opportunity to dispense with the second pastry.

She shook her head, returning her attention to the man in front of her. "Is there any other way we can assist in your enquiries today, Mr. Price?"

"No, Judge Hartwell, you've been most helpful."

Bracken spoke up, "I do have triplicate copies of all my incident reports, Mr. Price. I would be willing to part with one copy if it would help in your own report."

Mr. Price's face twisted as if he had just bitten down on a lemon rind. "That would be... courteous of you, Sheriff Bracken."

Bracken smiled, "Courteous to a fault, that's me. I'll just get those ready for you."

Mr. Price took the copies that Bracken handed him and slipped them into his folio, then nodded politely and retreated outside. He'd been gone for almost a whole minute before either Judge Hartwell or Bracken released their collective breaths.

"Sheriff Bracken, I think we may have pulled that off."

"Judge Hartwell," Bracken laughed softly, "I do believe that we did." He limped over to the breakfast offerings and took the whole plate of pastries with him to the table, then melted into the chair.

"He took the bait just like you said he would," she said.

"Not my first audit," he mumbled, sleepily. Bracken had taken his sling off and draped himself awkwardly across the table, too bone tired to keep upright anymore.

"First time with only twelve hours notice, though, and having to create an entire precinct's worth of paperwork out of thin air and wishful thinking... so that was special. But we never have to do that for the first time ever again. Gets easier after the first one... First one's always the worst..."

"Sheriff?"

"Mmm?"

"Thank you. For what you did today."

"S'why you buy me breakfast... gonna just... close my eyes for a moment..."

And he was asleep again.

Margaret Hartwell stood in the transformed church annex, watching Sheriff Thomas Bracken sleep face-down at the makeshift desk like a man who'd finally reached the end of his rope.

The morning's performance had been masterful—Bracken had handed Price exactly enough rope to hang himself, then stood back while she'd applied the judicial noose. But watching him now, collapsed over paperwork he'd spent the night perfecting, she realized the true cost of his competence. He was burning himself to cinders to prove he belonged here.

When the governor had first contacted her to inform her of Bracken's assignment to Cypress Run, she'd expected either a corrupt Chicago reject or a green fool who'd wash out within a month. Instead, she'd gotten a man who could rebuff a hostile audit while running on fumes and fever dreams, who dismantled his own lynch mob with calm words and a patient smile, and who turned gator bites into a suit of armor.

She'd misjudged him completely.

The annex door opened and Dr. Delgado stepped inside with his apprentice, Simon Finch, on his heels, the bulky wooden camera clutched in Simon's arms like unstable ordnance.

"Judge Hartwell, my wife tells me I missed the excitement last night, but that a commemorative picture might—"

Maggie lifted a sharp, silent hand—*stop*.

Diego halted mid-sentence. His eyes narrowed, then softened in that long-suffering way he reserved exclusively for Tom Bracken doing something ill-advised. He exhaled once, almost a laugh.

"Señor Finch," he murmured, dropping his voice, "tell me the plate is ready."

"Y-yes, Dr. Delgado," Simon whispered, tiptoeing despite the boards creaking beneath him.

"Good." Diego gestured toward Bracken—face-down in paperwork, bandaged arm curled protectively around the plate of *pastelitos* like a dragon hoarding treasure. "First you will take a photograph of *that*."

Simon blinked. "Of... the sheriff? Sleeping?"

"*Por supuesto.*" Diego's voice dropped even lower. "He will deny it later, and I want evidence."

"But—if he wakes up—"

"Simon," Diego said softly, his tone carrying all the gravity of his suffering, "I am the county physician and have survived three of his attempts at medical self-destruction this week alone. Take. The picture."

Hartwell cleared her throat, though the corner of her mouth tugged upward. "Mr. Finch, do hurry. Sheriff Bracken will be furious if he wakes to find us standing over him like mourners at a viewing."

Simon darted forward, set the tripod, and opened the shutter with the shaky solemnity of a boy lighting a fuse. The camera clicked. Bracken did not stir.

Diego nodded, satisfied. "Frame it well. I may need copies."

"We will all need copies," Hartwell added.

"Why?" Simon whispered.

"For leverage," she said dryly.

"For medical files," Diego corrected.

"For... blackmail?" Simon ventured.

Both adults glared at him.

Simon cleared his throat. "I'll just... go develop this now."

Diego shook his head and ushered him out, leaving Hartwell once again in the quiet of the annex.

She pulled a spare blanket from the supply closet and draped it carefully over Bracken's shoulders. Whatever political wolves had engineered his exile from Chicago, they'd done Cypress Run an unexpected favor. The man was sarcastic, irreverent, and utterly infuriating—but he was also exactly what this growing swamp town needed if it was going to survive.

She left him sleeping and stepped outside, where Price's black carriage was already disappearing down the dusty road. Another predator successfully driven off, thanks to the exhausted sheriff who somehow kept more professional tricks up his sleeve than a card sharp kept aces.

The hammering from the courthouse construction resumed outside, honest work replacing political theater. Perhaps that was fitting—they were all building something new in Cypress Run, brick by careful brick. And Sheriff Bracken, for all his sardonic deflections and billiards metaphors, might just be the cornerstone they needed.

CHAPTER TWENTY-FOUR

Sunday Reckoning

It had been two days since Price's audit, and the committee had spoken: Cypress Run would keep its municipal seat, Judge Hartwell her jurisdiction, and Sheriff Bracken his job. His methods had been noted as "unorthodox but effective." The real victory, though, was quieter: he no longer felt he had to fight to stay here. People nodded on the street now, the shopkeepers smiled, a few matrons had even invited him to Sunday dinner—offers he'd deflected with flustered graciousness.

Now the chapel bell called the town to Sunday worship.

Tom Bracken stood outside the whitewashed church, hat turning slow in his hands, watching families file past in pressed linen and gingham. He felt shamefully underdressed in shirtsleeves and his blue jacquard vest. His wool frock coat was still somewhere in the swamp, and he wouldn't stop feeling half-naked until he replaced it.

Stepping through that door felt like walking into a street gang's territory—new rules, unfamiliar faces, no sense of who might take offense. And the worst of it was that without his coat, the shoulder harness rig with his twin gun holsters hung out in the open where God and everyone could see them. A sheriff was expected to be armed, yes, but he preferred folks not to *see* it. The exposure itched at his skin.

When the last families disappeared inside, there was no putting it off.

He lingered in the doorway, hat twisting in his hands. Twice he counted the crowd, memorized the exits, and debated whether showing up was worse than staying away. Mrs. Mills made the decision for him, spotting him from a pew and waving as if he were a stray chicken needing to be directed to the roost.

He slipped across the threshold just as the opening hymn began—a bright, jaunty thing, worlds away from the Latin drone of Masses. The melody bounced off the whitewashed walls, all wrong angles and unfamiliar rhythm.

Every head turned to look at the tall outsider in the back. The congregation's singing faltered slightly as Tom instinctively genuflected in the aisle—thirty years of Catholic habit impossible to kill—then slid into the last pew with the stiffness of a man walking on broken glass.

The hymn recovered, voices rising in cheerful clamor while Tom mouthed along a beat late, catching at words like clues in a deposition. Across the aisle, Diego stood with Julietta and the girls—their stillness a calm island amid so much swaying and clapping. Diego caught his eye and lifted a brow, subtly checking in with his fellow exile in this sea of Baptists. Tom shook his head. Diego's small shrug and the bounce of his eyebrows that followed promised it would feel less strange—eventually.

The preacher's sermon came fast and fiery, a man selling salvation like a basket full of dry goods with plenty to go around. He spoke of gratitude—for rain, for harvest, for "the steady hand of law that keeps our county peaceful."

When Sheriff Bracken's name rolled through the room, applause broke out, a scattering of *Amens* following close behind. Tom nearly bolted from his seat. *Peace* wasn't the word he'd use for the past week, but the warmth in those voices—sincere, insistent, undeserved—loosened something in his chest that had been wound tight since Chicago.

When the service finally ended, Tom tried to escape through the side door like a man fleeing a crime scene. No luck. A battalion of church matrons descended on him the moment he left his pew, armed with covered dishes and determined smiles that brooked no argument. They moved with the coordinated precision of a military operation, cutting off his retreat with tactical efficiency.

Pies materialized in his hands as if conjured from thin air. Someone—he thought it might have been Mrs. Patterson—declared he looked "half-starved for a good woman's cooking," and the crowd took his weak protests as invitation for further assault. Each feeble attempt at refusal only seemed to encourage them.

"Mrs. Henderson, this is really too much—" he managed before another dish was tucked into his arms.

"Nonsense, Sheriff," she replied with the authority of a woman who'd been feeding reluctant men for forty years. "Look at you—thin as a rail."

"But I couldn't possibly eat all this—"

"Apple butter," announced Mrs. Mills triumphantly, adding another jar to his growing collection with the satisfaction of a general claiming territory. "My grandmother's recipe. Been in the family since before the war."

Tom found himself drowning in a mire of gingham-covered dishes and motherly concern, each woman apparently convinced that the sheriff's survival depended entirely on her particular contribution to his pantry. Someone at some point had taken pity and collected his gifts into a large basket so he wouldn't have to juggle it all.

From her spot under the church eaves, Ellie Harper watched the siege with poorly concealed amusement. The sight of the proud Chicago sheriff buried beneath a mountain of potluck dishes was medicine for her soul. When their eyes met across the crowd, she offered him a broad, mischievous smile—the kind that made his stomach flutter.

Tom finally extracted himself from the maternal ambush, basket heavy with enough food to feed a cavalry unit, and took refuge by Ellie.

She grinned at him, "Well, you survived your first church service down here. What'd you think?"

Tom laughed. "What a question. Let me think..." He shook his head in bafflement. "I think shouting at God to get His attention's a novel approach to religion. Sisters at the asylum used to say if God was paying attention to you, it meant either you'd done something particularly naughty and were about to get a lashing—or you were going to have a very short, very miserable life."

"Or maybe He just likes troublemakers. Ever thought of that?" Tom just shook his head. Ellie couldn't help a niggle of curiosity and asked, "Did you work at an asylum before you became a policeman?"

"Grew up in one."

"You grew up in an asylum?" Ellie laughed. "That explains a lot."

When he only looked at her, the smile slid from her face. "Oh. You're... not joking."

"Never found it particularly funny, I guess," Tom said, head tilting a little. Then realization dawned, and his tone lightened again. "Oh—oh, you mean *that* kind of asylum, the ones with the padded walls and the straightjackets. Okay, yes, I can see that being a good joke, but no, I wasn't talking about Bellevue or any place like that. Angel of Mercy Asylum for Boys—Catholic orphanage. So much worse than padded walls and straightjackets."

For a few solid moments she just watched him, struggling to find a response. Her instinct was to offer sympathy, but she knew better—he'd take it like salt on an open wound. Instead, she forced a small smile and ventured, "So... when you say worse than straightjackets... what you mean is that they forced you to keep your mouth shut for longer than ten minutes at a time."

Tom gave her a look bordering between startled she was playing along and grateful she was. He gave her a wide smile, "Those nuns'll pray the sarcasm right out of you if you let 'em. Had to stay on my toes."

"Doesn't seem like it stuck very well."

"Guess I was a lost cause."

"Lost cause? If a small army of nuns can't teach you to stay out of trouble, I'm guessing the rest of us don't have much of a hope, do we? It's funny, though," Ellie continued, "I remember you and Diego talking about confession in my kitchen the other day, but it didn't register in my mind that you're Catholic."

He looked at her mischievously and slipped into an exaggerated Irish brogue, "Ah now, Mrs. Harper—did the red hair and me smilin' eyes not give me away? Come away with ye, then."

"Well, I hardly ever see the red in your hair, usually you keep it hidden under swamp water and fever sweat." Her smile turned coy, her bottom lip catching lightly between her teeth. "Although, you do have very lovely eyes. So maybe I *should* have noticed something."

Tom let out a startled half-cough, half-laugh and looked away, grinning at the flirtation in spite of his embarrassment at how she'd turned the tables on him. "Yes, well..."

"Looks like you made quite an impression on the rest of the congregation," Ellie said, nodding toward the basket in his arms.

"An impression, huh?" Tom's mouth tugged wry. "Why do I get the feeling you had something to do with all this?"

"It wasn't me—this was your own doing. You were the one foolish enough to fall asleep in public with your arm wrapped around a plate of food like a stuffed toy. Mrs. Henderson got one look at you and every gossip in town knew our poor sheriff was starving before the sun was down. You brought this entirely on yourself."

Bracken chuckled. "So, you're telling me I've been worrying myself sick about how to eat 'til payday, and all I had to do was make myself look pathetic enough?"

"That's about the size of it. Don't tell me you're really that poor off, though—are you?"

Tom groaned, staring down at the floorboards.

"Don't tell anyone I admitted this, but I can't afford a new coat until the county decides to pay me. If some swamp badger takes a liking to the last shirt I own, I'm done for. But now that Mrs. Henderson's apparently adopted me, maybe I can stretch my five dollars into a few wins at the billiard table. Get myself a coat before I die of embarrassment."

Ellie's eyes widened at his confession, then narrowed with something between maternal concern and professional indignation. She glanced around to make sure no one else had overheard, then stepped closer, lowering her voice.

"Five dollars? Is that all?" She was mortified. "Tom, that's not poor—that's destitute."

"Well, when you put it like that, it sounds downright pitiful." Tom shifted the basket to his other arm, trying to play off her concern with his usual grin. "But hey, look at this bounty! I'm practically rich in preserved peaches."

She wasn't buying it. "The county should have advanced you something when you arrived."

"Knowing what you know, I'm sure you can think of just a few reasons why they might not have bothered. Judge Hartwell mentioned it might take a few weeks to 'process the paperwork.'" Tom smiled cheerfully. "So, one week down; maybe somewhere between one and three weeks left to go. Maybe. Probably."

Ellie studied his face, reading the careful humor that didn't quite mask the embarrassment underneath. "The government sent you here to fail, didn't they?" The question came out quiet, matter-of-fact, like she was stating the weather. "Stuck you in a place where you'd have no connections, no backup, no resources—just enough rope to hang yourself with."

"More like that gentleman from Illinois who's probably gnashing his teeth back in D.C. livid as all hell that his auditing trick didn't work. But the beauty of it is, all I have to do to piss that man off is keep on surviving. And let me tell you, I plan on taking all kinds of comfort in really pissing him off."

"You could have said something," she said quietly.

"To who?" he asked. No anger. No heat. Just quiet curiosity.

The question was awful in its simplicity. Ellie's hazel eyes searched his face, reading the careful neutrality he'd perfected in Chicago interrogation rooms. Around them, families scattered toward Sunday dinners and afternoon naps, their voices fading into the cicada hum.

Tom took her silence as its own answer. "Don't get too maudlin on my account, Mrs. Harper." He shifted the basket again, the weight of all those covered dishes suddenly feeling heavier. "Truth of the matter is that asking for help's a luxury I can't afford. Word gets back to the wrong ears that Sheriff Bracken's living hand to mouth, and suddenly every two-bit cattle rustler and smuggler knows exactly how desperate I am. Makes a man seem... negotiable."

He glanced down at the food—jaw set like steel. "And I'm not."

Tom looked back over at her, voice quiet but firm. "So, all this needs to stay between you, me, and the fence post, alright?"

Ellie had seen that look before—in her own mirror, back when the debts left behind after Harlan's arrest had threatened to swallow their homestead whole.

"Five dollars," she repeated sadly, shaking her head. "Tom, that's not even enough to replace your coat."

"Well, now you're just rubbing salt in the wound." His grin came back, lopsided and self-deprecating. "But, hey! Now the sling's off, I can start using my arm again. Small bets at the billiard table add up—should have enough set aside to get myself a jacket by Christmas. Something in a nice swamp-resistant, gator-resistant, heat-resistant fabric that isn't wool. I might even let you pick the color for me."

Despite herself, Ellie laughed. "You're impossible."

"I prefer 'resourceful.'" Tom tipped his hat to Mrs. Mills as she passed. "Trouble is I can't seem to find my cue stick. Everything was moving in such a flurry the night we dragged all the furniture up from the Sheriff's Office, but I can't for the life of me remember anyone grabbing my cue case and I haven't figured out where it went."

Ellie went perfectly still.

Tom turned toward her. "Ellie, you okay?"

Her voice came low, uneasy. "Tom, I know where your stick went."

Something must have registered as concerning, because he put the basket of food down and turned to face her, giving her his complete attention. "What's wrong?"

"The night you were out of town—taking Dooley to Everfield Junction—Harlan came to my house."

He stiffened, but there was only concern in his eyes when she met them. No judgment, only the quiet readiness to listen.

"He told me you were hurt," she went on. "That you might be dying. He said his men had found you on the road, that he'd either taken you hostage or left you in the swamp to die. And he had your cue stick to prove it—snapped the head clean off."

Tom made a small, pained noise. "He broke my stick? Well, that's just plain damn mean..."

He was joking, trying to ease the sharp edges, but Ellie couldn't laugh. "God, Tom, I was so scared."

Tom looked around quickly, then picked up the basket with his good hand and took her gently by the wrist with his healing one, leading her to the church annex building where the joint law office was still set up. He pulled her inside and the door closed behind them, cutting off the hum of voices outside.

Without hesitation, he drew her into his arms, her face fitting against his chest. His heartbeat thudded steady beneath the smell of laundry soap and cologne.

"It's okay," he murmured into her hair, pressing a soft kiss at her crown. "I'm here. I'm alive. Harlan was lying."

She stayed there until her trembling eased, then drew back enough to look at him. Her eyes were bright, wet at the edges.

"He was so convincing," she whispered. "Standing there with your broken stick, saying you were hurt or worse, and I—I thought I'd never see you again." Her voice faltered. "I thought you wouldn't make it back. That it was my fault."

Tom's arms tightened, one hand smoothing her hair. "Hey now. Takes more than a few swamp rats to put me down permanent. Actually, I take that back. The thought of what you Floridians have for rats down here is genuinely terrifying."

She pulled back just enough to look at him, her hazel eyes bright with unshed tears. "Don't joke. Not about this."

"Who's joking?" He cupped her face, thumbs brushing the damp from her cheeks. "Although, now that I think more on it, I'm not sure what it says about me that you thought I'd haul my billiards cue through twenty miles of swamp on a midnight prisoner transport."

She stared at him. "Tom."

"What? I love the game, but not *that* much."

"You're making fun of me."

"I'm not making fun—just trying to figure out if I should be offended that you think I'm that enamored with my stick. I'm genuinely confused."

She slapped lightly at his arm. "I can't believe you're making fun of me! I was terrified!"

"I'm trying to make you laugh," he corrected gently. "Just trying to show there's nothing to be scared of. See? Safe and upright. Breathing—mostly—and apparently the proud owner of enough peach cobbler to feed half the county."

That coaxed a fragile laugh from her. "That's not funny either." She blinked away the last of her tears and made herself look into the basket again, chasing steadier ground. "You have to be careful about the peach cobbler down here. If you get too much of it, somebody's got designs on you."

Tom chuckled. "What—you think it's poisoned?"

"Worse," she said. "It probably comes with marriage proposals."

Tom laughed outright at that, stepping back to allow Ellie to compose herself and straighten her skirts. "How do you figure?"

"Southern hospitality isn't just about kindness," Ellie said, peering inside the basket, "it's about having legitimate excuses to examine your business up close."

"Ah. So this is reconnaissance, disguised as apple butter."

"Pretty much. You can tell an awful lot about a woman's intentions by what she's trying to feed you." She poked through the assortment with mock severity. "For example, this apple butter from Mrs. Mills says she wants to know if you're planning to stay past your first year. Mrs. Patterson's cobbler means she's half convinced you need a wife. And Mrs. Henderson's chicken casserole is a sure sign that she thinks you're too skinny to survive a proper Florida rainy season."

Tom leaned in the doorway, watching her with that crooked half-smile. "What's your professional opinion, Nurse Harper?"

"About which part?"

"Any of it. All of it."

She looked up, gaze frank, measuring him. "I think you've been looking after yourself alone so long, you forgot what it feels like when other people want to help."

That landed deeper than he expected. Tom cleared his throat, pretending to study a jar label.

"And the wife situation?" he asked.

"As for the wife situation..." Ellie continued, drawing the words out playfully, a smile tugging at the corner of her mouth, "I suspect Mrs. Patterson's going to be disappointed. Most of the unmarried ladies in town are either too young for you or too set in their ways to appreciate a man who thinks billiards strategies are at all flattering when courting a girl."

"Most of them?"

The question slipped out before he could stop it, and Ellie's smile widened into something that made his chest feel tight and loose all at once.

Ellie's smile turned gentle, predatory in a way that Tom had no defense against. "Most," she confirmed. "I can think of one or two that might be charmed despite themselves. And besides, they're all forgetting one tiny detail."

"And what's that?"

"I fed you dinner first." Her grin was quick, proud. "Means I claimed my stead before any of them did."

Tom's grin came slow, genuine. "'Claimed your stead?' Guess I should've read the fine print on that supper."

"And what if you had?" she asked, genuinely curious.

"I reckon I still would've eaten it. Would have been heartbreaking to turn it down. It was a particularly fine meal, as I recall."

Ellie's laugh slipped out light and unguarded. She remembered perfectly well that she'd only served him beans and cornbread that night—more warm and filling than anything. She straightened, taking a step toward him. "You really can't have much experience if you call beans and cornbread a particularly fine meal."

Tom huffed out a laugh, "Mrs. Harper. I will concede that you were correct in my lack of kissing experience and your education in the matter was appreciated, but you are just going to have to accept that a man knows a good meal when he sees one and that was the best damn meal I can recall having eaten in my life, fine print and all."

She took one more step into his space, color touching her cheeks. "Best be careful, Sheriff. You flatter a girl about her cooking that way, she might just have to feed you again."

"I'll risk it," he said easily.

Outside, the last of the congregation was dispersing, voices carrying through the open windows as families made plans for Sunday dinner and afternoon visits. The normal rhythm of a town at peace.

"Ellie…" He started, lost the rest of it, the thought catching somewhere between his chest and his throat. He had words—he just couldn't seem to find the right ones…

The crash of the door slamming open cut through the moment like a gunshot. Jake Henley burst in, face flushed and breathless.

"Sheriff! You gotta come now—courthouse—there's something—" He bent over, hands on his knees, gulping air like a man who'd run the length of Main Street.

Tom stepped away from Ellie, instantly alert. "What kind of something, Mr. Henley?"

"Dead man on the courthouse steps. Got a badge on him." Jake panted, wiping sweat from his forehead. "Just come."

Tom's blood went cold. He grabbed his hat from the desk.

"Stay here," he told Ellie, but she was already following him out the door.

They ran through the Sunday-quiet streets, their footsteps pounding against boardwalk and dust as they ran toward the half-built courthouse. The brick structure loomed against the afternoon sky, its scaffolding casting long shadows across the town square. A crowd bunched at the steps, whispering, but parted fast when the sheriff strode through.

The smell hit him first—sweet rot and swamp decay, thick enough to taste.

A decomposed corpse sat propped against the bottom step like a drunk sleeping off a heavy night. Except this drunk would never wake—he'd been dead for weeks. The flesh had turned black and waxy, peeling back from bone, but the clothes remained: work pants, cotton shirt, leather vest. And pinned to his chest, tarnished but unmistakable, a sheriff's badge.

"Jesus Christ," Tom breathed.

"That's Sheriff Brown," Jake said quietly. "Rode out for Tampa when the Carter gang shot up the old jailhouse."

"Doesn't look like he made it very far," Tom said.

He crouched beside the body. For a moment he just looked at the badge—the thing they both carried—then drew a slow breath.

He touched two fingers to his brow and traced a small cross in the air over the tarnished star.

"*Pax,* brother," he murmured. "I'll make sure they know you didn't cut and run. Best I can offer."

He shifted closer, breathing through his mouth to combat the worst of the stench. Something white protruded from the corpse's skeletal fingers—a folded piece of paper, tucked deliberately into his hand as if the dead man had been sent to deliver a message.

Tom carefully extracted the note and unfolded it. The handwriting was steady, confident, mocking:

This is what comes to men who forget their place. I do worse to those who take what's mine. Maybe my girl could stand to learn a lesson, too.

I have the boy.

You want him breathing come moonrise, bring yourself to the big camphor on Calusa Cypress Trail. Come alone, or collect the consequences.

"The hell—" The words dried up. Understanding hit like cold water to the chest.

Ellie had come up beside him. She read over his shoulder, then went white as paper. "Nate," she whispered. "Oh, God—Nate."

The note crumpled in Tom's fist. His voice came low, knife-thin. "Ellie, do you know where Nate is? Is Carter lying again?"

"He was playing behind the church after service—Sarah Mills said she saw him walking toward the creek with his pole, but that was over an hour ago—"

Her breath broke on the sentence.

A heavy stillness filled Tom's chest, cold as steel. Harlan Carter had just declared war—and he'd chosen the one weapon that could hurt them both.

Tom stood slowly, his movements controlled and deliberate, the kind of calm that preceded a storm of violence. Whatever the crowd saw in his eyes made them step back. This wasn't their charming sheriff anymore; this was the man Chicago had tried to chew up until it had been forced to spit him out.

"Jake," he said quietly. "Get the Doc—have him look at the body, see if he can tell us anything useful. And get Judge Hartwell—she needs to know about this."

Tom turned to Ellie, arms hanging still at his sides—offering nothing, because there was nothing left to offer. Nothing except the truth.

"I'm going after him."

No bluster, no charm, no clever plan—only the flat certainty of a man who'd already read the story and knew how it ended.

Ellie caught his arm, feeling the fury coiled beneath his careful control. Her grip tightened, as if she could anchor him by force alone.

"Tom, no. That's exactly what he wants—you alone, on his ground, by his rules."

Tom glanced from the crumpled note in his hand to Ellie's stricken face. Somewhere out there, Harlan Carter held his own son hostage.

The table was set, the break already made. There was no choice now but to play with what he had—and what he had was a murderer waiting for him somewhere in the cypress swamp dangling a frightened young boy as bait to catch a sheriff.

"He's got Nate." Each word clicked like the hammer of a Colt cocking back. "Of course I'm going."

Because what other option was there?

Act Five

THE FINAL GAME

CHAPTER TWENTY-FIVE

Behind the Eight

The church annex felt cramped around his fury, too small to contain what was building inside him, as Tom methodically loaded cartridges into his Lightning's magazine, the metallic clicks echoing off the makeshift courthouse walls. His movements were precise, automatic—muscle memory from a dozen Chicago raids where preparation meant the difference between walking home and not.

"Kid's in danger." Tom said, already weary of the argument, as if he'd been trying to explain single-digit addition for the last thirty minutes. "End of discussion."

"You're not thinking this through," Ellie said, watching him stuff ammunition into every available pocket. "Harlan doesn't do anything without everything stacked in his favor."

Tom slid the bolt forward, the slide action smooth as silk. "I'm thinking plenty. Harlan's got Nate. I go get Nate. Simple."

"Simple?" Ellie's voice sharpened. "You told me the night we met that thinking a few steps ahead wasn't trigonometry. So prove it. Use that billiards brain of yours instead of charging in like some half-cocked city cop pretending to be a cowboy."

Tom paused, a handful of cartridges hovering over his vest pocket. The comparison stung because it was accurate—he was reacting, not calculating. And it was something he hadn't done since Chicago.

Anytime a child was in danger, something primal kicked loose in his brain. He'd once stormed a warehouse full of kidnappers for a paper boy he'd never met. Spent three nights prowling tenements and rail yards to pull a six-year-old out of the Bellweather gang's hands. Kids getting hurt—it never failed to rewire his judgment, make him act stupid.

If he were thinking even halfway straight, he'd realize that somebody had studied his record well enough to know that, well enough to know exactly the right nerve to press, to use it against him. The thought should've made him damned uncomfortable.

And if he were thinking at least three-quarters straight, he'd know better than to let anyone make him stupid.

But that was the problem: he wasn't thinking straight at all.

Because this was Nate.

The boy who'd thrown himself at a gunman to save a stranger. Who asked questions like it was how he breathed oxygen. Who'd left his stuffed bear on Tom's pillow when Tom had been out of his mind with fever. The boy whose mother made Tom believe that maybe Florida was a place he could make a life and not just the place he'd been exiled to die.

"I can't leave him out there," Tom said quietly, more defeated than angry. "You know I can't."

"I'm not asking you to leave him." Ellie stepped closer, her voice urgent. "I'm asking you to be the man who outsmarted a big city auditor and solved John Fletcher's murder inside of a day. What's Harlan really after?"

Tom's hands stilled as he finally gave her question the consideration it deserved. "He wants me dead," Tom said slowly.

Ellie shook her head. "Dead is easy. Why the theater? The note, the meeting, the big camphor tree?"

Tom set the rifle on the table, the click of wood against wood providing the auditory cue he needed to rerack the thoughts in his head. Billiards. Angles. The shot you saw versus the shot that actually mattered. "He wants me away from town."

"There you go." Ellie's voice carried grim approval. "Harlan can only be in one place at once, but his gang can act while he's somewhere else. You ride out to save Nate—and what happens here?"

The answer clicked, as unpleasant and sickening as sinking the wrong ball or scratching the cue. Tom could see it now—the real play hidden behind the obvious one. "He hits the town while I'm gone. The courthouse, the saloon, maybe even the church." His eyes found hers. "Your place. Anyone who helped me."

"Including Judge Hartwell. Diego. Simon." Ellie's voice was steady, but Tom caught the tremor underneath. "Everyone he needs to make an example of."

Tom stared at the Lightning, the evening light sliding over the blued steel of the barrel. Classic misdirection—get the sheriff chasing shadows in the swamp while the real work happened in his absence. Like a pool shark lining up the table while his mark gets himself snookered.

"Sonofabitch," he breathed.

Ellie nodded grimly. "Harlan's not just planning to kill you, Tom. He's going to make it look like you abandoned the town, ran off into the swamp like a coward. Burn everything to the ground and your reputation with it. And if you play straight into his hands..." She drew a sharp breath. "I don't know what he'll do to Nate. To me. To this town. He could burn it to cinders if he wanted."

Tom's fingers traced the butt of his long-barreled Colt—the heavier one, built for distance and precision. Useless in tight corners, but capable of landing the impossible when he needed it most. He had a feeling he'd need every impossible shot he could find now that he saw the shape of the game: not revenge, not jealousy—*obliteration*. Harlan wanted everything Tom was reduced to ash, his death remembered as betrayal instead of sacrifice.

It wasn't just destruction. It was *mean*—like stealing his damned pool cue, snapping it in half, and using the pieces to terrorize the woman who cared for his safety.

"So your husband's set us a bad table and left us square behind the eight." Tom exhaled. "We'll need one hell of a kick-shot to break out of it. Any ideas?"

Ellie met his gaze, steady and fierce. "Kick his balls when he's not looking."

Tom blinked. Once, twice. Then the laugh came, low and exasperated. He dragged a hand down his face.

"That's—God help me, Mrs. Harper, that's not how billiards metaphors work."

Ellie lifted her chin. "Maybe not. But if he's going to cheat, I don't see why we can't. And it might even buy us a shot."

Tom drew a deep breath and let it out, letting the decision settle in.

"Then I guess we better make it count."

The mule stood patient as a cemetery monument while Bobby Keene adjusted the harness one final time, muttering about fool sheriffs and suicide missions. Tom tugged at the sleeves of his new sack coat, trying to coax another inch of fabric past his wrists. The thing fit like a hand-me-down from a shorter, broader man—which, given Cotton's inventory, it probably was.

"You look like a scarecrow dressed for a county fair," Diego said, circling Tom with the air of a surgeon examining a patient he couldn't save. "This is madness, you know that? Walking into Carter's trap with nothing but a mule cart and bad tailoring."

"The coat's got pockets," Tom said, patting the bulges where he'd distributed his ammunition. "Makes me feel prepared. Professional."

"Professional corpse, maybe." Diego's hands clenched into fists to keep them from shaking. "I'm not going to forgive you if you get yourself killed, Tom. I mean it."

Judge Hartwell stood apart from the group, her silver hair catching the last of the daylight. "The state government won't look kindly on losing a sheriff to vigilante justice, Bracken. Particularly after I just spent a day convincing them you were competent."

"Appreciate the vote of confidence, Judge Hartwell."

"This isn't a joke." Hartwell's voice sharpened. "If Carter kills you, he wins everything. The town, the railroad contracts, the smuggling routes. You're playing right into his hands."

Tom checked his rifle one more time. "Maybe. But he's got an eight-year-old boy that he's holding hostage. My hands are pretty well tied."

A small crowd had gathered despite the hour—John Cotton wringing his hands, Jake Henley shifting his weight from foot to foot, even Mrs. Henderson peering around Jennifer Starr's shoulder. The kind of crowd that formed when folks smelled disaster coming and couldn't look away.

"Sheriff's doing the right thing," Jake offered, though his voice lacked conviction. "Can't leave a boy out there with a murderer."

"Can't help the boy if he's dead," Mrs. Mills countered. "Ought to send word to the federal marshals, let them handle Carter."

"Marshals are two days away," Tom said. "Nate Harper doesn't have two days."

Ellie stood silent near the clinic steps, watching him with an unreadable expression. She'd been quiet since he'd started making his preparations.

"Mrs. Harper?" Tom called softly. "You got any last-minute wisdom for a fool sheriff?"

She looked at him for a long moment, her hazel eyes steady in the gathering dusk. "Don't get yourself killed."

"That's it? No lecture about thinking three moves ahead?"

"You already know what you need to know." Her voice carried something he couldn't quite name—not goodbye, but not see-you-later either. "Just remember who you're coming back to."

Tom touched the brim of his hat, suddenly aware of how the coat's stiff collar chafed against his neck.

Bobby cleared his throat. "Mule's ready when you are, Sheriff."

Tom climbed onto the cart's bench, the Lightning across his knees and his Colts riding easy at his sides. The cart looked ridiculous, the coat even more so. A pathetic state of affairs—but when had it not been this week?

"If I'm not back by dawn," he said to the assembled crowd, "bar the doors and send word to Everfield Junction. Tell the marshals that Harlan Carter's making his play."

"Tom," Diego said quietly, stepping in as he had once before. "Don't do this alone."

Tom didn't meet his eyes. "You upset that I'm cheating you out of another thrilling evening in mortal peril?"

"I'm serious."

"So am I." He gathered the reins, the humor thinning but not gone. "Last time—last time you nearly got crushed under a crate, shot at, burned alive in a warehouse fire, and blown up. And that was when we were just going in to *talk* to the guy. You've done your share for me, Doc, and it means more than—" He broke off, cleared his throat. "But you're not coming. Not this time."

"*Cabezón inútil, idiota valiente—no quiero que mueras.* You're not invincible."

The sheriff's jaw worked. For a heartbeat, the noise of the yard flattened to silence.

"Never said I was," he murmured, then added with a ghost of his old humor, "And whatever the hell else you just said, I'm sure I probably deserved it. Just... keep folks safe here till I come back."

"And if you don't?"

Tom finally looked at him—steady, calm, almost kind. "Then you'll get to say I told you so. Don't think I'd rob you of that, Doc."

He flicked the reins. The mule's hooves struck soft percussion against the packed earth as the cart rolled from the clinic yard.

He didn't look back, but he could feel their eyes on him—Diego's exasperation, Hartwell's cool calculation, the townspeople's uneasy admiration.

And Ellie's silence, the one sound that followed him furthest into the dark.

———— ★✹★ ————

The mule clopped along the dark road until Tom turned it into a stand of cypress trees. Spanish moss hung like funeral shrouds in the moonlight, and somewhere in the distance an owl called out its lonely question to the night.

Tom didn't have to wait long. Hoofbeats approached through the underbrush, and a horse emerged from the shadows carrying a familiar silhouette. The rider pulled up beside the cart, and Tom felt his heart do something complicated in his chest.

"Evening, Mrs. Harper."

Ellie swung down from the saddle with practiced ease, holding the reins of a familiar dark gelding. Tom hopped off the wagon bench and moved toward the horse, his face breaking into something that might have been relief if it weren't so tangled up with worry.

"Hey there, Old Boy." Tom ran his hand along the horse's neck, checking him over like a mother hen. "Miss me, did you? Course you did."

Ellie stared at him. "You named your horse Old Boy?"

"What else was I gonna call him?" Tom scratched behind the gelding's ears, his voice dropping into the tone reserved for beloved animals and small babies. "He's such a good Old Boy, isn't he? Yes, he is."

The horse whickered and nudged Tom's shoulder, clearly pleased with the reunion. Tom fished a piece of dried apple from his pocket and fed it to the gelding, murmuring nonsense endearments.

"You're ridiculous," Ellie said, but her voice carried warmth instead of scorn.

Tom looked at her, his hands still stroking the horse's muzzle. "You sure about this? Really sure? Because once we do this, there's no taking it back."

Ellie's chin lifted in that stubborn way he'd learned to recognize. "Of course I'm sure."

"Alright then." Tom shrugged out of Cotton's ill-fitting coat, the fabric catching on his holsters. "Arms up."

He helped her into the coat, his fingers brushing hers as he guided her arms through the sleeves. The thing hung on her like a tent, the shoulders drooping and the cuffs covering her hands completely. Tom rolled the sleeves back, his touch gentle and methodical.

"Now the hat." He lifted his battered felt hat from his head and settled it over her hair, tugging the brim low to shadow her face. He stepped back to assess the effect, his head tilted like an artist studying his work.

"You're too short," he said finally. "Way too short. But from a distance, in the dark..." He tried to laugh, but the sound came out strained and thin. "Hell, maybe Carter's eyesight's going bad."

The joke fell flat between them. Tom's face crumpled slightly, and before Ellie could say anything, he pulled her against his chest, knocking the ill-fitting hat from her head, his arms wrapping around her with desperate strength.

"Christ, Ellie." The words came out muffled against her hair, raw and honest in a way that made her heart clench. "What if this doesn't work? What if I'm sending you to die instead of—"

"Stop." Ellie's voice was firm against his chest. "Just stop. You're not sending me anywhere. I'm choosing to go."

But Tom held her tighter, his hands shaking slightly where they pressed against her back. In the coat and hat, she felt small and fragile, like a child playing dress-up in her father's clothes. The weight of what they were about to do settled over them both like the humid night air.

Somewhere in the swamp, a gator splashed, the sound echoing Tom's fear back at them from the dark water.

"You're shaking," she said against his chest.

"Course I am," he let out a small, miserable laugh. "Never been more terrified in my life."

"Tom—"

"Here, I need you to keep this hidden." He pressed a small derringer into her hand. "If he gets the drop on you, he's gonna take the obvious guns. Make absolutely sure this one isn't obvious, you understand me?"

Ellie looked at the miniature gun in her hand and laughed. "Tom Bracken, I have seen you half-naked more times than I've seen you fully dressed; where in the Lord's name have you been keeping this?"

Tom blinked innocently and managed the ghost of his usual grin. "Why, Mrs. Harper, you're going to have to get to know me just a little better before I let you get acquainted with my less than obvious hiding spaces."

Ellie laughed and buried her face in his shirt, wrapping her arms around him. "Don't tell anyone, but I'm terrified for you, too. Here, I made this for you." She pulled a talisman out of her dress pocket and slipped it around his neck before he could protest.

The thing was rough and small—a curved alligator tooth, cleaned to a pale ivory sheen and strung on a strip of leather darkened from oil and sun. A thin twist of copper wire bound the root, glinting faintly in the lantern light.

Tom's breath caught. That damned tooth. He remembered clutching at her in desperation while Diego dug it out of his arm with forceps and a prayer. The marks against the edge were still there.

"Knew you'd recognize it," she said quietly. "Figured if it tried to eat you once, it might as well warn off whatever tries to come for you next."

He closed his hand over it, the tooth cold against his skin at first, then warming. "You boiled it, too, didn't you? Cause Doc painted a vivid picture of the flesh-rotting toothpaste these guys use and it left an impression on me, I must say."

"Of course I boiled it," Ellie said, eyes bright with amusement that pretended to be irritation. "Twice, if you must know. Do you think I don't pay attention to how injury prone you are? Liable to survive the gun fight only to scratch himself to death with his own gator tooth. Tried to take *some* precautions."

Tom laughed softly, the sound breaking halfway through. "You're something else, Mrs. Harper."

"So are you, Sheriff Bracken." She gave the leather cord a gentle tug to tighten it. "Now keep it close. Whatever city luck has kept you alive so far, it's nothing compared to the swamp grit you've got now."

He touched the tooth once more, feeling its curve settle against his chest. "I'll do my best," he said. "But maybe you could use some city luck for yourself."

Tom pulled his pocket watch from his vest, the silver catching moonlight as he worked at something small attached to the chain. His fingers fumbled with the clasp, and Ellie heard him mutter a curse under his breath before a tiny medallion came free.

He held it up between them, the small disc spinning slowly on its delicate chain. "St. Christopher," he said, his voice carrying that particular tone he used when he was trying not to sound as worried as he felt. "Patron saint of foolish bastards who can't help wading into trouble on a regular basis."

Ellie squinted at the medallion in the dim light. The saint's figure was worn smooth from years of handling, barely visible against the tarnished silver. "Tom—"

"Always helped me make the crossing," he continued, ignoring her protest. "Reach the shore on the other side, you know? Figure it can't hurt, and if it helps...?"

The gesture hit her somewhere deep and unexpected. She looked up at his face, seeing past the swagger to the man beneath—the man who was terrified of sending her into danger but trusted her enough to let her go anyway.

"I haven't any way to keep it safe," she said quietly. "Don't want to lose it."

"When we make it through tonight, I'll get you a proper chain to wear it on." Tom's mouth quirked into something that might have been a smile if it weren't so fragile. "If I ever get paid, I mean. Assuming Hartwell doesn't dock my wages for all the property damage I reckon is coming."

He stepped closer, his hands gentle as he worked loose a strand of hair from her braid. "But in the meantime..."

His fingers moved with surprising dexterity, weaving the medallion's chain through the soft, brown strands as if he'd done this a thousand times before. The concentration on his face was almost comical—tongue caught between his teeth, brow furrowed in determination. When he finished, he tied the knot tight so it wouldn't come loose, then tucked the adorned strand carefully behind her ear.

"There." His hand lingered against her cheek, thumb brushing the line of her jaw. "Now we've each got some city luck and swamp grit both. And St. Christopher has a front row seat to keeping you safe."

The space between them seemed to collapse all at once, and when he kissed her, Ellie tasted fear and hope and desperation all tangled together. His other arm wrapped around her waist, pulling her against him like he could somehow keep her from harm through sheer force of will.

She felt everything in that kiss. His love, raw and honest. His admiration for what she was about to do. And his honest fear that this might be goodbye. The heartbreak of a man who'd finally found something worth keeping and had to let it ride into the dark without him.

When they broke apart, Tom pressed his forehead against hers, his breathing unsteady.

"Be safe," he whispered, half instruction, half desperate prayer to whatever saints might be listening in the Spanish moss above them. "Please... please be safe..."

He stepped back, his hands falling to his sides as if it was the only way he could force himself to let her go. The moonlight caught the sharp angles of his face, and for a moment he looked exactly like what he was—a man balanced on the knife's edge between hope and despair.

Tom stooped to grab the hat and settled it on her head again, then slowly, painfully, forced himself to walk away from her. He hid his face for a moment in Old Boy's neck before scrambling awkwardly up into the saddle, somehow getting himself settled without falling off. The horse stood as still as could be, as if well aware that his new owner just needed a little bit of extra patience and grace. Tom clutched at the saddle horn and Ellie couldn't help wincing at his form.

"Are you sure you're going to make it back to town?"

Tom grinned, petting the horse's neck. "Sure, I'm sure. I got the best horsey partner a lawman could ask for. Helped me get home through five miles of swamp. He'll make sure I don't fall off between here and town. Cause he's a good Old Boy, isn't he?" Tom patted the horse's neck as if it was nothing more than a big, loveable dog. Old Boy's ears flicked at the praise, so perhaps he didn't mind too much.

Ellie climbed into the cart and held out his rifle. "Don't forget this."

Tom's horse started forward of its own accord, moving close enough to the cart for Tom to take the rifle and sling it over his back. "Hey, Ellie?"

She looked up at him. "Yeah?"

"Don't miss your shot, okay?"

She smiled and shook her head—she wouldn't.

"Come on, Old Boy. Got ourselves a gunfight we can't be late to." The gelding moved off through no urging at all of Tom's, much slower and steadier than he's been when she'd ridden him out, following the path back they had taken to get here. She didn't know how it had happened, but Tom Bracken, a city boy who couldn't ride a horse, had thrown himself off a runaway wagon in the middle of the wilderness, and of all the horses of all the outlaws he could possibly have encountered, he had somehow lucked into the most considerate creature this side of the Mississippi.

Maybe St. Christopher knew what he was about after all.

She touched her fingertips to the medallion in her hair as Tom and his horse disappeared from sight. "Please be safe," she whispered after him. Then she took the reins and urged the mule toward her own troubled waters that lay ahead.

CHAPTER TWENTY-SIX

Double-Bank

The cart's wheels creaked against cypress roots as Ellie guided them deeper into the swamp. Moonlight filtered through Spanish moss, casting silver shadows that danced with each step. Every few minutes, a low whistle drifted from the treeline—Carter's men tracking her progress like wolves following wounded prey.

She sat as tall as she could manage in the driver's seat, Tom's coat hanging loose around her shoulders, his hat pulled low over her eyes. The disguise felt fragile as paper, but it only needed to hold until she got close enough. Close enough to do what needed doing.

Her thoughts drifted to Nate—somewhere out there in the dark. Eight years old and being used as a weapon by his own father.

What kind of man did that?

The kind who hadn't always been this way.

The memory came unbidden: Harlan's hands, gentle once. Cradling Nate like spun sugar, steadying his tiny steps, tucking blankets around him at night. Resting almost tenderly over her pregnant belly before their son was born.

But those same hands had later counted stolen bills, loaded guns, and left widows and orphans in their wake. Not for the first time, she wondered what had happened. Had he always been this underneath, and she'd just never seen it? Or had something inside him truly changed?

She had loved him once—honestly, fiercely, with everything she had.

But had the man she loved ever existed, or was he just the lie that looked like love?

Brooding on who Harlan used to be wouldn't help her now. The man waiting ahead wasn't the one who'd held his child; he was the one using that child as bait. And she couldn't afford to forget it. Not even for a breath.

She'd have to remember that tonight—when his voice went soft, when he said her name the way he used to. He would lie. Twist. Reach for the version of her that used to flinch at his disappointment.

That woman was gone.

And Ellie would keep her gone.

The road jolted; the mule snorted, steady as ever. Ellie kept her hands firm on the reins, even as she shook her head—as if the motion could convince her future self that listening to him talk had been a foolish idea.

The movement freed the lock of hair where Tom had woven his St. Christopher's medallion. It swung loose, brushing her cheek. She tucked it back behind her ear, fingers lingering on the braid he'd tied with such clumsy care. His hands had trembled the whole time. He'd tried to hide it with that easy grin, but she'd seen straight through him—pale as his shirt, scared out of his mind, holding himself together just long enough to let her go. It had cost him plenty, she could tell.

That was the difference between Tom and Harlan.

Harlan would've sent her into danger without blinking, already counting the profit before she was out of sight. Tom would've thrown himself between her and the bullet if he could. Charging into danger to save someone he'd never met came as naturally to him as being an insufferable, stubborn jackass. Guns, gators, rum-runners, explosions—every damned thing the world hurled his way—he could face it without losing his smile. But letting *her* walk toward danger? That was the thing that terrified him.

And the damnedest part... he'd done it anyway. Terrified or not, he'd stepped back because she'd asked—because he trusted her. The bastard. God help her, she hated how much she loved him for it.

Maybe that wasn't the only thing she loved. Maybe she loved all the ways he wasn't Harlan.

Harlan had been all promise and no follow-through—grand gestures that crumbled the moment life demanded substance. He'd wooed her with moonlit rides and stolen kisses, then left her to explain his absences to their boy.

Tom was... well, Tom. Awkward with new experiences but never afraid to try them. Always racing to make the first joke at his own expense. Could tell a story about *anything* if you let him warm to the audience. Far too good at landing on his feet for anyone's peace of mind, and far too good at hiding pain even from the people who cared.

Where Harlan spun tales to justify his choices, Tom admitted his mistakes straight—then spun tales to distract from the embarrassment. Where Harlan charmed his way *out* of trouble, Tom charged right into it—and *then* charmed his way out again by apologizing for bleeding on her floor, by being hopeless with oranges, by answering all ten million of Nate's questions as though each one mattered, and by sharing his wonder over a sky full of stars.

Damn the man. She wasn't this far gone already. She refused to be.

She'd been in love before and hated what came after. But this... this wasn't the same. How could it be?

Harlan had loved her like a prize to be won, something pretty to possess between jobs and schemes. Tom looked at her like she was the only steady thing in a world gone crooked—as if her good opinion mattered more than seeing another sunrise. And if that opinion didn't include him, he'd respect it anyway.

He looked at her as if she were the solids to his stripes.

And now she was using billiards metaphors.

God damn the man.

Tom Bracken was everything Harlan Carter wasn't. The difference sat in her chest like a physical weight. And she wasn't ashamed to admit that carrying the weight of Tom Bracken in her chest was far more of a comfort than it was a burden.

But comfort couldn't be the thing she carried in there now. Not tonight. She needed to forge that weight into armor and use it to shield her heart from what was coming.

Harlan would talk first—he always did. He'd try to own the conversation, turn her heart against her head, and make her question what she already knew. And if she let him in, even an inch, he'd take the rest.

The cart wheels hit a rut, jolting her back to the present.

Time to stop thinking about what she might lose and focus on what she aimed to save. A whistle echoed through the trees, closer now. She adjusted Tom's hat on her head and urged the mule forward.

The clearing opened ahead, moonlight washing everything silver-white. The massive camphor tree stood like a sentinel in the center, its trunk wide enough to hide three men. Harlan waited beneath its branches, lean silhouette unmistakable even at a distance.

Ellie's hands tightened on the reins. She asked herself one last time: Did she have the strength for this? To face down the father of her child, the man who'd taught her what both love and betrayal tasted like? To pull a trigger if it came to that?

And the answer was more simple than she thought it would be. She could do this. She had to.

The gunfire reached Tom's ears before he topped the last rise into Cypress Run. Sharp cracks of rifle fire mixed with the deeper boom of shotguns, punctuated by shouts and the crash of breaking glass. Smoke drifted above the buildings like morning mist, except morning was hours away and this smoke carried the harsh bite of gunpowder.

Tom urged Old Boy faster, though the horse needed no encouragement. The animal sensed the violence ahead, ears pinned back, nostrils flaring. They crested the hill and Tom saw muzzle flashes winking from windows and doorways along Main Street. Carter's raiders had spread through town like a plague, turning Cypress Run into a shooting gallery. Unfortunately for them, the shooting gallery was one carnival attraction where Tom never failed to take the prize.

He counted at least six men from his vantage point, maybe more hidden in the shadows. They moved with purpose, not the random chaos of drunken brawlers. This was military precision applied to mayhem.

Tom slid from Old Boy's back and grabbed his Lightning from the scabbard, then patted the horse on the neck and told him to stay safe and be good.

The familiar weight of the rifle steadied him as he surveyed the battlefield below. The jail sat dark and empty—his office serving as the perfect sniper's perch if he could reach it.

He sprinted down the slope, keeping low, using the scattered buildings for cover. A raider emerged from Cotton's store carrying an armload of supplies, whistling like he was on a Sunday picnic. Tom put the rifle to his shoulder and squeezed the trigger. The whistle cut off mid-note as the man dropped.

The others noticed their friend's sudden silence. Shouts went up, but Tom was already moving, circling toward the jail. He reached the building's rear wall and climbed quickly, using the bars on the windows to leverage himself up. The roof offered a commanding view of Main Street, and more importantly, clear lines of sight to the raiders below.

Tom settled into position, using the chimney for support. Through the Lightning's sights, the street transformed into target practice. A raider crouched behind a water trough, reloading his pistol—Tom's bullet found him before he could finish the job.

Another man darted between buildings, but didn't live long enough to dart back out again. Every slide of the pump action on his rifle was another raider in the dirt.

He worked methodically, picking off Carter's men with the dispassionate proficiency of a clerk filing papers. Two more down. Reload, careful to keep the magazine from jamming.

Movement at the corner of his eye—a man stepping from the alley beside the jail, something stick-shaped in his hand. A heartbeat later the man lobbed it through the open door.

It took Tom an unflattering length of time to realize someone had just thrown *dynamite* into his jail.

Another moment to realize that *he was standing on top of the damn place.*

"Oh, shit."

Tom didn't think. He vaulted from the roof, hitting the ground hard and rolling to absorb the impact. His shoulder screamed in protest, but nothing felt broken; he didn't stop to check—he was too busy lurching to his feet and desperately scrambling away from the building.

The dynamite exploded just as Tom cleared the blast radius, lifting him off his feet and slamming him hard into the street.

His ears rang like church bells, and dust filled his mouth with the taste of powdered brick. The jail's front wall bulged outward, then collapsed in a thunderous cascade of debris.

Tom shook his head to clear it, spat dirt, and climbed to his feet. His Lightning lay somewhere in the rubble, but his Colts remained secure in their holsters. Time to get closer to the action anyway.

He jogged across Main Street, dodging between abandoned wagons and overturned barrels. The Cypress House blazed with lamplight, its doors thrown wide. Inside, he could see figures moving—not raiders, but townspeople tending to their wounded.

Tom pulled the heavier wooden door shut behind him and tried to sort through the organized chaos of a field triage center in full operation. Diego knelt beside a man with a bloody leg, wrapping the wound with a cloth towel—bandages must have run out already. Jennifer Starr directed traffic, sending women with water basins toward the injured while keeping curious children well back from the violence.

Diego looked up as Tom approached, his face cycling through surprise, relief, and exasperation in rapid succession.

"Tom! What are you—how did you—"

"Long story," Tom said, checking his ammunition. "What are they hitting?"

"Started with the jail, then spread out. But they keep circling back toward the courthouse."

"The courthouse?" Tom repeated with a shake of his head. "Of course they are."

Carter wasn't just trying to burn down the town.

The jail. The courthouse. The spine of legitimacy that turned this patch of swamp into a county seat instead of another godforsaken crossroads.

Burn those, and Cypress Run would slip right back to whatever the hell it had been before folks started believing it could be more.

Tom ejected the spent casings from his Colts and reloaded with fresh cartridges.

"Keep them safe," he told Diego, nodding toward the wounded. "I'm going hunting."

He stepped back into the street where gunfire still echoed off the buildings and somewhere up ahead, Carter's raiders were making their play for the courthouse.

The mule's hooves squelched through marsh mud as they approached the tree. Harlan stepped forward, cocky smile already spreading across his face.

"Well, well. Didn't think you had the stones to show, Bracken. Figured you'd send a deputy—or hide behind that judge's skirts." That voice—the same honey-eyed drawl that once made her pulse quicken.

Ellie slowed the mule and set the brake, keeping her head down, hat brim hiding her face. When she spoke, her voice came out calm as creek water.

"You have my son, Harlan. Of course I showed."

Silence stretched taut as a bowstring. She felt his shock ripple across the clearing, his certainty cracking like thin ice. When she finally lifted her head, pushing the brim back, Harlan's expression shifted from smugness to surprise.

For the first time in all the years she'd known him, Eliza Harper held the upper hand.

His face ran through confusion, recognition, then something like admiration before settling back to that crooked smile she'd once thought charming.

"Well now, Eliza. Look at you—sitting tall in the driver's seat." He stepped closer, hands loose at his sides in a gesture meant to look harmless. "Though that hat doesn't suit you near as well as it does our sheriff friend. Letting him keep his boots under your bed wasn't enough? You had to wear his clothes too, just to show the world what a faithless wife you are?"

"Can't be faithless to a man who isn't my husband anymore, Harlan."

His teeth caught the moonlight. "Well, darling, if *faithless wife* offends you, I could call you a *lawdog's whore* instead. Would that suit?"

He didn't wait for an answer before snapping, "And yes, Eliza, I *am* still your husband. Paper don't make you free of me. You can sign a hundred times, you're still mine in all the ways that matter—until I say otherwise. You understand me?"

Ellie's jaw tightened.

"You're right about one thing, Harlan. Paper didn't dissolve our marriage—your choices did. The night you chose to be a murderer and a thief, to trade your family for recklessness and greed. When you chose to do the things that landed you in prison. Those are the choices that ended our marriage. Paper just made it official."

Harlan laughed. "Thing about paper, darling, it's so fragile, isn't it? One spark and it all just goes up in smoke. You wouldn't happen to keep that paper in that new courthouse with all those other fine county records, would you?"

Ellie frowned. "Why?"

"No reason." His grin spread slow and poisonous. "Just want to make sure it stays safe—if that's all you think's keeping me from reclaiming our marriage bed."

"I wouldn't say that's the *only* thing, Harlan."

Ellie lifted the shotgun from the seat beside her and leveled the barrels square at his chest.

"Now. I've had about enough of listening to you talk. You're going to tell me where Nate is."

Harlan laughed. "Ooh, boy, that's an adorable look on you. You gonna shoot me with that, Liza?"

"I'd rather not. But I will. Where's Nate?"

"Safe as houses. Safer, actually, considerin' what happened to yours." His eyes glittered in the moonlight. "Amazing how quick a place can burn when the right people ain't around to put out the fire."

"You always did enjoy making threats, Harlan. Never could just say what you meant."

"Threats?" He laughed again, the sound echoing off the water. "Darlin', I'm just making conversation. Reminiscing. Remember how you used to trust me enough to follow me anywhere?"

"That was before I learned where you were leading."

He stepped closer, hands raised in false entreaty. "Eliza, if I could just explain—tell you how much I thought of you while I was gone, how much I needed you. Missed not havin' you. Thought of you near drove me crazy."

His expression softened, sliding into the gentle mask she remembered from their courting days. When he spoke again, the smooth cadence was pure memory—gold spun from straw, the voice that had made her believe every lie he ever told.

"Remember the first night I asked you to follow me out here? Carved our initials on this very camphor tree." He turned his back and touched the bark's scarred letters. "Look—they're still here."

"Harlan—"

"I'd left a picnic basket for you, remember? Saved my wages a whole month—wine, candles, those candied strawberries you loved. Made your lips so sweet when I got to kissin' you."

Ellie closed her eyes. She did remember that night. She remembered him promising her the world, that he'd make his fortune and buy her jewels to match her eyes, and nice dresses so everyone could see how pretty she was—flattering things that sounded like forever to a young girl. "I remember," she said softly.

He took another step, voice low, coaxing. "We got up to more than kissin' that night, remember? I laid you down on the blanket right here under the tree and made a woman of you—made you mine. You were such a pretty little thing—God, you still are—just look at you."

The memory washed over her like warm rain, and for a heartbeat she was sixteen again, dizzy with young love, first kisses, and flattery. She remembered laying on her back when he was done with her, aching and shivering, but proud of herself for making such a grown-up choice and pleasing the man who loved her. Remembered looking up at the stars.

Then she remembered Tom, looking up at those same stars on the road to her house—his eyes bright with wonder, his voice quiet with it. Sharing, not taking. Expecting nothing at all.

The weight in her chest closed around her like armor. She tightened her grip on the shotgun, snapping her eyes open and banishing the memory to the past where it belonged. "That was a long time ago, Harlan. And tonight, the only thing I want to hear from you is the promise that you'll give me back my son and then leave and never come back. Now, where's Nate?"

Harlan's smile faltered before sliding back into place. "Safe, like I said." He gestured toward the swamp. "Got him tucked away nice and cozy while we have our little reunion."

"This isn't a reunion, Harlan. It's a trade. You want something, and I want my son back. So skip the sweet talk and get to business."

"Always practical. That's what I love about you." He leaned against the cart wheel, close enough for her to smell the familiar blend of tobacco and leather.

"Thing is, Liza, you don't have anything to bargain with. You already belong to me. Always did. Just need to scrape that sheriff's stink out of you and remind you where home is."

"I know where my home is. And I don't want to have to kill you to get back to it—not after everything. Please, Harlan, just let Nate go, and walk away. We'll call it even."

He laughed—low, dangerous. "Oh, darlin'. Is that what you think we are? *Even*? We ain't nowhere close."

Somewhere in the darkness beyond the tree, a branch snapped.

Ellie turned instinctively toward the sound.

Harlan moved faster. He caught the shotgun barrel, wrenched it free, and yanked her from the cart in one brutal motion. She hit the ground hard, the breath punched out of her.

He flung Tom's hat into the darkness and seized a handful of her hair, hauling her upright.

The smile he gave her now showed too many teeth to be human.

"Remember what I told you about the swamp, Eliza?" he said. "Sometimes what you're huntin' ends up huntin' you instead."

Tom moved through the chaos of Main Street like a blind man threading needles—guided by muscle memory and his urban instincts more than sight and conscious thought. Doorways offered cover, shadows swallowed movement, and every window could hide a rifle barrel. Chicago's back alleys had taught him to read violence like sheet music, and this nocturnal symphony played in familiar keys.

A raider emerged from behind the blacksmith's forge, rifle raised toward a family fleeing with their children. Tom's Colt spoke first, the bullet spinning the man around before he could fire. The family scattered toward the church without looking back.

"Get to the saloon or the church," Tom called to anyone who'd listen. "Stay low, stay together."

Another gunman crouched behind Cotton's overturned wagon, taking aim at the courthouse steps. Tom flanked wide, using the general store's shadow for concealment. The raider never saw him coming.

The courthouse blazed ahead like a torch in the swamp darkness. Flames licked at the wooden scaffolding surrounding the brick structure, and the air tasted of smoke and burning pine. Judge Hartwell stood in the street directing a bucket brigade, her voice cutting through the chaos with courtroom authority.

"More water on the north wall! Keep those buckets moving!"

Tom reached her just as part of the scaffolding groaned and twisted, timbers snapping like kindling. The wooden framework collapsed inward, trapping at least three people beneath the burning debris. Screams echoed from inside the building.

Tom grabbed two men from the bucket line. "Help me get them clear!"

They plunged into the smoke-filled courthouse, the heat hitting them like a physical blow—and for one stupid instant he was nineteen again, a rookie patrolman watching an entire city turn to hell around him while the people he was supposed to protect screamed for help he couldn't give.

But this wasn't then.

Tom shook the memory from his eyes and forced himself deeper into the building.

Inside, Tom found a railroad surveyor pinned beneath a fallen beam, his leg twisted at an unnatural angle, eyes wide with panic and pain.

"Can't... can't move it..."

"Hold still," Tom told the surveyor, then positioned himself at the fulcrum point. He wedged his shoulder under the support beam and pushed up, shifting the heavy timber just enough for the other men to drag the surveyor clear.

"Get him to the saloon," Tom shouted, trying to make himself heard over the fire. "Doc's treating people there."

They carried him outside as fresh gunfire erupted from the far end of Main Street. More muzzle flashes in the darkness—Carter's second wave arriving to finish what the first had started. But it wasn't the sound of the bullets that set his teeth on edge—it was their horses, their sounds of exertion warping until they became too close to the screams of the ones that had drowned in fire.

He set his jaw. *Not again.*

Tom moved further into the building.

Smoke rolled low as river fog, clinging to the floor. Tom kept low under it, cloth pressed to his mouth, scanning through the haze until he spotted two more workers backed into a corner behind a fallen joist. One waved weakly, the other sat slumped against the wall, half conscious.

"Hang on," Tom said, voice muffled by the cloth. He tested the weight of the timber pinning them—too heavy to lift straight, but one end rested over a tool chest. Simple leverage. He found a crowbar near the door and jammed it under the plank, angling for the right purchase. "When I say go, pull him clear."

He leaned his weight into the bar. The timber rose with a groan. The free man dragged his partner out, both stumbling into Tom's chest. They coughed and blinked through the smoke, faces streaked with soot and disbelief.

"Come on. Gotta move," he said, steering them toward the doorway, heat crowding up close behind him like ghosts in the firelight.

They made it to the threshold; the workers staggered into waiting arms, and Tom took one last look back down the corridor—the flames breathing harder, testing the walls—before turning away.

Something stopped him. The hairs crawling up the back of his neck. A chill down his arms. *Something.* He turned back toward the fire again.

A voice calling for help. A real one, not a memory.

"Shit."

He took a breath and forced his legs to move.

Smoke churned thicker the farther he went in. The hallway rattled like a furnace pipe, every nail popping in the joists overhead. From beyond a half-collapsed doorway came coughing and the frantic scrape of boots. Two men—bricklayers, he thought—were huddled under a fallen section of scaffolding, one trying uselessly to lift a crossbeam off the other's shoulder.

"Don't move," Tom said, dropping to his knees beside them. He glanced once at the sagging ceiling—already spitting embers—then at the barricade: a tangle of planking and wire, too heavy to shift clean. He braced a boot against the wall, grabbed a jut of timber, and heaved until pain shot down his spine. The beam grudgingly lifted an inch, maybe two—enough. "Now! Pull him free!"

They dragged the trapped man out as sparks exploded around them. Tom slung him over his shoulder, shoved the other worker ahead, and ran blind for safety and clear air, the roar behind him swelling into a single, endless sound—fire, wind, and every voice he hadn't saved in Chicago, all at once. He didn't slow until his boots hit mud outside.

"Everyone out!" Tom ordered the bucket brigade. "Building's lost—no sense dying for brick and mortar!"

The townspeople scattered, some carrying wounded, others grabbing what supplies they could manage. As the bucket line dissolved, the flames spread faster, consuming the scaffolding and reaching for the courthouse roof.

Judge Hartwell shoved past him toward the burning building. Tom caught her arm; she twisted free and lunged for the flames a second time.

He didn't think—just grabbed her around the waist and slung her over his shoulder like a feed sack.

She hammered his back with both fists. "Put me down! There's *paperwork* inside—"

He carried her behind a water trough while bullets whined past, set her on her feet—and had to catch her again when she tried to charge right back.

He finally pinned her against the wall, the fear and fury combining in a bellow that could be heard over the screaming hell, "What the goddamned *hell* is wrong with you? There's nothing in there worth burning alive for!"

The outburst startled them both. He swallowed hard, and added, "Respectfully. Your Honor."

"You don't understand!"

"Of course I don't!" He slammed his hand against the brick wall. "Why the hell would I understand? If it's just paperwork—hell, I'll write you new paperwork every night for a week, I'll make triplicate copies till my fingers fall off!"

He caught her arm again, more to anchor himself to something real than to make any sort of point, fingers trembling with adrenaline.

He exhaled hard, voice rough from smoke.

"I'm missing something here, so I need you to explain it to me," he said quieter, dragging a soot-blackened hand down his face. "What in God's name is so damned important?"

Her composure cracked; her voice thinned with real fear. "If those documents burn, the town ceases to exist. *Legally.* The charter, the deeds—everything that proves we're more than a group of buildings. The railroad pulls out, the state revokes our grants. Cypress Run becomes *nothing*."

Tom stared at her, the truth hitting like smoke in his lungs. Not a building burning, but a whole idea.

"Sonofabitch."

His eyes and lungs burned with smoke—some real, some imagined. The building was coming down; there was no saving it. And when it fell, it would take Cypress Run with it—unless some miracle found a way to save a city from the flames. But Tom had never held his breath waiting for one of those. He couldn't see himself starting now.

He swallowed hard, bile rising in his throat and practically choking him on the words he forced out, "If you could only save one thing—if you only had time for *one*—" God help him, he couldn't believe he was saying it, "—what would it be?"

"The county charter and the land deeds," she said without hesitation. "Black leather book, about this thick." She held her fingers apart. "Proves every homesteader here actually owns their land. Without it, they're all just squatters on federal territory."

Tom grabbed a cloth and soaked it in the water trough. The courthouse blazed higher, but the main brick structure still stood. The finished section where legal documents would be stored might yet survive if he moved fast.

"Wait here," he told Hartwell, then sprinted toward the flames.

The dying courthouse was breathing fire and Tom ran straight into its open mouth.

The heat hit him like stepping into a furnace. He held the wet cloth over his mouth and nose, but smoke still filled his lungs with every breath, and the crackling of burning timber popping like gunfire as the ceiling split open in a rain of sparks.

The part of him that had run back then wanted desperately to run again now. The rest of him, older and meaner, shoved through the heat instead.

Inside, the courthouse had become a maze of fallen debris and dancing shadows. The rafters above him pulsed orange, sagging like breath about to give out. Tom followed the wall toward what had been Hartwell's office, counting doorways through the smoke.

The black leather book still sat on the shelf behind an overturned desk, miraculously intact. He pulled off his vest, wrapped it around the book to protect it, and held it close to his chest.

Time to leave. The swamp might eat everything eventually, and fire might take the rest, but he had no intention of dying here. Not tonight. Not if he could help it.

Just as he turned, a groan rolled through the beams.

A heartbeat later, half the ceiling came down in a roar of sparks—his route back vanished under a wall of cinders and twisted scaffolding.

Heat wrapped around him. For a second he was on Michigan Avenue again—terrified, winded, watching the whole sky turn scarlet.

"No... no, no. Please no—not like this."

The smoke was the same: tar, paint, hair—God, the smell of it!

His lungs locked, muscles seizing with old memory. He looked up, instinct screaming to climb, to tear through the rafters before the fire could bury him alive.

Then something sharp and cold thumped against his chest—the gator tooth.

Shaking fingers found it, slick and solid.

Mud, he thought, *not sky. Down, not up.*

Different rules—this wasn't the city; this place had crawlspace and swamp under it, not cellars.

He dropped to his knees, coughing hard enough to hurt, palms sweeping the boards until he found where water from the bucket line had pooled. They were warped but loose. If water could seep through, so could he.

He drew his knife, jammed it between planks, pried until one cracked free. His fingers scrabbled at the edge of the board, ripping, tearing, desperate to create a way out. He shoved the book through first, followed with one arm, then his shoulders. Splinters tore his palms, but desperation lent brute speed where calculation would have failed.

One more twist, one more desperate pull, and he fell through the hole he'd made in the floor, dropping into mud and black water, half sobbing from the shock of cold—*a Catholic city boy saved from the fire by a baptism in swamp water.*

He held the book to his chest and coughed desperately to clear his lungs, the gator tooth slick against his throat.

Then came the sound that he had never wanted to hear again in his life—a long, thundering rumble as the world above gave way and the building folded inward with a noise like all the life in the world exhaling at once.

CHAPTER TWENTY-SEVEN

The Kick-Shot

Harlan stood over Ellie with the easy confidence of a man who'd broken horses and women alike. He hadn't bothered with ropes—why would he? The shotgun leaned against the camphor tree within his reach, and Ellie sat in the mud where he'd shoved her, skirts torn, braid coming loose from its pins.

Ellie's head snapped up as one of Harlan's men emerged from the cypress shadows, dragging Nate behind him. Her boy stumbled forward on unsteady legs, hands bound tight behind his back, a dirty rag stuffed in his mouth and tied around his head.

"There's my boy." Harlan's voice warmed with genuine affection as he crouched. "Look at you—grown near half a foot since I been gone."

Nate's eyes went wide above the gag, darting between his father and mother. He tried to speak, the sound muffled and desperate.

"Easy there, son. Rope's just temporary." Harlan reached to ruffle his hair; the boy flinched away. "See, your mama's been filling your head with stories about your old dad. Made you forget how families work."

Ellie's hands clenched in the mud. "Harlan, please—"

"Let me paint you a picture of our future, Eliza." He straightened, voice slipping into the smooth cadence she remembered from their early days together. "First, I'm gonna kill that sheriff for putting his hands on my wife. Then we're going to be a family again. You, me, and Nate—like it should've been all along."

Nate jerked against the ropes, a strangled sound rising behind the gag.

"Don't fret, boy." Harlan's tone stayed gentle, almost tender. "Those ropes ain't forever. Just till your mama remembers how to be a proper wife again. How to be loyal. The faster she learns, the faster you're free."

"Don't do this." Ellie's voice cracked. "Please, Harlan. Forget about us. Just take your men and go."

"And leave your sheriff breathing, you mean?"

The words hung heavy in the thick air. Ellie met his pale blue-gray eyes and saw nothing of the man she'd once loved in their cold depths.

"Yes."

Harlan shook his head with that stubborn tilt she'd known too well. "Can't do that, Liza. You and the boy belong to me—always have, always will. And I'm getting paid a lot of money to burn this town to the ground. More than I ever saw from rustling cattle or robbing coaches. What would my employer think if I ran off with the job half finished?"

He stepped closer, his shadow folding across her in the moonlight.

"But mostly?" His smile stretched wolfish, all teeth, no warmth. "I'm going to really... *really* enjoy killing that sheriff. Make him hurt a good long while before the bullet. And if you behave? You be good enough for me? Well, maybe I won't make you watch."

The blood in Ellie's veins went to ice. This wasn't the reckless outlaw she'd married, the charming rogue who'd swept her off her feet under this very tree. This was something else entirely—something that had learned to wear Harlan's face while the man she'd once loved rotted away in prison.

Somewhere in the distance, smoke threaded the wind.

"Please, Harlan... If you ever loved me, if you ever loved our son... don't do this. Don't *choose* this."

"The only choice here, Liza, is how soon you want me to take those ropes off our boy." He gave a careless shrug, washing his own guilt away. "You make amends right now—start being the good wife I remember—and he's free tonight."

His tone hardened. "But if you make me wait too long, make me mad... Well, boy's fingers'll go numb before sunrise. Who's to say if I get to them before the tips turn black. Like I said, that part's up to you."

Ellie closed her eyes. Tears pricked hot at the corners as the weight in her chest throbbed.

"What do I have to do?"

Harlan's voice slid into that honeyed cadence sweet enough to drown flies. "You can start by showing me you remember a wife's duty to her husband—have ourselves that little *reunion* I mentioned. Right here where I made you mine the first time."

"Really? Here? In front of our son? In front of your lackey over there?"

"Nobody's gonna have a doubt in their mind that you belong to me, darlin', not when I'm done with you. Get used to it. Or don't."

She laughed bitterly, anger keeping her from sobbing, but only barely. She turned away from him and his ugliness, facing the tree.

Harlan had been right. Their initials were still here. She pressed a hand to the carving, a symbol of the past and all that had been between them. Half of her wanted to cut it down and burn the roots. But it wasn't the tree's fault Harlan had left his scars there. It was the only other being in the world that had seen what their love had been like when it was fresh and blossoming. Now it was a solemn witness to that same love turned to rot and ruin.

Her fingers brushed the lock of hair behind her ear, grazing the St. Christopher medallion woven into her hair with Tom's trembling handiwork. It was there, still—the weight she'd carried with her into this clearing—strands of iron, coiling around her heart and becoming the armor she needed it to be.

She took a shaky breath and turned. She set her back to the camphor tree. "Well, come on then. Let's get this over with."

Harlan crossed the distance in two long strides.

She reached down, lifted her skirts, steeling herself for what came next.

He leaned in, the heat of him pressing close, his body pressing against hers—

—she pressed the derringer to his temple and pulled the trigger.

The sound was tiny—nothing more than a muffled pop—far too quiet for how completely it changed her world.

Harlan's body pitched sideways into the dirt.

Before it hit the ground, Ellie had the shotgun in her hands again, sights trained on the man holding her son. She didn't even wipe the blood from her face.

"I don't know you," she said, her voice colder than a gator's eyes. "But I hope your momma taught you better than to stand between a mother and her boy."

He froze, then dropped his gun and lifted both hands.

"Good. Now go. And stay gone."

The man didn't need telling twice; he disappeared into the swamp.

Ellie kept the gun up, listening. The silence pressed close, restless with night sounds but no voices. When she finally believed they were alone, her arms went slack. She dropped to her knees beside Nate, pulled the gag free, and worked at the knots binding his hands.

Nate's wrists were raw where the ropes had cut into them, but his hands were steady as Ellie worked the knots free. She kept glancing over her shoulder at Harlan's body, half-expecting him to sit up and laugh at his own joke.

When Nate's hands came free of the ropes, he collapsed forward into Ellie's arms, trembling like a spooked colt. She held him tight against her chest, feeling his rapid heartbeat through the thin cotton of his shirt while her own pulse hammered in her ears.

"Mama." His voice cracked on the word. "I thought—when he said he was gonna—"

"Shh." She stroked his hair, damp with sweat and fear. "It's over now. You're safe."

But even as she spoke the words, Ellie knew they weren't true. Harlan's body lay crumpled ten feet away, his blood seeping into the black earth beneath the camphor tree—but his death wouldn't solve everything. His men were still out there, and Tom—

"Mama?" Nate's voice came out soft and small. "Is he really dead?"

Ellie's hands stilled. The question crackled between them like a dying fire. She could lie—tell him his father was just sleeping, buy herself time to figure out how to explain that she'd killed the man who'd given Nate life. But it would be the most bald-faced lie she'd ever told in her life and lies had a way of festering in the swamp air.

"Yes, baby. He's gone."

Nate stared at his father's body, his young face struggling to process what he'd witnessed. "You killed him."

"I did."

"Because he was going to hurt you."

"Because he was going to hurt all of us." Ellie cupped his face in her hands, making him look at her instead of the corpse. "Your father made his choices, Nate. Every one of them led him here."

He nodded slowly, though she could see the questions forming behind his eyes—questions she'd have to answer eventually, when the immediate danger passed. The fact that he was keeping them from spilling out was as much a sign of his ordeal as anything else.

Nate rubbed his freed wrists, and stared at Harlan's still form with a clinical focus uncommon for a boy his age. But he'd grown up around Dr. Delgado's work and knew that looking away when things got ugly didn't make them disappear. "Good," he said finally. "He scared me. He scared us both. And he had no right to."

The words hit Ellie harder than Harlan's fists ever had. Her eight-year-old son—who'd once begged her for stories about his daddy, the hero—was relieved his father was dead.

She pulled Nate against her chest, breathing in the familiar scent of his hair. Somewhere in the distance, orange light flickered between the cypress trunks like trapped lightning, and the smell of burning wood seeped slowly into the clearing, carried on the night wind from the direction of Cypress Run.

The town was burning.

"Pa said—" Nate pushed back from her embrace, his brown eyes wide. "Sheriff Bracken—"

"Is exactly where he needs to be." Ellie forced steel into her voice, the same tone she used when Nate argued about his arithmetic. "Tom can handle himself."

She hoped to God that was true.

Ellie stood and shouldered the shotgun, scanning the shadows between the cypress trees. Somewhere in the distance, she could hear the faint crack of gunfire like thunder from a far distant storm. Her place was where Tom was fighting for his life, not here keeping company with the dead.

"Can you walk?" she asked Nate.

"Yes, ma'am."

"Then we're going home. And if anyone tries to stop us—" She breached the shotgun and checked that it was still loaded. "Well. They'll learn what your mama's made of. Come on."

She helped Nate into the cart and climbed in behind him. Then she turned the mule toward town, not once looking back at the body she left for the swamp.

Ellie's first glimpse of Main Street told her everything she needed to know. The sheriff's office gaped like a broken jaw where dynamite had torn through the front wall, leaving jagged timber teeth and a scatter of brick dust across the boardwalk. Smoke still ribboned from the wreckage, gray and thin against the predawn sky.

Nate pressed closer to her side, his small hand finding hers. "Mama, where's Sheriff Bracken?"

"I don't know, sweetheart." The words tasted like ash.

The smell of smoke hung thick in the air, mixed with the acrid bite of dynamite residue. People moved through the streets like survivors of a hurricane, their faces drawn and dirt-streaked.

The courthouse drew them like a funeral pyre.

What had been the pride of Cypress Run now resembled a broken tooth, its front arch standing defiant while the rest lay in smoking ruin. The back half had collapsed entirely, leaving a crater of charred timbers and shattered masonry that steamed in the morning air.

People moved through the debris like undertakers, grimly attending their duty. They worked in pairs, lifting beams with careful coordination, calling out when they found something worth preserving. No one spoke loudly. No one joked. The silence carried the weight of searching for the dead.

Ellie guided Nate toward the wreckage, her borrowed coat hanging loose around her shoulders.

Judge Hartwell stood near what had been the main entrance, her usually pristine appearance streaked with soot and sweat. She directed the salvage efforts with quiet authority, pointing here and there as workers pulled county documents from the wreckage. Her face looked carved from stone.

Diego knelt beside a pile of rubble, meticulously checking each beam before it was moved. His shirt clung to his back with perspiration, and ash had turned his dark hair gray at the temples. When he straightened, Ellie caught sight of his expression—the careful neutrality he wore when patients needed his expertise more than his humanity.

When Diego spotted her, his face transformed with relief. He crossed the rubble-strewn ground in quick strides, pulling both her and Nate into a fierce embrace.

"*Gracias a Dios,*" he murmured against her hair. "I've been looking for you since the attack started. When I couldn't find you anywhere..." He pulled back, studying her face with his physician's eye. "Are you hurt?"

Ellie shook her head, though everything in her felt bruised. Diego's gaze dropped to the coat she wore—too big, too like the one Tom had grumbled about spending money on not even an hour before riding out of town—and understanding flickered across his features.

"You switched places with him," he said quietly. "You went to meet Carter."

"I had to. The trap he set was for Tom, not me. I was the only one of us who could wiggle out of it." Her voice came out hoarser than she'd intended. "And he had Nate."

Diego's jaw tightened, but he didn't lecture her. Instead, he squeezed her shoulder gently. "Are you okay?"

Ellie thought of Harlan's breath on her face, the fear in her son's eyes, the moment when everything could have gone wrong. "I think I will be."

She looked past him to the smoldering wreckage, to the people still digging through debris with increasingly hollow expressions. "Where's Tom? I don't see him. Is he—"

"We don't know, *mija.*" Diego's voice was soft, not in the way it would be if he was the doctor giving bad news to patients and their families. It was soft in the way that he spoke to his own daughters when life seemed particularly cruel or unfair.

"He was in the building when it collapsed, but we don't know anything for certain. We haven't found—" he broke off, rethinking his words. "We haven't found anything one way or the other."

Judge Hartwell approached them, her face gray with exhaustion and something deeper—regret that sat heavy in the lines around her eyes.

"It's my—I'm responsible," Hartwell said, her usual authority stripped away. "He asked me what was in here worth dying for." Her voice cracked slightly. "I asked a man to die for a pile of papers."

Diego shook his head. "You didn't ask him to do anything, Maggie. Tom saw something that needed to be done and he accepted the risk."

Hartwell turned away, refusing the offered comfort. "We've been searching for hours," she continued, her gaze drifting back to the wreckage. "No sign of him yet."

Ellie spoke softly, trying to fill her voice with something that might have been hope even if that was the last thing any of them were feeling right now. "Which could mean he made it out somehow."

She stared at the collapsed courthouse, trying to imagine anyone surviving that cave-in. The rear wall had folded inward like a house of cards, burying everything beneath tons of timber and masonry. If Tom had been inside when it fell...

The tears came without warning, hot and sudden—not the careful, controlled crying in the dark that she'd mastered through years of Harlan's worsening abuse and imprisonment, but the raw, helpless sobbing of a woman who'd found something precious just in time to lose it.

Diego pulled her close again, one arm around her shoulders while his other hand rested protectively on Nate's head.

"Shh," he whispered, his voice rumbling against her ear, steady and sure despite the uncertainty they faced. "Don't cry, *pobrecita*. We don't give up yet."

Ellie pressed her face against Diego's shoulder, breathing in the familiar scents of carbolic soap and coffee that always clung to him. For a moment, she let herself be held—let someone else carry the weight of worry and fear that had been crushing her since she'd left Tom at the cypress stand.

"He promised you he'd be safe, Mama," Nate said quietly, his voice small but certain. "Sheriff Bracken doesn't break promises."

Through her tears, Ellie almost smiled. Her son's faith was absolute, untainted by the knowledge of how easily promises could be broken by circumstances beyond anyone's control.

She looked down at her son's dirt-streaked face, then back at the smoking ruin where Tom Bracken had last been seen alive. Somewhere beneath that wreckage lay the man who'd kissed her goodbye three hours ago and woven his good luck charm into her hair.

The man who'd promised not to get himself killed and then ran into a burning building to save not just a single person, but the whole town—as if Cypress Run was a living thing just as worthy of rescuing from the flames as any of the folks who lived here.

And he'd left Ellie standing in the cinders with her heart held together by hope that a man who'd already survived everything else trying to kill him this week might still have enough left in him to survive the collapse of a burning building, too.

Hope that St. Christopher—whoever he was—was still looking out for that poor city cop he'd protected all these years, the one who couldn't stop himself from wading into trouble.

*S*ilence. Stillness.

Not the kind born of peace, but the kind that follows a fight—the pause when you realize you're still breathing, when you have to force yourself to stop so you can listen for anything else coming to kill you.

Something dripped against his cheek. Water, cold and insistent. His ears rang; every sound was far away and under glass. The air above him shimmered red through cracks in the wreckage.

Tom lay half in mud, half in water, the black book wrapped protectively in his vest and clutched against his chest like a swaddled baby. The rest of him was pinned down by too much weight. His body refused to move yet. Every muscle was waiting for the next ultimatum.

When he thought he'd stayed still for more than long enough, he tried to move, but the effort stopped as soon as the pain hit and he fell back with a groan that ripped through his ribs. He pressed his face into the mud and breathed through his mouth. Once. Twice. Forced the pain back to where he could manage it. The muck smelled of silt, not smoke, and that alone was a God send.

The gator tooth hung heavy at his throat. It had dragged him downward, saved him from the fire; now the sharp point of it pressed lightly against his skin, as if it knew it had more to teach him. A gator waiting in the depths, hidden until its prey got close, only making itself known by the warning growl that Tom still heard in his dreams.

Delirium was useful for all kinds of things. Some of his best ideas came when he'd lost too much blood to think through them properly.

But whatever the hell connection his brain was trying to make here, he wished it would just spit it out already.

When he finally opened his eyes again, the timbers moaned above his head, echoing in soft percussion—the courthouse's heartbeat muffled beneath its own grave. Somewhere beyond it, faint and steady, came the calling of frogs. But more than that, the calling of voices. Water sloshing, wood creaking... dim and far away. Somebody calling his name.

"...help..." His voice was useless, his throat burned dry by smoke and heat. He couldn't move enough to take a proper breath, couldn't bellow like a gator. But his hand was free and his gun was within reach. Could probably beat a gator on the nose again if he had to. Or something else. If he had to.

Tom moved his hand, the effort of positioning it making him dizzy. He tapped the Colt's barrel against the beam pinning him in place—*short-short-long, short-short, rest.* A rail-wire pattern, half Chicago telegraph, half billiard table rhythm—enough for anyone topside to know a man was under there, still playing to stay alive.

short-short-long, short-short, rest.
short-short-long, short-short, rest.

Voices grew louder. Ash and cinder drifted across his face, mixing with the water. Daylight twisted down in thin ropes.

Then the pressure lifted. Hands seized him; someone dragged him upward and he was pulled from the depths.

For a moment, all he could see was the courthouse's front arch still standing—tilted, stubborn, haloed in smoke. Half gone, half alive. Like the town. Like him. And somehow still standing.

CHAPTER TWENTY-EIGHT

Corner Pocket

The hands that pulled Tom from the wreckage belonged to Jake Henley and Bobby Keene, their callused fingers gripping his shoulders with desperate strength. Their faces were streaked with soot and worry, sweat cutting pale tracks through the grime.

Behind them, half the town pressed forward in a tight semicircle—men still clutching buckets, women with their hair escaping hastily-pinned braids, children peering between adult legs. All their faces were lit by the orange glow of dying fires, embers still dancing in the smoky air, eyes wide with the kind of relief that comes after you've already started grieving and measuring plots in the cemetery.

Tom's legs buckled the moment they set him upright, his knees hitting the ground with a wet thud. He'd inhaled so much smoke, his lungs felt like they'd become charcoal and the rush of fresh air after being trapped for so long in that dank crawlspace made them spasm. Violent coughing wracked his body, black phlegm spattering the mud as he fought to clear the smoke from his chest.

"Jesus, Mary, and Joseph," someone whispered from the crowd, the words carrying across the sudden hush that had fallen over the gathering. "He's alive. The man's actually alive."

More voices joined in—prayers, cries of gratitude, exclamations of disbelief—but Tom barely heard them over the ringing in his ears. He fumbled with the bundle pressed tight against his chest, his scorched hands shaking as he tried to maintain his grip. His vest, once a beautiful blue, was now scorched, muddied, and torn, wrapped around the precious black leather book like a burial shroud.

The charter. The deeds. The survey records and land grants. Everything that made Cypress Run more than just a collection of buildings someone could burn down and walk away from, more than another failed settlement swallowed by the Florida wilderness.

"Judge Hartwell." His voice came out as gravel. He thrust the bundle toward Hartwell, who stood frozen, her silver hair wild with ash. "Your paper—" he broke off coughing, tried again, "Your paperwork. As requested."

Hartwell's hands shook as she unwrapped the vest. The leather book's cover was blistered, its edges charred, but the pages inside remained intact. She pressed it against her chest like a prayer book, tears cutting clean tracks through the soot on her cheeks.

"Sheriff Bracken," she said hoarsely, "you reckless, infuriating man... Chief Killigan was right about you. Spectacular. Unpredictable. Fit for crusades—and followed by the smell of burning."

Tom choked out a laugh, "That's not all he said about me."

Hartwell shook her head. "I'm redacting the rest."

The crowd stirred, voices rising in a mixture of amazement and celebration. Their sheriff had walked into the flames for them—for papers most of them couldn't even read, for the legal standing of a town that half of them had never expected to last the year. Word rippled outward: *The sheriff saved the charter. The county's still ours. We're still here.*

Diego pushed through the crowd, his usually composed face cracking with raw emotion. Without a word, he wrapped Tom in an embrace that was part relief, part fury, part something deeper than either. Tom could feel Diego's shoulders shaking against him.

"*Idiota,*" Diego whispered in his ear, his voice thick. "Absolute *idiota.* Do you have any idea—" He pulled back, hands gripping Tom's shoulders, eyes bright with unshed tears. "Don't you ever do that again. Ever."

Tom tried for a grin, but it came out more like a grimace. "Can't promise that, Doc. Job description's a little vague on the suicidal heroics clause."

Diego's laugh was half sob. "Of course it is. Of course you'd joke about it." He wiped his eyes with the back of his hand, leaving streaks in the soot. "Come on. Let me look at you properly."

But Tom barely heard him. Through the crowd, through the smoke and celebration, he saw her. Ellie stood twenty feet away, Nate pressed against her side, both of them staring at him like he'd risen from the dead. Her face was pale beneath the grime, her eyes wide with something that looked like disbelief.

The crowd seemed to sense the moment. Voices quieted, bodies shifted, creating a path between them. Tom took a step forward, then another, his legs steadier now. Each step hurt, but not the kind of hurt that would stop him.

Ellie's composure cracked first. A sob escaped her lips, and then she was running, pushing past the onlookers, her boots splashing through the muddy street. She hit him with enough force to stagger them both, her arms wrapping around his neck, her face buried against his shoulder.

Tom felt the tremor run through her shoulders, the way her breath hitched against his neck. He could feel a million aches and pains in his body where she pressed against him, but all that mattered was the solid warmth of her in his arms.

"Hey, it's okay. Everything's okay," he whispered, his voice still rough from the smoke. "I'm here. I'm right here, Lovely."

She pulled back just enough to look at his face, her hands framing his jaw, thumbs brushing away streaks of ash to make sure he was real. Her eyes searched his features like she was memorizing them, cataloging every scrape and burn that would have to be cleaned and treated with antiseptic and she knew he was hurt in places she couldn't see and—

"I thought—" Her voice broke. "When they said you were inside when it collapsed, I thought—"

Before he could answer, she kissed him, hard, desperate, relishing the salty taste of tears and smoke that proved he was no ghost. When she broke away, the tears came in the raw, shaking sobs of someone who'd been holding their breath for too long.

"Don't cry." Tom's thumb caught the tears on her cheek, his own voice unsteady. "Please, Ellie, it hurts to see you cry."

"I can't help it." The words came out between gasps. "I thought you were dead. I thought I'd lost you before I even—" She pressed her face against his chest again, her shoulders shaking. "Nobody could have survived that. Nobody."

Tom wrapped his arms tighter around her, one hand stroking her hair. "Well, almost nobody. I had city luck *and* swamp grit keeping me safe, remember?"

He squeezed her tightly, "That gator tooth you gave me saved my life. Reminded me not to be a foolish city boy when I most needed to hear you saying it." His voice dropped to something softer, more serious. "You saved my life, Elle. Even when you weren't there, you saved me."

"You saved me, too," she said. "Derringer you gave me came in handy. And when I needed to remember what was important and why I needed to not let him spin his lies around me again, it was thinking of that goofy look on your face that kept me safe."

"Oh? Which one?"

"When you tried to eat that orange peel, I think."

"Oh, Christ, woman. Fruit was trying to kill me, and all you can say is that I looked goofy while choking on it? Mighty unkind of you, Mrs. Harper."

The tears came unbidden again and Ellie buried her face against his chest. "God, Tom, I didn't think I'd see your face again," she whispered. "I wanted to, so badly, but I didn't think I would. I didn't think you were coming back to me this time."

Tom held her tightly, resting his cheek against her hair. "Shh. It's alright now. Remember what I told you the other night? I'd crawl through worse than five miles of swamp to get back to you." He pulled back so he could see her face, so she could see his smile. "Meant what I said. And it doesn't get much worse than that, so any other scrapes I have to face going forward are gonna be cakewalks in comparison."

She huffed out a startled breath, not quite a laugh but aiming in the right direction.

"Now, granted," he went on, determined to pull a real laugh out of her. "Lying around like a stick in the mud waiting to get rescued doesn't ring quite as heroic as crawling through hell to reach you, but I hope it still counts as a romantic gesture."

That did it. She laughed—watery but real—wiping her eyes with the back of her hand.

"There's nothing romantic about it at all."

"No?"

"No." She shook her head emphatically, though she was still smiling through her tears. "Bringing me flowers is romantic. Surprising me at lunch with my favorite meal is romantic. Teaching me how to play your stupid billiards game so you can let me win and I can understand your silly metaphors—that would be romantic. But getting squished by buildings absolutely is not, and I expect you to never do it again."

"I'll try to remember that for next time."

"There won't be a next time." Her voice turned stern, though her hands were still gentle on his face. "Promise me."

Tom took her face in both hands, brushing his thumbs across her cheeks where the tears had left their marks. He kissed her tenderly on the brow, then softly on the lips, with none of the desperation, fear, or uncertainty of other kisses they'd shared. This was a kiss that demanded nothing, offering only a solemn vow of enduring affection. It was a kiss that felt like coming home.

He pressed his forehead against hers. "I can't promise there won't ever be a next time," he said softly. "But I can promise I'll always do my damndest to get back to you. And my damndest is pretty damned good, Mrs. Harper, if you'll pardon my language."

"Your language isn't the problem, Sheriff, it's your ego that gets insufferable."

Tom smiled, weary and luminous beneath the soot and ash streaking his face. "I suppose I should consider myself fortunate that you like me in spite of my ego."

"You absolutely should."

A small tug on Tom's sleeve broke the moment. Nate stood beside him, his young face streaked with ash but his eyes bright with relief and something that looked suspiciously like hero worship.

"Sheriff?" The boy's voice was small but determined. "Are you really okay? Mama was crying, and she don't cry much."

Tom looked down at him, then back at Ellie, who was wiping her eyes with the back of her hand, trying to compose herself. "Well, Nate, I'm a little singed around the edges, but nothing that won't heal. Your mama's got every right to be upset—I scared her pretty bad."

"You do look kinda like you got chewed up and spit out."

Tom crouched, wincing as his ribs protested. "Fair assessment. Though I'd say it was more like getting stomped on by a very large, very angry building."

Nate's serious expression cracked into a grin. "Buildings don't get angry."

"You didn't get to meet this one. It had a real mean streak." Tom ruffled his hair, leaving a gray smudge in the boy's dark mop. "But I kept my promise, didn't I? Said I'd come back, and here I am."

"Yeah." Nate's grin widened. "Mama cried when she thought you were dead, but I told her you wouldn't break your promise. Did you really save the whole town?"

"Well, maybe not the *whole* town, but an important part of it."

Nate drew a deep breath, suddenly earnest again. "Mama says you need someone to teach you how to stay out of trouble."

"Oh, hell." Tom smiled fondly at her. "She's not wrong."

"I could teach you," Nate said brightly. "If you don't mind me showing you how."

"I'd be honored, kiddo. I bet if I have you showing me the ropes, I won't get flattened by an angry building next time."

"There won't be a next time," Ellie said firmly, though her voice was still thick with emotion.

"Course not," Tom agreed, winking at Nate. "Your mama's the boss."

Diego cleared his throat nearby. "Speaking of being the boss, you're coming to the clinic. Now." Diego's tone brooked no argument. "That smoke inhalation needs proper attention, and I can see at least three burns that require treatment."

Tom opened his mouth to protest, but Diego cut him off with a raised hand. "Don't. Just don't. You've done enough heroics for one week."

Ellie stepped closer, her arm sliding around Tom's waist to support him. "He's right. You can barely stand." The gesture was comforting in a way that made Tom's knees just a little wobbly. As if the kisses and the tears and the trauma and every other thing he'd subjected his body to wasn't already enough to make a man's knees weak—having Ellie tucked in close to his side was the thing that did him in.

"I'm standing just fine," Tom protested, though he leaned into her touch more than he'd probably admit.

Judge Hartwell approached, the rescued charter still clutched against her chest like armor. Her silver hair caught the firelight as she studied Tom with something approaching respect. "Sheriff Bracken, I believe I owe you an apology. And a considerable debt."

Tom managed a tired grin. "Well, if it's a debt you owe, you might consider advancing me a loan till my first pay. This was the last shirt I had and I don't think there's any saving it. Not to mention I sacrificed my vest to save your ledger. A small clothing stipend is the least you can do."

Hartwell chuckled, tension breaking between them like a fever. "I'll manage something."

Diego and Ellie helped Tom hobble to the mule cart parked on the street. There was no earthly way he was capable of walking as far as the clinic, but the cart he could manage.

Tom looked around at the crowd still watching them, at the smoldering ruins of what had been the courthouse, at Judge Hartwell clutching the rescued charter like it was made of gold. A place he thought he'd never fit. But now here he was, thinking of Cypress Run as his own. His town. His people. Still standing, despite everything—same as him.

Tom hefted another piece of charred timber from the courthouse rubble, sweat already beading on his forehead despite the morning air still carrying the night's coolness. Eight days of hauling debris had cleared maybe a little more than half of the mess. His body still felt every inch of his recent encounter with collapsing architecture, and his ribs protested every lift with sharp reminders that no amount of pure thoughts and clean living could make broken ribs heal faster than they intended to.

"Sheriff Bracken!" Mrs. Cotton's voice rang across the square like a dinner bell. "You put that down this instant!"

Tom glanced over his shoulder to find the store owner's wife bearing down on him with the determination of a locomotive, a glass of orange juice clutched in one hand and maternal fury blazing in her eyes.

"Now, Mrs. Cotton, I'm perfectly—"

"You are perfectly exhausted is what you are." She plucked the timber from his hands as if it weighed nothing. "Come sit in the shade and tell me how you're feeling."

Tom opened his mouth to protest, but Mrs. Cotton had already linked her arm through his and was steering him toward a chair someone had dragged into the courthouse square's only remaining patch of shade. A small table sat beside it, laden with the orange juice, a plate of cookies, and what looked suspiciously like a hand fan.

"Mrs. Cotton, I appreciate the concern, but—"

"Nonsense. You're a regular hero, Sheriff. You saved my John, and so many more besides. The least we can do is make sure you don't work yourself into an early grave." She pressed the glass into his hands. "Now drink that up. Citrus is good for the constitution."

Tom caught Diego's figure passing on the street, medical bag in hand. The doctor paused, took in the scene of Tom being fussed over like an invalid, and burst into quiet laughter.

"Excuse me just a moment," Tom muttered, setting down the orange juice and rising from the chair. Mrs. Cotton made disapproving noises, but he was already limping across the square to intercept Diego.

"Don't say a word," Tom warned as he caught up.

Diego's grin widened. "Wouldn't dream of it."

"This is ridiculous. I'm fine. A few bumps and bruises never killed anybody."

"That's what happens when you nearly die," Diego said, adjusting his grip on his medical bag. "People start thinking they need to take care of you."

Tom fell into step beside him, favoring his left leg slightly but otherwise moving well enough. "I don't see how this is any different from all the other times I nearly died. Got shot at, bit by a gator, half-strangled in a swamp—nobody made me sit around drinking juice and discussing my feelings."

Diego stopped walking and looked at him with the expression of a man trying not to laugh out loud. "Tom, this time you caught a cold."

"So?"

"On top of everything else." Diego's professional composure cracked, and he chuckled. "It's one thing to shrug off bullets and concussions and gator bites, because you were always laughing them off. Made you look invincible. But then you caught a head cold on top of nearly burning to death, and it was the most pitiful thing most of these women have seen in their lives."

Tom stared at him. "A cold."

"Sniffling, sneezing, voice all rough and gravelly. You sounded like a dying raccoon that morning when you tried to give orders about the cleanup." Diego wiped his eyes. "Mrs. Mills actually teared up watching you try to blow your nose without moving your ribs."

"Jesus Christ."

"You're doomed, *amigo*. They're going to coddle you for the next few months at least." Diego clapped him on the shoulder. "Better get used to orange juice and concerned inquiries about your constitution."

From across the square, Mrs. Cotton's voice carried on the morning air: "Sheriff! Your juice is getting warm!"

Tom looked at Diego, who was trying and failing to maintain a straight face. "This is worse than getting shot," he muttered.

"Much worse. Bullets you can dodge. Maternal instincts?" Diego shook his head gravely. "No defense against those."

Salvation came from a truly unexpected quarter: Judge Hartwell bearing down on them from the direction of the church. "I'm afraid Sheriff Bracken will have to drink his juice while we walk, Mrs. Cotton. I need him for official business, I'm afraid."

Tom could have kissed her. "Sorry, Mrs. Cotton. Duty calls."

She frowned but brought him two cookies wrapped in a kerchief and the glass of juice. "Don't worry about bringing the glass back. I'll collect it myself from the church later. Just be sure you drink it all and make sure you sit down and rest."

Tom could have sworn he heard her mumbling something about "the poor boy" as she walked away.

Judge Hartwell's amusement radiated from her like heat off summer pavement. "I can see the matrons of Cypress Run have you well in hand, Sheriff."

Tom grimaced, taking a deliberate sip of the orange juice to avoid her knowing look. "I almost preferred it when they called me 'that poor idiot' in passing conversations. At least then they left me alone to make my own mistakes."

"Oh, but this is so much more entertaining." Hartwell's eyes sparkled with rare humor. "I'm glad to see you were able to put your clothing stipend to use."

Tom glanced down at his new shirt—a sensible blue cotton that actually fit his shoulders without pulling tight across his back. "Me too. Mr. Cotton only had two shirts in his store that were close enough to my size that they could be let out a bit in the arms, but he's got a shipment of goods arriving from Tampa today. Said he'd add some clothing in my size to the order."

"Excellent. Can't have our sheriff looking like a scarecrow indefinitely." Hartwell paused at the church annex door. "Though I suspect the ladies would find even that charming at this point."

Tom muttered something unflattering under his breath as Hartwell opened the door to their makeshift office. The scent of old wood and lingering incense greeted them, along with something else—expensive tobacco and sea salt.

Tom's hand moved instinctively toward his gun before his brain caught up.

Mercer sat in the guest chair in front of Tom's desk, looking perfectly at ease despite being in what amounted to enemy territory. The smuggler wore a crisp white shirt and dark vest, his hair pomaded to perfection, as if he'd stepped out of a Tallahassee gentleman's club rather than a burned-out shipping warehouse.

"Your Honor. Sheriff." Mercer rose with fluid grace, offering a slight bow to Hartwell before meeting Tom's eyes. They regarded each other like cats eyeing the same patch of sunlight—wary, territorial, but not quite ready to draw claws.

"Mr. Mercer." Tom's voice carried the careful neutrality of a poker player checking his cards. "Didn't expect to see you in our humble establishment."

"I thought it appropriate to pay my respects." Mercer reached into his coat with deliberate slowness, producing a bottle of amber rum that caught the morning light streaming through the church windows. "A small token of goodwill between neighbors."

Hartwell's eyebrows climbed toward her hairline. "We will not accept illegal goods as bribes, Mr. Mercer."

Tom stepped forward before she could continue, a smile tugging at the corner of his mouth. "Judge, I believe you misunderstand our guest's intentions." He accepted the bottle, examining the label with apparent appreciation. "This is clearly a kind gesture of good faith from a fellow businessman. We can and will accept such generosity in the spirit it's offered."

Hartwell's expression suggested she thought Tom had taken leave of his senses, but she held her tongue.

Tom looked around his sparse office, searching for something that could reasonably serve as a reciprocal gesture. His gaze finally dropped to the kerchief-wrapped cookies Mrs. Cotton had pressed into his hands. Perfect.

"Mr. Mercer, please, have a seat." Tom unwrapped one of the cookies and placed it on a clean piece of paper before sliding it across the desk. "Mrs. Cotton's finest. Oat cookies with a vanilla orange glaze—family recipe, I'm told."

Mercer's eyebrows rose fractionally, but he accepted the offering with the same solemnity he might show a diplomatic treaty. "Most kind."

Tom rummaged through his desk drawer until he found three clean glasses, then carefully poured two fingers of rum into each. The scent that rose from the liquid gold spoke of Caribbean sunshine and careful aging.

"To neighborly relations," Tom said, raising his glass.

"To mutual understanding," Mercer replied.

Hartwell looked between them as if watching a chess match where she couldn't see the board, but she lifted her glass nonetheless. "To keeping the peace."

The rum burned smooth and warm. Tom could taste the money in it—real money, the kind that bought silence and favors and made problems disappear.

Mercer bit into the cookie with evident surprise. "Exceptional. Mrs. Cotton, you said?"

"Store owner's wife. Taken it upon herself to ensure I don't waste away from poor nutrition and overwork." Tom leaned back in his chair, studying Mercer over the rim of his glass. "Funny how people suddenly care about your wellbeing once you nearly die saving their property deeds."

"Ah yes, the courthouse fire. Tragic loss. Though I understand you managed to salvage the most important documents?" Mercer's tone was conversational, but Tom caught the subtle probe beneath it.

"Enough to keep Cypress Run on the maps." Tom took another sip of rum.

"That's good. It certainly makes it easier for commerce to continue."

Tom closed his eyes and took another sip of his rum.

Mercer set the glass down, the sunlight flashing off the rim.

"You'll forgive me for dispensing with pleasantries," he said, tone all silk. "We share a problem, you and I—a gentleman from Illinois named Clayborne. Seems he's been telling Tallahassee that Everfield County's law enforcement is delinquent, that the fires were... a failure of moral governance."

Hartwell's mouth thinned. "The senator has been championing my removal for several weeks. I am aware. And I'm afraid our Sheriff is not a person the senator is fond of either."

Tom smiled and shrugged his shoulders as if the troubled history between them was as simple as a property dispute over a fence line.

"Then you'll be delighted to know," Mercer continued, "that my employers in Tampa have acquired certain documents tying the Gentleman from Illinois to one Harlan Carter. Letters, receipts, bank vouchers—showing the good senator paid our late friend to create your little conflagration. We might call that a mutual thorn removed, if these papers were to come to light."

He smiled the way men do who know they're holding the high card, letting the option breathe before continuing.

"However. Tampa proposes a simpler approach. We keep those papers where they won't trouble Washington, or your courts. In return, Tampa shields this town. For a price, yes—but one that serves everyone's interests."

Hartwell's eyes narrowed. "Serves?"

Mercer spread his hands, congenial as a banker discussing interest rates.

"My principals intend to expand the docks—modern cranes, new storage sheds, proper dredging of the east channel. The improvements bring trade, shipping, investors—the sort of growth that makes newspapers call a place *promising* instead of *godforsaken*. Naturally, we must continue to manage the docks ourselves; we ask that the legal oversight here will... refrain from interference."

Hartwell stiffened. "In plain language: you keep running your smuggling ring."

"You mischaracterize the scope of our operations, Judge. Let's say: commerce unencumbered by excess paperwork. The same lumber company supplying your courthouse project has been happily laundering our accounts for years—proof enough that the law already shares in the enterprise. Tampa proposes simply to continue that contract honestly—no wash, no markup—and donate a handsome portion of the profits to rebuilding. Consider it a civic investment."

He slid a folded sheet across the desk; neat receipts and signatures bore out his claim.

Tom exhaled hard through his nose. "I'm gettin' a headache from all the window dressing, Mercer. Try me in plain speech."

Mercer inclined his head, amused.

"Very well, Sheriff. The senator made this mess; Tampa can keep him from sweeping your town off the map. We'll front lumber, money, and a whisper or two in Tallahassee to make sure Cypress Run stays the county seat. In exchange, the docks stay *ours* and no one in uniform pokes about unless something on two legs is bleeding. Honest enough?"

Tom looked at Hartwell. Her jaw worked once before she spoke.

"Protective corruption in lieu of destructive corruption," she said dryly. "How civilized."

Mercer's smile didn't move. "Civilization is an expensive hobby, Your Honor."

Hartwell exhaled through her nose. "I'm sure you have thoughts, Sheriff?"

Tom leaned back, rubbing a smudge of ash from his sleeve.

"I think it's only a matter of time before Tallahassee shuts us down. Senator Clayborne'll use the fire and the damage to pull federal funding for the courthouse construction. I think there might be a middle ground between clean as a whistle and drowning in corruption. It may only be about a boot-width wide, but I can keep my balance on it if you can."

Hartwell studied them both—the smuggler polished as a harbormaster, the sheriff soot-stained and unshaven—and finally reached for her glass.

"You will submit to a quarterly inspection of manifests," she said.

"Naturally."

Tom added quickly, "No weapons shipments, no flesh trade."

"Perish the thought."

Hartwell finished, "And if Tallahassee asks—"

"You never met me," Mercer agreed, raising his drink. "To progress."

Hartwell touched her glass to his, the faintest clink. "To pragmatism."

Tom lifted his own, wry smile returning. "To whatever fresh hell this is—long may it hold."

After Mercer departed, Tom corked the rum bottle and put it away in his desk. He laughed.

Hartwell looked at him, eyebrow raised. "Something funny, Sheriff?"

Tom smiled and shook his head. "Just remembered you telling me to keep an eye out for corrupt, trigger-happy, bribe-taking lawmen wandering around your swamp. Think I finally found one, but I can't for the life of me remember what message you wanted me to give him."

Hartwell glanced at him, looking him up and down the same way she had when he'd first stepped foot off the train. "I believe the message was 'keep up the good work' and to mind that his ego doesn't cost him a favorable job performance review in six months."

Tom grinned. "Yes, ma'am. Message received. Question withdrawn."

T he best part of working up at the church annex building, even if only temporary, was how close it was to the school room.

Tom knocked on the schoolhouse door frame, peering inside where twelve children hunched over their slates. Ellie stood at the blackboard, chalk dust on her dark skirt, working through nouns, verbs, and proper sentence structure with the patience of a saint.

Every small head swiveled toward him like sunflowers tracking light. Ellie's hazel eyes narrowed with that particular brand of exasperation she reserved for his interruptions.

"Afternoon, young scholars. Sorry to interrupt, but could I borrow your teacher for just a moment?"

"Children, keep working on your sentences. I'll be right back." She set down her chalk and followed him outside, crossing her arms. "What's so important that you had to disrupt my lesson?"

Tom rubbed the back of his neck, suddenly feeling foolish. "Well, I wouldn't call it urgent business or anything, but I was nearby—"

"You're always nearby."

"—and I wanted to bring you flowers." He pulled a bouquet of spiky purple blooms from behind his back, their stems still dripping swamp water.

Ellie's stern expression cracked, and she covered her mouth as laughter bubbled up. "Tom Bracken, did you really wade into the swamp to pick me a bouquet of pickerelweed?"

His face fell slightly. "This is a weed?"

"About as weedy as they come."

"Sonofa—" Tom sighed, shoulders sagging. "Well. I tried. I thought they were pretty."

Ellie stepped closer, her voice softening. "They *are* pretty. And seeing as they survive damn near everything and always grow back, I think they're perfect." She rose on her toes and kissed him sweetly, her lips warm against his, her hand briefly touching his cheek.

A chorus of giggles and whispers erupted from the schoolhouse window where twelve small faces pressed against the glass.

Tom's ears reddened as he glanced at their audience and he rubbed the back of his neck, color creeping up from his collar. "Well, that's embarrassing."

"They've been watching us all week," Ellie said, taking the dripping bouquet. "Nothing stays secret around here for long."

Tom cleared his throat, attempting to recover his dignity. "Speaking of which, I do have some actual business. I've noticed the townsfolk acting strange lately. You know anything about that?"

Ellie's expression turned mysteriously innocent. "Can't say I do."

"Can't or won't?"

"Won't."

Tom studied her face, noting the way her eyes crinkled at the corners when she was keeping secrets. "You're enjoying this, aren't you?"

"Maybe a little."

"So you're not going to tell me why Mrs. Patterson nearly jumped out of her skin when I walked past her on the street? Or why Jake stopped hammering and started whistling the second he saw me coming?"

"Nope."

"And the fact that Mr. Cotton practically shoved me out of his store this morning has nothing to do with whatever's got everyone whispering?"

Ellie picked a piece of swamp moss off one of the pickerelweed stems. "I'm not revealing any secrets. You'll just have to find out later today."

"What's happening later today?"

"Something."

"Ellie."

Ellie smiled, that same mischievous look Nate got when he'd hidden a frog in someone's desk. "Something's happening at the town hall meeting tonight. You should probably be prepared for it."

"Prepared for what?"

"You'll see." She smiled and kissed him again, then smoothed her skirt. "Thank you for the flowers. You're getting much better at the romantic gestures. But I do need to get back to my students before they decide grammar is optional."

Tom caught her elbow gently. "You're really not going to give me any hint?"

The mischief in her eyes softened into something warmer. "It's nothing bad, Tom. Trust me. But you might want to wash the swamp mud off your boots before tonight. Just a suggestion."

Tom watched her disappear back into the classroom, leaving him standing in the schoolyard with more questions than answers. Through the window, he caught sight of twelve small faces quickly ducking below the sill.

Whatever the town was planning, it involved children keeping secrets and grown folks acting like they'd swallowed canaries. In his experience, that combination usually meant trouble.

Or worse—a surprise.

It bothered him all the way up to the evening when the Town Hall Meeting was called to order.

The meeting convened with unusual energy, folks filing in with barely contained grins and sideways glances at Tom. Judge Hartwell called for order, but her own mouth twitched with suppressed amusement.

"First item of business," she announced, consulting her notes with theatrical formality, "a presentation to Sheriff Bracken."

Tom's stomach dropped. In his experience, presentations from grateful townsfolk usually involved either a gold watch or a one-way ticket out of town. Given recent events, he wasn't placing bets on the watch.

Mr. Cotton rose from his seat, carrying a large wooden box with both hands. "Sheriff, we took up a collection the day we pulled you from that courthouse. Figured it was time Cypress Run showed proper appreciation."

Tom approached the front with the caution of a man expecting either applause or a lynch rope. The assembled crowd watched with the eager attention of children on Christmas morning.

"You didn't need to do anything," Tom said, accepting the box. "Just doing my job."

"Open it," called Mrs. Patterson from the back row.

Tom lifted the lid and stared. Inside lay an assortment of clothing, all in his size—work shirts in sturdy cotton, a crisp white dress shirt for court appearances, and a vest of deep brown brocade that wouldn't shame him in front of visiting dignitaries.

But at the bottom, carefully folded, was a coat that made his breath catch.

Dove gray linen, lightweight but expertly tailored in the style of his ruined Chicago frock coat. The cut was unmistakably Northern—formal enough for a sheriff, practical enough for Florida heat. Someone had taken considerable time and expense to have it made specifically for him.

"Well, I'll be damned," Tom murmured, lifting the coat with a reverence he usually reserved for fine billiard cues. His eyes itched and he briefly considered putting on his dark spectacles to hide what was clearly an attack of dust aggravation from the crowd.

"Language, Sheriff," Ellie called from her seat, but her eyes sparkled with mischief.

Tom slipped off his patched jacket and pulled on the new coat. The fit was perfect—sleeves hitting precisely at his wrists, shoulders sitting square, the length falling just where it should. He turned in a slow circle, arms spread like a debutante showing off her first ball gown.

"How do I look? Respectable enough to arrest the better class of criminal?"

Laughter rippled through the crowd. Tom caught Ellie's eye and saw her satisfied smile. She was one of the few people who'd had the opportunity to take his measurements while he lay unconscious and feverish in her guest bed.

"You clean up nice, Sheriff," Jake called out. "Almost civilized."

"Don't get carried away," Tom replied, adjusting the lapels. The coat moved with him like it had been made for his frame—which, he realized, it had been. "Still the same disgraced Yankee beat cop underneath."

Mrs. Mills stood up, her expression softer than he'd ever seen it. "Sheriff Bracken, this town deserves representation that isn't going to be an embarrassment to us. We all decided that since we've already got the finest lawman this side of the state line, we should make sure he looks halfway decent at doing his job."

Tom felt heat rise in his face that had nothing to do with the Florida climate. He cleared his throat, suddenly finding the floorboards fascinating.

"Well," he managed, "appreciate the vote of confidence. And it does feel good to have sleeves that actually reach my wrists again."

He gathered the rest of the clothes back into the box, acutely aware of twenty pairs of eyes watching his every move. The gesture touched him more deeply than he cared to admit—not just the expense, but the thoughtfulness. Someone had paid attention to what he needed, what would make him feel at home in this strange place.

"Thank you," he said simply. "All of you. This means more than you know."

Judge Hartwell cleared her throat. "Well, now that our sheriff's properly dressed for the job, perhaps we can move on to actual business?"

But Tom barely heard her. His fingers traced the fine stitching of his new coat, and for the first time since arriving in Cypress Run, he felt like he might actually belong.

THREE MONTHS LATER

CHAPTER TWENTY-NINE

A Shot of Irish Courage

Ellie finished cleaning the last of the surgical instruments when Simon burst through the clinic door, face flushed and hair wilder than usual.

"Mrs. Harper—I mean—" He stopped, gulping air. "You need to come quick. It's the sheriff."

Her hands froze on the cloth. "What happened? Is he hurt?"

"He's at the saloon, and he's—" Simon's eyes went wide. "Nobody's ever seen him this drunk. Something's gotta be wrong with him. Real wrong."

Ellie set down the instrument and grabbed her medical bag without another word. She'd seen Tom drink plenty of times—a whiskey here, a beer there—but never to excess. The man treated alcohol like he treated everything else: with calculated control.

They hurried down Main Street, Simon jogging to keep pace with her quick strides. The Cypress House glowed bright against the evening darkness, raucous laughter spilling through the transom window above the door. But as they got closer, Ellie heard something that made her understand Simon's concern—a sound she'd never expected to associate with Tom Bracken.

Giggling.

She pushed through the doors to find a crowd gathered around the billiards table, their faces split between amusement and concern. Tom was bent backward over the green felt at an impossible angle, head hanging upside down as he lined up a shot that defied both gravity and good sense.

"Twenty dollars says he can't make it," someone called out.

"You're on." Tom's voice came out strained from his precarious angle. "Physics is just... suggestion anyway."

He drew back the cue and struck. The ball ricocheted off three cushions, kissed two other balls, and somehow found its way into the corner pocket. The crowd erupted in cheers.

Tom started laughing—a bright, helpless sound that made Ellie's chest tighten with worry. He tried to push himself upright, failed, and slipped sideways off the table to land in a heap on the floor, still giggling.

"See?" he said, waving the cue stick from his prone position. "Told you... Every drunk worth his liquor knows gravity's negotiable."

Ellie knelt beside Tom, who was now reaching up to feel at the edge of the table above him for his whiskey glass. When he saw her, his face lit up with a grin that was equal parts charming and concerning.

"Ellie, my Lovely, perfect timing! You should join me for a drink!"

She pressed the back of her hand to his forehead. No fever, but his pupils were dilated and his coordination was shot to hell. "Tom, what happened? Have you eaten anything today?"

"Eaten? Ate?" He blinked slowly, as if the concept was foreign. "Depends? Is it still yesterday or is today tomorrow already?"

Tom used the billiards table to haul himself upright, his knuckles white against the green felt as he swayed. The room tilted like a ship in rough water, but he managed to stay vertical through sheer determination and what felt like divine intervention. He patted his vest pocket reflexively, feeling the small wooden box that had been sitting heavy there all evening.

"Tom." Ellie's voice carried that tone he'd learned to recognize—the one that meant she was about to start using her medical training on him whether he liked it or not. "How much have you had to drink?"

"Define 'much.'" He attempted to lean casually against the table and nearly missed entirely. "Because if we're talking about volume versus intent, the mathematics get complicated."

Tom tried to focus on Ellie's face, but she kept blurring around the edges. The freckles across her nose seemed to dance in the lamplight, and her hazel eyes held that mix of exasperation and worry that made his chest tighten in ways that had nothing to do with the whiskey.

"Come on," he said, reaching for her hand and missing it by inches. "One drink. Life's too short to spend it all sober and sensible."

"Life's also too short to spend it face-down in a gutter." Ellie stepped closer, close enough that he could smell the lavender soap she used and see the way her lips pressed into a thin line when she was trying not to smile. "Why have you been drinking tonight, Tom?"

The question hit him like cold water.

"Sometimes a man needs a little liquid courage," he said finally, the words coming out more honest than he'd intended. "Irish tradition."

"Courage for what?"

The saloon had gone quiet—or maybe the whiskey was just drowning out the noise. Tom looked at Ellie's face—the lamplight in her hair, the small scar on her chin she'd never explained.

"For admitting that some questions are worth asking," he said, "even if you're terrified of the answer."

Simon cleared his throat behind them. "Maybe we should get him some coffee? And possibly a chair before he falls over?"

But Tom barely heard him. The box seemed to pulse in his pocket like a second heartbeat, and Ellie was still looking at him with those eyes that saw too much, understood too much, forgave too much. He let out a helpless laugh and lost his grip on the table, slipping back down to the ground.

Ellie knelt, checked his pulse and pupils, then said, "Tom—what did you eat today?"

"Coffee," he said, blinking slowly. "Maybe some jerky this morning? Time gets... slippery when you're contemplating life's eternal mysteries."

Jennifer snorted from behind the bar. "He'd been nursing that first whiskey for twenty minutes before he threw it back and ordered another. Then another. Man's been drinking like he's trying to drown something."

"I am drowning something," Tom said with a giggle that made Ellie's chest tighten. "My good sense. It was getting too uppity anyway."

"Coffee, if you don't mind, Jennifer," Ellie said. "Strong as you can make it." She turned back to Tom, who was squinting up the cue stick like it might explain the ceiling.

Ellie's eyes sharpened. She'd seen Tom drunk before—tipsy after a long day, loose after a particularly difficult case—but never like this. Never giggling and philosophical and touching his pocket like it contained either salvation or damnation.

"What question, Tom?"

He blinked up at her. "Question?"

"You said you had a question worth asking. What kind of question?"

"The kind that changes everything." He tried to focus on her face, but the lamplight kept shifting and her freckles kept dancing. "The kind that makes a man feel like he's lost under the stars, but he keeps looking up 'cause they're still so beautiful even though they make him so small."

Jennifer appeared with a steaming mug of coffee black enough to wake the dead. "Drink this," she ordered, pressing it into Tom's hands.

Tom wrapped his fingers around the mug, grateful for something solid to hold onto.

Ellie studied Tom's face, noting the way his fingers kept returning to his vest pocket like a nervous habit.

"What's in your pocket, Tom?"

He froze, his hand stilling against the fabric. "Pocket? Don't know what you mean. Pockets are for... pocket things. Normal sheriff pocket things."

"Normal sheriff pocket things don't make a man drink half the saloon's inventory." She reached for him, but he twisted away with the unsteady grace of the thoroughly drunk.

"Ellie, my Lovely, listen." He struggled to sit up straighter, gripping the billiards cue like an anchor. "Some questions are like loaded guns. You carry them around, knowing they could go off at any moment and change everything."

Simon reappeared with a plate of bread, setting it down carefully beside Tom. "Mrs. Harper, should I fetch Dr. Delgado? He might have something for—"

"No." Tom's voice sharpened, cutting through his drunken haze. "No Diegos. Doc knows too much. He'd take one look with those judgy eyes and judge me with them."

Jennifer watched from behind the bar, polishing glasses with mechanical precision. "Been sitting on something for weeks, haven't you, Sheriff? Man doesn't drink like that unless he's trying to wash down his pride."

Tom laughed, but it came out hollow. "Pride's the least of it. Try terror. Good old-fashioned, bone-deep terror of asking a question that might get answered."

Ellie knelt closer, voice soft, "Tom, whatever it is—"

Tom stared into Ellie's eyes, his mouth opening and closing like a fish pulled from the Calusa River. Words formed on his tongue—the question that had been burning in his chest for weeks—then died before they could reach the air.

"I—" He stopped, swallowed hard. "Ellie, I—"

Her hazel eyes were so close he could see the gold flecks scattered through the green, could count the freckles that dusted her nose.

"Tom?"

"I need—" His voice cracked. He cleared his throat and tried again. "Oh, God, I'm not drunk enough yet."

He twisted toward the bar, nearly losing his balance. "Jennifer! Could you add some whiskey to this coffee? Generous pour. Make it Irish coffee's drunken uncle."

"Absolutely not." Ellie's hand shot out to steady him. "It's time to get you home before you pickle yourself completely."

Tom turned back to her with a smile that would have charmed the devil himself, all crooked grin and twinkling eyes. "My Ellie, why won't you just have one tiny little drink with me? Just one." He held up his finger, wavering slightly. "Just one more drink and I think I won't be scared anymore."

Ellie's expression softened despite herself. She'd seen Tom face down armed outlaws without blinking, watched him walk into burning buildings to pull out survivors, seen him stare down a room full of angry townsfolk with nothing but a crutch and a fast tongue. Whatever had him this rattled went deeper than whiskey could reach.

"Scared of what, Tom?"

"Of asking a question that might change everything. Of finding out that some dreams are just—dreams."

Jennifer set down her dishrag, amber eyes sharp with the kind of attention she usually reserved for card cheats. "Sheriff, you've been nursing that same question for weeks. Whiskey won't make it any easier to ask."

"Won't make it any harder either," Tom mumbled into his coffee.

"No more drinks," Ellie said firmly. She stood and brushed off her skirt. "Come on, Tom. Let's get you sobered up so you can ask whatever question's eating you alive."

"No," Tom whined, clutching his coffee mug like a lifeline. "No sobering up. Absolutely not. I refuse to be sober right now."

He twisted away from Ellie's reaching hands, nearly toppling sideways off his precarious perch against the billiards table. "You don't understand—Sober Tom is a coward. Sober Tom thinks too much. Sober Tom would never—would never ask you to marry him because he's too much of a chickenshit to—oh shit—" Tom immediately clapped a hand over his mouth like he could stuff the words back in, eyes going wide as if he'd said something catastrophic.

The saloon went dead quiet. Even the piano player stopped mid-note, his fingers frozen above the keys. Every head in the place turned toward them, and Tom felt heat crawl up his neck that had nothing to do with the whiskey.

"Oh, no, no, no—No, I didn't say that," he mumbled through his fingers. "Nobody heard that. Especially not you, Ellie. You definitely didn't hear that."

Ellie sat back on her heels, her face cycling through surprise, confusion, and something else he couldn't quite read in his current state. "Tom—"

"Nope." He waved his free hand frantically. "We're pretending that didn't happen. I need more whiskey. Much more whiskey. Industrial warehouse quantities of whiskey."

He tried to push himself upright, but his legs had apparently decided to stop cooperating. "Jennifer! Emergency whiskey situation over here! Man drowning in his own stupidity needs immediate assistance!"

"Tom Bracken, you sit right there," Ellie's voice carried the kind of authority that could stop a charging bull. "You're not getting another drop until we talk about this."

"Can't talk about it sober," he said miserably, slumping back against the table. "Sober Tom knows you deserve better than a sheriff who plays billiards with criminals and argues with swamp gators. Drunk Tom thinks maybe—just maybe—you might say yes anyway—at least, he does when he's not thinking straight—cause when he's thinking straight he knows this is the worst idea he's ever had."

He looked up at Ellie with eyes that were glassy but suddenly, devastatingly sincere. "I want to marry you, Ellie Harper. Been too much of a coward to say it because what if you laugh? What if you say no? What if—"

"Tom."

"—you already know you could do better than a piano-playing, billiards-hustling fool who—"

"Tom."

"—reads math books because angles are more fun than people give them credit for and geometry is actually really helpful in police work—"

"Tom Bracken, shut up."

Ellie's voice cut through his rambling like a scalpel through silk.

Tom's mouth snapped shut like a bear trap. The silence stretched thin as piano wire, broken only by the distant clink of glasses and the wheeze of the saloon's regular crowd, all trying to hold their breath to hear better, waiting to see what happened when an unstoppable drunk met an immovable nurse.

Ellie stared at him, her hazel eyes wide with something between shock and calculation. The freckles across her nose seemed to stand out sharper in the lamplight, and Tom found himself cataloging every detail of her face like a man memorizing his last sunset.

Jennifer cleared her throat from behind the bar. "Perhaps I should—"

"Stay," Ellie said without taking her eyes off Tom. "Someone needs to make sure he regrets his choices tonight, and I have a feeling it isn't going to be me."

Tom tried to stand, failed spectacularly, and settled for leaning more heavily against the billiards table. The room spun like a roulette wheel, but Ellie's face remained steady at the center of it all—serious, thoughtful, terrifyingly unreadable.

"Tom Bracken," she said, and her voice carried that tone he'd learned to recognize. Not angry, not dismissive, but something else entirely. Something that made his chest tighten with hope and terror in equal measure.

"Present, ma'am" he said weakly. "Unfortunately."

She reached for his vest pocket, and this time he didn't have the coordination to stop her. Her fingers found the small wooden box, drawing it out like evidence from a crime scene. It sat in her palm, small and significant. Ellie turned the box over in her hands, studying it like she might examine a patient's wound—careful, thorough, looking for complications. "And asking me to marry you is the *worst* idea you've ever had?"

"Uhh," Tom said. "Well, I, uhhh... think saying that out loud is probably *actually* the worst idea I've had, now that you mention it."

The crowd around them had thinned to a few lingering cattlemen and Jennifer, who was pretending to clean glasses while obviously listening to every word. Simon had backed away to give them space, but his wide blue eyes missed nothing.

Ellie opened the box.

The ring caught the lamplight and threw it back in tiny rainbows.

For a heartbeat, the entire saloon seemed to lean in closer for a better look.

It was a simple gold-colored band with a small opaque white chip where a diamond might normally sit. Nothing fancy—nothing that would look out of place on the hand of a woman who spent her days teaching children and stitching up wounds—but pretty enough to show he'd put thought into it.

Tom huffed out the breath he'd been holding. "I, uh... well, I know it's not much to look at, but with... with everything that's been costing money these last few months, I couldn't afford anything fancy like you probably deserve, but Jake helped me."

Tom bit his lip and rubbed the back of his neck. "Had all those shell casings from the night at your house—when you kissed me that first time—and Jake melted them down for the band. The setting's just a little chip off my gator tooth, but I thought... oh, God, that sounds even stupider said out loud."

Her thumb stroked gently over the chip of tooth in its setting. "It's beautiful," she said quietly.

Tom's heart hammered against his ribs like it was trying to escape. "You think so? Because it doesn't have to be, you don't have to think it's beautiful just because I made a fool of myself, I can go bury it in the swamp somewhere and we can pretend this never happened, but oh, God, I don't think I'm drunk enough for this, Ellie. Just, uh... give it back and I'll make it disappear and we—"

"Don't you dare." Her voice was sharp enough to cut through the spiraling panic and his jaw clipped shut again.

Ellie looked up at him, and for a moment the whiskey haze cleared enough for him to see her clearly. The slight upturn at the corner of her mouth that meant she was fighting a smile. The way her fingers traced possessively across the edge of the ring box like she was afraid it might disappear.

"Tom," Ellie said again, her voice softer now, and he could hear something in it that made his whiskey-addled brain sit up and pay attention. "Look at me."

He lifted his eyes from the ring box to her face, expecting to see pity or gentle rejection or the kind of careful kindness people used when they were about to break your heart real slow. Instead, he found something that looked suspiciously like fondness mixed with exasperation.

"You beautiful, drunken fool," she said, and there was no sting in it. "If you want this ring back, you're going to have to pry it from my fingers, and medically speaking, you're in no condition to fight me for it."

Tom blinked. The words didn't seem to arrange themselves properly in his head. "Fight you for it?"

"This is mine, now." She closed the ring box with a soft snap and held it against her chest. "And when you sober up in the morning, you can ask me to wear it for you properly. But you're never getting this back, do you understand?"

"Uh, yes, ma'am, I think so, but—"

"But you're too drunk to know if you understand me for certain, which is why I'm taking you home and feeding you proper, then putting you to bed so you can sleep this off. Then, tomorrow when you're sober, you can ask me again. So I can be sure that you'll remember my answer, and understand what it means when I give it."

Tom stared at the closed ring box in Ellie's hands, his whiskey-soaked brain struggling to process what had just happened. The saloon's piano had started up again—a jaunty tune that seemed to mock his current predicament.

"You're keeping it," he said slowly, as if testing the words.

"I'm keeping it." Ellie stood and brushed off her skirt. "And you're coming with me before you fall through those floorboards and give Jennifer something else to charge you for."

Tom attempted to lever himself upright using the billiards cue, managed it on the second try, and immediately wished he hadn't. The room performed a lazy pirouette around him, and he gripped the table's edge to keep from rejoining the floor.

"Ellie, I'm not entirely sure my legs remember how to walk."

"Then you'll learn fast." She tucked the ring box into her pocket with the kind of decisive movement that brooked no argument. "Simon, help me get him vertical."

Simon appeared at Tom's other side, his young face bright with excitement. "Mrs. Harper, this is just like that time Mr. Patterson drank too much turpentine thinking it was gin, except the sheriff's romantic instead of poisoned."

"Romantic's debatable," Tom muttered, allowing them to haul him toward the door. "Stupid's more accurate."

Jennifer called out from behind the bar. "Sheriff, your tab's settled—but next time you want to propose, maybe try it sober. Less entertaining for the rest of us, but probably safer for your pride."

Tom managed a weak salute in her direction. "Noted for future reference."

The night air hit him like a physical thing—cool and damp with the smell of river water and cypress bark. It should have sobered him up, but instead it just made his head spin worse. Ellie's hand on his arm was the only thing keeping him upright, and he found himself cataloging the warmth of her fingers through his shirt sleeve.

"Where exactly are we going?" he asked.

"My place. You need food, coffee, and about twelve hours of sleep before you're fit for human company again." She glanced at him sideways. "And tomorrow morning, when you can form complete sentences without giggling, you're going to ask me properly."

Tom's heart performed some complicated maneuver that felt like a cross between hope and terror. "And you'll give me an answer?"

Ellie's mouth curved into something that wasn't quite a smile but wasn't exactly not one either. "Oh, I'll give you an answer, Tom Bracken. Whether you like it or not."

Tom's liquor-slurred brain latched onto the one thing that seemed crystal clear in the spinning world around him. "Ellie, can I kiss you?"

"Absolutely not." Her answer came swift and decisive as a scalpel cut. "You smell like you fell into a brewery and decided to stay for the tour. I don't even want to imagine what that tastes like."

He blinked, processing this information with the careful deliberation of the thoroughly drunk. "So, if I didn't taste like a brewery, you'd let me kiss you?"

Ellie's mouth quirked at the corner—not quite a smile, but close enough to make his heart stutter. "That's highly likely. Maybe you'll think of that before you go drinking this hard next time."

Tom considered this wisdom for a moment, then lifted her hand to his lips with surprising steadiness. He pressed a gentle kiss to her knuckles, his whiskey breath warming her skin. "There. Respectful compromise."

Ellie didn't pull away, which Tom took as an encouraging sign even through his alcoholic haze. Her fingers were callused from years of work, steady and capable, and he found himself wanting to memorize the texture of them.

"Tom?" She waited until he lifted his eyes to hers. "Can you walk the mile to my house, or should I get Simon to wake up Bobby Keene and have him hitch up his mule cart?"

Tom straightened with what he hoped looked like dignity. The world performed another lazy spin, but Ellie's hand in his felt like an anchor. "I can walk. As long as I don't have to let go of your hand."

"Then don't." She squeezed his fingers. "But if you fall in the river, I'm not fishing you out until morning."

Simon appeared at Tom's other elbow, still wide-eyed with excitement. "Should I come with you, Mrs. Harper? In case he needs medical attention?"

"I think I can handle one drunk sheriff," Ellie said dryly. "But thank you, Simon."

They started down Main Street, Tom's boots finding the rhythm of walking only because Ellie set the pace, and for the first time all evening, his terror was beginning to edge toward something that might have been hope.

"Tomorrow," he said—more to himself than to her.

"Tomorrow," Ellie agreed.

The walk to Ellie's house stretched longer than Tom remembered, though that might have been the whiskey making every step feel like he was walking through molasses. The moon hung low over the cypress trees, casting silver shadows across the dirt road, and somewhere in the distance a night heron called out like a rusty gate swinging in the wind.

"You're awful quiet," Tom observed, his words only slightly slurred now that the night air was working its sobering magic. "Usually you've got opinions about my poor life choices by now."

Ellie's hand remained steady in his, guiding him around the deeper ruts in the road. "I'm thinking."

"That sounds dangerous."

"For you? Probably." She glanced at him sideways, and in the moonlight he could see something calculating in her expression. "You realize what you've done, don't you?"

Tom's free hand drifted automatically to his vest pocket, finding it empty. The absence of the ring box felt strange, like he'd forgotten to strap on his gun belt. "Asked the prettiest woman in three counties to marry me while too drunk to remember my own middle name?"

"You've given me time to think about my answer." Ellie's voice carried that tone he'd learned to recognize—the one that meant she was working through a problem like she would a difficult patient. "A whole night to consider whether I want to spend the rest of my life married to a man who thinks billiards is a suitable metaphor for courting a girl."

"It's a very good metaphor," Tom protested weakly. "Angles, pressure, reading the table—"

"And what happens when you scratch?"

Tom stumbled slightly, caught off guard by the question. "You... lose your turn?"

"Exactly." Ellie stopped walking, turning to face him on the moonlit road.

The weight of her words settled over him like morning fog rolling off the river. Here he was, drunk and fumbling through the most important conversation of his life, and she was already three moves ahead of him.

"Ellie," he started, then stopped, because suddenly he wasn't sure what came next.

She reached up and touched his cheek, her fingers cool against his whiskey-flushed skin. "Ask me tomorrow, Tom. When you're sober enough to mean it."

The night sounds of the swamp filled the silence between them—frogs and insects and the distant splash of something large moving through dark water. Tom found himself holding his breath, waiting for her to say something else, anything else that might give him a clue about what she was thinking.

Instead, she just smiled and started walking again, leaving him to follow and wonder if he'd just made the best decision of his life or signed his own death warrant.

Just before they reached the porch steps, Tom tugged gently on Ellie's hand, pulling her away from the worn path that led to her front door.

"Wait," he said, his voice softer now that the night air had begun to clear some of the whiskey fog from his head. "There's something I want to show you."

He led her around the side of the house, past her small vegetable garden and the chicken coop where her hens roosted quietly in the darkness. His steps were still uneven, but more purposeful now, like he knew exactly where he was going.

"Tom, what are you—"

"Here." He stopped beside a patch of ground near the back corner of her property, where the grass grew thick and soft beneath a gap in the cypress canopy. Moonlight filtered through the Spanish moss, casting lace patterns on the earth below. "Softest grass in your whole yard. I checked one afternoon when you were teaching and Nate was fishing."

Without ceremony, he dropped down onto his back, arms spread wide like he was making a snow angel in the grass. His vest fell open, and his shirt collar worked loose, making him look younger somehow—less like the sharp-eyed sheriff who could read a man's guilt in the angle of his shoulders, more like just another soul trying to make sense of the world.

"Join me," he said, patting the ground beside him. "Please?"

Ellie hesitated, glancing back toward the house where lamp light glowed warm and welcoming through the windows. Her practical nature warred with something else—the same impulse that had made her pocket his ring box instead of handing it back.

"The grass'll stain my dress."

"It'll wash." Tom's eyes found hers in the moonlight. "When's the last time you just... looked up? Really looked?"

She considered this for a moment, then carefully lowered herself to the ground beside him, mindful of her skirts. The grass was indeed soft, and cool against her back after the warmth of the walk. Above them, the Florida sky spread out like black velvet, scattered with diamonds—more stars than city folk ever dreamed of.

"There," Tom said, his voice barely above a whisper. "Worth a grass stain, don't you think?"

Ellie found herself nodding, though he couldn't see it. The ring box pressed against her hip through her pocket, solid and real as the man beside her breathing whiskey-scented air into the humid night.

Ellie kept her eyes on the stars, watching them blur and sharpen as her vision adjusted to the darkness. "The last time I looked at the stars was that first night you stayed in my guest bedroom," she said quietly.

Tom's head turned toward her, though he kept quiet.

"You couldn't go more than five feet without stopping to gawk at them again," she continued, a smile creeping into her voice. "I wanted to see what you'd found so interesting up there."

"I'd never seen the stars until that night," Tom said, his voice sobering despite the whiskey still flowing through his system. "Not really. In Chicago, there's too much smoke and light. The sky's just... black. Empty."

His hand found hers in the grass, fingers threading through hers with surprising steadiness.

"You always make me feel like I'm walking in starlight," he said, thumb tracing across her knuckles. "Even when we're just standing in your kitchen arguing about whatever it is you want to argue about that day. It's like you carry some of that light with you."

Ellie's breath caught. The whiskey had stripped away his usual deflection, leaving something raw and honest that made her chest tighten.

"Tom—"

"I know I'm drunk," he said quickly. "I know I'm saying things I probably shouldn't say until tomorrow when I can ask you proper. But lying here with you, looking up at all this…" He squeezed her hand. "I wanted you to know that's why I need to ask. Because you make everything brighter, and I'm tired of pretending I don't need that light."

The night sounds of the swamp surrounded them—a symphony of frogs and insects that seemed to pulse with the rhythm of her heartbeat. Above them, the stars wheeled on in their ancient patterns, indifferent to the small human drama playing out in a patch of soft grass behind a modest house at the edge of civilization.

Tomorrow, she would give him her answer. Tonight, she would let him hold her hand under the starlight and pretend that time could stand still.

Tom's head felt like someone had used it for billiards practice—repeatedly—and the morning light streaming through Ellie's guest room window drove spikes directly into his brain. He groaned and rolled over, immediately regretting the movement as his stomach performed an impressive rebellion against gravity.

Fragments of the previous night drifted through his consciousness like scattered cards from a busted deck. Whiskey. The saloon. Something about physics being negotiable. And Ellie—Christ, what had he said to Ellie?

He stumbled toward the kitchen, following the blessed aroma of coffee like a man searching for salvation. His legs felt unsteady, his mouth tasted like he'd been chewing on old leather, and every step sent fresh waves of misery through his skull.

Ellie stood at the stove with her back to him, already dressed for the day in a simple blue dress, her honey-brown hair pinned back in its usual practical style. She glanced over her shoulder as he shuffled in, her expression unreadable.

"Coffee's ready," she said, pouring a steaming cup from the pot.

Tom managed to lower himself into a chair without collapsing entirely, accepting the coffee with hands that shook only slightly. The first sip burned his tongue, but the second began to clear some of the fog from his brain.

Silence stretched between them—not the comfortable quiet they'd grown accustomed to, but something heavier. Tom stared into his coffee cup, trying to piece together the evening's events through the pounding in his head.

Tom nursed his coffee, eyes bleary. "Ellie," he rasped. "Did something... happen last night? Everything after that third whiskey's a fog."

She didn't answer right away. Instead, she lifted her left hand, sunlight sliding across the ring on her finger—his ring, the one forged from spent shell casings and crowned with a chip of gator tooth.

The cup froze halfway to his mouth.

"You solved a tough case," Ellie said lightly, though her voice held steady restraint. "Bit of a messy struggle, but you got your suspect in irons."

Tom eased the cup down. The ring looked different on her—less like a gamble, more like it had been meant for her all along. "Did I now?" he managed, hoarse.

Her mouth tugged into the faintest smile. "Question is, Sheriff, what are you planning to do about it?"

A lump caught in his throat. "Depends whether I made a good enough case before the judge—and what the sentencing is."

Ellie turned from the stove, studying him as she might a wobbly patient. "Well," she said, crossing her arms, "you fumbled your closing argument. Mixed your facts, repeated yourself. Pretty sure you giggled twice."

He winced. Images rose like storm debris: the billiards table, the upside-down shot, blurting it all like a confession.

"But," she added, her voice softening, "you argued well enough to win a conviction."

Silence swelled—the tick of the clock, the distant cluck of chickens. Tom didn't breathe. "And the sentence?" he asked, barely above a whisper.

Ellie's smile grew until it gentled her whole face. "Lifetime incarceration. No parole, no time off for good behavior. You're stuck serving your sentence until you die of old age."

He blinked. "That's a mighty harsh sentence."

"The punishment should fit the crime," she murmured, stepping close and brushing her fingers against his jaw. "And that's exactly what you deserve for making me fall in love with you."

It hit like a shot of raw whiskey—hot, staggering, impossible to set down. "Fall in love?" he croaked. "When did that happen?"

"Somewhere between you stepping off the train and making me watch the stars with you last night." She perched on his lap, light as breath. "Hard to say exactly."

Her arms looped around his neck. "You make me laugh when I shouldn't. Argue every bit of my advice, then follow it to the letter. You let Nate hero-worship you when you can't see why he should. And you once waded through swamp water to bring me weeds because you thought they looked romantic."

Tom's hands found her waist; his voice turned rough. "Those are terrible reasons to fall in love."

"The worst," she agreed, grinning. "Especially with a man who proposes while upside down on a billiards table."

"I wasn't upside down," he muttered.

"Close enough," Her forehead touched his. "Life sentence, Sheriff. You ready for that kind of time?"

Warmth spread through him like sunrise over water. "Ma'am," he said, steady now, "I think I've been ready to serve that time since the night you first kissed me."

The ring glinted on her hand as she cupped his face, and Tom swallowed against the sudden swell of emotion in his chest.

"Ellie," he said quietly, "are we really doing this?"

Her smile softened, unflinching. "Depends. Are you really asking?"

He drew a breath that felt brand new. "Will you marry me, Eliza Harper?"

She gave a short, certain nod that carried every ounce of her usual resolve. "Yes, Tom Bracken," she said, voice low and sure. "I believe I will."

And when she kissed him, the whole room tasted of coffee, sunlight, and home.

The End

CYPRESS RUN
Circa 1883

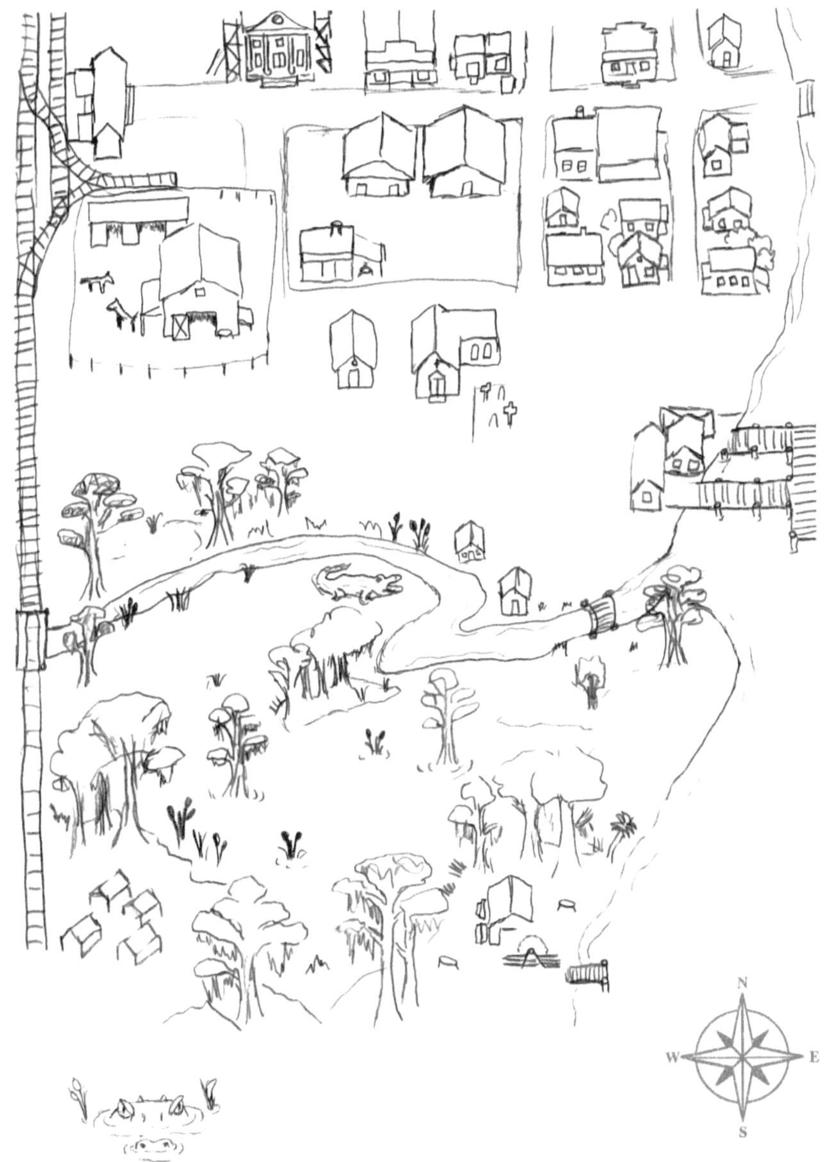

Questions for Discussion

The following questions are intended to spark conversation and reflection about the characters, setting, and themes of *Cypress Run*. Feel free to use as many—or as few—as you like.

1. Tom Bracken arrives in Cypress Run as an outsider with a damaged reputation. How does the town change him over the course of the story? Do you think his exile to Cypress Run is a punishment or an opportunity?

2. Tom struggles to adjust to Florida after coming from Chicago. What moments best show how out of place he initially feels? If you were suddenly dropped into Cypress Run in 1883, what would be the hardest thing for you to adjust to?

3. Ellie Harper has a unique role in the Cypress Run community as both a nurse and a schoolteacher. What challenges has she had to overcome to fill that role? How does it affect her interactions with other characters?

4. Tom and Ellie often challenge each other's assumptions. How does their relationship shape the choices they make?

5. Diego's background may give him a different perspective on authority, loyalty, and survival than the other characters. How does that influence the way he navigates life in Cypress Run?

6. Several characters in the book are hiding secrets or protecting their pasts. Do you think secrecy is necessary for survival in Cypress Run? Which character do you think has the most intriguing backstory?

7. The Florida frontier is almost a character in the story. How does the environment—the swamp, the frontier conditions, and the town's isolation—affect the events of the novel?

8. The novel takes place during a time of railroad expansion and rapid change in Florida. How do those forces shape the conflicts within the town?

9. In many ways Cypress Run operates under its own rules. Do you think the town benefits more from Judge Hartwell's or Sheriff Bracken's ideas ideas about law and justice? How does justice in a frontier town differ from justice in a big city like Chicago?

10. Many of the characters in Cypress Run form bonds that go beyond simple friendship. Which relationships surprised you the most? Which felt most meaningful?

11. If you lived in Cypress Run, which character, faction, or location would you enjoy interacting with the most?

12. If you were to write a survival guide titled *"How to Keep Tom Bracken Alive,"* what rules or advice would it include?

—

Not quite ready to leave Cypress Run?

There's a short interlude set between Book One and Book Two:

"Urgent Business"

Scan or visit:
tndaigle.com/urgent-business

Author's Note

When I was a baby author, someone gave me the worst writing advice known to man: *"Write what you know."* If I'd stuck to that, this book wouldn't exist. I have absolutely no idea what life was *actually* like in 1880s Florida. I've never even seen Hollywood try. It takes every ounce of imagination I have to turn Arizona backlot "Old West" movie sets into swampland, and I've had to remind myself "less dust, more foliage" more times than I can count.

So here's better advice: write what you **want** to know.

The moment I started wondering what a Western set in Florida might look like, my brain took off. Every chapter sent me down another rabbit hole about the state's history and the strange, wonderful people who shaped it. (Don't laugh, but growing up in the Pacific Northwest, our history classes treated "the South" as if it stopped somewhere around Georgia. Florida was *news* to me.)

So please allow me this small disclaimer: I am not a historian. I don't write strict historical fact—I write historical realism, which occasionally involves a little narrative hand-waving. Any remaining mistakes are, of course, my own. (And for the cowboy gunfight enthusiasts out there: I just learned you're only supposed to load five rounds in a revolver after it was far too late to recount the bullets. My step-dad taught me to count the shots, not how to keep my characters from shooting themselves in the foot. My apologies!)

But if you're anything like me, and a stray detail here or there sparks your curiosity and sends you exploring, then I'm glad to share the journey.

Florida is wild, weird, and endlessly fascinating. I hope reading this book is as fun for you as learning about it has been for me.

Acknowledgements

Thank you so much to everyone who has made this book possible. Your support, your love, and your well wishes are truly the things that keep me going.

To my mom, who has always supported and believed in me. To Christina, who is always down for an adventure and a long and excited chat about anything on my mind. To Lil, who gives the best brainstorming feedback ever in exchange for gay pirates. To Tony, who taught me more about quirky police detectives than I wish I knew. To Chey, Sky, Tabs, and Lyn, who all love me when I need to feel loved even if we haven't spoken in ages. To every single one of my library friends, who have had to listen to me gush excitedly about every scene I've written. To my awesome editor, Serena, who is awesome at what she does.

And to my husband, who reads and asks questions and underlines every single sentence so you can't tell what he thought was interesting because he thinks it all was interesting. You're the best.

And to my kiddo. You're pretty cool, too, I guess.

T. N. Daigle was born and raised in the outskirts of the SeaTac area of Western Washington, giving her a healthy appreciation for moody weather and the use of dark chocolate and coffee as coping mechanisms—she has yet to face a challenge that could not be overcome given enough caffeine. Her love of westerns and immersive literature are the result of Saturday mornings spent alternating between watching John Wayne movies with her dad and raiding his library for Tolkien novels and Dick Francis mysteries.

An Air Force veteran and military spouse, she has hopscotched around the world before finally settling on the Gulf Coast side of Tampa Bay. In hindsight, it was only a matter of time before she wrote a book about what it's like to be a northerner transplanted into the weird and wild country of Florida.

—

For town gossip, research notes, bonus stories, and updates on future books, visit *The Cypress Run Gazette*:

tndaigle.com/welcome

The Cypress Run Quartet

Four books. One sheriff. So many alligators.

Cypress Run

When a disgraced Chicago detective gets exiled to a Florida swamp town, he expects to quietly disappear into obscurity. Instead, he finds murder, conspiracy, alligators, and the love of his life—not necessarily in that order. Too bad his past won't stay buried—and someone powerful wants him dead before he can even unpack his bags.

Cypress Tide

When Sheriff Tom Bracken follows a trail of missing supplies downriver to Port Calusa, he expects a smuggling dispute and a few broken crates. Instead, he finds a city on the brink of collapse—fever spreading through the docks, bodies turning up where they shouldn't, and a criminal network that may be using disease as cover for something far worse.

Cypress Blood

When a Treasury inspector turns up murdered and incriminating ledgers vanish from his locked office, Sheriff Tom Bracken becomes the prime suspect in a conspiracy he was trying to expose. With Ellie's quiet strength holding the town intact and a haunted new deputy hiding deadly secrets, Tom must outmaneuver a ruthless political machine before Cypress Run is swallowed whole.

Cypress Crown

When a federal summons pulls Sheriff Tom Bracken into Tampa, he discovers Senator Clayborne has come south to finish what Chicago started. To survive, Tom and Ellie must navigate political lies, criminal power, and a city where even the gators would think twice before biting.

—

To learn more about *The Cypress Run Quartet*, visit:
www.tndaigle.com

SCRIBOMANCER
GUILD PRESS
Verba Incantant